A Chimerical World: Tales of the Seelie Court

A Chimerical World: Tales of the Seelie Court

Edited by
Scott M. Sandridge

Editor: Scott M. Sandridge

Published by Seventh Star Press, LLC.

ISBN Number: 978-1-937929-47-3

Seventh Star Press
www.seventhstarpress.com
info@seventhstarpress.com

Publisher's Note:
A Chimerical World: Tales of the Seelie Court a work of fiction. All names, characters, and places are the product of the author's imagination, used in fictitious manner. Any resemblances to actual persons, places, locales, events, etc. are purely coincidental.

Printed in the United States of America

First Edition

Dedication

To Ruby Delk, a.k.a. "Mammy," for feeding me encyclopedias, novels, Shakespeare plays, and faerie tales from the moment I first learned how to read. And to Linda Walters and Virgil Sandridge for being the best parents they could be while under messed up circumstances. R.I.P. all three.

To Stephen Zimmer and Seventh Star Press for giving me the opportunity to edit this anthology. And to all the writers, for without you there would be no anthology.

Last but not least, to the rest my family for having the patience to put up with my ornery arse.

The Tales of the Seelie Court

Foreword
by Scott M. Sandridge

When coming up with the idea for an anthology about faeries (and I *refuse* to use the Americanized spelling for that word), my thoughts were on the Elves of J.R.R. Tolkien (especially how they were portrayed in *The Silmarillion*), the mischievous Fey of Shakespeare, and all the old tales pre-Disney. And I didn't want just the "good" faeries to get all the love like usual, but both Courts. Anyone who's read the old tales—indeed anyone who's ever played *Changeling: the Dreaming* from White Wolf Game Studio—knows that faeries are more than just Tinkerbell stereotypes: they come in all shapes and sizes and forms.

Without Elves, Dwarves, Goblins, Trolls, Centaurs... and yes, Sprites...the Fantasy genre would be nowhere near as interesting as it is. There's just something about them that, despite how different they seem, remind us so much of, well, *us*: the good, the bad, the ugly, and the just plain dumb. They're just as popular as the dragons, undead, angels, demons, and all the other common staples of the genre; and they just never manage to become clichéd (not even Tink). And whether it's the drunkard sprites in *Willow* or the selfish but goodhearted pixie in *Legend*, they never seem to get boring. And they'll likely continue to have a place in our imaginations for a long, long, time—perhaps for happily (or not-so-happily) ever after.

As for the two Courts, this anthology is about the *Tales of the Seelie Court*, and not to be confused with its darker brother. But do not think that all the Fey in this Court are all goody-goody-three-shoes, for that is just not the case (and is probably a racist view anyhow). As with Tolkien's Elves, they are not always the "good guys." They can be just as prankish and vengeful as their Unseelie brethren when they need to be; they just happen to be more "proper" about it. For they are the embodiment of Daylight and Twilight, and some even have their likenesses written in the sky (you know, those shiny "stars" you see up there?). We humans are mere children to them, pets even, and we should never be so foolish as to forget that.

But that does not mean you should be sad about gaining the attention of the Seelie Court. It could be worse, you know. It could be that "other" court: the ones who like to play with their food.

So let us open the gate to that magical Land of Faerie, that place of dreams and nightmares where we desperately wish we could be but also fear to stay too long.

Just try not to eat the food, or you might be stuck here forever.

Here, have an apple while you stay....

Extra-Ordinary

By B.C. Brown

Marcus Samuel Simon, with brown hair and brown eyes, a generous smattering of freckles across his cheeks, is what some would call an extraordinarily ordinary little boy. He walks away from school with rounded shoulders, hands crammed into the pockets of his too short blue jeans. The toes of his red and white sneakers leave wakes in the dirt as he drags his feet. The day is quiet—solitude and silence a sad companion in the fall air. The shades of his new classmates taunt him during his long trudge down the road leading back to his home—a trailer park named Oakview Courts that housed not a single tree, oak or otherwise, nor a single view, unless one was fond of staring at rusted scrap metal in the junk yard next door. The shades' taunts echo off the mounds of abandoned refrigerators, dismantled bicycles, and stripped cars, multiplied and amplified.

"*Marcuth Thamuel Thimon,*" the shades mock.

A new year at a new school because his dad has a

new job at a new refinery. Marcus had anticipated the ridicule; this is the fourth school in as many years. He'd been an Indian Brave, a fighting Tiger, a ferocious Husky, and something called a Salukis. He still doesn't know what a Salukis is, but he thinks it most closely resembles a rabid dog. At this new school, Marcus found himself a fighting Tiger symbolized by a cartoon tiger with razor-sharp teeth and claws. It is simultaneously inviting and frightening.

He sighs as his vision takes in the faded lime green pull-behind camper; his home since his mom left. His dad, Stephen Simon, did what he could but work was hard to find with refineries closing all across the U.S..

Marcus rubs the back of his neck, sweat and grit beneath his palm, as he takes in his trailer.

Twenty-two minutes and eleven seconds….

A piece of cardboard, that neither kept out the rain nor the cold, is duct-taped over the busted window (the window where his "bedroom" is) at the front of the camper. Two rusted lawn chairs stand guard outside the dented front door, sad sentinels. The duct tape that holds the broken shards of window in the door glints in the afternoon light.

Marcus strides across the green outdoor carpeting that constitutes their lawn. He retrieves the house key tucked inside the shirt that, if he doesn't grow too much this year, might last the rest of the school year. He keeps the deadbolt key on a long necklace comprised of two of his dad's old bootlaces. A ghost of a smile graces his face at the faded scratched "smiley" face his father had etched into the key's metal last year. The smile that reaches his eyes, however, is more wistful than happy.

Nineteen minutes and six seconds....

He slides the key into the lock and twists. The deadbolt makes a loud thunking sound, signifying the lock's disengagement. Pushing his way into the dim interior, the door only squeaking lightly since he'd oiled it yesterday, Marcus reaches for the kerosene lantern to his right. The lantern hangs on a rusted nail his father has driven into the fake wood paneling; the book of matches for the lantern is in a brown glass ashtray. The ashtray is from the local (as in two states and three schools ago) bowling alley. It is balanced on the backside of the bench seat that joins its mate and a small orange table making up their "living/dining room".

Lighting the lantern, the pungent odor of the kerosene burning his nostrils, Marcus closes the door and hangs his key on the hook. He will need it tomorrow; his dad is never home to let him in. Climbing the two stairs that bring him into the center of the trailer, he sets the lantern on the table. From his position he can touch the table, the hot plate, and the bathroom door all at once if so inclined.

Marcus is not inclined. He is never inclined.

Fourteen minutes and thirty-seven seconds....

Looking at the table, he sees his dad left him a note.

Notes are the only way the two ever communicate. They hadn't had a phone in years.

'Dear son. Chance for overtime. Eat your dinner, do your homework, and wash your face before bed. Here's a dollar; get yourself something sweet from Chuck's. Love, Dad.'

Chuck's is the convenience store down the road from their trailer park; it would be visible from the trailer park if the junk yard didn't separate the two. Marcus moves the four quarters used to hold down the corners of the paper and sighs. A dollar might get him a pack of Bubble Yum gum if the old man who works there takes pity and doesn't charge tax. Marcus deposits the quarters back into the change jar sitting beside the hot plate. He stirs the jar, making it look as if he spent the coins—not that his dad would check.

Stephen Simon works from three each afternoon until three in the morning, six days a week. Overtime meant an additional four hours; he will be ready to drive the hour and a half back to their trailer about the time Marcus will be getting ready for school. The boy will then be in class when his dad pulls into the driveway. Marcus knows Stephen Simon will be too tired to check his change jar to see if Marcus spent the money or put it back like always.

Marcus opens the door on the miniature refrigerator; the refrigerator shares the same counter as the hot plate and a small, one-compartment sink. The three items make up their "kitchen". A small gas generator runs the tiny water heater in their bathroom and the refrigerator. It will run the lights in the trailer too, but Marcus uses the kerosene lanterns instead to save the gas in the generator.

Removing a package of bologna and pouring a glass of concentrate-made apple juice, he closes the door to the refrigerator. Bread is in the cupboard above him. Within five minutes, his dinner is made; five minutes later, his dinner is eaten and his mess cleaned.

Four minutes and eighteen seconds....

There is no schoolwork for the night; it's the first day of school, and the teacher has taken pity on her class. Marcus heads into the bathroom to get ready for bed.

The bathroom consists of a small commode, a child-sized shower, and a sink the size of a sand bucket. The mirror on the wall is tinged yellow and peeling at the corners; it has a warped spot near the center that makes his face resemble a carnival mirror. Marcus removes the washcloth from the edge of the sink and wets it. His eye catches on the full laundry basket sitting in the hallway between the bathroom and his father's room, and he makes a mental list to take the clothes to the laundry mat tomorrow after school. As an afterthought, he sets down the cloth and checks the bottle of laundry detergent sitting beside the basket and frowns; the bottle has little more than a coating of soap left in it. He sighs and removes the cap from the bottle, sticking it under the tap of the sink, and refills the bottle. Shaking the jug to mix the remaining detergent with the added water, he recaps it, calculates he can get three or four more loads of laundry before he'll need to buy more, and places it back beside the dirty clothes.

Marcus turns back to the bathroom, picks up his washcloth and scrubs at his face, turning the skin pink and tingly, then wrings the water from the cloth. Placing it back on the edge of the sink, he exits the bathroom. To his right, beyond a moth-eaten curtain and the basket of dirty laundry, is his dad's bedroom. His dad's room houses a bed and a small two-drawer cardboard dresser; the dresser has decorative pink and purple flowers. His dad found it sitting on the side of the road, and it only has one stain on one side. His dad conceals it by pushing it against the wall of his bedroom.

Marcus turns and makes his way to his bedroom. His room is past the main room, and he turns off the kerosene lantern as he moves beyond the living room. Marcus's dad had hung him a sheet too; the sheet is 'Strawberry Shortcake' but Marcus doesn't mind. He likes the privacy. He bats the sheet to the side and climbs into his bed, kicking his sneakers off as he pulls himself up. With a glance and a frown, he sees the small hole forming in the sole of his left sneaker. He makes a mental note to duct tape a piece of cardboard into the inside of his shoe in the morning before school. If he doubles up on the cardboard, he might get six more months out of that shoe—if the weather isn't too wet, that is.

Two minutes and three seconds….

Marcus draws the curtain shut, closing himself in, shutting himself off from the rest of the world, the holes in his sneakers, the dirty laundry, and the plain bologna dinners. His room is made up wholly of his twin-size bed and the small storage space beneath it. Two small porthole windows are at the front corners on either side and let in enough light from outside that he can see without the lantern despite the cardboard duct-taped into the busted window in his room. He sits Indian-style on his mattress. Marcus reaches down and opens the door to the space beneath his bed. He pulls out a battered shoebox, clearly one of his dad's old shoe boxes, and settles it in his lap. The boy caresses the battered cardboard box, sliding his hands along the top of the cardboard, before he removes the lid. Light engulfs Marcus, seeping out around the seams of his 'Strawberry Shortcake' sheet to illuminate the tiny interior of his home, and he closes his eyes.

Seven seconds….

Marcus opens his brown eyes to the sea of adoring faces tilted upwards at him from inside. Salutations of greeting drift to him in melodious harmony, sending waves of warmth coursing through his body.

The tiny people stand upon gently swelling green hills dotted with red and white checkered picnic blankets; mothers bounce babies on their hips or wipe dirt from the childrens' faces; fathers wear baseball mitts and drape arms over sons' shoulders. A full circus plays upswing music in the distance, and white Christmas lights twinkle in the green, full branches of the trees dotting the landscape like stars pulled to Earth. The only thing separating the scene from reality are the gossamer wings nervously trembling at the backsides of each individual present there.

"Hail Marcuth Thamuel Thimon! Hail King Marcuth, the Portal, the Creator!" the people inside the shoebox cheer. As the jazz band next to the winding river springs into action, upbeat swing music trickles out of the shoebox and fills the silence of his quiet trailer.

A female with a beaming grin and iridescent blue eyes takes to the air, leaving the confines of the shoe box, and alights on his forearm.

"*Grand evening, King Marcuth, we are humbly at your service.*" Her voice is bells and perfume.

Marcus sighs. The dented front door with its duct-taped window melts into oblivion; the thick smoke from the kerosene lantern fades from his nostrils and is replaced with the scents of carnival; the tired, plain bologna sandwiches night after night are replaced with the mouth-watering flavors of cotton candy, funnel cake, and popcorn. His eyes sparkle, his freckled cheeks plump, and his face splits into a grin. Marcus is home.

You see, Marcus Samuel Simon, with his twinkling

eyes and sunny grin, is what some would ordinarily call an extraordinary little boy.

Dead Fairy Doormat

By George S. Walker

Andrei's problems with Vanessa started when her cat left the dead fairy on the doormat.

"I'll only be gone a week," she'd told him. "A business trip to Paris. Would you look after my house and cat while I'm gone?"

Vanessa was a beautiful, enchanting woman. Andrei was just a bicycle messenger who picked up courier parcels at her office downtown. He'd known her only a few months, and had a crush. He said yes without a second thought.

"Just bring in the mail and feed Mephyst," she'd said sweetly. "He stays outside, because I don't want him clawing the furniture." She gave Andrei a key and showed him where she stored the cat food.

Vanessa flew to Paris on Sunday morning, and he fed Mephyst that evening. It was the next morning, when he went to refill the dish before biking downtown, that he found the skeleton.

Mephyst was on the doormat, with a twisted framework of tiny bones resting between his paws.

"What have you got there, boy?" Andrei asked the cat.

Mephyst looked up at him warily. The silver bells on his collar sparkled in the morning sun.

Andrei crouched down for a closer look, careful of his bad knee. The tiny bones were clean and white, as if scoured by acid. They had a ghastly beauty. There were delicate wings, but it wasn't the skeleton of a bird. The skull was missing, but even without the skull, he could tell. For one thing, there were too many limbs. Was that what bats looked like? He reached out to touch it, and Mephyst scratched him.

Andrei jerked back and sucked the scratch on his hand.

The cat growled, and only thoughts of Vanessa kept Andrei from booting it off the step. He filled the food dish and limped to his bike. His left knee hadn't worked right since he'd been sideswiped by a hit and run driver a year before.

Vanessa called his cell mid-morning, as he was waiting to pick up a parcel.

"Bonjour, mon chéri," she said. "How's Mephyst?"

"He scratched me."

"Were you teasing him?"

"No. Does he often leave dead animals on your doorstep?"

"He likes to hunt birds."

"I don't think this was a bird."

"Well, I can never tell. I don't have my contacts in first thing in the morning. Did you—Oh, I have another call. Bye!" She hung up.

* * *

That night, Andrei had a dream. He was in a tunnel or cavern, with only a faint glow to see by. From somewhere in the distance came the most beautiful music he'd ever heard: Chimes like a bell choir, and though he didn't recognize the melody, it drew him irresistibly.

He wasn't alone. Others were in the cavern, too, and he saw the soft glow of their lights. Like him, they were moving toward the music, but he had a sense of foreboding.

Then the screams began.

Andrei sat bolt upright in his bed, uncertain whether the screams had been in his dream or outside his apartment.

It took him a long time to get back to sleep.

* * *

Another morning, another skeleton. Or was it the same?

Using his phone, he took a picture of Mephyst with his prize and sent it to Vanessa.

Then he found a broom and gently prodded

Mephyst off the doorstep. The cat hissed at him, scampering off with a jingle of silver bells and leaving the skeleton behind.

Andrei knelt, careful of his bad knee.

This wasn't the same skeleton as the day before, because it had a skull. Sharp teeth had pierced it, and as Andrei looked more closely, a shiver went down his spine.

The tiny skull was humanoid.

The arms and legs were proportioned like a Halloween skeleton, but there were wings attached behind the shoulders. The wing bones were much finer, almost as thin as threads, and badly broken. The skeleton was about three inches tall.

Mephyst sat just out of range of the broom, glaring at him.

"Bad kitty," Andrei muttered. "Where'd you find this?"

The cat couldn't have killed it. The bones were too clean. Besides, it couldn't possibly be real. He examined it carefully, hunting for a tiny "Made in China" stamp. But it didn't feel like plastic; it felt like bone. He wrapped it carefully in paper towels and put it in his backpack.

He fed the cat and biked downtown.

Vanessa called enroute, and he stopped to answer.

"Bonjour, Andrei. Your picture was gross."

"Looks like a *CSI: Doormat* case. Mind if I ask you a few questions, ma'am?"

He'd meant it as a joke, but she replied, "You're not getting all Audubon Society on me, are you?"

"So far, birds seem safe. How often does Mephyst bring you little gifts like this?"

"From time to time."

"Every morning?"

"Aren't you going to ask me about Paris?"

"Sure! How's Paris?"

"The food is *fantastique*! Oh, another call. Bye!"

Andrei sighed and got back on his bike.

* * *

In the evening, he carefully unwrapped the paper towels around the skeleton. But within, there was only bone-colored dust. How had that happened? It hadn't seemed that fragile in the morning.

Later that night, he dreamt he was in the dark cavern again. Faintly, he heard the bells playing. Glowing lights moved around him. But this time, he remembered it was a dream, and that it would end with terrified screaming.

In lucid dreams, you can change the ending. Even as he was drawn toward the music, he willed himself to have a weapon in the dream. He wished for something big and powerful, like Rambo's M60 machine gun.

What he found in his hands was a bow and a single arrow.

The music was so beautiful he wanted to just close his eyes and listen. But in this dream, he struggled to keep them open, and fitted the arrow to his bow. The lights moved all around him, but they weren't the source of the music. He heard something move in the darkness ahead.

As the bells reached a crescendo, huge jaws opened before him. He drew the bow—.

The screaming woke him.

* * *

In the morning, Mephyst had another skeleton.

Andrei was about to get the broom when he noticed a quill protruding beside the cat's nose. It was thicker than a porcupine quill, more like a long splinter of wood. He knew if he tried to remove it, Mephyst would bite him.

Vanessa's ring tone interrupted him.

"*Bonjour, chéri*," she said. "Has Mephyst eaten?"

Andrei looked down at the skeleton. "I think so. Do you ever have weird dreams?"

Silence from the phone.

"Like being in a tunnel?" he added quickly.

"Oh, were you riding through a tunnel the time you got hit by a car?"

"This isn't about bikes. It's about your cat."

"You were dreaming about Mephyst? How sweet!"

"Where did you get him? From a shelter?"

She laughed derisively. "I bought him on a business trip to Romania. He was the most adorable kitten. From the Lambrino branch of the royal family. Do you know what a hassle U.S. Customs makes you go through?"

"Did this royal family have anything to do with fairies?"

A long pause. "Andrei, are you turning gay?"

"People don't turn gay, Vanessa. It's not a disease you catch."

"Have you fed Mephyst?"

"I was just about to."

"That's probably more important than worrying about fairies, don't you think?"

"I'm on it."

"*Au revoir*, Andrei." She hung up.

"*Adios,*" he muttered.

After he fed the cat, he limped to his bike and pedaled downtown.

He couldn't afford a data plan for his phone, so between messenger jobs, he stopped at the library and did a Wikipedia search for Romanian Royal Family. The Lambrino branch was the illegitimate Russian branch of the House of Hohenzollern. Kicked out of the castle, along with their cats, presumably. Wandering the forests of Transylvania.

That link led him to a paragraph about dogs and cats in Transylvania raised to hunt down "creatures of the other realm," which apparently included anything from wood sprites to werewolves.

Mephyst's niche in the ecosystem seemed to be

hunting wood sprites. There wasn't a lot of scientific data on wood sprites, but faerie queens were fond of silver bells. And they were positively allergic to cold iron. Cold iron, which sounded like it might be related to refrigerator magnets, turned out to be any kind of iron, even steel. Iron nails were what kept vampires in their coffins. Old graveyards were surrounded by iron fences for the same reason.

Andrei decided to buy Mephyst a new collar: one with lots of iron on it. To repel fairies instead of fleas.

After work, he biked to Vanessa's house with the new collar.

Mephyst was on the doormat, waiting to be fed. The skeleton was gone.

He held out the new collar for the cat to sniff, but Mephyst took no interest. Andrei unlocked Vanessa's door, filled the food dish, and set it on the step.

"Nice kitty," he said, and gently unbuckled the old collar as the cat ate.

Mephyst gave a low growl. His tail twitched.

Andrei got the collar off. The silver bells jingled. He picked up the new collar and slipped one end under Mephyst's neck.

Quick as a rattlesnake, Mephyst sank his teeth into Andrei's thumb.

Andrei swore.

The cat had jaws like a pit bull. Andrei fought to pry them open with his other hand. His face was near the cat's. Baleful yellow eyes stared into his. As he shifted for a better grip, his bad knee went down on the cat's tail.

With a screech, Mephyst let go and fled across the lawn.

Andrei sucked on his bleeding thumb, then looked at it. The teeth marks went clear to the bone. He was going to need alcohol. Both kinds.

* * *

That night he had another dream in the cavern with the moving lights. But there were no chimes this time. He looked down and found the bow and arrow in his hands again. He heard the creature moving quietly ahead of him in the darkness. He felt a sense of anticipation, a phantom memory that preparations had been made. He floated forward, realizing he was flying, and fitted the arrow to the bow. Sounds of the creature's breathing reached him. Lights flitted all around him.

Suddenly there was a monstrous howl, and the sound of something heavy sliding into a pit, scrabbling to stop its fall.

All the lights darted forward, Andrei included. Hovering over the pit, he fired an arrow down into it. The beast roared in fury and tried to leap out, but slid back into the pit.

* * *

In the morning, he stopped at Vanessa's house. His bandaged thumb still throbbed.

Mephyst wasn't there. Andrei was pretty sure he knew why, but went inside anyway and filled the food dish. He put it on the doorstep along with the two collars.

His cell rang.

"*Bonjour,*" said Vanessa. "Have you fed Mephyst?"

"I put food in his bowl. He hasn't shown up yet."

"He always shows up."

What could Andrei say? *Fairies kidnapped your cat?*

"I'll bet you're starving him," she accused.

"No! The bowl's full!"

"Prove it. Send me a picture right now."

Andrei took a photo and sent it to her phone.

A minute later, she exclaimed, "You took his collar off!"

Andrei kicked himself for leaving the collars on the doorstep. "The old one is a girl collar. I thought Mephyst would like something more macho."

"You were going to use the one on the photo? The one with steel spikes on it? That's a dog collar!"

"Actually, it's a puppy collar," said Andrei.

He'd never heard a woman swear like Vanessa.

"I'm sure when this is all over," said Andrei, "we'll look back at this and laugh."

"No," she snapped. "We won't. When I call tomorrow morning, Mephyst had damn well better be on my doorstep, wearing his original collar and eating out of his bowl. Or I swear you'll wish you were never born!"

"He's a free-range cat! How am I supposed to find him?"

Vanessa hung up.

Andrei put the collars in his backpack and limped to his bike, muttering, "How do I locate a Transylvanian psycho cat being held hostage by fairies?"

He managed a bit of online research between messenger runs, but found no references to fairy sightings in the state, let alone the city. The only way to find the fairy hill was with Mephyst, and fairy archers had probably turned him into a splinter pincushion by now.

After work, he biked around Vanessa's neighborhood, calling Mephyst's name. He found a small park with a hill nearby, but though he searched every square foot of it, there were no burrows. Mephyst and the fairies could be anywhere, even in a storm drain. The dream hadn't provided many clues.

It was getting dark. He was tired, fed up with both Mephyst and Vanessa. He went home to his apartment.

* * *

The dream began as soon as he fell asleep. The beast had been digging and climbing all day, and dirt from the eroded sides of the pit was filling the bottom. It was only a matter of time before it escaped. He could sense the beast's fury, and joined other lights flying out of the tunnel.

It was night out, and they darted up into a tree, perching on the branches. He heard frogs and crickets, a dog barking in the distance. By the light of the moon, he saw a hill below him.

It was the hill in the park near Vanessa's house.

* * *

He managed to wake himself from the dream and looked at his clock radio. It wasn't even midnight yet. He dressed hurriedly, put on a jacket, and got his bike.

It was a long ride to Vanessa's neighborhood, but he found the park. He unclipped his bike light and ran toward the hill, hobbled by his bad knee. As he did so, a swarm of fireflies swooped down from a tree toward the hill. They hovered over a large opening in the ground as he approached, then darted inside.

Andrei knew the hole hadn't been there when he'd searched after work.

"Mephyst?" he called.

Vanessa's cat yowled. It was not a welcoming meow or a "come rescue me" mewing. It was a yowl that proclaimed, "*I'll kill you all.*"

Andrei wished he'd brought leather gloves and a leather jacket. Maybe a hockey mask. He stripped off his jacket, hoping to use it as a cat containment vessel.

He shined his bike light into the subterranean entrance and saw creatures flitting through the beam. They were a lot bigger than fireflies, but his eyes couldn't focus on them. He saw a pit in the dirt floor of the tunnel. Another yowl emerged from it.

The tunnel wasn't tall enough to go on hands and knees. It was a claustrophobic belly-crawl. Light in hand, he scooted in, glad that the pit wasn't very far ahead.

As he crawled forward, his left arm crunched on a birdlike skeleton. He wondered if it was a recent kill by Mephyst. Did fairy flesh evaporate when one of them died?

Another yowl, and he heard the cat leap and slide back into the pit. Tinkerbell lights flitted warily above the pit.

His own breathing was loud in the tunnel. He smelled musty raw earth. If the tunnel collapsed, the fairies couldn't dig him out. They probably didn't know CPR, either.

He crawled down toward the pit and shone his light into it. It was a lot deeper than he'd expected. He couldn't reach Mephyst without climbing in. And if the hole in the hill closed when the cock crowed at dawn, he didn't want to be trapped down here.

"Nice kitty," he grunted. Awkwardly, he pocketed his bike light so he wouldn't lose it, and pulled his jacket forward. He dangled it into the pit and Mephyst leaped.

The cat's claws snagged the fabric and Andrei pulled up. He wrapped his jacket around the squirming cat before it could get away. Then he tied the sleeves together and began scooting backwards. Mephyst screeched, fighting furiously to free himself.

When Andrei reached the exit, he staggered to his feet. He was covered in dirt. The cat was starting to get free. He re-secured it inside the jacket, fastening the zipper and tightening and tying all the drawstrings. He limped to his bike, wedged the cat in one of his panniers, and pedaled home to his apartment, the cat screeching outrage to the night the whole way.

At home, he locked Mephyst in the shower stall and shut the bathroom door.

* * *

There were no more dreams that night.

The next morning, he reattached Mephyst's original collar, put a leash on him, and stuffed him into a cardboard box. Then he bandaged all the new places the cat had scratched and bitten him, secured the box to his bike rack, and pedaled to Vanessa's.

He refilled Mephyst's food bowl, tied the leash to Vanessa's front door, and waited.

His cell rang.

"Show me Mephyst," Vanessa ordered.

He took a photo of the leashed cat eating from its food dish and sent it to her phone.

Vanessa swearing lasted almost a full minute.

"Are those quills stuck in his skin? He needs to see a vet! What is *wrong* with you?! My six-year-old neighbor boy did a better job of taking care of Mephyst than you do!"

"How many stitches did the boy need?"

"I'll be back tomorrow night, Andrei. My cat had better be there, and I never want to see your face again." She hung up.

Andrei decided it was time to call in a professional. He made an appointment with a vet.

* * *

The next afternoon, he picked up Mephyst after an overnight stay at the vet. The splinters had been removed, and an angry Mephyst was wearing a plastic cone around his head. That made it easier for Andrei to replace his collar.

It was Vanessa's old collar, except he'd carefully replaced the silver bells with steel bells from a craft store. The collar looked the same as before, but he hoped the fairies would know the difference.

He'd taken the liberty of having a couple other medical procedures done as well, though it had cost him over a week's pay. Mephyst was now neutered and declawed.

He took Mephyst back to Vanessa's, locked him in the house, and dropped her key in the mail slot.

* * *

After that, there were no more parcel pickups from Vanessa's office. And no more tunnel dreams at night.

He went back to the park in the middle of the night, searching the fairy hill for the entrance. It wasn't there.

But as he left the fairy hill, he discovered his limp was gone.

His knee never bothered him again.

Taggers

By Christine Morgan

"Not again," Edgar said. "Not a-goddamn-gain."

He stopped on the cracked sidewalk, about halfway between a paper bag with empty beer cans spilling out of it, and a pile of dogshit that had been there so long even the flies didn't bother with it anymore.

Morning traffic rolled by on the expressways above, the rumble of tires and the drone of engines a constant steady vibration interspersed by the occasional blat of a horn, brake-screech, siren-wail or crunch of a fender-bender. Down here, in the part of town now known as The Gulch, few cars moved. Plenty of the ones lining the streets *couldn't* move, or hadn't in years. Rustbuckets, husks, and stripped hulks, for the most part.

Not much sunlight made it through the gloom-shadow cast by the maze of concrete, asphalt and steel overhead. What did was thin stuff, tinged like old newspapers from the perpetual fug that hung in the exhaust-smelling air. It didn't flatter what hadn't been a nice neighborhood even before the so-called marvel of urban renewal and modern engineering had gone in.

Still, there was more than enough to show Edgar Norris in all-too-clear detail what had been done to the side of his locksmith shop.

Again.

A-goddamn-gain.

Where they got those colors…so son of a bitching *bright* it about made his eyes bleed…who would even make spray paint in such vivid, garish hues…?

And what the hell were any of the designs supposed to be? Oh, they couldn't be contented with some hasty outline of titties, or initials in a heart, or clever witticisms about who sucked what anymore. No, it had to be this kind of crap.

Fantasyland murals, illegible letters, undecipherable symbols, images of who-knew-what….

Reminded him of those posters from the 60's, those psychedelic head-trip ones, Day-Glo on black velvet, the kind of thing the unwashed hippies hung on their walls as they basked in pot smoke and incense by the glimmer of lava lamps, while good and decent hard-working American boys supported the war and fought and died in fetid swamp-jungles half a world away. Peace and love, man, far out, Age of Aquarius, tie-dye, and if we hold hands and sing we can make the world a better place.

Yeah. Grow the hell up, put on some damn clothes,

get a damn haircut, get a damn job.

The same could be said to kids today. To kids ever since, for that matter. Spoiled, sulky brats, the bunch of them. Everything handed to them on a plate, and they still whined for more. And if you expected them to actually earn any of it? If you expected them to have any respect for others?

They all needed a good swift kick in the seat of the pants, and Edgar wished he was young and spry enough to do it. If he could just get his hands on the little bastards who'd decided they had every right to scribble their nonsense up and down the cinderblock he'd only repainted last week....

Street art, they called it. Or had that term, like 'graffitti,' been deemed socially hurtful and politically incorrect? No, this was the creative expression of inner-city youth, which ought to be fostered and encouraged as a positive outlet for energies that might otherwise be stifled, or turned toward drugs and crime.

Enough to make a grown man sick to his stomach.

Otherwise turned toward drugs and crime?

Like you didn't have to be drugged out of your mind to do something like this, or consider it 'art'?

Like this wasn't a crime? Vandalism was what it was. Theft, too. The theft of his time and money to have to cover over their goddamn mess, robbing him as surely as if they broke into his shop or stuck a gun in his face and demanded his wallet.

Looking at the unwelcome decorations on the wall gave him a headache. They almost seemed to float there, and glow there.

Float and glow.

Flow and gloat.

Swirls. Starbursts. Stick-figure letters. Intricate, interweaving, interlaced patterns. Circles and lines. Something that was probably meant to be one of those devil-pentagrams, only with too many angles, and in a shade of pink his mind wanted to identify as 'electric bubblegum.'

All the colors were like that. Electric bubblegum, acid lemonade, neon watermelon, hyper-lime, fiery creamsicle. Even the darker shades weren't dark. He didn't know how that could be—how could you have bright indigo or incandescent black?

What mattered most to Edgar was the certainty that they'd be a bitch to cover up. Probably need three or four coats. Damn it.

He trudged to the front door, up three cement steps flanked by windows behind barred grates. The glass had dulled to a murky opacity that showed little of the interior, which was fine by him. Faded sheets of cardstock tilted on the sills announced hours and services, and the emergency number, written in plain felt-tip marker. No website. The sign mounted above the door read: ABLE LOCK AND KEY followed by the motto, "If you're willing, we're ABLE."

Irene's idea: the name and motto. Back then, he'd been so young and besotted-in-love that he would have named the business anything she wanted. Didn't even mind her answering the phone that way, chirping it in her sweet, cheerful voice. He would have given her the moon on a string.

Times changed. Live and learn.

Over the years, he'd come to hate it so much he got heartburn every time he saw the motto, but never badly enough that it was worth replacing the sign. He figured it would fall down eventually. Everything did, in this decrepit place. The trick would be seeing if the sign fell down before or after the shop itself did.

He unlocked the metal security gate, which creaked on its hinges, and then the inner door. Before going in, he spared a last glance up at the looming network of highways, on-ramps, off-ramps, interchanges, cloverleafs and express lanes.

A marvel of urban renewal and modern engineering, they'd called it. Something destined to revitalize the struggling central district, bringing more business while improving the commute. A boon for this and future generations.

All for a small tax hike certain to pay for itself within the first three years, yada-yada prosperity, yada-yada working families, yada-yada progress and property values and improving the schools.

So they'd said, but the improved commute sped

people past the central district faster, bringing less business, and the result was this. The Gulch. Just another lump of forgotten dogshit.

Smack in the middle of it was ABLE LOCK AND KEY. It sat along a block of similarly run-down establishments, some boarded up, some struggling along; only the pawnshop on the corner could be said to be thriving. An alley split the block between ABLE and the closed bail-bondsman's. It was this alley wall where the 'street artists' did their thing.

Edgar went inside, turning the placard to 'Open' with the reflexes of long habit as the door swung shut behind him. The interior wasn't much, a front room and a back room, dim and cluttered, smelling of dust, metal and nicotine.

In the front room, display cabinets with their glass almost as murky as the windows held padlocks, bike chains, lockboxes, hide-a-key containers, a gun vault, jewelry boxes, lockable diaries, and other such assorted odds and ends like those mock-safes made to look like a can of soup. Keyblanks hung on a labeled pegboard, the ink on their tags old, smeared and smudged. On the counter, beside the phone and register, were racks of keychains and novelty accessories. The key grinder squatted on a sturdy worktable, surrounded by drifts of brass shavings.

The back room, windowless, was even grungier. Shelving lined its walls, packed with cardboard boxes, spare parts, and tools. A desk of the dented battleship-grey sort Edgar remembered from his long-ago school days overflowed with files, receipts, paperwork and bills. The trash can and bulletin board also overflowed, one with wrappers and junk mail, the other with business cards, calendars, take-out menus, and notes. A squeaky swivel chair was tucked into the desk's kneehole. A larger chair, a battered vinyl recliner mended with duct tape, faced a folding table with a TV, radio and coffeepot on it.

Wedged into the far corner of the back room was a bathroom the size of a phone booth. The condition of it was about three inches short of a health hazard, but Edgar didn't care. It flushed. That was what mattered.

He went about the routine of settling in for another lucrative and productive day here at ABLE LOCK AND KEY, but damned if his gaze didn't keep being drawn to the wall that faced onto the alley. Damned if he was fancying he could still *see* those garish colors and symbols, as if they shined right through solid cinderblock and everything else.

The knowledge of them was like an itch he couldn't reach, a scent he couldn't quite identify, the title of a song he could almost remember, a persistent sound just annoying enough to be impossible to tune out. Switching on the radio didn't help, neither did making coffee.

After puttering around for a while, Edgar gave up,

knowing he wasn't going to be able to get his mind off the mess until he'd gotten rid of it. He had some paint left over from last time, probably not enough but a start. He took the can, tray, and roller back outside.

The alley wasn't as squalid as usual, which he supposed was a silver lining of sorts. Come to think, it hadn't been that bad lately. The bums had moved on, or *been* moved on, including the space-case who used to mumble about little tiny aliens and their flying saucers all lit up like Christmas. It didn't stink of piss anymore, there wasn't much of a roach or rat problem, and he couldn't remember the last time he'd seen bloodstains or busted vials.

Edgar's grudging gratitude toward whichever gang might be responsible for that did not, however, extend to forgiving them leaving their goddamn Day-Glo scribbles all over his goddamn wall.

Only *his* wall, too, he noticed. The opposite wall, the closed bail-bondsman's, was far from pristine, of course. It sported layers upon decrepit layers of events posters, fliers, band logo decals, bumper stickers, and such a tangled scrawl of the ordinary kind of graffiti—titties, dicks, for-a-good-time-calls, so-and-so RULZ, so-and-so SUX—that the original color could barely be discerned. But there was none of the eye-bleeding, needles-to-the-brain neon psychedelic folderol on that side.

Lucky him.

Grumbling, he got to work. He painted over

something that looked like a woven wreath of willow branches with stars or jewels twinkling in it. He painted over a bunch of swoops and dots that might have resembled script, to someone into those hippie head-trip hobbit movies. He painted over a dark circle that gave the effect of peering down into a deep well, where ripples tried to suggest a face framed in flowing hair. He painted over what he thought was a speckled mushroom with arms and legs, and a diminishing inward spiral of tiny shapes like hummingbirds or butterflies…or tiny airplanes, how the hell should he know?

Then he was out of paint, and he'd only managed one coat over about two-thirds of the wall. The vivid hues were muted but visible. The largest piece of 'street art' left was an oval border of sharp gold interlocked triangles, with a pair of ultra-turquoise handprints in the middle…not normal handprints, but stylized ones, very thin and with elongated fingers. Under those, in a blinding yellow-blue, were words that Edgar could at least read, even if they still made little sense.

Umbriel was here.

Whatever or whoever the hell *that* was. Good for Umbriel. If Edgar ever caught Umbriel out here again, Umbriel better be ready to run.

He got out-called for some lock changes—landlords and bitter breakups made for his main source of business—and stopped by the hardware store on the way back for another couple cans of paint. He also stopped by Dave's to pick up a pastrami-on-rye, reasoning that if he was going to have heartburn anyway he might as well earn it.

The activist nutballs across the street had set up one of their petition booths again. Edgar surprised them sometimes by signing his name to whatever their cause-of-the-day might be. He knew he was regarded in the Gulch as a grouchy old fart, which was true enough, but on some matters his beliefs were apparently downright progressive.

Legalize marijuana? Sure, why not? Everybody else had to pay taxes on their smokes and booze, so why should the hippies get a free pass?

Birth control and abortion? Damn right, and the more of it the better. Someone wanted to slut around, that was their concern, and why burden the world with the perpetual cycle of their mistakes?

Women in combat? Absolutely; they wanted to fight, let them fight. Whoever thought they were too frail and sensitive must never have gotten into it with the missus. All Edgar hoped was that once they were allowed to shoot terrorists, they'd start squishing their own damn spiders.

Gay marriage? Only fair. Let them suffer same as anybody else. Let them get nagged at day and night. Let them be screwed over for alimony, too. Let them shell out child support for a bunch of mouthy, ungrateful little shits who thought the world owed them whatever the hell they wanted.

Let them find out decades after the fact that it was no coincidence after all the middle brat looked more like the manager at the Stop-n-Shop where Irene had worked part-time as a checker....

He shoved that thought away and trudged across the street to see what the current crusade was. Some of them, naturally, he wouldn't touch with a ten-foot pole. Who gave a crap about animal testing, or chemicals in food? No cell phones while driving, sure, to keep everybody else safe...but if someone didn't want to wear a bike helmet, well, it was their skull and their neck. More gun laws would keep people safe from criminals? That was a joke; since when were *criminals* impressed with laws in the first place? Illegal immigration, same deal, otherwise it wouldn't be *illegal,* would it?

Last time, it had been a 'Save the Rave' rally, when a nearby warehouse converted to a dance club got shut down after a raid and drug bust. Edgar hadn't cared either way, so he signed with the idea that if the kids were going to be drinking and drugging up anyway, it would be better to have them all in one place to keep the damage localized. So far, nothing had come of it; the warehouse was still boarded over and locked up tight.

This time, it turned out they were over there now collecting signatures protesting the slap-on-the-wrist sentencing of a city official who'd been caught not just with a hand in the cookie jar but with both arms elbow deep. Edgar was glad to sign that one. If a cushy salary and expense account still wasn't enough, good riddance. Not like *he'd* voted for the greedy idiot anyway.

After lunch, he went back to the alley and finished the paint job. Three coats should have done it, seemed to have done it, but damned if he didn't think he could still see some of the colors bleeding through. Probably a trick of his tired eyes, the lingering effect of having had to look at them, having them practically seared into his retinas.

Tomorrow, if necessary, he'd do another coat. For now, he ached from the exertion. All that bending and stretching and reaching played hell on the old back.

Now, if they had a petition for health care reform, that was another he'd be glad to sign. Used to be that a person could go to the doctor without having to about take out a loan. Edgar knew he was lucky enough to have escaped many of the ailments of age thus far, but even so, keeping up with his regular prescriptions was a big enough bite out of the dwindling budget. He'd make do with aspirin.

A couple of customers came by in the afternoon to get keys duplicated, but the rest of the day was quiet. Edgar didn't mind. Channel Four was running a *Judge Janice* marathon—he enjoyed watching her rip the deadbeats a new one—and after that was the news, then game shows.

Between *Wheel of Fortune* and *Jeopardy*, he ordered in a pizza because the heartburn still hadn't abated. He crunched some token antacids while waiting for the delivery kid and washed down more aspirin with a warm leftover soda.

At some point, he must have dozed off, because he woke in the recliner with the television showing one of those medical dramas where the doctors spent more time having sex than treating patients. He burped pepperoni, coughed, checked the clock, and discovered it was almost nine.

Well, not like anybody was waiting for him at home. No one had come in to loot the register while he slept, either, not that they'd have gotten much for their troubles.

His back felt better, that was what mattered. Also, he had to piss like Old Faithful.

The bulb over the bathroom sink, a yellowed and flyspecked thing on its last legs, had finally given up. Edgar pissed in the flickering light from the television screen, then noticed that the water in the stained porcelain bowl had a weird silvery shimmer, as if reflecting moonlight through a window.

Ridiculous, since there was a.) precious little moonlight down in the Gulch and b.) no window in the bathroom.

He realized then that it was coming from the wall,

just behind his left shoulder.

Edgar finished up with a squirt and a dribble, put the pipeworks away, and turned his head.

Irene had chosen the wallpaper when they first opened the business, all those years ago, and it had never been changed since. Originally robin's egg blue with cream-colored pinstripes, it had gone to musty grey, split and peeling to reveal cheap, splintering wallboard beneath.

Shifting spots of multi-colored brightness wavered on the wallpaper.

No.

Wavered through the wallpaper. Coming from behind it. Where it encountered one of those peeling splits, it spilled into a slanted ray of microscopic twinkling motes, the way dust looked in a sunbeam.

Through the wallpaper and the wallboard…as if flashlights were being played across holes from outside.

But there were no goddamn holes through to his bathroom from the cinderblock alley wall. Hadn't he spent half the damn day out there, painting over? Wouldn't he have noticed?

It came to him then—the 'street artists' were back! They were out there right now, thinking he'd gone home for the night, thinking the block deserted, so they could beam their flashlights and shake their spray cans with impunity.

His hours of hard work…the cost of the paint…the

last coat probably wasn't even goddamn *dry* yet…!

The nerve!

No point calling the police. They had crackhouses and raves and gangfights and domestic violence to deal with—*real* crimes. They'd only laugh at one of the neighborhood old farts bitching about kids doing graffiti.

Unless, of course, he stormed out there to confront them, and the kids proved to be gang members after all and *shot* him….

He stormed out there to confront them anyway. If they wanted to risk gunshots that was their problem, and if they tried coming at him with switchblades that was why he paused long enough to grab a hammer from the worktable.

The sidewalk was empty. Overhead, on the expressways, commuters had been replaced by truckers, semis, and long-haulers crossing the city. A souped-up car stereo whumped and thumped bass thunder from blocks away.

Edgar went to the corner of the building, saw nothing, took another step, and the alley was suddenly awash in glimmering lights and colors. Bright neon blurs went swooping and sweeping and swirling around, leaving streaky after-images. He thought of kaleidoscopes and prisms, rainbows, mirrored disco balls, those glowstick things kids cracked and shook, laser light shows.

Strange sounds filled the air too…a whirring-humming-twittering-chiming-tinkling-buzzing…

something like tiny bells, and something like the fluid trill of harpstrings...high girlish giggles and pure choirboy notes...

Whiffs of scent and taste, quick and fleeting, teased his senses and vanished. Sweet ones like cotton candy, lemon drops, roses, cake frosting, a kind of berryblue taffy he hadn't found since he was a child. Warm ones like toasted marshmallows, lit candles, cinnamon, laundry fresh from the dryer, buttered popcorn.

He felt the tingle of a brisk sea breeze, and the crisp crunch of autumn leaves, and the invigorating chill of winter air, and green grass in the sun.

Reeling, Edgar squinted and blinked. He shaded his eyes with his free hand, peering into the dazzle in hopes of finding the source.

Shapes...

Indistinct shapes in a sudden flurry.

Shrill cries of alarm.

Panic and confusion rushing at him, whirling around him, and Edgar couldn't see, couldn't hear.

Something whizzed past his ear like a wasp and maybe someone had thrown a rock or maybe someone had taken a shot at him and something else smacked into his shirtfront and clung there whapping and flapping like a piece of windblown paper and he slapped it away and another piece flew into his face, a whirlwind of tatters and scraps whipping around him.

He shouted, shielding his head with one arm and

taking wild hammer-swings with the other, connecting with nothing more substantial than a styrofoam cup, until it struck the wall and was painfully jarred from his grip. He hunkered down, both arms over his head now and wondered if he was going crazy, or if he'd walked into a cloud of drug fumes, interrupted an Alice in Wonderland hallucinogenic party.

Then it was over.

Darkness and calm silence descended. Edgar crouched, gasping, heart walloping in his chest, pulse doing drumbeats in his neck and ears, not sure if he was having a goddamn heart attack or not.

When he decided he wasn't, and that he hadn't been shot either, he cautiously looked around. The alley was empty except for him.

But, even in the shadows, he saw the unfinished markings on the painted cinderblock. Jigsaw scribbles and designs, crosses and stars and curved triangles. They weren't as vivid as before, not luminous with that floating glow or flowing gloat.

He straightened up and touched one of the images. It smeared. A pale green residue came away on his fingertip. It did not seem like paint at all but some kind of glittery, oily chalk. Didn't smell like paint, either, but like a...ghost, or echo...of the scents that had teased at him before.

The hammer lay where it had fallen. Edgar picked it up and saw residue on its flattened round head as well, though this was much brighter, and red instead of green. Not red like blood, but red like the artificial color of maraschino cherries or strawberry syrup.

More red caught his eye, a brilliant shine that reminded him of brake lights on the back of a car or the red of a traffic signal. But, even if a broken chunk of the plastic covering of one had been left in the alley, without a bulb behind it...even if it caught some random beam of light, it shouldn't have gleamed with such intensity ...

It wasn't a chunk of red plastic.

It was....

A doll?

About five inches high, thin as a twig, its skin and clothes and hair reddish, its translucent glassy-looking butterfly wings patterned with veins and traceries of ruby light.

Edgar bent closer and curled his fingers around the tiny figure crumpled at the base of the alley wall. It weighed next to nothing in his hand, a soap bubble or twist of tissue paper. It draped limply across his palm, slender legs dangling.

He remembered the sensation of the hammer striking something no more substantial than a styrofoam cup.

Was this what he had hit?

What was it?

Was it a doll? A fairy doll, a character from a Disney

cartoon?

The body thrummed as if with a barely-perceptible vibration. A wind-up thing, one of those new remote-controlled gadgets?

He had no idea toys had gotten so intricate—.

The fairy-doll twitched. The ruby shine of its wings strengthened.

It…felt…not like a toy at all.

Alive?

Was that what he was thinking?

It felt alive in his hand, inert but tingling with vitality. Weightless as a hummingbird, moth or mouse… so delicate and fragile…yet he'd whacked it with a hammer….

The thought occurred to him again that he was going crazy, or had been drugged, or this was somebody's idea of a smartass practical joke. Maybe he was dreaming, still sound asleep in the recliner, and this whole bizarre scene was the result of acid indigestion.

Whichever it was, he decided he'd rather deal with it inside than out here in the alley. He went back in, shut and locked the door, switched the placard to 'Closed,' and indifferently shoved papers off the desk until he'd made a clear space. He put the…

…fairy…

…in the clear space, then trained the goosenecked desk lamp full on it, a concentrated spotlight like an interrogation or autopsy scene from a movie.

The tiny red face squinched up in unconscious but reflexive reaction to the glare.

Edgar considered.

Okay, say it *was* real, say it *was* a living thing. Never mind the how or why or they didn't exist. Just go with it.

Fine. A fairy. A real, live fairy.

He couldn't let it get away until he had some answers.

The thinnest length of chain and smallest padlocks he had in the shop were big and clunky by comparison, but he fashioned a manacle around the fairy's ankle and looped the other end of the chain through a ringbolt in the desktop.

Only then, when it was secured, did he let himself thoroughly scrutinize his captive.

Five inches tall…skin an opalescent pinkish-red… upswept spiky-feathery hair like a cardinal's crest…a teardrop-shaped face with lash-fringed large eyes, the barest nub of a nose, ears flat to the head and tapering to a point, the mouth a lipless slit. The body was long-legged and slim, the chest flat and the hips narrow.

He thought again of Disney cartoons, not Tinkerbell but that other one, the fantasy one set to classical music, with Mickey and the brooms. That was what this reminded him of.

Edgar couldn't tell if it was a boy or a girl. Maybe it was neither, or both, or something weirdly in-between. Its clothes weren't much help. The shiny red pants were so tight it might have been dunked in latex paint. The knee-high high-heeled boots fastened up the sides with intricate rows of the smallest buckles he had ever seen. Its shirt was a red halterneck-style garment of lacy mesh finer than medical gauze.

The wings were like soft glass, or hard clear jelly, resilient but slightly giving when poked with a fingertip. The glowing ruby lines ran through them like the branching veins of a leaf or thread-thin tubes of neon gas.

Nothing about it seemed damaged or injured, despite what had happened. It was obviously much tougher than it looked.

Not to mention impossible.

Edgar wondered again if he was dreaming or drugged, but reluctantly concluded this was all too detailed and precise for such an easy explanation.

That left crazy…or real.

The fairy's eyes opened. They were scintillating shades of red, faceted like jewels, without whites or pupils…glittering crimson orbs like beaded drops of crystallized blood.

His face must have been looming over it like a giant moon, and probably not the prettiest one either. With a darting whirr, the fairy tried to take off, but was brought up short at the end of the chain.

It went nuts.

Fluttering and spinning, buzzing in all directions,

yanking to the end of the chain, snapping back, it went utterly nuts.

Edgar had seen someone put a cat on a leash once. The result had been similar to this, only noisier, with more fur and claws. And without ambulance-flasher wings giving off such bright bursts of emergency red that they lit up the whole room.

Finally, it stopped its frenzied flight. It landed on the desk, as far from Edgar as the chain would permit, and tugged with both hands at the manacle. No use. It glared up at him.

Despite his distinct size advantage, Edgar leaned back, unnerved by what he saw in those glittering red eyes.

"Settle down," he said. "I'm not going to hurt you."

The glare continued, piercing. In a high piping-clear voice, the fairy said, "You hit me with a hammer, you big fuckhead."

He sat back further, jaw dropping, not sure if he was more surprised by its speech or its language.

So much for Disney.

The fairy tugged at the chain again, fixing its gaze on the links. Twin hair-fine beams of red light shot from its eyes. Edgar thought of gun-sights and laser pointers, and security grids in heist movies. He winced in anticipation of melt-sizzling metal and acrid smoke, the plink of a link breaking, the fairy's rapid escape.

But the chain held. The red light gleamed harmlessly

along it.

"Shit!" The fairy looked back at Edgar.

His wince worsened, now with the anticipation of those beams searing his skin. Or blinding him; hadn't he read somewhere that shining a laser pointer into your eye was worse than staring directly at the sun? He raised his hands protectively in front of his face as if that would do any good.

"Settle down," said the fairy, mimicking his voice in unflattering caricature. "I'm not going to hurt you."

They studied each other. An uneasy feeling of détente crept in as their speculative pause extended.

"You called me a fuckhead," Edgar said.

"*You* hit me with a hammer, and chained me up."

"Hitting you was an accident. I was defending myself."

"We were just trying to get away! You surprised us. You weren't supposed to be here. You weren't supposed to see."

"We?" Edgar remembered the kaleidoscope blurs of motion, the colors dancing and whirling. "Us? How many of you are there? And what are you, anyway? What were you doing in the alley? You're the ones who've been doing all that damn psychedelic graffiti, aren't you?"

"We're taggers," the fairy said, as if Edgar was the stupidest thing he'd ever met. "It's what we do!"

"It's vandalism, painting all that nonsense on

people's walls."

"It isn't paint; where would we get paint, why would we need paint?" The fairy crouched and swiped a hand in a smooth stroke across the desktop, leaving an arc of vivid red on the scarred surface. It was just like the stuff on the wall outside, both oily and chalky, iridescent.

"Fine, so it isn't paint, it's still *my* wall you scribble all over!"

Its little shoulders hitched in a shrug, shifting its glassy ruby-marbled wings. "Well, yeah, where else? And it'd help if you'd leave it alone, you know. Think that's easy? Think we like having to keep coming back to re-do it?"

Edgar sputtered. "Leave it alone? It's on *my* wall! What, are you going to give me a lecture next about not appreciating street art and the creative expression of inner-city youth?"

"You don't have to appreciate it," the fairy said. "You shouldn't even be seeing it, really, but I guess since you've *been* here so long, it's seeped in over the years."

"What's seeped in?"

"Magic, what else?"

"Magic," Edgar said.

"Dude. I'm a fairy."

"Right. And a tagger. And you tag my wall, *my* wall, with pixie dust."

A tiny hand flicked up in warning. "Fairy dust. We don't mix with pixies, and you don't want to either, old man. We're non-violent. Pixies? Pixies will fuck your shit right up."

"This is insane," Edgar said. "I'm getting a goddamn headache."

"Look, tell you what…unlock this chain, let me go… you can forget this whole thing ever happened."

"You'll go tag someplace else?"

The tiny red face twisted uncertainly. "Welllll…that might be a problem."

"Oh, come on, I'm not asking for three wishes or a damn pot of gold—."

"Dude, that's—never mind." Evidently, fairies could get headaches too, judging by the way this one pressed its fingertips to its temples.

"I just want you and your…your little fairy-friends to…to *tag* off and leave me alone."

"I told you," the fairy said, "you shouldn't even be seeing the tags. It's nothing personal. Ignore them."

"Ignore them? Those colors? Those designs like—like I don't know what? Letters nobody can read, or if they can, don't make any sense? You want me to ignore them, there on my wall, damn near glowing in the dark, for all the world to see?"

"Not all the world. Only us."

"What?"

Tiny fingertips massaged harder at tiny temples. "Why me? Why'd he have to catch *me*?" muttered the fairy. "Why not Strobe, or Neon? They'd be able to explain. Or Glowstix. Shit, even Emo."

"Those are your names?" Edgar asked, eyebrows lifting.

"Not our real names. You couldn't pronounce our real names even if you wanted to, which you wouldn't."

"Strobe? Emo? What's yours?"

"Laser."

"Pff. I should have guessed."

"Yeah, well, in the olden days it was shit like Cowslip, Cobweb, Moth and Mustardseed," Laser said. "Times change."

Edgar took a deep breath. "If you say so. Just tell me how come, if only fairies are supposed to be able to see your scribbles, I can."

"Because, like I said, some of the magic here must have seeped in, since you've been here so long. This place, this shop of yours, it's at a thinning."

"At a what?"

"Like those fuck-ugly highways up there," Laser said, pointing past the roof. "A junction, an interchange, a merge. For the commute. For the rush-hour traffic flow. You know."

"Here? My shop sits on a gate to Fairyland?"

"Don't flatter yourself. It's a thinning, yeah, a shortcut to the low road, but it's not a great one. We had one of those, but now that we can't use it anymore, we have to make do. This is the best we've turned up so far. We tag it so the others can find it and cross over."

"Because they, these 'others,' they can see your scribbles. Like me."

Laser nodded, that feathery cardinal's crest waving. "Exactly. It's been here long enough, and so have you, and enough magic's come through from our side, that you've gotten used to it."

"The hell I have!"

"You could see our tags. You saw us, when you came into the alley. Dude, you're talking to a fairy right now."

"Or maybe I've gone crazy, like that bum who used to camp out there, the one who was always going on about...," His words trailed off.

Little tiny aliens, their flying saucers all lit up like Christmas....

"Look," said Laser, "I'm sorry I called you a fuckhead, okay? Just let me go. Maybe we'll find a better thinning soon, and you'll never have to deal with us again. Sound good? Sounds good. Deal? Deal."

"Hold on, not so fast!"

"Aw, c'mon, you said you wanted to get rid of us."

"But what *you* said makes it sound like I'm stuck with this until you find a better option. What happened to your old path?"

Though Laser's mouth was only that tiny, lipless slit, it turned down in a disgruntled scowl. "They shut us down! Closed the club, boarded it up, and now we're S-O-L!"

"S-O-L?"

"Shit-outta-luck!"

"Wait...club? Boarded up? You don't mean that rave warehouse, do you?"

Again, the red crest waved with the fairy's vigorous nod. "It was the greatest! The lights, the music—."

"The drugs?"

"Fuck yeah! Couple hundred or so kids blissed out on E? That kind of uninhibited energy, we used to only be able to get with a dance in a full-on fairy-ring. We took care of them, too. Nobody died, nobody messed with anybody else. Umbriel made sure of that. He ran a safe place."

"Umbriel," Edgar said. "I remember that one from the wall. About the only damn thing out there I could read, not that I knew what it meant."

"Our DJ. Best spinner ever to cross over from Underhill. The trolls always had it in for him, though. The raid? The bust? It was total trollshit, dude! Total trollshit."

"The hell's a troll?"

"Mean-ass fairy haters. A lot of them become cops, and nothing gets them off like ruining our fun."

The idea that there were trolls on the police force somehow didn't seem as surprising as it probably should have been.

He was about to ask—though he was sure he'd regret it—how much *else* of this hidden world of trolls, fairies, and magic there was, especially down here in the Gulch, but before he could, there was a sharp knock at the door.

It was followed by a brief but bright pulse of ultra-turquoise light flooding in through the grimy front windows. The interior of the shop lit up with a wavering, eerie shimmer like an illuminated swimming pool at night.

"And what the hell's *that*?" Edgar said instead.

"That," said Laser, grinning, "is Umbriel. You didn't think my friends would ditch me, did you? They went for help."

"Oh...."

He went to the door and opened it, and found himself face to face with Umbriel. Or, at least, with a tall, pale, slim, elfin-featured pretty-boy he could only assume was Umbriel.

Certainly *looked* like someone who'd have a name like that....

Shock-platinum hair in a spiky mane fell over one of his heavily-eyelinered gold-flecked blue eyes. He wore skinny jeans and high-top sneakers, a thin jewel-studded belt that looped three times around his narrow hips, and a form-fitting black tee shirt with a logo on it of stylized turquoise handprints inside an oval border of interlocking gold triangles.

"Mr. Norris."

Umbriel did not, however, *sound* like someone who'd have a name like that. His voice was deep, low, resonant and husky. Not the voice of a person to screw with. Nor were those gold-flecked, eyelinered eyes the eyes of a person to screw with. They were…old…old, and wise, and filled with a kind of terrible, powerful knowledge that made Edgar instantly accept as truth everything Laser had told him.

He wasn't sure how any of this worked, so, took a guess. "Uh…come in?"

With a slight chin-dip of acknowledgment, Umbriel stepped into the shop.

"You've captured one of our own," he said, in that deep don't-screw-with-me voice. "Will you relinquish what is ours and show yourself a friend, or keep fairy bound by mortal hand and make yourself our foe?"

Edgar gazed a moment longer into those terrible gold-flecked eyes.

We're non-violent, Laser had said…and whether that meant just the little taggers, or whether that meant all of them, Edgar decided he'd rather not find out. Besides, skinny and girly though Umbriel might appear, there were probably plenty of magic tricks in his arsenal that could make Edgar's life miserable even without resorting to violence.

He indicated the other room, doing a shuffling backward walk through the cluttered shop to avoid taking his attention off his visitor as much as possible. Umbriel followed, moving with a poised, lithe, gliding silence.

Once at the desk, Edgar had to turn away to focus

on unlocking the miniscule manacle. The nape of his neck prickled. His usually-deft fingers felt huge, thick and clumsy, bumbling logs of dumb meat compared to the fairies' grace.

He got it, though, finally. The chain hissed into a pile on the desktop. Laser took off with a gleeful trill, zipping around Edgar's head in a streaky red blur of motion.

"Ah," said Umbriel, smiling in satisfaction.

No sooner had he than an entire host of small, glassy-winged bodies swept past him. "Laser!" cried a shrill, piping multitude in ecstatic chorus.

They were all the glowing colors Edgar had seen in the alley, vivid green and electric bubblegum, acid lemonade, neon violet and nuclear tangerine, incandescent black, a silver-white like magnesium, rainbows and prisms in a flickering-fluttering dance of lights. Some were dressed similar to Laser, some wore tight vinyl miniskirts and fishnets, some skimpy shorts and tank-tops, or went bare-chested in loose saggy-baggy pants.

Laser joined the kaleidoscope dazzle of fairies. They swirled giddily, joyful, darting back and forth, weaving intricate patterns in the air, chattering, laughing their effervescent champagne-fizz laughs.

"Glowstix! Binkie! Blinkie! Jitter!"

"Laser, yay! You're okay!"

"When he caught you—."

"Me and Neon wanted to come after you, but

Strobe said—."

"—so worried!"

"Emo thought you were a goner!"

"...well duh, hammer-whack to the face..."

"—it hurt?"

"—he hurt you?"

"All good, he's cool, we worked it out," Laser said. "He's not so bad for a cranky old grouch."

This brought the others swarming around Edgar, engulfing him once more in that cyclone of scents, tastes and sensations as they jostled to inspect him up close. Some, he noticed, sported nearly microscopic tattoos and piercings. Others had fuzzy moth-antennae. One buzzed right into his face on dragonfly wings like fans of radioactive Mountain Dew, the little inquisitive head topped by some kind of Dr. Seuss crazy hairdo. It patted him on the end of the nose, leaving a green fairy dust smudge.

Edgar recoiled, peripherally aware of Umbriel watching with a pretty-boy smirk that was half insolent, half indulgent.

"We should help him, then!" the patter chirped, not at all put off by his recoiling.

Another, bright indigo and twinkling like a skyful of stars, agreed. "The shoemaker-and-the-elves thing, only with keys!"

"This could be our new hangout!" added a pink-and-yellow one wearing a frilly tutu and ballet slippers, clapping tiny hands.

"What a great idea!"

"We can come here all the time!"

Laser laughed, and Umbriel smirked, and Edgar's mouth went dry.

Early the next morning, to the immense surprise of his neighbors in the Gulch, a folding table stacked with flyers had been set up on the sidewalk outside ABLE LOCK AND KEY. Posters decorated with brilliantly-colored designs had been taped to the grimy windows.

By the end of the week, Edgar had collected over five hundred signatures in support of 'Save the Rave.'

Wormwood

By Alexandra Christian

Freedom Jenkins wanted to kill Gerald Wilkins.

He was the overseer at Wormwood, the plantation where Freedom was born. She couldn't remember a time when she hadn't wanted to see the old man's blood flow into the black pluff mud in the depths of the swamp beyond the indigo fields. All the slaves called Wilkins "the Butcher," and it was the truth. He delighted in doling out cruel punishments that would leave even the heartiest of fieldhands crippled. They would whisper and hiss behind his back, making the sign of the cross or even cookin' up some hoodoo whenever he passed. The Butcher would hobble around, squinting at you through his one good eye. The other was a dead, sightless orb tinged with red. The old folks said he got poked with a pitchfork by the devil and Freedom could believe it. His hands were gnarled and wrinkled and always clutched around the handle of a whip he'd made special just to torture them. Eight long tails fashioned from strips of thin leather that would cut right across your skin, making it crack open and bleed down your back. If that wasn't bad enough, at the end of each tail was a bit of steel that had been sharpened to cruel points. Some people said that he had killed a little slaveboy with that whip at the plantation he used to oversee down in Louisiana.

"Freedom," he'd sneer, staring at her with that glassy eye. "Like an uppity little girl like you'll ever be free."

Freedom would clench her fists and grit her teeth, staring right up into those yellowed eyes and showing no fear. She might be just a little thing, but her will was as strong as a fieldhand's right arm. Though her skin was dark brown, the color of fresh gingerbread, her little cheeks would blush bright red as she tried to hold back her rage. Her sister Ady's firm hand at the small of her back would always calm the fire. Slaves that talked back to the Butcher often got themselves lost. Wilkins chuckled, seeing how Freedom struggled to hold on to her anger. He taunted her with it, wanting her to give him a reason to beat her, but she was smarter than that. She might be just a baby, barely out of shirttails, but she could see right through to that old man's rotten soul.

"I may not be free now, Missah Wilkin', but someday my spirit be flyin' wit' the angels."

He shook his head, kicking up dirt onto her apron as he passed. "Maybe sooner than you think, little girl," he mumbled. He peered over his shoulder, but this time it wasn't Freedom on which his dead gaze fell. It was Ady. Something about that toothy grin made her blood run cold. It was the look of a sly old fox, staring at the newborn spring lambs. A hungry look. He'd lick his lips and run a single fingertip down Ady's arm, never saying a word with his voice, but that look said it all. If the Butcher hadn't been at Ady yet, he soon would be.

When he was gone, Freedom grumbled. "I don't like when he look at you that way," she said, glowering. "Like you a pig ready for the slaughter."

Ady chuckled and put her arm around her baby sister's shoulders. "Don't your face look sour!" she said, trying to hide the small tremble in her voice. "Careful you don't let it stick that way."

But Freedom continued to scowl. She had heard Cook talking about all the scandals and lurid goings on around Wormwood—usually in hushed tones and subtle innuendo, but Freedom knew what they were talking about. Just last spring one of the girls, just about Ady's age, had hung herself by the neck in the barn rather than giving birth to that old Butcher's baby. And now it seemed his eye was falling on Ady.

Ady was one of the most beautiful creatures God ever put on the Earth. Tall and slender, she had the air of an African queen as she walked, slow and steady toward the Big House each morning. Everyone, white and black folks alike, marveled at the graceful slope of her nose and the full rosette bow of her mouth. And then there were her eyes. Ady had the most beautiful, catlike green eyes. They were so unusual and so other-worldly, that folks thought she must be touched by the wood sprites that lived down by the marsh. Even more beautiful than her eyes or her skin, was her soul. Ady was about the kindest person you could ever meet. It didn't matter how hard she worked out in the kitchen or the laundry, she always had a smile and a kind word. But lately, something had changed. Freedom had noticed a sort of fear behind her smile. At night, she was keeping to the quarters. Even on the Sabbath when the slaves could gather 'round the fire and sing songs and tell stories, Ady was nowhere to be found. She used to walk with her head held high, but now she looked down toward the ground and would only speak when spoken to. Ady had become an empty shell of what she once was, and now that Freedom had seen that greasy expression on Gerald Wilkins's face, she knew why.

"If I was you, I'd poke his other eye out," Freedom said.

"And you be dead before the mornin'," Ady hissed. "Just you hush up about that, girl! It ain't none of your business."

Freedom knew that her sister was scared. She could smell it on her like the sweat running down the backs of the men working in the fields below the house. Freedom had been just three when her Mama had been killed trying to escape. Even though no one had ever said so, she knew that Gerald Wilkins had murdered her Ma. Ady knew what the Butcher was capable of and therefore she tried to shield her little sister from whatever hidden horrors were being inflicted upon her.

The two sisters began the long walk toward the expanse of indigo fields that spread out along the horizon. The sun was low in the sky and soon they'd be able to hear the voice of Boone, the foreman, calling in that sing-songy way, "Quittin' time!" The evening cool was setting in and Freedom was glad. It was her and Ady's job to take the water buckets out to the field workers two times each day. Usually, by the time they made the morning trip, the sun was already high in the sky and sweltering. Especially for such a little girl with two big buckets full of freshly-drawn water slung over her shoulders. Of course, with the coolness of the impending night came the dread of passing through the edge of the wood on the way to the well. The shadows of twilight would descend, giving the trees the look of gnarly arms that would reach out to grab Freedom and carry her away into the darkness.

"Them trees looks angry," Freedom said, keeping her voice low, as if she were hiding. "Like witches' fingers."

Ady laughed at her little sister and shifted the yoke that weighed heavily on her muscular shoulders. "Ain't no such things as witches. You know that, Freedom."

"Yes there is," Freedom replied. "Caroline and Stuart told me that there was witches in them woods that would snatch you up and throw you in a big boilin' pot and make soap outta you!" Freedom nodded, her face so dark and serious that Ady burst into peals of hearty laughter. Caroline and Stuart Kilpatrick, the master's two children, were known to be skilled in the art of mischievous storytelling of a most good-natured sort. They loved Ady and Freedom with no reservation or regard for the color of their skin, but they dearly loved to give Freedom the heebee-jeebees.

"Caroline and Stuart are just teasin' you, chile! There ain't nothin' bad in them woods."

"How do you know for sure?"

"Because I know what's really in them woods." Ady leaned in close. A gleam of conspiratorial glee sparkled in her eyes and Freedom couldn't help but return her sister's smile. "And it ain't witches." Ady winked and hurried up the hill toward the large stand of trees that shaded the well.

"What is it, Ady?" Freedom shouted, stumbling after her, forgetting to be afraid of the long shadows that crept up around them. The heavy yoke over her shoulders and the awkward buckets nearly tipped her over as she tried to keep up, her face aglow with a childlike curiosity.

Ady turned and gracefully set down her burden. She rolled her shoulders back and forth before stretching her back like a sleek cat basking in the sun. Her body was silhouetted against the fiery pink sunset and a sprinkling of perspiration glistened on the back of her neck. Freedom was struck by her sister's beauty and suddenly had no doubt that she was privy to all sorts of magic. "Well," she began, "some folks call 'em wood spirits or brownies, but I call 'em fairies."

"What's a fairy?" Freedom asked, dropping her buckets and lighting on the grass at her sister's feet. She whispered the word again. The new word felt strange on her lips.

"Why, a fairy is the most beautiful thing God ever put on this Earth. They got pale skin and silver eyes, hair that's fine and soft like cornsilk and wings so's they can fly wherever they get a mind to go."

"They can fly?" Freedom asked with a breathless sigh.

Ady smiled and began lowering the smaller bucket down into the well. "I 'spect they can do whatever they please. They knows all the secrets of the woods and... they can do magic."

"What kind of magic?" Freedom looked skeptical. She had heard about some folks that had "the Gift." Hoodoo folks that could heal the sick and hurt the wicked. Conjure women that could work roots and carried bags full of gris-gris. But nobody, not even the most powerful of the Voodoo Queens could fly.

"All kinds. But most of all...they likes to play tricks on

folks."

Freedom started to ask her sister to tell her a story about the fairies. Ady had a particular gift for telling stories, but they could hear that old Butcher Wilkins calling out to them. "Ady! Get up here, girl!"

The sisters looked at each other with worried expressions. They never knew what would happen when Wilkins called like that. He might give them a new chore to do or he might be waiting with that whip of his. It didn't matter if you were doing what you were supposed to or not. Sometimes he'd beat a slave just out of pure meanness. Men like Gerald Wilkins never needed a reason.

Ady immediately stopped and wiped her hands on the apron tied around her waist. "I better hurry on," she said, forcing a reassuring smile toward Freedom. "If I'm late, that ol' devil will never let me hear the end of it."

Freedom scowled. "Please Ady...don't go up there. I got a bad feelin'...."

Ady shook her head and rolled her eyes as if to shrug off her sister's warning. "I ain't got no choice, baby girl. I got to go...." As if to accentuate the point, Wilkins bellowed again for her.

"We got to run away, Ady," Freedom hissed, grabbing Ady's arm and pulling her back. "We got to get away from here. I heard some of the others last night...they plannin' to leave just as soon as it gets warm at night. We can go with 'em, Ady! We can be...."

"Hush up!" Ady growled. "Don't you talk about runnin' away. You know what they do to folks that run off. You'll be dead before summertime, one way or another! You know what happened to Ma and Pa."

Freedom heaved a big sigh. This was an old conversation.

She jerked her arm away from Freedom and began to run toward the Big House. She called over her shoulder, "Get that water out to them field-hands!"

Freedom watched her sister disappear over the hill, running to her uncertain fate. Again she shook her head, wishing that she could talk some sense into Ady. She kicked the grass as she went over to the well, humming to herself as she began to pull the cool, clear water up from the well.

After a few minutes she was singing loud, trying to keep herself from thinking of the burning ache that had started in her shoulders and crept down her back. The song was so familiar now. She had heard it so many times in the night around the cooking fires. Cook had told her to sing it 'til she could say it in her sleep. She said that the words to the song would someday show her the way to freedom up north. The song's words had wings, and soon Freedom was soaring up above the fields and into the clouds with the birds. Her voice soared too, ringing out among the trees and giving her hope. It was her own special magic.

"God's gonna trouble, the water," she sang,

pouring the water from the well into her heavy wooden buckets. Each was full to the brim by the end of her song and sweat stood out on her brow. Now came the task of getting all that water out to the fields.

"Four buckets and only one of me," she grumbled, another pang of hatred for Gerald Wilkins stabbed her temples. She'd have to make two trips with those heavy loads on her back. And she was already tired.

Freedom dipped the drinking gourd into one of the buckets and took a long drink of the cold well water. She lay down on the lush, green grass there at the edge of the forest, resting herself for a moment before setting out on her long walk to the indigo fields that lay on the other side of the plantation. Looking up at the sky, she wondered if the sky looked the same up north. Some folks said that up in Canada, the air was chilly and crisp, but you could see forever in the sky. Freedom hoped that was true and that someday she'd get to see it for herself. But she couldn't leave without Ady. And Ady was too scared to leave. Their Ma and Pa had died trying to run away from Wormwood.

Freedom had only been three years old and Ady nearly ten. Gerald Wilkins had just come to work for Mr. Kilpatrick and his nickname preceded him. All over the quarters, people were scared. Wilkins had taken an immediate dislike to the sisters' father. Their Ma had begun to fear that The Butcher was going to kill him soon. Every day he would take out his frustration on their daddy's back with that cruel whip until finally he had no choice but to escape up north. He'd promised them he'd be back to get them and stole away in the blackest part of the night.

It was storming so bad that the whole sky was lit up with lightning. Ma had begged him not to go, but he left, knowing that it was his last chance. A little while after he left Ma noticed that he'd left the little knapsack of food that would last him until he got to the river had been left behind. Without that food, Pa would starve before he ever reached the boatman that would carry him across to the first stop on that rumored railroad to the Promised Land. Ma put on her kerchief and took off after him, hoping that she would catch him before he got too far. Freedom remembered her Ma kissing the top of her head and Ady crying and holding her tight.

It was the last time they saw her alive.

The next morning, both of them were hanging in the trees out behind the slave quarters as a warning to others that might try to leave. There were whispers that Wilkins had killed them, but no one would dare say anything. And as long as Kilpatrick's crops got harvested, he didn't much care one way or the other.

Freedom closed her eyes tight and willed the dark thoughts away. There was no time to wallow in the sorrows of her past just now. Now there were workers out in the fields that were thirsty. She sat up and started to stand when she saw movement just out of the corner of her eye. Her breath caught, and for a moment she was afraid that Wilkins, himself had been watching her slacking off under the trees. But when she turned, there was nothing there, save for the well.

"Hello?" she called out, but there was no answer. She stood up slowly, remembering the old witch woman and her boiling pot. A chill breeze whipped her cheeks and she shivered. There was no sound, save for the rustle of the new spring leaves. A soft voice, seeming to travel on the wind, just barely a voice at all, whispered past her ear, calling her name.

"*Freedom...,*" it called, and suddenly she wanted to run to the woods. "*Come and play....*"

"I got to go," she shouted back, immediately feeling silly for shouting at the trees. But she waited for the voice to come back. Her hands shook as she bent over to pick up the heavy yoke again, so much so that she nearly dropped one of the pails full of water. She could feel whatever it was lurking in the woods watching her. She hoisted the heavy load over her shoulders and backed away from the well slowly, keeping her eyes on the tree line, afraid to blink for fear she'd miss it. Once she was away and scaling the hill toward the fields, she started to think about the strange encounter she'd just experienced. Though she'd been afraid upon seeing the shadow move and hearing that odd, breathy voice on the breeze, Freedom was sure that whatever it was, it was friendly. Almost playful. She turned once more, staring back at the well and for a moment it was there—a shadowy silhouette against the trees that seemed to wave. And then gentle laughter that wrapped her in a warm shawl of reassurance.

"Steal away, Freedom."

* * *

The moon was high by the time Freedom got back to the meager quarters she shared with Ady, Cook, and her boy Chaz. She could hear the other slaves laughing and singing around the cooking fires, but she was much too tired to join them. Her back ached from the heavy yoke and the muscles across her shoulders and down her arms were on fire with fatigue at dipping out bucket after bucket of water from the well. It was all she could do to make it through the ragged door to lay down across the bedstraw by the fire. She was comforted by the sweet scent of the straw and the crackling sound of the kindling as it popped in the low flames. Closing her eyes, she let the exhaustion and worry of the day slip away until she was nearly asleep.

"Freedom!" She opened one eye and tried to pretend she hadn't heard. It was Chaz, coming to pull her away from bed. Night time was the only time that the children had to play, and he'd been waiting for her since sunset, she reckoned. Chaz wasn't exactly a child, though. When he was around her age, he'd fallen down and hit his head on a rock, making him perpetually a child of ten even though he was now well over twenty. "Come play, Freedom!"

She sighed and covered her head with her hands. "I don't want to play now, Chaz. Go find you somebody else to play—."

"C'mon, Freedom! We play hide and seek in the dark. Ady play too!"

Freedom sat up and stared at Chaz and his goofy, lopsided grin. He was bouncing with excitement and tugged at her arm gently. "Ady ain't gon' want to play no hide and seek, you silly boy," she sighed. "And I'm too tired...."

Chaz began to laugh, covering his mouth and trying not to let the sound escape as his shoulders shook.

"Why you crackin' yo' teeth boy?" Freedom asked, suddenly peeved at the thought that Chaz might be laughing at her.

"Ady play too," he giggled, pointing off in the direction of the barn. "She go hide wit' Missuh Wilkins."

He must have been able to sense Freedom's alarm and immediately his laughter dissolved into more of a sheepish grin. Chaz was so childlike, but he could sense that something more sinister than hide and seek was going on in the barn.

A shard of ice worked its way painfully down Freedom's spine, making the tiny hairs on the back of her neck stand on end. "Where, Chaz? Where did Ady go hide?"

"She and Missuh Wilkins was up in the barn. I hear Ady makin' all kin'a noise, so I sneaked in to see, and they was in there."

Freedom's heart hitched in her chest and for a moment she could see nothing but darkness before her eyes. Shaking her head, she steeled herself, clenching her fists. "Show me where," she hissed.

Chaz shook his head, wringing his hands and backing away from Freedom. "No'm... you don't want to be goin' up there, Freedom. We ain't s'pose to go up there. Missuh Wilkins say so."

"I don't care what that ol' Butcher say or don' say, you bes' show me where he took my sister!" she exclaimed, grabbing Chaz by the ear and pushing him out the backdoor.

They stumbled out into the mucky lane behind the two rows of slave cabins. Chaz started to squeal, but Freedom elbowed him in the side and pressed her fingertips over her lips. He took her meaning, and they both crouched down low so as not to be seen by the groups of people sitting by the cooking fires. They would have to be careful if they wanted to make it past the keen eye of Cook. That old woman sat on the stoop every night dozing in an old broken down rocking chair while she mended the clothes. Even when she looked like she was sleeping, she didn't miss a thing. Many nights Freedom had been scolded by Cook when she stole away in the night, playing chase with Chaz. If she caught them sneaking back toward the barn, she'd bend their ears good.

"Freedom...," Chaz hissed. "What if we gets caught?"

"We ain' gon' get caught," she replied. But she wasn't so sure. The Butcher had eyes like a hawk and would surely see them coming if they weren't extra careful. But the danger didn't matter. Something deep down in Freedom's gut told her that her sister was in trouble. Bad trouble. And she was willing to kill the old bastard if that was what she had to do.

She shivered, rubbing her hands together as they crept slowly, careful not to let her feet make a single sound against the graveled lane that led up the hill toward the barn. It was only April, and the wind that whipped around them was cold and damp. The sounds of the crackling cooking fires and the laughter of the other slaves faded away as they approached the hulking shadow of the barn up ahead. It was like an ominous, craggy old stone castle, full of ghosts and goblins, looming in the distance. Freedom didn't want to go in. She had a sense that whatever she found inside would alter her path, for good or ill. A dim flicker of fire shone in the window at the hayloft. A single lantern light, but no shadow.

"Freedom," Chaz whined, tugging at her apron strings as he followed close behind. "We shouldn't be 'round here."

"Don't be such a baby," she scolded. "Ady needs our help." She started to say more when they heard voices coming from the barn. Freedom's breath caught in her throat, and for a moment everything stopped. A soft, meek whimper came from somewhere above and then the gruff voice of Butcher Wilkins. She listened hard, trying to make out the words, but there were only muffled sounds. "Come on, Chaz! We got to save Ady!"

She tried tugging at his arm, but the boy wouldn't move. She was reminded how much larger he was than her when she couldn't make him budge. "I need your help, boy!"

"I...I can't...." His eyes glanced toward the window and shadows moved across the light of the lantern. With a small whimper, Chaz broke away from Freedom's grasp and he took off over the hill.

She started to shout his name, but then thought better of it, dropping to her knees on the mossy earth and catching her breath. The heady scent of the hay and the animals wafted through the air. She could almost taste it. And just underneath there was blood—coppery and bittersweet. Freedom wrinkled her nose and continued, slogging her way through the narrow path that led to the back of the barn. Her knee went down on something soft and she cursed under her breath. Mud or manure, she wouldn't be sure until this was over.

If she lived through it.

After what seemed an eternity, she finally made it to the small door in the barn, just behind the stalls where the sheep bayed low. They seemed to understand when she pushed through the door and into the stall, her fingertip still pressed to her lips. One of the lambs nudged at her hand, but did not make a sound. Making her way through the maze of muck and feedboxes, Freedom finally emerged at the ladder that would lead to the hayloft.

"I got to get back, Missah Wilkins."

Freedom recognized Ady's voice and her heart seized, but one small sound and she'd be given away. Then both of them would be in trouble. She looked around for something, anything that she might use to defend her and her sister. A sickle lay on a workbench by the door. Freedom picked it up and turned it over in her hands.

She knew if she had to use it, she'd better kill Wilkins because he would surely kill her and Ady both if given a chance. Not to mention that running away would be the only option. Slaves were hung for less than raising a sickle to the overseer. Gathering her strength and balling it up in her hot little hand, Freedom began to climb the ladder slowly, the sickle laying heavy in her deep, apron pockets.

"You ain't goin' nowhere 'til I'm done with you, girl," Wilkins growled. His snarling threat was followed by the sound of fabric ripping and Ady's quiet whimpers.

Tears already rolled down Freedom's cheeks as she slowly ascended to the hayloft, her arms aching with the exertion. She breathed slowly, ignoring the heartbeat that pounded in her ears.

"Please…stop…." Ady panted.

Freedom cringed and peered over the edge of the loft floor. Wilkins gave no response, but reared his hand back to deliver a sharp blow to Ady's cheek, hard enough to make the girl fall backward. He lay on top of her, his back to Freedom, and his grimy work pants had fallen down around his ankles. Ady lay beneath him on the rough wooden floor, straw and filth stuck in her hair and in the streaks of tears on her cheek.

Freedom wanted to close her eyes, to block out the sight, but her anger wouldn't let her. She took the last rung as stealthy as a tomcat and began to creep toward them. The air was thick and humid and Freedom could smell the sour smell of Wilkins's sweat as he bent over Ady, his meaty hands all over her. Ady had stopped crying and now just lay there, letting Wilkins use her body until he was through. He grunted and growled, occasionally stopping to bite down on one exposed breast. He had her pinned tight, her wrists scraping against the rough boards until they were bleeding.

Freedom wiped her hands on her apron before delving inside to seek out the sickle. Just a few more steps and she would be able to bury that sickle in his back. She prayed to God that she would have enough strength and that the blade wasn't dull. Her eyes stung with the drying tears and she stopped, wiping across her face with the back of her arm.

Her movement must have caught Ady's eye because she gasped and looked straight at Freedom. Luckily, Wilkins was too far gone to notice. She took a step forward, raising the sickle so that it caught the firelight. Ady's eyes went wide, and she shook her head wildly.

"Good girl," Wilkins growled. "I knew you'd get the hang of it."

Ady narrowed her teary eyes and mouthed "no," but Freedom paid no mind. In another heartbeat it would be done, and they would never have to fear again. They could run away. It was nearly springtime. It would be easy.

"Please," Ady whispered. Her eyes pleaded, and Freedom lost her nerve.

Wilkins let out a sickening groan and it was over. Freedom dropped the sickle on the hay strewn floor. It made a loud noise that startled her. Her gaze darted back to Wilkins, but he hadn't heard. He still lay there panting and looking down at Ady with that greedy look. She stepped back toward the ladder on the tips of her toes, careful not to make a sound as he began to gather himself. Ady made a big show of replacing her clothes in an attempt to distract him just a little while longer.

Freedom held her breath as she climbed down the ladder and took off from the barn. She wanted to scream, to cry out, but she knew that she'd best not until she was well away. She ran toward the forest, her hair whipping around her head, coming loose from the ragged ribbons Cook had used to tie her braids that morning. Her chest hurt, but she pushed herself faster and farther with no thought for her imagined boogeymen. She looked behind for a moment, sure that Wilkins had come after her, but there was no one. She was safe for the moment.

She finally emerged into the grove of trees behind the well where she had seen the shadow earlier. Freedom stopped, looking up at the tower of trees that surrounded her. They were a cavalcade of guards, protecting her from the ugliness of the barn and the despair that threatened to descend. Directly overhead the moon shone like an enormous eye, staring down at her. That feeling of being watched was there again, but this time she was not afraid. Whatever lurked in the dark was watching her, watching *over* her.

In the safety of the trees she fell to her knees on the soggy ground. The wet grass dug into her skin, and the early spring frost wet her face. She lay on the ground and sobbed into her hands. She sobbed for her childish innocence, for her mother and father and for Ady. Ady who was going to be doomed to be an evil man's plaything until age and mistreatment released her in death. Visions of a young girl hanging in the barn, hung by the neck, flashed in Freedom's mind's eye. This time it was Ady, her catty green eyes bulging from their sockets as the noose squeezed the life from her body.

Freedom screamed into her fists, shaking her head back and forth violently, trying to displace the image that had burned into her mind. She wouldn't let Ady suffer that fate. She couldn't. Ady was all she had left and without her, Freedom may as well be dead.

"Lord, what is I goin' to do?" Freedom sobbed, rocking herself back and forth on her skinned knees. "Help me, Lord. Please help me."

She hid her face in her arms, crying until she couldn't cry anymore. The voices of the slaves back at the cabins carried lightly on the breeze and soon died out altogether as the inky night descended. She was all alone now. How easy would it be to slip through the shadows and down the river with no one to see her passing?

But she couldn't leave her sister. If Freedom disappeared, Wilkins would torture Ady to try and figure out where she'd gone. And Ady had suffered enough already.

"Are you going to sit there like that all night? Don't you know it's nearly midnight?"

Freedom's head snapped up at the unfamiliar voice. She looked up, and a blurry figure stood before her, leaning on one of the gnarly old oak trees. She rubbed her eyes to clear them of the grit that tears sometimes leave behind.

"Well?" The voice said again, a touch of impatience tempering its tone.

"Who are you?" she croaked, pulling her knees in tighter. "I'm not supposed to talk to strangers."

The shadow came forward into the moonlight and Freedom gasped. The most beautiful creature she'd ever seen came fully into view. It was a boy, but not a human boy. For a moment she thought he might be an angel. Of course, no angel would have such a mischievous grin. His skin nearly glowed with the light of the moon and his features were fine. His jet colored hair fell in careless waves over his brow and he had a long, slim pipe perched between his lips. The smoke from the end curled around him like a plume of silvery feathers.

His only clothing was a pair of mossy green trousers that fell low on his hips, almost a part of the skin underneath. Most amazing were his wings. They looked like skeletal twigs covered in dewy spiderwebs that sprang from his back. They flapped so quickly in the still air as he lit on the branch just over her head. They hardly looked to be moving at all. "I am Robin Goodfellow. And you are Freedom Jenkins," he replied matter-of-factly, taking a long pull of his pipe. "And now we're not strangers."

"How you know my name?" Freedom asked, standing up quick.

"Your sister told me."

"You know my sister?" He seemed to ignore her question and jumped down to the ground. As he began to pace, Freedom watched him back and forth, unable to tear her eyes away. Was he even real? His silvery skin and almond eyes were like nothing she'd ever seen before and she sat there transfixed.

"What are you?" she blurted, not considering her rudeness.

"Me? Well I'm a creature of the forest. Your kind call us woodfolk or sprites—."

"A fairy? You're a fairy!" Freedom cried, for a moment forgetting about her predicament.

Robin gave a perturbed scowl and turned his nose up snottily at Freedom. "I prefer Fae, for I am, in fact, the prince of all Fae. A most cunning sprite and knavish Puck, at your service."

He gave an exaggerated bow and nearly fell over, making Freedom giggle in spite of her sadness. He stopped and looked up at the girl, his mouth curled into a thoughtful sneer. "You are so very sad, just as your sister said." He shook his head and inhaled deeply on his pipe again. This time when he exhaled, the smoke formed a sparkling, silver bird that fluttered toward Freedom. Just before it lit on her nose, the bird blew apart into an entire flock that fluttered around her head for a moment before dissipating. "No little child born of the Fae should be so sad as you. It isn't natural." With a graceful leap, he alighted on the low bough of the oak and squatted there. "You have a touch of our magic, of course. You and your sister."

"What kind of root you got in that pipe, Suh?" Freedom asked, her eyes bugging. "If'n we had magic, we be out of this place long ago." She sighed miserably and put her head in her hands. "It's hopeless, Robin. Me and Ady gon' die here, and that nasty old Gerald Wilkins is goin' to git away wit' his mischief."

The sprite had a roguish grin that was almost too large, and Freedom couldn't help but return it. "Sometimes magic is hard to see, but it was magic that brought me to you. If you hadn't called, I wouldn't have come. What do you think about that, Freedom Jenkins?"

She shrugged. "I don' 'member callin' nobody."

"I heard you sing, of course. And Ady said you'd need my help. So here I am."

"Ady say? What did Ady say?"

The Fae prince smiled again, chuckling in a manner that suggested playful condescension. "Surely you know that your sister is Charmed. She has great power, as do you. Both of you were born of the Fae. Yours and Ady's great-grandmother was a favored concubine of Oberon himself! Ady, of course, is my betrothed and as such, you're my little sister as well."

He perched the pipe between his lips once more and sighed heavily as he realized that the fire had gone out. With a quick snap of his fingers, a small blue flame alighted on the tip and he lit the end. He began to smoke once more, blowing out circles of silver smoke as he leaned back against the trunk of the tree. She watched his every move, pausing to rub her eyes every now and again to be sure that she wasn't dreaming.

"Now, what help would you ask of Clever Robin?" he asked, turning his round, silvery eyes on Freedom again.

"I want to kill that ol' devil, Gerald Wilkins," she replied, her childish voice so cold and humorless that Robin shivered. "I want to make him pay for what he done to my sister and all of us. I want him to know that I ain't scared of him no more!"

"But you are, Little Sister. Very scared, indeed," he said thoughtfully. "Not that you shouldn't be. If you intend to kill Wilkins, you'd better be sure because that old Butcher will have no trouble at all killing you." Robin hopped down from his perch and stared into Freedom's eyes with a burning gaze. The world around them darkened, and Robin seemed to grow until he blocked what little moonlight there was. "And he won't just kill you, little one. He'll torture you. Humiliate you. You'll wish for death before the end, and I fear I wouldn't be able to stop him." Every bit of mirth was gone from the fairy's expression, and Freedom could barely breathe. She knew he spoke the truth. She *was* afraid. "And besides," he continued, once again the impish sprite, "for some, death is far too lenient a punishment. An eternity of sleep and rest seems...inappropriate for one such as Gerald Wilkins."

"I want him low," Freedom huffed. "So low that he know what it feel like to be a slave."

"Ah yes," Robin chuckled, kneeling before the little girl. "Walk a mile in another man's shoes if you want to know the journey. But to make him a slave would be much too noble. Hmm...."

Robin stood up, grabbing Freedom's wrist and pulling her to her feet. They began to pace back and forth, each one mirroring the other.

"What's lower than a slave?" he mused.

Freedom let out a hearty guffaw. "You funny, Missuh Robin. Even that ol' white trash down the road ain' lower than no slave. Ain' nothin' lower than no slave," she said. After a pause she added, "'ceptin' maybe that mule be pullin' the plow."

Robin stopped and turned slowly to face the child. His eyes sparkled with mischief, and his mouth grew into a malicious grin that was nearly grotesque. After several moments, he began to laugh wildly. Robin twirled Freedom 'round and 'round in a riotous reel until she was laughing too.

"My dear little sister!" Robin exclaimed. "What a clever girl you are!"

Robin kept spinning until they were both dizzy and tumbled to the ground.

"Why is I so clever, Missuh Robin?" she asked, breathing heavily as she lay on the ground, staring up at the early morning gray-blue sky.

"Because you, dear one, just gave me the most wonderful idea. A most whimsical, just and *terrible* idea. But you must be careful and use that fae wit. For only you can save our love, Princess Adhira."

Robin sighed and lay back on the grass beside Freedom, looking thoughtful. His nose wrinkled as he drummed his fingertips. "So many ways, so many tricks to play," he sighed. "But which one would be most deserved by the intolerable Mr. Wilkins?"

He leapt to his feet and began to pace back and forth. After several moments he stopped and stared at Freedom, his eyes growing wider. "Aha! There is a rare flower that grows just on the edge of the swamp. The nectar of this plant is most foul when distilled with just a bit of wormwood." Robin cupped his hands in front of his mouth and blew into them gently. A small, leathery bag appeared, tied neatly at the top. Robin's quick, sinuous fingers picked at the knot and dipped inside, gathering a bit of sparkling yellow powder just on the tips. He wrinkled his nose, inhaling the foul stench of the fairy dust.

"Made of rotting elderflowers, crocodile musk, wormwood, and the tears of dying children, this powder is among the most powerful and malevolent of all fae magic. It should just do the trick," he said with an ominous chuckle.

Freedom's eyes lit up with excitement. "You're going to put a spell on him?"

"Of course not, Little Sister!" Robin exclaimed, pulling Freedom to her feet. "You are."

* * *

It was the most beautiful time of the day, yet most folks didn't see it. That time just before sunrise when the moon has set and the sky has just started to fade from that deep India ink color down into a dusky blue, just the color of the flowering plants that covered the hills surrounding Wormwood. Overhead, little pinpricks of stars still twinkle, desperately hanging on to the night. The air is always the freshest at this time. Only freshly turned earth and the light perfume of dew on the early spring wildflowers. The livestock had not yet left the warmth of their straw beds to luxuriate in the morning sun.

It seemed disquieting that such a place was where Freedom knew she would find Gerald Wilkins. Behind the Big House and almost at the edge of the swamp was a working still that Kilpatrick used to brew whiskey for him and his Charleston and Atlanta cronies. Wilkins frequently slipped in unawares and stole a few bottles. Especially after a night of debauchery and rape. After his adventures in the hayloft with Ady, Freedom just knew he'd come on over and help himself to a jar of Kilpatrick's home brew.

Slowly Freedom crept into the still house, closing the door behind her. The room was tiny and the air was humid and close. The bitter stench of fermenting yeast was overpowering, and Freedom swallowed hard as it seemed to fill up her throat. She could taste the bile on her tongue, and if she'd had anything to eat it would surely have come up. Lined up along the window ledge was a group of glass jars waiting to be filled with the intoxicating spirits, and beside it was a wooden cup that Kilpatrick used to taste the finished product. It was also the cup that Gerald Wilkins used to get tight in the late afternoon or the dead of night when he thought nobody else was around. But Freedom had seen. One afternoon, her and Chaz and the Kilpatrick children had run upon him while they were wading in the creek. Drunk as a skunk and passed out on the grass, he was, clutching that old wooden cup in one hand and that nasty old whip in the other.

Freedom's hands shook as she reached out, taking the cup and one of the glass jars full of whiskey. Thoughts of what might happen swam around in her head until she thought she'd fall over with dizziness. For a moment she considered taking a drink herself, but she sat down on the dirt floor of the still and held the glass jar between her knees. Staring down at it, she could see her reflection in the sparkling, clear liquid. What if when she put the potion into the 'shine, it made it murky or discolored? What if the potion did indeed kill Wilkins? Would she be condemned to Hell as a murderess? And of course, there was always the possibility that Mr. Kilpatrick would get here first. Freedom gasped at the thought, and that feeling of nausea swept over her again. After all, the Kilpatricks had always been kind to her and Ady and she meant them no harm. She hesitated for a moment and almost put Robin's tiny, leather pouch back into her apron.

"No," she hissed, scolding herself. "Don' be gettin' scared now, girl. You got to do this for Ady."

There was no turning back now, even if it meant that somebody else got caught in her trap.

Slowly Freedom began unscrewing the lid off of the jar. Her nose wrinkled and tears sprang to her eyes as the fumes from the alcohol burned the inside of her nostrils.

"Lawd, have mercy!" she exclaimed, shaking her head and wondering how anyone could consume such foul stuff. When she opened Robin's pouch, the golden powder inside didn't smell much better. The scent of the rotting flowers put her in mind of seeing her parents laid out in those crude wooden caskets inside their cabin. It had rained for a week, and the ground was so sopping wet that they'd had to wait to bury them, so there they had laid, all ashen-faced and sleeping, until the wildflowers clutched in their hands had died away to nothing. Ady always said that there was nothing sadder than the smell of dead flowers.

Freedom did as Robin had instructed and dipped her fingers into the small leather pouch, gathering some of the powder on her fingertips. It felt like bee pollen or flour, so soft and sticky. Lightly, she sprinkled the essence into the jar of moonshine and watched it swirl down to the bottom. Replacing the lid, she shook the jar lightly, watching as the golden powder dissolved slowly in the liquid. To her surprise, there was no change. Old Wilkins would never know the difference. She held the jar in both hands, careful not to drop it, as she rose to her feet and replaced the jar on the shelf beside the others. She wondered if she should poison them all, but suddenly she heard a rustling in the trees behind the still house.

She sneaked quickly out the back, keeping low to the ground and using the shadows of the surrounding swamp as she made her way to hide in a thicket of brambles. Soon after she saw The Butcher ambling up the hill. He was whistling and singing to himself. Obviously his evening of frivolity with Freedom's sister had lightened his mood considerably. She watched as he pushed the door to the still house open, his eyes darting here and there to be sure that no one was around. Freedom strained her neck, stretching high to see what he was doing inside the tiny cabin. She couldn't see, but after several minutes, Wilkins staggered out from the still house with a jar of moonshine in one hand and that wooden cup in the other. Freedom tensed as he came closer to her, wandering down the path and nearly tripping over his own boots. He tried to pour more of the whiskey into the cup, but his drunken gait kept making him spill it on the grass. Freedom bit her lip, praying that he wouldn't pour the whole thing out, when Wilkins tripped on a root and sat down hard on the grass. Miraculously he didn't spill a drop but the stumble was so comical that a tiny laugh escaped from Freedom.

"Who's out there?" Wilkins roared, making a few attempts to get to his feet before succeeding. Freedom clapped her hand over her mouth and tried not to howl with laughter, watching him bumble, his big belly and wide posterior swaying and jiggling with his wobbly stance.

"Come outta there, you. I know you're out there!" His voice was low and took on an ominous musical quality. Freedom slowly began to back away into the shadows. Her heart pounded in her chest and she could barely breathe. If only Robin were here now. The mucky water began to soak through her skirts where she knelt and crawled along the ground. There was no moon, and she couldn't see a thing around her, but she could hear Wilkins. She could hear him stalking her. His footsteps on the grass seemed to be all around her. "You best come out here now or you'll wish you'd never been born!"

Freedom's breath came in short gasps, and she was almost into the swamp, away from danger when a pair of boots cut off her path to escape.

"I thought it was you," Wilkins snarled, snatching

her up by the collar with one meaty hand.

"You let me go, Missuh Wilkin'!" Freedom shouted, trying to sound braver than she was. "I done seen what you been doin'!"

He threw her to the ground hard, and the air was pushed from her chest with a sickening thump. "Oh yeah? And what have I been doin'?"

"I's gon' tell. I's gon' tell what you been doin' to my sister!" Freedom replied, desperately trying to crawl away.

Wilkins kicked her hard against the backside, making her fall forward on the soggy ground. "Nobody's gon' care what I do with a little slave whore!"

"I care!" Freedom shouted, clutching Robin's leather mojo hand in her fist as if to hold onto some of his strength. She got up to her knees and tried to get to her feet, but he kicked her again, this time two heavy blows to her kidneys. This time she stayed down. Freedom could taste the blood in her mouth and she was sure that this time he'd kill her. If only she could get him to drink the rest of the potion. "And I bet Missuh Kilpatrick care if you be drinkin' his moonshine!"

Reaching down, Wilkins grabbed Freedom by the hair, pulling her up savagely. She screamed, willing herself not to cry. She'd never let Gerald Wilkins make her cry again.

"I tell you what, little girl. I'll just finish off this jar of whiskey, and then we'll see if you scream as good as your sister."

Freedom struggled in his grasp, but he held onto her scalp so tight that she was certain he was tearing her hair away from the skull as he guzzled the last of the potion. Freedom stopped thrashing and looked up, watching as the last drop of the liquid slid down his gullet.

Wilkins coughed and snorted, taking in the rank potion. On his tongue it began to bubble and foam until it ran over his lips and down his chest. He inhaled deeply, trying to catch his breath, but this time when he ingested the potion deep within, the yellow substance spewed forth from his nose and even rained down from his eyes like tears. He loosed his grip on Freedom, and she stumbled away. She began to chuckle, just slightly at first, but then just the sight of Gerald Wilkins, the Butcher of Wormwood Plantation, stumbling to his knees and panting like a dog at her feet was just too much. She doubled over and began to howl with peals of laughter.

Wilkins reached for her, but was unable to speak from the spume of fetid liquid that poured from every orifice. He coughed and spit, wiping the potion away as he stumbled toward Freedom. "Help me, girl!" he sputtered. "God help me!"

"What help does God have for a mule?" Freedom snarled.

"What's happening?" He clawed at his face and

eyes, trying to clear the thick, milky globules away.

"You hear me, Gerald Wilkins? You ain' nothin' but a ragged. Old. Mule." As she said it, Wilkins doubled over in pain. Freedom stood back, darting out of the way as he groped around, trying to grab at her wrists. It was of little use, as his hands had already begun to change. His groping, gnarled fingers that had been so greedy as he pawed at Ady, had melded into one hardened hoof and turned black. Going down on his knees, his spine twisted, and she could hear the bones in his pelvis pop and crackle as they were rearranged. The skin along his shoulders burst open and coarse, gray hair sprouted and grew in its place. A continuous scream issued forth from Wilkins even as his jaw elongated and his teeth pushed forward, cutting his lips and dripping blood on the grass. From the ruins of his skin, the bubbly yellow pus had turned a black color and continued to ooze over his new fur. Every joint beneath crackled and groaned before finally coming to rest. The old man inhaled, trying to scream again, but this time all that would come forth was high-pitched baying.

* * *

There's a line in an old book that says, "And this weak and idle theme, no more yielding but a dream."

Freedom often thought that her life before Robin came was but a dream. A very long, tenuous nightmare from which her and Ady had finally awakened. Once found by the fairies, Princess Adhira and her little sister were welcomed back into Ablach with open arms. They could live there happily, without fear and care, until the end of all things. Yet it happened that one day, many years hence, that Adhira and Freedom stumbled upon Wormwood again. A boy and his sister stretched in the fields, the sun beating down upon their backs. As Freedom stared, she could see the vestiges of her childhood friends. Their eyes, once so bright with wonder and mischief, were now darkened with care and long years of struggle. The house behind them was a shadow of its former self, the skeletal remains silhouetted in the sunset. There was no singing or chanting of the slaves in the fields, only a mere whisper of wind. This place was a memory of a time long past. War had come and with it, the glory and radiance of the Old South was gone. Here it was obvious that only desolation and despair remained.

The boy and girl were plowing the fields. Their shoulders slumped, and the ragged clothing that was draped around their wasted bodies was sticky with sweat and nearly transparent. But they were determined. Like always, Stuart and Caroline Kilpatrick had always been blessed with a sense of hope. Caroline bent over, pulling the leaves carefully from the skimpy plants that grew near the ground.

Freedom wanted to go to them, but Ady held onto her sister firmly. "They couldn't see you even if you spoke to them. We are but a childish fantasy to them and therefore remain unseen, little sister."

"I miss them," Freedom sighed. "Do you think they remember me?"

"I'm sure they do," Ady replied, taking her sister's hand and leading her away into the depths of the forest.

As the fairy princesses turned to dance along the path back into that gauzy plane between what is real and what is fantasy, a breeze caught the scent of wormwood and carried it along. The honeysuckle sweetness made Caroline look up from her work and off toward the edge of the great wood that surrounded them. She wasn't quite sure, but she thought she saw the slightest sparkle of light flutter just below the tree line and then wink out.

"What is it, Caroline?" Stuart called out from where he stood behind the old mule.

"Nothing...I just thought I saw...it was nothing," she sighed, giving a weak gesture toward the trees.

The mule brayed a long, sorrowful noise and pulled at the reins held tightly in Stuart's fist. He shrugged and tapped the mule's haunches with the cruel, eight-tailed whip. "C'mon, you old one-eyed beast! Times a-wastin'!

The Harpist's Hand

By Steven S. Long

Through Killdraigan forest came Thomasin Blythe, seeking sage counsel.

Tall she was, nearly as tall as a man, with fiery red hair and a face and form most pleasing to look upon. She wore a fawn-colored tunic laced in front, grey breeches, and fine black leather boots; against the chill in the air she covered herself in a grey cloak lined with fox-fur. In a special pack slung over one shoulder she carried her most prized possession, the Black Harp of Ulon, and on her right hip she wore a dagger. Her green eyes flashed with anger at the predicament she found herself in.

* * *

Some days previously Thomasin had been at Mac Ferla's hostel in Conhaile, enjoying a tankard of Mac Ferla's good crisp ale during a respite in the evening's singing. The warmth inside was far better than the cold outside, and a full belly better than an empty one, so glad she was to have reached the hostel after three long days' walking across the Moy Conroy from Cathair Kildare. Perhaps there was more work to be had here in the northern lands, and if so Mac Ferla's was as good a place as any to start looking for it.

A man approached her. Well-favored and well-dressed, with a heavy black cloak over his shoulders, he carried himself with a fine air of assurance. His belt-pouch was embroidered with an axe entwined by holly—the arms of Conhaile. "Lady Thomasin Blythe?" he asked.

"It's no lady I am, to loll about some king's hall in a fancy gown, but it's Thomasin Blythe you've found. Sit."

He took off his cloak, draped it over the chair, and sat down. "My name is Lachlan, m'lady. I serve King Crogher."

"So I'd seen. What does Crogher of Conhaile want of me? Does he need music for some great feast he's planning?"

"No, m'lady—he wishes to marry you."

Thomasin stared at him in disbelief. "He wants *what?*"

"Your hand in marriage, m'lady."

She laughed then, not the gentle peal of merriment the Tualans call "Thomasin's Bells," but a laugh laden with scorn. The patrons of Mac Ferla's hostel shuddered to hear it; they bent their heads low over their meat and beer to keep their eyes off her. But Lachlan merely flinched, then looked at her again.

"Aye, m'lady Thomasin, Crogher the Strong seeks you to wife! All Tuala Morn knows the beauty of your face and voice, and King Crogher desires that such beauty should be with him always. All Conhaile shall be your dowry!"

Again she laughed. "Crogher of Conhaile would no more give up his kingdom to me than eat scraps from the floor with his dogs."

Lachlan grimaced at her words. "But you will consider his offer, m'lady Thomasin?" he said. It was more a statement than a question—he knew even a bard dared not refuse a king outright.

"I will," she said with a sigh. "Meet me here at the next full moon, and you shall have my answer."

Satisfied, Lachlan nodded to her, got up, donned his cloak, and left the hostel. All the rest of the night her hands would play only songs of sorrow and longing.

* * *

Dawn found her on the road, heading south across the Moy Conroy as fast as her feet would carry her. There was no desire in her to wed King Crogher, and she had no intention of remaining within his lands while she was still able to leave.

Two days later she passed through Balag Dornoch,

crossed the River Glaishin at Ath Drolada, and found herself in the Moy Gavrach—the Plain of Crows, where the armies of Conhaile and Seanclough had often clashed through the centuries of their long feud. In better times she would have followed the River Mointarc south to green-roofed Dunrioga, seat of the High King. There a dozen lords would compete to have her grace their feasts with her music, but she was in no mood for company just yet. For now all she wanted was to get far away from Conhaile.

As she crossed the plain, an idea came to her: where better to seek refuge from Conhaile...than Seanclough? If Crogher came after her there, King Sitric would fight him out of sheer spite. Even the King of Conhaile wasn't foolhardy enough to start a war over her—was he?

Pleased to have some plan other than flight, she turned her footsteps more toward the east. By late morning she reached Drocade Dareg, the Red Bridge over the eastern arm of the Mointarc which flowed from Loch Kilkarry. She stopped by the bridge and had herself a meal of bread and cheese, then continued on eastward down the Balath Moinu.

Shortly after mid-day she spied a rider heading toward her on the road. He sat his horse with a careless air that bespoke great skill at riding. He wore a blue cloak over his chainmail, and he carried a spear. He was not known to her, but no sense of menace lurked about him.

He reined in his horse as he approached her. "Thomasin?" he said, looking at her intently. "Thomasin Blythe?"

"And who would be wanting to know?"

"My name is Turlagh. And if you are the Lady Thomasin, I ask that you play for me."

"As you will, sir," she said, inwardly cursing a storm as she retrieved her harp from its case. Whoever this Turlagh was, he knew her *geas,* the strange curse placed upon her long ago—that she could not refuse a request for music. She seated herself on a stone next to a roadside thicket and brushed a hand across the harpstrings. They held true, so she began to play, and continued for half a glass. "Are you satisfied, m'lord?" she asked when she was finished.

He chuckled at that. "Oh, satisfied I am indeed. It's the Lady Thomasin you are. Only you would have to agree to a request to play by the side of the road. And only Thomasin Blythe could draw the birds with her harping." He pointed to the branch above her head. When she turned to look, all the birds seated there flew away in a flurry of wings and bright feathers.

"Why were you seeking me, Lord Turlagh?"

"No lord, Lady Thomasin, merely Turlagh of Seanclough, and it's on behalf of Seanclough that I was sent to find you. King Sitric seeks your hand in marriage."

Her head reeled. "Himself as well?" she asked.

Turlagh frowned. "As well? King Crogher's messenger has already found you?"

"Aye, two days ago, at Mac Ferla's hostel."

"Will you be marrying Crogher, then?" he asked, his voice taking on an ugly tone when he said the king's name.

"I've not said yet. I'm to meet his messenger at the hostel at the next full moon to give my answer."

His face brightened a little. "Good! It's too fine a woman you are for a dog like Crogher, Lady Thomasin. Marry my king Sitric, and you'll be happy and content all your days."

"I believe that no more than believe Crogher's honeyed words. But Sitric shall have the same as he. Meet me at Mac Ferla's hostel when next the moon is full, and I will tell you my decision."

"If such is your choice, Lady Thomasin, I shall await your pleasure there." He took something from one of his saddlebags. "Pray accept this as a token of King Sitric's faith," he said, handing her a small package wrapped in soft leather. Then he remounted his horse, turned, and rode back to the east.

Inside the leather was an object wrapped in ivory-colored silk. Inside the silk was a small silver pin in the shape of a harp. Thomasin wrapped it back up and put it away.

* * *

This was a pretty kettle of fish! Now she had not one but two kings to deal with, and bitter enemies at that. She had no wish to marry either of them, or any other man, but a spurned king is as deadly an enemy as one could have in Tuala Morn. No matter what choice she made, there seemed no way to avoid earning one ruler's wrath…and perhaps starting yet another war between Conhaile and Seanclough. Her head filled with gloomy thoughts, she turned her feet yet again, this time west and south. It was time to seek advice from the wisest…person…she knew.

She slept that night by the cool waters of the River Rathware, and the next day forded it and continued her journey. Soon she left the High King's lands behind and crossed into Duneane, a realm where the ground was often soft and boggy, but whose king did not want to marry her, at least. It pained her to be so close to Cathair Duneane and not go visit King Ernan—and perhaps see his son, Prince Callahan—but her troubles drove her, and she had little time before the moon would be full once more.

Several more days' walking brought her to Dundelgan, the castle of Aith MacLeith, one of King Ernan's vassals. "Ho, Thomasin Blythe!" one of his guards called as she approached the walls near sunset. "Come to play for us again, have you?"

"Sure, and I have," she replied with a smile she didn't feel inside. "There'll be dancing tonight, you may be sure!"

"Worse the luck," the guard said ruefully as he signaled his comrades inside to open the gates. "I'm on duty all night."

Thomasin walked through the gates and into the castle courtyard, where Aith's steward met her. "So good of you to grace Dundelgan's halls again, Lady Thomasin," he said, bowing to her.

"So good of you to have me, Glaisne," she replied. "Could the Lord's hall use a bit of music tonight?"

"Always, if it's you who plays it. It will delight Lord Aith to hear of your arrival."

"How is he?" she asked, a note of concern touching her fine voice.

"Back to his irrascible old self. His fever passed weeks ago, and now you can scarce tell he was ever sick. He even plans to go hunting with his war-band in a few days."

"Gods be praised," she said. "Or is it the Golden Temple that holds sway here now?"

"No, we still revere the Dronnach Lanva in Dundelgan. For now, at least."

Glaisne led her into the castle and up to the room she usually occupied when she came to Lord Aith's castle. She spent a few minutes working with her harp, tuning the strings and warming up her fingers, then went down to the feast-hall to await Lord Aith's pleasure.

She had not long to wait. Lord and Lady MacLeith came in just a few minutes after she did, followed by their sons and retainers, and they all took their seats at the large MacLeith feast-table.

Lord Aith looked much better than the last time she'd seen him, when he was still in the grip of fever. He had his old air about him, at once noble and sour-tempered—few there were in Tuala Morn as quick to speak their minds or express their displeasure as the Baron of Delgan. But like his wife he smiled when he saw her. "Thomasin Blythe! Glaisne told me you'd be here tonight. Play us something to set our hearts to leaping!"

"Aye, m'lord, gladly." She began with a sprightly tune, one to make toes tap and heads bob, but soon settled down into more sedate tunes as her audience began to eat. After the feasting was done, she picked up the pace again so the lords and ladies could dance. She kept at it for several hours, but no matter how well she played her mind was not on her music. Crogher's and Sitric's offers of marriage sent her thoughts wandering down dark and foreboding paths.

"The harpist's face should match the beauty of her music," said a voice beside her, "not a summer thunderstorm." It startled her out of her reverie, but her fingers faltered for not even a second on the harpstrings. She glanced to her right and saw Lord Aith sitting next to her on the hearthstone.

"M'Lord?" she asked.

"Your spirit is not as light as the music you play, I can see it in your face," Lord Aith said. "What troubles a bard of Tuala Morn so?"

"A trifling matter, Lord Aith," she said, not wanting to draw him into her troubles.

"Not so trifling, if it causes such a frown as you've worn most of the night, Thomasin. What is it?"

She sighed. "King Crogher of Conhaile has asked me to marry him."

His eyes widened. "Why so glum, then?"

"King Sitric of Seanclough has made me the same offer."

He laughed then, but in commiseration rather than mockery. "That's a pretty problem, but not so terrible as you make it out to be, I think. Taking one of them over the other is like choosing between two vicious hounds—but whoever's offer you accept, you get to be a queen. And the life of a queen is a fine thing."

"That's not the life I want! It's my hand they've asked for," she said, holding up her right hand so he could see it clearly. "But this isn't a queen's hand, it's a harpist's hand! I've no desire in me to be a queen, for all their riches and strength. Gilded cages are cages still."

"Turning down Crogher is a dangerous thing to do. His temper's more famous than mine. And Sitric, he has the tenacity of a badger."

"Aye. But I'd rather risk it than go to one of their

beds just because they think they can have me for the asking."

Lord Aith stood up. "Those who play with fire often get burned."

She smiled at that. "Not Thomasin Blythe! The Lady of Fire smiles on me, so I've no fear of her daughters."

He chuckled. "As you say. But play with them carefully naetheless."

* * *

She left Dundelgan the next morning with two new pieces of silver in her purse and a sack of good food in her hand in recompense for her music. To the west lay Killdraigan, and so west she went.

By midmorning she was hard upon the forest. She entered it carefully by an old trail she knew, alert for any of a thousand dangers—many a thing that dwelt within Killdraigan cared naught that she was a bard. She walked slowly but steadily, eyes trying to penetrate every shadow beneath the leaves in case some troll or goblin lay in wait for a succulent morsel such as she. Once she came upon an ancient ruined tower and gave it a wide and careful berth, for it had the malicious smell of old magic.

After two more hours' walking she reached her destination: a small clearing amidst the mighty trees, with a low hill next to a silver spring. This was Connalleigh Shee.

Thomasin bent down, cupped water in her hands, and had a long, refreshing drink from the spring. When she stood up again she saw a small, thin man with light green skin seated on a rock near the forest's edge. "Pining for us, Thomasin Blythe?" he asked with a grin.

"Aye, too long it's been since I visited Connalleigh, good sir," she said. "Is the Lady Islaine presently at the shee?"

"I shall have to see," the green man said with a sniff. "She may not wish to talk to a Dullard even if she is." He hopped off the rock and disappeared. Thomasin sat down next to the spring and waited patiently.

Later that afternoon she finally saw the Lady Islaine walking toward her, down the hill and across the clearing. Behind her on the hilltop rose the grand faerie castle of Connalleigh. More fae folk than she could count worked and played on and around its broad lawns.

Islaine wore her usual semblance: a woman of middle age who in her youth would have been ravishingly beautiful, but whose features age had softened into merely head-turning beauty. She was dressed in a sweeping gown of white, and upon her head was a diadem of star-diamonds made by faerie smiths. "Thomasin, my dear, have you come to stay with us at last?"

"Not to stay, my Lady, but only to visit. It's sorely troubled I am, and I need your wisdom."

"Surely, then, you shall have it—but first you must sing for your supper!" The faerie queen clapped her hands once, and tables laden with a wondrous feast appeared. Laughing and cheering, her subjects came rushing down the hill to seat themselves. One of the goblins the shee pressed into service offered Thomasin a goblet of wine. She declined, knowing that if the merest sip of faerie drink or bite of faerie food passed her lips, she would never again leave Connalleigh Shee.

"Now play for us, Thomasin Blythe!" Lady Islaine said, and all the faeries cheered.

Thomasin took the case off her back and brought forth the Black Harp of Ulon. The finest of harps it was, a clarsach made of ebony alder-wood and strung with silver. Carved along the length of its curved pillar was a serpentine dragon writhing among knotwork, and along the neck more knotwork designs surrounded the silver tuning pins. Five generations of harpists' hands had played it since Ulon MacGrath crafted it in the time of King Dualtach—perhaps, some said, with the help of magic. She meant to keep playing it until she passed it on to a student, as Murchadh had to her. She'd be damned if it was going to languish in some closet while she did a queen's work!

The first song she played was slow and sweet, like a summer breeze over a moonlit meadow. The Connalleigh faeries listened enraptured, but she knew they wouldn't sit still long for more of that. So when she was done she swung into a sprightlier tune that set their feet a-tapping. For the next song she picked up the pace again, and soon the faeries were dancing and capering with joyful abandon while their queen looked on approvingly.

After two hours of music the Lady Islaine signaled for an end, much to the dismay of her subjects. "I think Thomasin Blythe has paid in good coin and plenty of it for what she seeks—off with you now!" The faeries scampered, strode, or flew away, back to whatever they were doing before the festivities began, and the tables faded from existence like a bad dream in good morning sunshine.

"Come, Thomasin," Islaine said. "Leave your harp there for now, no harm will come to it." Thomasin gratefully put the harp down, shook her hands to relieve the tension of so much playing, and hurried after the queen. "What is it that troubles you so, child, to bring you all the way through the forest to Connalleigh?"

Thomasin told her story then, quickly so Lady Islaine's faerie attention would not wander, but with all a bard's skill to evoke as much sympathy as she could—if the Good Folk could truly feel sympathy for a Dullard.

"Such a mortal foolishness of ceremonies and rings!" Islaine exclaimed when Thomasin was done. "Just take whichever one you want and let the other be."

"But I don't want *either* of them, Lady. And I fear that whatever choice I make, one king will become my bitter enemy."

The queen considered. "Then you must arrange it so that neither of them wants you. I could take away your beauty so that kings and commoners alike would turn their eyes away from you."

"No, thank you, my Lady," said Thomasin with a shudder.

"Have Treboso inflict a few scars upon you with the whip? Just a few."

"No, thank you, my Lady."

"A pox, perhaps?"

"No, thank you, my Lady."

"If you won't let me make you undesireable, you shall have to find a way to do it yourself. Though I caution you, my way is simpler and more reliable."

A thought came to Thomasin then. "It's truth you speak, my Lady...but there's undesireable and undesireable. I think I do not have to change myself, merely put a condition upon the union neither Crogher nor Sitric will meet. It's a fine idea you've given me." For the first time in many days she felt the weight begin to lift from her heart.

"So it shall always be, dear Thomasin; faerie wisdom has no equal among mortals. And now that you have your answer, you must go. Come back again when the summer moon is full and bright, and play for us once more!"

"I shall, my Lady," said Thomasin, bowing her head

in homage. Lady Islaine kissed her once on the forehead; she could feel her skin tingle from the touch of faerie lips.

When the fire-haired bard looked up again, queen and castle were gone. All she saw was a hill in a clearing with a spring beside it, and the forest beyond. Eager to be gone from Killdraigan before nightfall, she put her harp in its case, the case on her shoulder, and her feet on the path leading back out of the forest.

* * *

As full of energy as if she'd just awakened from a long and restful sleep, Thomasin walked swiftly and made it back to Dundelgan just as twilight arrived, much to the delight of the castle's residents. She asked to see Lord Aith at once.

"I didn't expect to see you back here so soon, Thomasin Blythe. Has something happened?"

"No, my lord, but I may have found a way out of my worries. I must ask a favor of your lordship."

"Of course, lass, what do you need?"

"The services of a messenger to go to Mac Ferla's hostel in time for the next full moon. He must tell both Crogher's and Sitric's men that I will give them my answer two weeks from that day at the ford over Talacorrie stream in the midst of the Moy Gavnach."

"That I can do. I have a good fast horse in my stables, a get of the Grey of Cora Mala himself, that I'll put the messenger upon to make sure he arrives in time."

"Thank you, my lord," Thomasin said with a beaming smile, then prepared herself for a night of harping.

* * *

Four weeks later, on the appointed day, Thomasin Blythe sat on the soft, grassy ground next to the shallowest part of Talacorrie, playing a flute she'd just made from a reed. The morning was cool, and thick wisps of fog drifted over the plain.

From the north came the sound of horses, and Thomasin ceased her flute-playing. Standing up she peered northward, her keen eyes straining to see through the mists. Soon the outline of men on horseback appeared, and a few moments later she could see them clearly. This was Crogher of Conhaile and his retinue—a scant dozen spearmen, as Thomasin's messenger had instructed. The king led them, his harsh, proud face displaying a grim smile of satisfaction at the sight of the beautiful bard.

At almost the same time, she heard similar sounds from the east. Glancing over her shoulder she saw another group of warriors. At their head rode Sitric of Seanclough, easily distinguished by the grey at the temples of his otherwise dark black hair.

A breeze blew from the south, momentarily clearing away the fog. The two kings and their men saw each other at the same time. Shouts of anger went up on both sides, followed by the sound of swords being drawn.

"Hold!" shouted Thomasin, walking out to the center of the stream so that she stood on neither king's side. Only a fool would disobey the command of a Tualan bard, and a double fool when that bard was a woman. The warriors settled down and fell silent, though none sheathed their weapons.

"What is that dog Seanclough doing here, my lady?" asked Crogher with a snarl. "This is to be an engagement, not a battle!"

"Dog?" Sitric shouted. "You dare to insult me, you pox-riddled bastard? The lady Thomasin is to be *my* wife, and I'll cut your heart out if you try to take her."

"Be *silent!*" Thomasin said, her bardic voice not raised, but pitched so her command carried over the kings' blustering. "Both of you have asked for my hand, and before I deign give it to either of you, you will hear my say."

"As you will, m'lady," Sitric said. Crogher snorted angrily but said nothing.

"Choosing between two kings is too perilous and difficult a task, even for myself. So it's the two of you who'll do the choosing for me."

"What do you mean?" Crogher asked, not taking his eyes off Sitric.

"What I mean is this, King Crogher. I will give my hand only to the one of you who meets my terms. He who will not meet them must swear to leave this place at once, without bloodshed. And if you break this oath, I will satire you from one end of Tuala Morn to the other, and neither peace nor respect shall be yours for the rest of your days. Do you swear?"

"Very well," said Sitric in a dry voice.

"Aye," Crogher quickly replied.

"So be it. My terms, then, are this: my hand I will give to whichever one of you first swears to abandon the long feud between Conhaile and Seanclough, and to renounce all claim of vengeance against the other. Who will so swear?"

She held her breath, awaiting the response. Neither king spoke. Crogher's face became redder and redder, and Sitric looked as grim as a stormcloud. Thus they stood for nearly a minute…and then, almost as one, each king turned his horse and rode back the way he'd come, his warriors trailing behind.

Thomasin Blythe let out her breath. Picking up her harp and flute, she headed west to Dunrioga with a light heart.

Sanae's Garden

By Chantal Boudreau

Sanae stood amongst the cherry trees in her garden, enjoying their fragrance. She often went there to seek solace, before or after a day's work. When everything around her seemed like struggle, a dying parent, a cold bed and an empty womb, the colour and scent of the cherry blossoms reminded her that there was beauty in life, if you sought it out. This knowledge didn't make her life any less lonely, but it made the loneliness easier to bear.

She was her parent's youngest child, and while one of three, she had not been third born. Her mother had been plagued with miscarriages, stillborn births and frailer offspring who had not lived to see their fifth birthday.

"It's not fair," Sanae had remarked as a child, as they had laid to rest the tiny body of what should have been her younger sibling. "Why does this keep happening to us?"

"There's a reason, even if it is one we do not understand—even if it brings us great pain," her mother had said tearfully, placing a steady hand atop Sanae's head. "Natural processes are never evil. They are what they are. If a child does not live, there was something that went wrong with it to begin with. But you and your brother and sister? You're what went right. We should be grateful for that much."

Aside from this loss of life, fate had not been unkind to Sanae's family in the beginning. Her parents had been skilled farmers, and their farm had flourished. She and her brother, Akio, and sister, Yuko, had grown tall and sturdy, like the cherry trees in the garden. Nature had granted them many gifts in exchange for what it had taken from them. Their world was bountiful and serene.

Yuko was the first to leave the farm, but for pleasant reasons. Her parents were able to find her a husband of higher status, and she left her family to live a life of privilege. She would often send gifts, though, and she had already given birth to five strong children. Yuko had not had to suffer the same sorrows as their mother.

Yuko's marriage and resulting family was where the extension of their blessings and joy had come to an end. With only Sanae and Akio left to help their aging parents with the farm, the arrival of army recruitment officers had come as quite a blow. They had travelled to the area to demand one son from every family, and since Akio had been the only son they had had to offer, he had been forced to go.

Those memories brought stinging tears to Sanae's eyes as she gazed upon the pinks and whites that filled the sky above her. She missed Akio. She still felt anger and angst at his loss. Unlike with the tiny bodies of her other dead siblings, there had been nothing natural about his death—a casualty of war.

With Yuko living far away with her new family, and Akio lost in battle, Sanae had been left alone to support her aging parents and their small farm. She had been unable to maintain it at the size it had once been, the family poorer for it. They might have starved had it not been for Yuko's gifts.

This did not stop Sanae from keeping a small sacred garden at the edge of the cherry trees, one with a shrine for the kami in the form of a tree her parents had grown from a seedling. They had cultivated it to take the shape of an outstretched hand, reaching toward the sky, and had marked it with shimenawa, the traditional rice fibre cord. Sanae would speak to the spirit of Akio there every day, as well as to her father's spirit. He had passed on not long after news of her brother's death. Sanae's mother insisted it was age that had claimed him, but Sanae believed the man had died of a broken heart, because of Akio's loss.

Along with the prayers to lost family, Sanae would offer wishes to the kami there, too, before returning to her house to prepare supper for her and her mother. Today's offering included a wish for peace to visit the land so that all soldiers could return to their families and no more young men would die in battle like Akio. She also wished for fruitful growth and a bountiful harvest from her garden.

"And nothing for yourself?" The foreign voice that seemingly came out of nowhere startled Sanae, unaccustomed to visitors. All her neighbours were located several hours travel on foot away, because the rocky terrain that surrounded their farm did not welcome cultivation. "The blessings you ask for are always as much to meet others needs as your own. What about your happiness? No one has ever given you that consideration."

"That's not true. My parents were always kind to me. Until Akio was taken, we were never hungry or wanting for clothing or shelter. Yuko has been very generous. Mother and I might not have survived without her help."

"But what of love? You have sacrificed that to remain the dutiful daughter." The voice drew closer, but the speaker still had not shown himself. "Are you not lonely?"

"I have my mother for company." Sanae could not disguise all of the sadness that accompanied that thought. Her mother grew older and frailer with each day that passed and likely would not live to see another spring. Once the old woman joined her mate in the spirit-world, Sanae would be all alone.

"For how much longer? Besides, the love of a child for a parent is one thing, but the love of a man, sharing your bed with him, is quite another. So is the sensation of life growing in your belly, your child's heart beating in synch with your own, the bond you develop when it suckles at your breast, and you have had all these things kept from you."

Sanae was hoping the speaker would show himself, tortured by curiosity as she was. She glanced around the garden, but could not detect the source of the sound. The wind played tricks with her ears and her perception, the stranger's words seeming to come from one place at first, then another, and yet another.

"What does it matter? I'm too old to marry, too weathered to even consider bedding a man, and too far past my prime to bear my first child." That last part was only so true. While silver had already begun to dot her black hair, her body was still capable of conceiving. At her age, however, any birthing would be likely to kill her, her flesh unpracticed in such things.

"I disagree." The speaker chose that moment to finally reveal himself to Sanae, stepping out from behind the tree that was her garden's shrine. She couldn't understand how he had remained hidden to her there, or how he had managed to throw his voice as he had done. That was until he lowered the hat that shielded his face and hair. He looked about half her age in all ways but one. His eyes, the colour of jade suggested a wisdom that likely spanned centuries. The other thing she noted was that his hair was red. He was a demon… or at least a creature from the spirit-world.

Sanae recoiled away from him.

"Are you yokai…an obake…or yurei? Or are you kami?" she demanded, flinching when he approached her.

"Will that make any difference to you once you know of the gift I am proposing? I offer you life. I offer you renewed purpose. I offer you the opportunity to experience things you believed you never would. But most of all, I offer you an escape from loneliness." He grinned at her, extending his hand to Sanae to help her to her feet. She ignored it at first, continuing to kneel on the ground at the base of the cherry tree.

"What do you mean? How?"

"Lie with me, here in your garden, on the ground beside your shine. I will give you life. All I ask in exchange is that you grant me three favours. You can say no, but your mother will die before this season is through, and if you do not do this, the grief from her death and your loss of purpose will claim you soon after. You are too young to follow her, Sanae. I can grant you a new reason for living. I can promise you happiness again."

Sanae was wary. She had heard of spirits visiting mortals, of tricksters playing games with human hearts and desires. Some of them interfered for the sake of evil, wreaking havoc upon the mortals they visited. She didn't want to be the wretched pawn to some demon, a plaything he could ruin and toss away. However, despite how unsettling the encounter with this spirit-man was, she did not get the sense that he intended her any harm. Rather, he provided her with an unusual sense of well-being. Sanae longed to take him up on his offer, for he was handsome as well as charming, and his smile warmed her heart. She had always wanted a child of her own, envying Yuko for her five. Could she trust her instincts?

"And how will these favours work? I will not promise to work any evil on your behalf. I will not kill or hurt anyone for your sake," Sanae insisted.

"I'll ask nothing like that from you. It's not in my nature anymore than it is in yours," he assured her.

She decided to yield to his request, knowing the spirit-man was right about her mother not having much time left in the world. More than anything, Sanae did not want to be left all alone. With butterflies in her stomach, she allowed him finally to lift her to her feet, her first embraces awkward ones. Any hesitation on her part, any shyness, faded quickly in response to his charm.

The pair shed their clothing. He smelled of familiar things, things that brought her comfort, moss and wildflowers with a hint of cherry blossom. His touch was gentle and his soft words pleasing to her ear. Once she relaxed in his arms, banishing any resistance, he lowered her to the grass so they could lie together. Even though his skin was cool to the touch, his actions ignited a fire in her, one that burned blissfully and continued to grow until they both tensed and climaxed.

Sanae was surprised he had not just left her there, once the deed was done. She lay in his arms enjoying his scent and the sensation of the warmth of the fading sun on her bare skin.

"You won't be staying with me, will you?" she said.

It was a statement of fact as much as a question, because she instinctively knew the answer.

"I can't stay, as much as I want to," he replied. "But I will leave something with you, other than the new life inside you." He passed her a pouch that he pulled from their shed clothing. "The first of the three favours—you must plant this seed beside your garden's shrine. It will grow as our child grows, an emblem of that one's essence.

"What will I tell this child you have given me, when I show them this tree and tell them of your visit…when they ask about their father?"

"You can tell them my name is Haruo, and this is not the last time I will visit. I'll return to see our progeny, and you, from time to time…when I am able."

A gentle breeze danced around them where they lay in the grass. He smiled, kissed her forehead and when she turned to look at him, he was gone, his clothing vanishing with him. Sanae wondered then if loneliness was driving her mad, and he had been nothing but a figment of her imagination. The seed he had given her, however, was still there—physical proof of his visit.

Seeing the sun glowing orange in the sky, she realized it was time to return to her house. Otherwise, her mother would worry and would be complaining of hunger when Sanae did arrive, because her supper was late. As she dressed quickly, Sanae gazed upon the outstretched cherry-blossomed hand that was her garden's shrine. She then hurriedly dug a small hole close to the shrine and dropped the seed into it. She covered it over with the fresh earth before leaving, just as she had promised Haruo.

Then, with hope in her heart, Sanae left to see to her mother.

* * *

Haruo had been right about her mother. Just as Sanae began to feel the first stirrings of life inside her, the quickening that let her know that the spirit-man had not offered idle promises, she woke one morning to find her mother cold and still in her bed. She had no cleric she could fetch to perform the necessary funeral rituals, so just as her mother had once done with her stillborn children and her dead husband, Sanae wrapped her mother in a white shroud and laid her to rest in the garden, offering her prayers to the kami for her mother's safe passage into the spirit world.

The loneliness would have killed Sanae, if she did not have that life blossoming within her. It was the anticipation of the child she would one day hold in her arms that carried her through her grief. Haruo did not return to visit her in the months that followed—the winter a harsh one to endure alone while bearing her extra physical burden. But despite the hardships and the struggle, she managed to make it through to spring without falling victim to the cold or the strain of her pregnancy at such an advanced age. Although she did not succumb to melancholy or grief, she did often find herself wracked with worry and fear. She would have a hard enough time maintaining her garden on her own, until her child was old enough to help, but how would she manage to survive the birth without assistance, and if she did, what did she know about caring for babies? The only infants she could recall seeing were the ones her parents had buried in the ground.

Her fear worsened, turning to panic, when in early spring she was beset with the pains that alerted her to her child's impending arrival. They roused her from sleep at early dawn, when the spring air was still cool. Unable to restrain herself, Sanae cried out at their suddenness and intensity. A voice answered from outside, calling her name, and it lent her the energy to stumble from her bed and out into her garden.

Haruo stood beside the shrine and beckoned to Sanae, his hair ablaze in the early morning light.

"I've come to request my second favour," he told her. "I ask only that you lie at the foot of the shrine, beside the seedling that was once that seed you planted for me. You will birth our child here, and I will help you. I will make it easier for you, Sanae. I will make sure you and the child are safe."

Sanae was hardly in any place to deny him, the pains worsening with every moment that passed. She allowed him to help her down into the grass, the ground cold and hard beneath her already uncomfortable form.

"I'm too old for this," she said, struggling to breathe. "I told you—it's not something I can survive."

He touched a gentle hand to her damp and matted silvering hair and another to her belly. While the pressure did not cease, the pains faded, only a faint echo of what they had once been.

"I won't pretend that this will not be a gruelling task for you, but you are exceptionally strong for your age, and you have the will of a bull...an ornery one at that. Don't tell me you will give up because this will be difficult. Much of your life has been difficult, but you never faltered as long as what you were doing was out of love. You want this child. You love this child. Just like your garden and then your parents, this child will need your nurturing. Don't tell me you will fail a loved one before they are even born?"

As fearful and discouraged as Sanae might

have been because of circumstances, Haruo's words bolstered her spirit and stoked her inner fire. Without any further fretting, she drew motivation from his touch and writhed and strained stoically where she lay on the ground until her body demanded she bear down. It took most of her remaining strength to force the child from her tired and seasoned body, but eventually the baby spilled into Haruo's waiting hands, the sun now directly overhead.

"A boy," Haruo declared proudly. "You have delivered a fine son, and his name will be Masaki."

Once the afterbirth had been discharged, Haruo carried the still naked Masaki away from Sanae, resting the child gently in the grass beside the seedling she had once planted. Strange gestures and ministrations followed. Sanae attempted to lift her weary head to observe, but her weakened state forced it down again.

"What are you doing?" she murmured.

"The seed that you planted in your garden for me was a very special seed. It has grown into a magical tree. I'm anointing it with the birth blood. This act will strengthen it and make it grow tall and sturdy. It thrives on lifeblood and weft of spirit, you see. Masaki is now bound to it in essence, and he will grow tall and sturdy as well. As long as you tend carefully to this tree, as long as it remains healthy and whole here in your garden, so shall our son remain equally healthy." He paused, gathering Masaki back into his arms. "And therein lies the final favour I will ask of you. Guard this tree with your life. Protect it from the elements or anything that might wish to do it harm. I will do my part to watch over it as well. He is, after all, my son too."

Sanae thought about rising and returning to the house, but her fatigue was overwhelming. She believed Masaki was safe as long as Haruo was there with them, so when the midday sun made her groggy she allowed herself to doze where she still lay in the grass. She did not stir until Haruo prodded her awake much later, rousing to the sound of Masaki's hungry mewling and the gradual drop in temperature as evening approached. Haruo pressed the baby to her chest and waited for her to become alert enough to take him.

"I must go, but I'll return sooner than I did before. If you ever find yourself in need, come out to the shrine with Masaki and call my name. I'll come if I can."

Sanae glanced down at Masaki when he wriggled in her grasp, and once she looked up again Haruo was gone, not even offering her a good-bye. Her heart felt heavy for just a moment, until the soft sounds of her newborn distracted her and maternal instinct took over. Her spirit filled with joy from cuddling Masaki to her breast. All loneliness became a memory.

Finding her footing, Sanae carefully made her way back to the house, wary about starting her life over as a mother.

* * *

Masaki thrived as readily as the tree beside the shrine in Sanae's garden. Parenting came to Sanae much more easily than she had expected. She rarely called for Haruo's help as a result, although he would visit on occasion without her appeal.

There were a few times when she brought Masaki out into the garden with her to summon his father. One summer they suffered through a terrible drought. When Sanae ran out of water to drink and to irrigate Masaki's tree, and the plant began to wilt, she rushed her feverish son to the shrine, pleading for Haruo to come. He did respond to her pleas, but when he emerged from behind the kami shrine, he looked soul-weary and as bedraggled as Sanae's poor suffering garden.

"Your son and his tree need water, Haruo, or they will die," she told him.

The spirit man gathered his strength and uttered a spell, stomping the ground full force beside the shrine. The earth there split, water burbling up from the soil. A relieved Sanae would have thanked Haruo, but he fell into a faint beside the hand-shaped cherry tree. At first she thought him dead. He lay still until Sanae had done all she could to revive Masaki's tree, quench her son's thirst, and bathe away his fever. When Haruo would not respond to her attempt to give him water, she turned her attention to her ailing garden, bringing water to all the plants that needed it. Only after she had done this did Haruo start to stir again, finally accepting water from her. He was still very weak, and for the first time he did not leave her after giving her what she had asked for.

For days Sanae stayed close to the spring evoked by Haruo's magic, nurturing everything she loved until all was healthy again. She did not return to the house until Haruo left them, spending her nights curled on the ground at the base of the shrine beside Haruo, Masaki cuddled between her and him. It was the most time she had ever spent with the spirit-man, and she longed for him once he was gone, saddened that she could not have a constant family as Yuko did. Nevertheless, she was grateful for Masaki and the odd moment she got to spend with Haruo.

The only other times she summoned Haruo were when a winter proved particularly long and harsh and their food stores dwindled before spring allowed for their renewal, and when a task around the farm required more strength than Sanae's aging and work-worn body possessed, before Masaki grew old enough and large enough to help her. Life was good during these times for Sanae, and she was happy, just as she had been before Yuko had left for marriage and Akio had been taken off to war.

She wasn't expecting the same fate that had made a victim of her brother to befall her son. Not long after Masaki had grown into a strapping young man, the army recruiters arrived at the farm. Sanae tried to protest his recruitment.

"But he's an only child and I am an old woman. I can't tend this farm on my own," she insisted. "I need him with me."

"You have other family…nieces…nephews…have one of them come to your aid on your 'farm'. Your plight is meaningless in the face of war, old woman. This young man will serve a greater purpose defending our lands from our enemies than frittering his time away in your simple little garden."

They escorted Masaki away, the young man as sad to leave his mother as she was to see him go. As soon as he was out of sight, she rushed to the shrine in the garden and flung her elderly body to the ground, weeping and begging the kami not to allow her son to follow in Akio's footsteps. Through her tears, she eventually perceived a flare of red and knew that meant Haruo had come. While she had grown older and frailer over the years, Haruo hadn't changed at all. He was still as ageless and as handsome as ever.

He approached her and placed a comforting hand on her shoulder.

"They took our son—why didn't you stop them," Sanae demanded, her tone accusatory.

"I can only control nature to some degree," he replied. "And I have no influence over the affairs of men." Haruo crouched beside her. "But you have his tree, and now you will need to guard it more diligently than ever. As I told you, it thrives on lifeblood. Any time it seems weakened or shows wear, you can help it heal with blood of your own—a few drops here and there. Any damage you repair to his essence within this garden will be reflected in Masaki's own well-being. You can protect him from afar, Sanae, it just requires being a dutiful gardener."

After Haruo had left again and Sanae had purged herself of all tears, she took what Haruo had told her to heart. Although winter was not that far off, she decided she would not leave her garden again until Masaki returned safely home. She built herself a lean-to close to her son's tree so she could guard over it day and night, and spent much of her time offering prayers at the shrine there, asking only to have her son come back again hale and whole. Her vigilance took a toll on her physically, having grown wizened in her old age even before she set watch in her garden, the price paid for many years hard work and the strain of the occasional tragedy. Sanae endured the wet, the cold and the occasional storm, but she did not give up her post.

Every now and then the branches of Masaki's tree would sag a little or there would be a shallow rending of its bark from which deep red sap would run. Heeding Haruo's advice, she would press the point of a knife into her palm and once the blood flowed, she would treat the tree's wound. Just as Haruo had promised, the tree healed quickly for it.

One late autumn day, Sanae awoke to a disturbing chill in the air and an eerie silence to her garden. When she glanced up at Masaki's tree from her shelter, she found a deep rend etched solidly into its wood, one that spanned halfway up the length of its trunk. Crimson sap gushed from the wound, and she knew that if she could not repair it, Masaki would surely die. She tried a few drops of blood from her palm, and when that did not work, she gashed the skin open wide, increasing the flow from drops to a small stream. When the effects from that appeared to be negligible as well, she slit open her wrist, letting the blood pour freely. Sliding to her knees, she watched as the wood and bark bubbled and morphed in response to her offering, the wound finally healing because of her desperate act.

She waited until there was nothing left of the rend but a scar in the bark before trying to staunch the flow of the opening in her wrist. Her grip was weak by this point, however, and her fingers trembling. Add to that the growing cold around her that was leaching into her bones and she found herself afflicted by an overwhelming fatigue and dizziness that forced her to lie on the ground. Unable to even find the strength to drag herself back into the shelter, she lay at the foot of Masaki's tree, watching the blood continue to pool around her shivering fingers, her wrinkled skin growing deathly pale.

She fell into a faint, and the next thing she was aware of was Haruo murmuring her name.

"Sanae, open your eyes. I am here for you."

She struggled to focus on him, recognizing him quickly by the red of his hair.

"You've come to help me bind my wounds and return me to my shelter?"

"No, love, I've come to claim you. I've come to take you home with me."

"Home with you? But what of Masaki? What of his tree?" She was stunned by the fact that Haruo had called her love. He had never mentioned the word with regards to her before. The spirit-man laughed softly.

"Still putting the welfare of others before your own, I see. Masaki will be fine. He is on his way home. The army has discharged him with what they believed to be a lethal wound. They did not expect him to survive, but he did, thanks to your devotion and your sacrifice. He has met a young woman, the daughter of the teamster charged with bringing him home. They are already falling in love. Before long, she will agree to marry him, and they will settle here on the farm. Don't worry—Masaki will tend to your garden and keep it growing. He will do it out of love and for your memory. In a few years it will ring with the voices of children again." He paused, taking her hand. "You will not be here to see it all, but we will visit. I couldn't make this my home, even though I wanted to. I never belonged here, but I was able to make the journey from time to time, just as you will from now on. You belong with me now, in a different world."

Sanae looked longingly at her garden, not wanting to leave it or Masaki behind.

"I meant what I said," Haruo added. "I watched you grow into a woman, Sanae. I loved the devotion you always showed your family, giving up your wants for the sake of your siblings and your parents. I adored the attention you lavished upon your garden, a labour of love. I wanted to be here to keep you company when the rest of your family left you, but since I couldn't, I gave you Masaki. You have lived a good life. You have been a worthy gardener. It is time to pass that legacy on to your son. You'll leave a part of yourself here when you go. You spared Masaki not only by feeding his tree your lifeblood, but your weft of spirit as well. You'll live on, in a way, in this garden, always a part of both Masaki and that tree. Now join me."

When Haruo helped her to her feet, it was only her spirit that followed. Shedding her physical form like an unwanted husk, a flower free from its seed, she allowed Haruo to guide her into the world that lay beyond the kami shrine, ready to be welcomed by her many ancestors who had passed that way before her. Perhaps she would be able to start a new garden on the other side.

Mark of Ruins

By S.D. Grimm

Olivia's shoes tapped against the sidewalk as she made her way closer to the monstrous building. Her stomach flip-flopped—as if she shouldn't be used to this by now. Another foster home meant another high school. It also meant a fresh start, and this time she wasn't going to mess it up.

She stopped in front of the towering structure. Staring up at the steeple made the sky spin. The black spire pierced heaven. White bricks, streaked dark from age and weather, crumbled. Tall trees from the woods behind surrounded the building in a wild, overgrown frame. Was it a school or a Catholic church?

Two gargoyles glared her, sticking out their sharp tongues. A chill prickled her skin when she looked into their sightless eyes.

"Ugly, aren't they?"

She spun around. A guy stood behind her. His unzipped varsity jacket revealed pecs that pulled his white shirt just right.

Even his smile was perfect. "Those huge, pointy ears freak me out."

Heat flushed Olivia's face. Her hand flew to the side of her head to check the bobby pins. Her weird birth defect remained hidden. Relief left her blood tingling. He just meant the gargoyle's ears. Pointy ears that freaked him out.

Hot varsity guy extended his hand. "I'm Ty."

"Olivia."

A group of five guys and four girls wandered over. Every one of them wore the same blue and white varsity jacket. Popular clique identified. And they were talking to her?

Olivia wiped sweaty palms on her uniform skirt.

Ty faced his friends and draped his arm around her shoulder. "Meet Olivia."

Hot guy was touching her? By the way his arm curled around her neck it was more like claiming. A shiver rippled through her body. The popular kids were accepting her? Holy awesome! Goodbye Olivia the freak. Hello private school in a creepy church.

"So, Olivia, need someone to show you around?" Ty's perfect lips stretched into a smooth smile as he pulled her closer.

Ignoring her accelerating pulse, she nodded.

His arm slid off her shoulder and, like a gentleman, held out his hand to help her up the cement steps and toward the dark, wooden double doors. "What's your first class?"

Class, right. Her schedule crinkled as she unfolded it. "Homeroom 213 with Watkins."

"I'm in that class." A stick-thin girl who wore her uniform skirt way above her knees looped her arm through Olivia's. "I'm Hailey."

Olivia glanced at her linked arm. Maybe everyone in the cool group was a little...possessive.

* * *

Olivia slid her lunch tray across the smooth surface of the table and joined Hailey. After three weeks she still couldn't believe she was sitting at the popular table.

She glanced toward the east wall. He sat there already, alone—in a crowded lunchroom—with his sketchbook. Who was he? The only thing she'd heard her new friends call him was loner or...freak. That word heated her blood. And made the compassion in her heart surge. No one should have to sit alone.

"Earth to Olivia." Hailey's voice cut her thoughts.

Olivia sucked in a breath and tore her eyes away, hoping Hailey hadn't seen where she was looking. "Yeah?"

"No staring at loner boy." Hailey slurped the last millimeter of coke through her straw. The slurping stopped. "I've seen you looking."

"What? I think he's cute."

"Yeah, but Jason Westman is damaged goods. Besides Ty's been holding doors and carrying books for you for three weeks. He's totally into you. And trust me, you want Ty to be into you."

Olivia's stomach twisted. Trust? That wasn't something she gave out easily. But this was what she wanted, right? To fit in. More than that—to be popular. That meant she couldn't trust them with her secret. "Ty's nice."

Cold hands gripped Olivia's fingers. Hailey finally parted with her coke can. "Securing a spot on the nice list isn't his agenda. He likes you."

Olivia couldn't shake the feel of Ty's arm resting around her neck like a leash made of a boa constrictor. "He's a little possessive. Isn't he?"

Hailey rolled her eyes. "He's a quarterback. It's in his blood. You like him, right?"

What was she supposed to say? Hailey's judgmental eyes narrowed to slits and Olivia's heart sped. "Of course."

The scent of Ty's cologne suffocated Olivia before his strong grip closed around her neck. "How's my girl?"

Olivia pulled back, but her bobby pins pushed into her scalp. No way she'd let those come undone. She smiled at Ty. He might be possessive, but the leash was better than rejection. Right?

* * *

Olivia checked the class transfer form, making sure this was the right room, and then held her head high as she walked into advanced English. Packed, floor-to-ceiling bookshelves lined three walls. More like a library than a classroom, except for the desks.

She gave her class transfer form to Mr. Hastings.

He smiled. "Welcome, Olivia. There's an open seat in the back."

She scanned for the empty desk, and her stomach jumped off the high dive. A head of dark messy hair bowed over a sketchbook. Jason Westman. And he was right next to her open seat. Hailey's "damaged goods" warning echoed in her thoughts, but she pushed it away.

She slid into her new desk and gave Jason her friendliest smile. "I'm Olivia."

He bobbed his head once without even looking in her direction.

Olivia leaned closer. Dang, he smelled good. "So, what do you draw?"

He closed his sketchpad.

"Not into sharing?"

"Not into making friends, Olivia." He crossed his arms on his desk and buried his head behind them.

Not awkward at all.

"Mythological beasts," Mr. Hastings dove right into

the lesson which was their first paper's subject. Any beast of her choosing. Cool. She picked up her pen.

The list of creatures to choose from was three miles long, and Mr. Hastings started naming each. Apparently he wanted to be sure they knew the correct pronunciations. Boring. At least it gave her a chance to try and crack Jason's shell.

When Mr. Hastings reached the "R's", she elbowed Jason for the fifth time. "What are you going to write about, Sleeping Beauty?"

At least he smiled this time. "You don't give up, do you?"

"Everyone needs a friend."

The smile vanished. "Your friends and me—oil and water."

"My friends are kinda…suffocating."

His eyes, blue like a warm summer sky, searched her face. "So find new friends."

Her lungs tightened. "I don't think Ty would let me go that easily."

The muscles in Jason's jaw popped. "And *Ty* gets to decide for you? That's a lot of power to give one person." He shook his head. "Is it worth it? Being one of them instead of being yourself?"

She stared at him. Why did he suddenly care anyway?

The bell made her jump.

Jason shouldered his backpack.

Everyone started shuffling out of their desks while she sat there stumbling over his words. Olivia gathered her things and hurried to catch him.

She found him walking down the hall. "Jason, wait. You never answered my question."

He chuckled. "There were so many."

Heat hit her cheeks, she had been relentless. "What are you going to write about?"

He stopped. Students swirled around them while she waited for his answer. Someone bumped her backpack, but she kept Jason's gaze.

The hint of a smile tugged his lips. "Changelings have always fascinated me."

Before she could ask him what a changeling was, he left.

* * *

Olivia pulled open the public library's huge wooden door and inhaled that familiar book smell. Now to find the section on mythology. Mr. Hastings was old school, so they had to use at least one physical book in their paper on monsters. Olivia didn't mind. Libraries comforted her. And they were quiet. She'd already started her search on changelings at home, but her foster siblings had no concept of keeping playtime below ten decibels.

Her gaze landed on a familiar face beneath a black hood, and her heart stumbled on a beat. Jason Westman. Of course he'd be here, listening to music and drawing in his sketchpad.

The taste of strawberry chapstick hit her tongue as she chewed her lip. Maybe she should say hi. Why? What about him made her want to? It wasn't like he'd been nicer in class today. Well, more talkative, but anything more than three words was a conversation with him. It was annoying, actually. But she'd gotten him to smile, twice. His eyes brightened when he smiled.

Her feet moved closer to the oversized leather chair and bobbing black hoodie.

"Hey, baby."

She spun around. Ty stood there grinning.

Though her blood pounded in her ears, Olivia stood tall and met Ty's gaze. "Please, don't call me baby."

He leaned closer—too close. "Why not, babe?"

Olivia shifted her backpack, which suddenly seemed to carry bricks, to her other shoulder. "Because it sounds very boyfriendish."

His perfect lips slid into a devious smile. "So *be* my girlfriend."

Her jaw dropped. What would happen if she said no? Would she lose Hailey too? All of her friends? Jason's voice echoed in her head. *Is it worth it?* "I—I don't—."

"Come here." His thick fingers closed around her wrist, tightening.

Pain pulsed through her arm. "Ty—."

"Don't make a scene." His words escaped through clenched teeth, and he yanked her between two rows of books, away from prying eyes.

Olivia's heart sped. "Ty, you're hurting me."

He tossed her against a bookcase and leaned close. "Everyone knows I want you."

"Ty, please. I don't—."

"I don't get rejected."

Bookshelves jabbed her back. Ripped arms flanked her. Why couldn't she breathe? His cologne choked her. She pushed against his chest.

"Like what you feel?" His breath heated her hair.

Panic coursed through her blood. She needed him off, now. "Ty, leave me alone."

"Or what?"

"She said, leave."

Olivia looked up, over Ty's shoulder. Jason stood there, jaw clenched. He grabbed Ty's shirt collar and pulled. Ty stumbled and crashed to the floor in front of the opposite bookcase. Books he'd grabbed at while falling landed near him.

Free, Olivia sucked in gulps of air. Her weak knees guided her to the floor.

Before she could react, Ty jumped to his feet and lunged. A thump resounded as Ty's hands met Jason's chest.

Jason rocked back. His fisted hands came up like a boxer's. "You gonna push me around now?"

Ty laughed. "You gonna stop me?"

Jason smirked. "You know I can." He glanced at

Olivia, those blue eyes softened. "You okay?"

"Of course she's okay." Ty reached for her and she scrambled away. His nostrils flared.

A gentle touch tugged her arm, and Jason guided her behind him. "Walk away, Ty."

Her fingers dug into Jason's shoulders. With him between her and Ty she felt…safe.

Ty punched at a row of books, and a chorus of thuds hit the floor on the shelf's other side. "This isn't over, freak."

He stalked off.

Jason's tense shoulders relaxed.

Holy crap! She was still hanging on to him? She released her grip. "Sorry."

"Don't apologize for that jackass."

Her legs shook. And her hands. She leaned against the bookcase and massaged her sore wrist. Jackass was right.

Something soft brushed her arm. "He hurt you?"

She whipped her hand behind her back. "I'm fine."

Jason touched her elbow. "Let me see?"

His fingers slid down her arm, so gentle compared to Ty.

He stroked her wrist, sending a surge of flutters through her chest. "It's red, Liv. Let's get you some ice."

Liv? Her stomach warmed like she'd eaten a bowl of soup. "I'm fine. Really."

His eyebrows pulled together. "Don't cover for him.

He hurt you."

A tingle rushed through her arm. Jason's thumb traced the tattoo on the inside of her wrist. A mystery in blue ink that she'd never been able to unravel.

He dropped her hand. "I better get going."

Just like that?

"Wait." She grabbed for his sleeve, but he dodged her. "I didn't get to thank you."

He scratched the back of his head. "You don't need to."

Olivia stepped closer, in case he tried to dart away again. Ty had been scared; otherwise, he would have fought back. "Ty's afraid of you."

Jason shrugged. "Only when he's alone. Which is never."

"Why?"

Jason leaned against one of the bookshelves. A smile tugged one corner of his mouth. "Questions are your thing, aren't they?"

Heat warmed her face, but she wasn't embarrassed enough to drop the subject. "And yet you let him call you freak? Why don't you stand up to him?"

"What do you think that was?" He motioned toward the fallen books and the whole scene played through Olivia's mind again.

She shuddered as the fear shot through her again, and then the feeling of safety. "I think you were protecting me. That's different."

He pushed off the bookshelf. "I take care of myself when I need to. Besides, I don't really care what *they* think. And neither should you."

Easier said. He couldn't be happy as a loner with no friends. She never was. Her stomach squeezed. Standing up to Ty today may have ruined everything. She rubbed her bruised wrist. Was it worth it? Could she pretend not to care what Ty and his friends thought?

Not alone.

Jason cleared his throat. "You hungry? There's a great burger place a few blocks over." He looked so unsure watching her with his eyebrows pulled together.

Maybe she didn't have to be alone. "I thought you had to go?"

He smiled. "It can wait."

"A burger sounds good."

* * *

Nothing beat the smell of fried meat and potatoes. Yum. Just yum.

Olivia sipped her Sprite. Jason was awfully quiet. Maybe she'd have to prod him with conversation like she did in Mr. Hastings' class. Their mythological beasts paper seemed a good conversation starter. "So I looked up changelings."

Jason smiled. "Yeah?"

"Creepy that some*thing* could steal your baby and replace it with one that looks like yours."

His blue eyes grew wide. "Yeah."

"I might write about them."

"Really? What angle?"

"Well, it seems like most beasts replace babies with changelings for terrible reasons and the changelings do awful things, but…there was at least one mythological race whose motives seem more mysterious than harmful."

His eyes narrowed. "Yeah?"

"Elves."

Jason almost choked on his pop.

"Are you okay?"

He nodded, still coughing.

She couldn't help but smile. "Trick is to swallow."

"I'm good," he finally managed.

The waitress set two plates down. Grease dripped over the bun, and the fries sizzled. Olivia rolled up her sleeves. Jason did, too.

"Cool wristbands." She squinted at the picture embossed in the leather.

"Uh, thanks."

"What's the design of?" Olivia reached across the table.

Jason dropped his burger and pulled away.

"O…kay. I don't bite."

He closed his eyes. "Sorry."

He held out his hands so she could see the wristbands. They both had different designs.

He pointed to the left one first. "This is a sword on fire. It represents a guardian."

"Like a guardian angel?"

He laughed and motioned to the other band. "This one's a live oak."

Olivia traced her finger over the smooth, worn leather. Her finger froze. She chanced a closer look. Her heart jumped off the starting block. The runes beneath the tree matched her tattoo. "What does this mean?"

His arm pulled back slowly. "You don't know what your tattoo means?"

Right. He'd seen that. How embarrassing. Olivia stared at her burger and shook her head.

"They're Elven runes. It says: heart of a wood elf." Jason picked up his burger. "I have a friend who has this huge, dusty book that translates the stuff."

Her tattoo was Elven runes? How did it get there? She dipped a fry in her catsup. For as long as she could remember, she'd always had the mark. The ink never distorted as she grew, like it was a living part of her. Like magic. Which was not real. Unless she was some changeling elf baby switched at birth. Wait.

"Wouldn't the babies have pointy ears?"

Jason smiled over his half-eaten burger. "You back on the changeling-elf thing?"

"Yes. And what makes a mother swap her baby?"

Jason set his burger down. "I don't think it's the mothers who swap them."

"You mean both mothers have their babies stolen?"

"Yeah."

"How sad."

Silence followed. Olivia looked up from her plate to see Jason frozen solid with one cheek stuffed full of food.

Heat flooded her face. "Well, not that any of that's real."

He swallowed. "Right."

* * *

The laptop's backlight brightened Olivia's dark bedroom. Two a.m. and still no luck on changelings with tattoos. Her head hit the back of the desk chair. Wait. Her fingers moved slowly as she typed *heart of a wood elf.*

The runes in her tattoo stared back at her…with a link?

She clicked it and was directed to a page with a story. Pulse racing, she read it. The last paragraphs chilled her core:

When the elven queen laid her babe in the basket that night, her spirit was restless. Not wanting any harm to befall her child, she put this blessing on him: "Flesh of my flesh, heart of my heart, may your heart always remember your home, may your guardian protect you and return you to me."

Tiny blue runes bled into the skin on the inside of his wrist, binding the blessing. They read: "Heart of a wood elf."

As she feared, the babe was taken from her, but a young maiden, marked as a guardian, returned the babe home. The maiden was gravely injured in the process and died soon after. The elven queen planted a tree in the maiden's memory, and carved the guardian's symbol in the trunk.

The flaming sword etched into the tree matched the sword on Jason's wristband. Goosebumps spread over her skin. Did he know about this story? Olivia closed her laptop and darkness enveloped her. She'd have to ask him.

* * *

Olivia headed to English class. Jason wasn't there yet. She took her seat. Everything she learned last night clawed at her insides. She hoped he knew something. She set her books under her desk.

"Special delivery for Olivia."

Her head popped up, and her heart leapt into her throat. What was Ty doing here? Judging from his slick smile, nothing good.

A folded paper landed on her desk. "Go ahead. Open it. It's from Jason."

Every eye glued to her desk where the strange

delivery lay.

The page was thick, rough, like sketchbook paper. The figure on the creased page made her stomach drop like a frozen lump. Her face…her ears.

Ty chuckled. "That's a pretty weird pastime, even for a freak."

"Stop calling him that!"

Ty leaned over her desk and whispered, "You can fix things, Olivia. You can still be mine."

Jason stood in the doorway, white knuckled. His cheek was purple and a sliver of dried blood caked his lower lip. Olivia's heart shriveled. So they had stolen the page from his sketchbook.

And he knew about her ears.

Tears battled to break free. Olivia would not give anyone the satisfaction of watching her cry. She balled up the picture, picked up her books, and headed out of the classroom avoiding Jason's eyes.

His hand brushed her arm. "Liv, it's—it's not what you think."

He was no different. He probably fed her that changeling crap on purpose. Just another person waiting for the right moment to tell the whole school about her ears. And Ty beat him to it.

"Really?" The balled paper crushed in her fist. She slammed it into his palm. "I think it's *sick*."

"That's my girl." Ty's voice followed her out.

* * *

The scent of rain and wet bark surrounded Olivia as she raced through the woods behind the school. Droplets misted against her skin, her hair, and washed away her tears. His girl? So Ty didn't believe those were her ears. Her secret was safe. Until Jason told. How could she have been so stupid to think it would be different here?

Leaving her backpack on the wet ground, she climbed into an ash's protective branches. No matter where she lived, the trees were always the same. Comforting, welcoming, and safe.

She huddled there until the sprinkling stopped. The sun peeked through and warmed her face. School would be over soon. Maybe she'd wait here until everyone was gone to avoid their stares and questions.

Searing pain shot through her wrist. Her arm jerked forward and she nearly fell. Gripping her wrist, she noticed her tattoo glowing like polished aquamarine. She stared at the foreign light.

Pain throbbed again, like something pulled against burned skin. The pull was so strong…like it was leading her.

Her shoes hit the soggy ground. The grip around her wrist urged her toward the school. Tentatively she took a step. The glow pulsed and grew brighter.

Shouts echoed in the school's back parking lot—right where the pull led her.

Olivia halted at the sound of Ty's voice.

"You should stop defending her, freak. I already won. You of all people should have seen that coming."

She stepped toward the parking lot, and her stomach lurched. Two of Ty's teammates, Bobby and Spike, held Jason's arms behind his back. Blood dripped from his face, staining the asphalt red.

She could run, or she could stand up to Ty. Jason had defended her. Maybe he meant to keep her secret.

She stepped forward. Her fists shook. "What did you win, Ty?"

He caught sight of her, and his lips slid into that smooth smile. "Olivia, you're just in time for your rescue."

"What?"

"I'm saving your reputation." His fist hit Jason's puffy face.

Pain squeezed Olivia's heart. "Stop!"

"Or what?"

"I'm not yours to save, Ty!"

His chuckle started low and grew louder. "You don't get to break up with me."

Is it worth it? No. Popularity wasn't worth this. "You really think you can control me? You can't because I don't care what you think." With a shaky hand, she held up her phone. "I called the cops."

Ty lunged at her. "You little—!"

"Time's ticking." She stood her ground.

The boys bought her lie and ran, leaving Jason

slumped on the ground. An engine revved and tires squealed.

"Jason?" Concrete bit into her knees and tiny rocks ate at her legs as she knelt near him.

"Liv, I—."

"Shh." Her voice trembled. Tears blurred her vision. This shouldn't have happened. She touched his swollen face. Warmth, like basking in the sun on a summer day, caressed her skin. Blinding light blanketed her. What was happening? It was so comfortable…so normal.

The light faded. "Your face…."

Jason stared at her like a dog ready to bolt. He was totally healed.

"H-how—?"

His Adam's apple bobbed several times. "You were glowing. Like a comet."

Her shaking hand flew to her mouth. "I did that?"

"It's all right." He grabbed for her hand, but she pulled back.

No it wasn't! She stood, breathing like she'd run a race. This couldn't be happening. She'd stood up to Ty and lost Jason all at once. Because there was no denying who she truly was—a freak. Gravel crunched under her feet and tears streamed down her cheeks as she raced away. She hadn't made it to the woods before strong fingers gripped her arm.

"Let me go!"

He did. "Liv, look."

She glanced over her shoulder.

He pulled off his wristband and blue elven runes inked into his skin stared back at her. Her mouth went dry.

* * *

Olivia's legs ached from running. Her lungs burned. Wind rippled her blouse and teased her hair. Under the giant trees' shade, the air cooled. The creek's nearby babble calmed her. She climbed a tree and nestled in the crook of a limb.

Leaning against the moist trunk, she pushed up her sleeve. The dark blue tattoo peeked out. Was she really an elf? Jason had one, too. Did that make him the guardian? Already he'd done nothing but protect her, get hurt for her. And she'd run from him, again. How could she have believed he wanted to expose her secret and hurt her?

And now he probably thought she was like one of the monsters from Mr. Hastings' list.

Footsteps, too heavy for a wild animal, thudded close. Olivia peered out of her tree. Someone in a familiar black hoodie came into view below.

Jason brought his hands to his mouth. "Olivia!"

Hope exploded in her chest. "Look up."

His blue eyes found her. "You had me worried. Come down?"

She bit her lip.

"Do you trust me, Liv?"

Yes. Everything inside her screamed yes, but the word stuck in her throat.

He winced. "I'd like to explain…the drawings."

As in, more than one?

His shoe dug a groove in the dirt. "If you want me to leave you alone—."

"No." She dismounted the tree and walked over to him, those eyes watched her intently. She placed her palm on his chest. So warm. He breathed deep and stared at her hand.

"Afraid I'll light up again?"

He smiled. "A little."

"You aren't going to tell, are you?"

"Your secret's safe with me."

That was all she needed to know. "I trust you."

Under her palm his heartbeat sped. "You do?"

"Can I see your tattoo?"

His eyebrows pinched together. "Didn't you get a good enough look?"

"It was kind of far away." She reached for his arm.

Jason pulled away. His chest heaved like a frightened rabbit's, but he said nothing. Still hiding something?

"Let me explain?" He sat on a rock near the creek, pulled his sketchbook out of his backpack, and opened it.

A drawing of the runes stared back at her. Fancy

calligraphy behind them read: heart of a wood elf.

The paper was rough like the one Ty gave her. "We have the same tattoo?"

"Mine's a little different."

"Wait. You drew my tattoo?"

"I didn't know it was *your* tattoo."

Then what did his look like? If he wouldn't show her, she'd find out herself. Before courage left, she grabbed his arm and yanked the wristband. It unsnapped and fell to the ground.

No tattoo.

He tore his arm away.

It was too late. She'd seen it.

Her palm pressed against her lips, and she stared at the side of his face because he wouldn't look at her. Not that he could be blamed. She'd intruded on something very, very secret—a long, thin, white scar.

No wonder Hailey called him damaged goods.

"Jason, I'm sorry. I shouldn't have done that. I—."

"You didn't know." He shook his head, still not looking at her.

"I still shouldn't have...I won't tell anyone."

He scoffed.

"Jason, I won't say a—."

"Can you just drop it?"

She bit her lip and nodded.

"I imagine you were looking for this?" He pulled up his other sleeve and removed the leather wristband. He turned his face away and thrust his arm under her nose.

The tattoo was there. And another scar right through it.

She cradled his hand in her palm. Her fingers traced the indelible blue ink. The ridge of the scar hit each groove of her fingerprint like an echo of its presence. Why had he done that? And did he ever think of doing it again? A shiver rippled through her.

His weight shifted. Clearly this made him uncomfortable.

She dropped his hand. "What does yours mean?"

"Wood elf's guardian." He turned the page in the sketchbook and there was his tattoo.

The scent of pencil, lead, and book glue mingled with the woodsy aroma around her. "Why did you show me yours if you drew it?"

Finally his eyes met hers, if only for a moment. "You're the kind of girl who would've demanded proof."

She smiled. "I guess."

His return smile was sad. "When Ty was threatening you at the library—."

"Your tattoo started glowing?"

"Yeah."

She turned a page.

"Liv—."

"I already know my face is in here, is there anything else I should be worried about?"

He shook his head.

Olivia stared at the picture of herself. Except it wasn't really her. The girl in the drawing was beautiful. And her ears peeked out of her hair, free. Olivia traced her finger over the drawing careful not to smudge it. The drawing was dated. June third? As in before they met? How could he have…?

"I've dreamt about her."

Olivia's gaze snapped to Jason. "What?"

"The elf-girl that looks like you. I've been dreaming about her for—well, forever." He rolled his eyes and the smallest smile tugged on the corner of his mouth. "I don't draw weird pictures of *you*. I draw your elven doppelganger."

"Elven?"

"There's the obvious difference." His finger traced the outline of her ear so delicately, like the way he touched Olivia's wrist after Ty hurt her.

So he didn't know about her secret? "Jason, do you think elven changelings are real?"

His eyebrows pinched together and he stared at her. "Why would you even ask that?"

"Are you forgetting what just happened behind the school?"

"Are you saying…?"

Olivia touched the drawing, the pretty ears that the elf girl wasn't afraid to wear. Her heart pounded. Wood elf was tattooed on her arm. Would she scare Jason away if she told him about the story—and that she believed it? "So, where did you get your tattoo?"

Jason's eyes met hers. "I don't know. I've always had it."

"But you know what it means?"

His mouth dropped open, but no words came out.

Olivia scooted closer. "You just found a guy with an old dusty book on runes to tell you what it meant?"

Jason bowed his head. "Wouldn't it be crazy if he was actually an elf?"

Olivia's heart missed a beat. "No."

His head popped up. "Really?"

"Would it be crazy if I was actually a changeling?"

"No."

She held his gaze. "And what if I had to find my real home?"

Jason leaned close. "I'd make sure you got there."

"Really?"

He nodded, his face serious.

Her breath caught as he touched her hair. The bobby pins moved. Her blood turned to ice water. A stinging sensation shot through her nose and eyes. What if he thought she was ugly? Her eyes squeezed shut and warm tears trailed down her cheeks.

Arms enveloped her, guided her to his chest.

He smelled like woods and boy and comfort and she never wanted to leave.

Olivia pulled the sketchpad closer. "She doesn't look like an ugly freak in your drawing."

Soft fingers brushed her cheek. "That's because she's not."

"But I am."

"No." His finger trailed up and down her arm. So smooth. "Look."

He rolled up his sleeves. His scarred arms stared back at her.

"When I was ten, I ran away because my parents were punishing me for—," his voice wavered, "for some stupid thing that was my fault. They found me and asked me to get in the car. On the way home a drunk driver hit us. They died."

His body shook. "They adopted me. They picked me, and I killed them."

"Jason." She lifted her head from his chest and threw her arms around him.

His chin hit her shoulder. "If anyone is an ugly freak, it's me."

"No. You taught me to stand up to Ty. To be true to myself. Ugly people don't do that. They beat people up for doing what's right." She squeezed him tight. "I'm sorry that driver robbed you. And you almost robbed... you don't need to pay for what that driver did. People need you. I need you."

He swallowed.

"I mean, not that you'd ever want to be with someone like me." She dropped her hold and backed away.

His hand stopped her. The grip was strong, but not harsh. He reached for her hair. One of the bobby pins slid out. And another. He laid them one by one in a pile on a stone by the brook.

The ache pressing against her head dissolved with every gentle touch.

When each pin lay on the rocks he cupped her face in his hand. His fingers glided over her ear's pointy edge, soft, like he'd touched his drawing. A shiver rippled through her.

"You're beautiful, Liv."

Her breath caught.

"There's no need to hide yourself from me."

She touched the scar on his wrist, and he didn't pull away. "I'll promise not to rob you if you promise never to rob me."

"Deal." Jason's fist curled around the pins, and he hurled them into the water.

Birdie's Life at the School for Distressed Young Ladies

By J. H. Fleming

Her dead sister stared at her with sightless eyes, their black depths immobilizing her. Ravens swooped around her, their voices chilling her blood. She wanted to scream, wanted to run home and pretend it was all some sick nightmare. But she couldn't move, and her sister was coming closer.

Her limbs jerked as she moved, like she was some ragdoll come to life for the first time. Her once blonde hair fell in sweaty strands around her face, darkened by grime and dirt. Her skin appeared gray from the ashes that covered her, and the stench was worse than she could have ever imagined. She doubled over, gagging and gasping for air. She could see her sister's feet, her unnatural gait moving them closer, closer. At any second she would touch her, she could already sense her arm reaching as a scream built in her throat....

* * *

Birdie sat in isolation for the fourth time that week. She supposed the time spent alone was supposed to cure her of her "intolerable nighttime behavior." She couldn't help that she woke screaming every time she dreamed of Morgan. Miss Tobin, the headmistress, believed punishment and proper penitence fixed any problem, and Birdie wished she were right.

The room was dim and cold, hidden away in a little-used part of the school. She couldn't count the number of times she'd sat in that exact spot, stared at the same peeling gray wallpaper and dusty floor. Memories of her life before were always strongest in isolation. No meaningless chatter to distract her, no endless lessons on etiquette and embroidery. The ghosts of her past could consume all her attention.

She remembered being happy once, before Father died. The four of them had gone on picnics, had family vacations to the beach or the country. Her parents had taken her and Morgan to the zoo, the museum, the opera. Then Grandmother had gotten sick and had to come live with them, and they didn't go out as often, but they were still happy. It wasn't until Father had died that things had really changed. Until then it had seemed to Birdie that the world was a magical, interesting place, where nothing bad ever really happened. After, she saw that it most closely resembled a bubble, beautiful and mysterious, but fragile, gone before you knew it, and then as though it had never existed in the first place.

Grandmother got worse, Mother stopped eating, and Morgan looked to her to assure her that everything would be okay. But it wouldn't, and it never had been. If they were "lucky" they'd marry, have kids, grow old, die, and be forgotten, just like everyone else. Happily ever after didn't exist, and those who believed in it were fools.

The lock on her door unbolted and light streamed over her as Miss Tobin peered in. "Feeling better?" she asked, her voice an annoying singsong. Her dress and hair were as dusty and gray as the room Birdie crouched in, more proof that time would wear them down in the end.

"Yes, much," she answered, her own voice creaky from hours of disuse, her throat still raw from that morning.

Miss Tobin smiled and stood aside for her to enter the hallway. They saw her as a poor, pitiful young girl who only needed a little love to make everything better. That she loathed them all, considered them nothing more than bags of dirt, herself included, never crossed their minds.

* * *

"Hey, Screamer! Did the boogeyman come for you this morning? Did you wet the bed? I bet they could hear you all the way in the city!"

Birdie ignored the taunts, which were lead by a simpering girl named Catherine Sherwood. She'd been sent to the school after a series of fainting spells and "undignified behavior" toward her new stepmother. Catherine and her ilk were the type who thought they knew what suffering was, and who considered themselves superior to others because of it. She passed by them without a glance, finding a table in an isolated corner near the window as a servant brought a plate over.

She could see the forest at the edge of the grounds, a forbidden place that most of the girls had no desire to see anyway. Birdie wondered how deep it was, what sorts of creatures lived in it, and how long it would take someone to find her if she ventured there. She almost didn't notice when the other girl sat beside her at the table. With an effort she drew her gaze away from the glass and looked at the younger girl who'd joined her. She was just a little waif, maybe eight or nine, with straight blonde hair that reminded her so much of Morgan. No one knew the girl's real name; she answered only to Goose.

Since she'd arrived at the school the girl had latched onto her, following her everywhere, keeping her company even though she preferred solitude. She wouldn't say why she'd been sent to the school, but Birdie supposed it didn't matter. The truth was they were all mad, haunted by one thing or another. The rest of the world just hadn't admitted it yet.

"The pudding's good today," Goose offered, her voice high and hopeful, another similarity to Morgan.

Birdie only nodded in response. She ate mechanically, without tasting her food. It was all sand and ashes anyway. Goose started to say something else, but Birdie stopped listening. She was thinking about the forest again, how lonely and empty it must be. She was thinking how, if one walked far enough and long enough, she could disappear entirely, leaving not even a memory behind.

* * *

The hallways were abandoned when Birdie slipped from her room late that night. If one of the staff caught her she'd get much worse than isolation, but what did she care? She intended to lose herself in the trees, and they couldn't stop her if they tried. She wore only a thin shawl over her nightgown, and the flimsy slippers they'd been given in case a call of nature came over them during the night. Her room was on the second floor at the end of a long hallway, so she had to creep past the rooms of the other girls and then down the stairs.

She was lucky to have a room all to herself. It saved her from having to explain herself to a roommate. Being sent away for attacking another girl in a fit of rage definitely had its advantages.

She paused on the middle landing and listened for the school's resident hound, Moxie. The dog usually slept in the kitchen, but Birdie didn't want to take chances. She would explore the forest, tonight, and no one was going to stop her. She strained to hear the softest movement, the smallest breath of air, but there was nothing.

Satisfied, she tiptoed across the short distance from the stairs to the front door and slowly turned the lock. It made an audible click, and she froze again, expecting to hear someone stirring, for Moxie to come investigate. Silence.

She opened the door in one swift movement, hoping the hinges wouldn't have time to decide to creak, and closed it just as quickly behind her. The night air was cool and blew steadily from the north in a gentle stream that just avoided being annoying. Dark clouds hid the moon, which had just reached its fullest the night before. Birdie thought she could already smell the forest, the leafy, pure scent of nature that held no trace of human taint.

She walked freely across the grounds, no longer worrying of waking anyone. None of the staff would find her now. She'd been to the edge of the forest once before, when she'd first arrived at the school. Every girl was told exactly how far from the school she could go, and warned of what would happen if she broke that rule. With a smile on her face, Birdie stepped beneath the trees' branches, feeling that she was a part of some grand joke.

It was darker among the trees, and a bit colder. Any other girl at the school would've turned back already, and even Miss Tobin would've thought twice before venturing further into that uncertain darkness. For Birdie each step was easier than the last. All the rules and expectations and illusions of the school fell away, leaving, finally, just Birdie, and the quiet forest.

The relief lasted all of a second, for Morgan was there with her, occupying the empty space with her unwanted presence. Birdie thought she could almost see her dead sister, serving as a quiet shadow at her side. "Go away," she whispered, never slowing her determined stride. Her sister had depended on her more than ever after their Father died and Mother abandoned them. It fell to Birdie to be the parent, though they'd never been close and she didn't have a maternal bone in her body.

Sometimes she'd resented her sister, but never for long. It wasn't Morgan's fault that everything had gone to hell. In a way it had been a relief when the girl had died. Nearly. At least Birdie only had herself to look out for, now.

The wind barely touched her, not quite able to maneuver between all the trees to reach her, and the smell of pine and honeysuckle grew ever stronger. She could feel every rock and twig through her slippers, assuring her that her shoes would likely be ruined before the night was through.

She'd been in a forest once that she could remember, when her Father had taken them hiking. That had been a tamed forest, closed to the public at night and cleansed of any dangerous plant or animal. This forest was wild, pure as the day it had formed, and all the more alluring for that. It could contain wolves, bears, perhaps even panthers. Even a wild dog would be something exciting she'd never encountered before. Birdie didn't fear death or pain. The worst had happened, and she'd faced it and survived. If only the dead would leave her be....

The trees parted, opened up to reveal a good-sized clearing before her, only to come back together in the barely discernible distance. Shadowy shapes filled the clearing, their forms small and indistinct. She approached one, reached out a hand to touch it. Cold, rough rock brushed her fingertips. The front of it was smooth, indented all over in small, consistent patterns. It was a gravestone.

She wondered if any of the staff knew of the cemetery's existence. She didn't imagine they'd tell the girls if they did. For some it would be an effective way to ensure they never ventured into the forest. Bur for those like Birdie, it would only incite curiosity. Either way, imaginations were sure to run wild. Tales of ghosts and monsters would circulate, the more delicate among them would have "episodes" and be forced to endure more long hours of therapy. It amused Birdie, imagining the havoc that could ensue from one slip of the tongue.

A laugh echoed across the cemetery, as if some lingering spirit had shared her amusement. She turned in the direction she thought it had come from, thinking that perhaps she'd only imagined it. She felt the forest and its cemetery were *hers*, a place she could escape from the school and the ridiculous girls who lived there. Anyone else was an intruder. With a resolve to forcibly remove the person if need be, she walked across the cemetery, careful to not trip over gravestones and random rocks.

The laughter started up again, guiding her step and irritating her all at once. By the time she finally saw the two blurry outlines on the far side of the cemetery she was ready to throw a proper fit.

"Hey!" she called. "You there! What do you think you're doing?"

The shadowy forms turned to look at her, their faces still hidden in the darkness. "Why, look Mr. Chezelwhip, it's a human."

"Indeed."

The first voice was feminine, youthful. The second was male, which couldn't bode well for the girl. He sounded at least twice her age.

"You shouldn't be out this late," Birdie said. "Especially with a man."

The girl laughed. "What nonsense is this? There are no men here. Come, what's your name?"

"I didn't come out here to exchange pleasantries. If I wanted company I would've stayed at the school. It's your business if you want to sneak out with men, but I won't be your accomplice."

The girl laughed again. "I like her, don't you Mr. Chezelwhip? Here, let's have some more light. I want to see her face."

A glowing ball appeared, held aloft in the girl's hand and illuminating their faces. Pointy ears poked out beneath white hair, and it looked as though the girl's body was pale green. Her short dress was of a darker shade, its hem torn and tattered. Behind her two green and black wings rose into the air, full of spirals and odd designs. Her companion was even stranger. It appeared to be a large teddy bear, its fur covered in patches and matted in many places. It wore a monocle and a top hat, and even a red bowtie around its neck.

Birdie just stared at them for several long seconds. They couldn't be real. Faeries didn't exist, and she'd never heard of a talking teddy bear. Both had black eyes, which stared at her in silent appraisal. The girl smiled then, her teeth even whiter than her hair.

"I'm Pip," she announced. "Do you like scones? We brought plenty." She moved the light to reveal a blanket spread out on the ground and covered with tea cups, plates, a tea pot, and a small assortment of food.

"You don't honestly want to share with it?" the teddy bear asked, a tone of disgust in his voice.

"Oh Chez, stop that. I officially declare…Uh…. What's your name?"

"Um…Birdie."

"Right. I officially declare Birdie my guest, so you have to be nice."

The bear sighed dramatically and Birdie took a deep breath. "I've finally gone mad, haven't I? You two aren't really here, are you?"

"And the questions begin," Chez grumbled, resuming his seat on the blanket. "You try to have a nice picnic and instead get bombarded with inane questions. Soon it will be, 'What's your name? How old are you? What's your favorite color?' What rubbish."

"Chez, please," Pip said. "I'm sorry," she added, turning to Birdie. "He doesn't take to strangers. We're members of the Moon Court. Lower ranking I'm afraid, but the free time is nice, and we get out of the less important ceremonies."

Birdie shook her head, more convinced with every second that she'd finally snapped. When the staff found out they'd keep her locked up all the time, and then the nightmares would get worse….

"Give it a rest, Pip," Mr. Chezelwhip said. "She hasn't the faintest idea what you're talking about. She doesn't even believe we're real."

"Oh dear! I didn't mention I'm a faery, did I? Sometimes my mouth runs away with me. Mr. Chezelwhip here is an abandoned toy. His owner's love brought him to life, and then he was discarded without a second thought. Quite sad, but it happens more often than you'd think. He's a good sort, and you can't blame him for being grumpy. Anyway, enough about me, tell me about you! And you haven't touched your tea yet, is it too sweet?"

"I'm sure it's fine," Birdie said. She could deal with this. Maybe if she just went along with it, acted like everything was fine, they'd disappear, and Miss Tobin would have no reason to put her in isolation. She sat on the blanket and sipped from a cup Pip offered her. The tea was actually quite good, much better than anything offered at the school. Her desire to be alone had been temporarily replaced by a curiosity of where this vision would lead. The girl was a cheerful sort, but not annoyingly so. The bear seemed to exhibit the same gloomy attitude Birdie possessed herself.

Pip was looking at her expectantly so Birdie shrugged and said, "There's not much to tell. I live at the school over that way. My Father and sister are dead, and my Mother and Grandmother are sick and depressed."

"Oh, you poor dear!

"Could be worse," the bear said. "She could be dead, or worse, sick and confined to a bed for life."

"Chez, please!"

"I'm just speaking the truth."

"I'm not asking for pity," Birdie said. "You wanted to know, so I told you."

"So how did you end up here?" Pip leaned forward, her hands cupped together in her lap, her eyes riveted on Birdie's face. Mr. Chezelwhip sipped his tea, his eyes wandering over the tombstones around them.

"I hurt a girl," Birdie said, not caring what a vision thought of her. "Pretty badly. She deserved it, but no one cares about that. They sent me here seven months ago."

"Have you seen your family since then?" Pip asked.

Birdie shook her head. "Not so much as a letter."

"That's deplorable! Completely unacceptable. I hereby adopt you as a member of the Moon Court. We will be your family, Birdie."

"Now Pip, I must protest-."

"Nonsense. It is done."

"But she's human. And what will the Queen say? This is hardly following Court Procedure."

"Rosehip owes me a favor. We'll make it official at the next Gathering."

Birdie shrugged. She saw no reason not to play along. And she liked listening to the two argue.

"It's settled then," Pip said. "I'll speak with the Queen and arrange your Induction."

"I really don't like this, Pip."

"It'll be fine, Chez. I'll be in touch, Birdie."

Pip stood and started grabbing up the cups and food. Mr. Chezelwhip stood slowly, sighing as he did so. "Can't even enjoy a good picnic," he mumbled. Birdie got off the blanket and watched the two pack everything away in a wicker basket. Pip moved quickly, tossing things in haphazardly. Mr. Chezelwhip was more careful, placing cups and plates in delicately so they didn't clash against each other.

Just how many plates do two people need? Birdie wondered as he reached for another one. The food was tossed in with all the rest, not even placed in a separate container.

"There!" Pip said when she finished. "We're off, then. Good evening, Birdie." The faery brushed past her toward the forest. The bear followed more slowly.

"Wish I could say it was a pleasure," he said.

"Same here," Birdie responded.

They disappeared quickly, the dark trees swallowing every trace of them, and Birdie was finally left alone.

* * *

Morgan lay in a pool of her own blood, her throat a mangled mess and still oozing. Birdie stood frozen, unable to look away, unable to cry out. A flock of ravens circled overhead, as though to protect the dead. Morgan stared at her with lifeless eyes, an expression of shock on her face. She hadn't expected to die, never thought her life would end so suddenly. Nothing bad could happen with Birdie watching over her, no one could hurt her....

Birdie doubled over and emptied her stomach, almost cutting herself on the bloody knife she still held in her hand.

* * *

After she was released from isolation that morning Birdie went to the library. Only a few of the girls ventured there very often, and they mostly kept to themselves. The library was a place of silence, and therefore most often resulted in solitude. The last thing the majority of the girls wanted was to be alone.

It wasn't very big, containing only a couple thousand books, and the quality of those was questionable. Miss Tobin didn't allow faery tales of any kind, claiming they were only fit to poison a young girl's mind. So Birdie grabbed a book randomly off a shelf and went to her favorite window seat. She never read the books she chose, but having one open in front of her lessened the chance that anyone would try to talk to her.

Usually she spent her time looking out the window, imagining she was somewhere far away, maybe by the sea. But today her thoughts kept returning to the odd pair she'd imagined the night before. She didn't believe they were actually real.

She wondered if she would see them again, or if her madness would conjure some new characters. She could sneak out that night and wait in the cemetery, see what happened.

Clink!

A small rock bounced off the window, interrupting her train of thought. She closed her book and leaned forward so she could see through the glass. Pip stood below, waving when she saw she had Birdie's attention. So it seemed her madness was the consistent type.

Pip was alone, dressed in the same outfit as the night before. She beckoned to Birdie and pointed toward the forest. Birdie shook her head. There was no way she'd be able to sneak out during the day. Pip frowned and rubbed her chin. After a moment she pointed off to the left where Birdie knew there was a door. It'd be risky, but she thought she could manage it. She nodded her head to show Pip she was on her way and stood to return her book, nearly running into Goose in her haste.

"Sheesh, Goose, you scared me," she said, sitting back on the window seat.

"What are you doing?" the younger girl asked.

"Um, nothing. I was just leaving. Thinking of taking a nap, actually."

"But it's not even noon."

"Well, I'm really tired. I feel like I didn't get any sleep last night, and reading hasn't helped."

"You never read." Goose knew her too well.

"I did today. Just a little bit. Anyway, I'll see you later, all right?"

She hurried past the girl and laid the book on the front counter. She didn't have to explain herself, and Goose wouldn't press her. Her thoughts quickly returned to Pip and whatever she'd come for this time.

***

"Ow!" a girl cried as Birdie pushed open the side door. Surely Pip hadn't been standing in the doorway. "Watch where you're going, Screamer!" Catherine Sherwood.

Birdie's initial thought was to say something witty and mean, but girls like Catherine relished that kind of thing. Anything to prove they were getting under your skin. So she pushed past her and looked around for Pip.

"Aren't you even going to apologize?" Catherine asked.

Birdie ignored her and walked around the corner. Pip stood just a little ways down and waved when she saw Birdie coming. "I have good news!" she said. "The Queen-."

"Hey! You can't just walk away from me."

Birdie silently groaned. Why couldn't Catherine just go away? Or better yet, fall in a swamp.

"Oh, is this your friend, Birdie?" Pip asked.

"No. Just a bully."

"First you run into me and take off without apologizing, and now you're not going to introduce me to your friend? It amazes me how rude you can be, Birdie," Catherine said, coming up behind her.

For a moment Birdie thought she hadn't heard her right. Catherine couldn't see Pip, she was Birdie's vision.

But then she crossed her arms and said, "I don't remember Miss Tobin announcing any new girls. Are you a crazy one, too?"

"You can see her?" Birdie asked. Catherine wasn't the crazy type. If she could see her, it meant Pip was real.

"Don't be stupid," Catherine said. "I'm not blind."

"We don't have time for this," Pip said, pulling Birdie aside and turning her back on Catherine. "The Queen wishes to meet you. Tonight."

"Excuse me," Catherine said behind them. "Just who do you think you are?"

Pip swirled around and closed her fingers together in front of Catherine's face. Catherine opened her mouth to say something, but no sound came out. Her eyes widened in alarm.

"I am Pip of the Moon Court, member of the Fifth Circle. I'm afraid I can't say it's nice to meet you. You choose such odd friends, Birdie."

"She's no friend of mine," Birdie answered, trying to wrap her mind around what was happening. "What did you do to her voice?"

"Hmm? Oh, nothing really. She'll be back to normal tomorrow."

She was real. She was real, and she could do magic. She could take Birdie away from this place. For the first time since her Father had died, Birdie felt a whisper of hope.

"Shame," she said. "I kind of like Silent Catherine."

Catherine glared at both of them. It was obvious there were several nasty things she'd like to say, but Pip's spell deftly stopped that. Birdie could get used to faery magic.

"Now, as I was saying," Pip continued. "The Queen wants to meet you. Come to the cemetery tonight. Chez will be there too."

"What does the Queen want?" Birdie asked. If Pip was real, then Chez must be real, and this Moon Court they talked about. If she wasn't mad, then what else must be out there?

"Why, to make you a court member, of course. Why else? I've got to go. Don't be late, Birdie."

With that Pip hurried off toward the forest. Birdie watched her go, then looked over at Catherine, who had given up trying to talk and was instead sulking and scowling. Birdie laughed in her face and went back inside. Catherine lived to make others miserable. It was about time she was on the receiving end.

* * *

Morgan's death had been as unexpected as their Father's. She simply failed to wake up one morning. The doctor told them later that she'd had a rare illness, one with hardly any symptoms. Left untreated, it had slowly killed her. He assured them there had been minimal pain. It was soon after this that that horrible girl at Birdie's school had laughed—laughed!—at the death of Birdie's family members. Only someone monstrous would do such a thing. Only someone with no soul.

Birdie didn't remember what had happened. She'd woken up in a hospital, strapped to a bed with nurses and doctors all around her. She'd been sent to the school after that. In some ways she was grateful. It was better than enduring the emptiness back home, pretending at school every day that there was nothing wrong. Here, it was assumed there was an issue, and no one had to pretend to be all right. Still, she would leave in a heartbeat if she could. The problem was she had nowhere to go.

Until now.

* * *

"Well you certainly took your time," Mr. Chezelwhip said. He and Pip stood among the gravestones on the far side of the cemetery when Birdie arrived. She'd had to wait a little longer to sneak out because Catherine Sherwood had thrown a fit and kept everyone up. Thank goodness no one had thought to give her a pen and paper, for Birdie was sure she would've told them of her plans. They'd finally knocked her out, certain she'd lost her voice from overexerting herself.

"There's no time to waste," Pip said. "The Queen is

waiting." She grabbed Birdie's hand and dragged her into the forest. Mr. Chezelwhip followed behind, keeping up with Pip's fast pace. Birdie was finally coming to terms with the fact that Pip really was a faery. She'd certainly used some kind of magic on Catherine. Mr. Chezelwhip was still a mystery, but she supposed if faeries were real, how unlikely were living teddy bears?

"We're passing through the Rift now," Pip said. "Not much further."

"The Rift?"

"The Court lies in a different plane than the one you live in. Mortals can't cross it on their own. Since it's dark you won't be able to tell much difference, but it's quite beautiful during the day."

There was a gentle pressure in the air, as though it'd grown denser, then Birdie's ears popped and the air was normal again. The stars were the first thing she noticed. There seemed to be so many more than normal, and each shone like a diamond on a black blanket. The air smelled sweeter too, scented with flowers and other growing things. She could swear she sometimes even caught a scent of something baking.

"Hurry up," Mr. Chezelwhip said, pushing her from behind.

Pip had continued on ahead of them, looking back at Mr. Chezelwhip's words. "Come on, Birdie!"

She caught up and strived to stay close after that. After a while the trees began to thin and she could see the full moon overhead, its light filtering through the leaves to illuminate their path. She could also see the glowing eyes looking at them through the darkness. There were dozens of them, with more appearing every second.

"Don't worry about them," Pip said, noticing Birdie watching them. "We're almost-."

One pair of eyes stepped in their path, its shadowy bulk blocking her view of the moon. It must've been at least seven feet tall, and it was fat. Beyond that she couldn't tell much about its appearance.

Pip stopped and glared up at it. "Kindly move," she said.

It chuckled. "I don't think so," it said, its voice gruff and male. "Smells like you've got a tasty mortal there. We want a bite."

"She is a guest of Queen Isadora," Pip said, her voice soft and fierce. "You will not touch her."

The other eyes were moving closer, their outlines revealing all shapes and sizes. Birdie scowled at them, hoping they could see her expression.

"Just a little taste," the big brute said as another reached out and pinched her arm. She slapped it and it squealed, causing the others to laugh.

"A sport! A sport!" they cried.

Pip yelled something in a foreign tongue and a ball of fire appeared in her hand. She threw it at the creatures, the flames regenerating in her hand as they screamed. "Chez, get Birdie out of here!"

The bear grabbed her arm, pulling her backwards through the throng of shadows.

"Wait," she said. "Pip–!"

"Can take care of herself. She'll do much better without having to watch out for you too, so come on!"

The shadow creatures reached for her, pulling her hair and clothes. She pushed and slapped them as Chez tugged her clear of them. Pip's fireballs lit the darkness and screams filled the air, but many still followed their retreat.

"We'll have to make for the Rift," the bear said. "It's closer than the Queen's court."

"Will they follow us through?"

Mr. Chezelwhip didn't answer. Birdie briefly thought of smacking him, but refrained, considering that he was probably saving her life, as reluctant as he most likely was about it. Her lungs strained with every step, and a ball of fire formed in her side. Still they pressed on, the creatures close on their heels.

"Almost there," Mr. Chezelwhip said, but she wasn't sure how much longer she could last. Her feet began to trip over the ground, and she nearly tumbled on her face. Mr. Chezelwhip caught her, cursing under his breath.

"I can't–."

"Come on!"

They struggled on, the burn in her lungs intensifying.

"We–."

Mr. Chezelwhip suddenly stopped, looking back the way they'd come. Birdie followed his gaze, but saw no sign of their pursuers.

"They're gone," she panted, taking the moment to rest on her knees and take deep breaths.

"For now," he said. "I wonder–."

Howls disrupted the temporary quiet, coming from a short distance to their left. Birdie couldn't see anything in the darkness, but they didn't sound too far away.

"Should we go back?" she asked. "Maybe Pip's alone, now."

"You stay here. I'm going to find out what's caught their attention."

"I can help."

"No! You'll only be in my way. Stay here until Pip or I come for you. I won't be long."

He wandered off into the darkness, leaving Birdie feeling angry and powerless. She was not some victim who could only wait for someone to rescue her. She could save herself. The howls of the creatures continued to echo through the forest, so she took a final look around, saw no sign of Pip, and set off after Mr. Chezelwhip.

She wanted to scold the bear for leaving her behind, give him a good shaking and maybe a slap or two. It was obvious he didn't like her, and she couldn't claim to feel any affection for him either. But was it really so hard to at least try to be civil?

The howls were getting louder so she slowed her pace, squinted through the darkness for any movement. The last thing she wanted to do was run right into one of the creatures. The shadows began to move ahead of her, the howls gaining volume with every step. They seemed to be circling something, but there was no way to tell what it was from her spot on the ground. In a flash of inspiration she climbed a tree, stepping carefully in the dark so she wouldn't slip. A faint light appeared in the middle of the shadows, but she had to climb even higher to see its source. A small girl stood holding a lantern in the center of the creatures.

Goose.

One of the shadows reached out, scratched Goose's arm. The girl recoiled, staring defiantly at all of them. They were still howling and laughing, their voices grating on Birdie's ears. One grabbed Goose from behind, tossed her in the air and swung her around. Goose smacked it in the face and it released her, but the others only laughed more, thrilled at the sport.

Birdie hurried down out of the tree, not as carefully as she had climbed it. She scraped her arms and hands in several places, and again and again branches lashed against her face. She could feel hot blood oozing from wounds in several places, but she ignored them all. She had only one thought: to get to Goose as quickly as possible.

Her feet hit the ground already running, and when

she reached the barrier of shadowy creatures she pushed through them as if they weighed no more than feathers. A second later and Goose was in her arms. Birdie scowled at the surprised faces all around her. In Goose's lantern light she could see they only distantly resembled Pip. Their faces were paler, their eyes a dull, solid white. Many had protruding, jagged teeth and sharp claws. Some appeared more like the monsters Birdie had imagined them to be. Some cross between a beast and a goblin from a faery tale.

"Back off this instant," she told them.

Many laughed. "Two for the price of one, boys," one said.

"It's so much funner when they fight," another said.

One grabbed at Birdie, and she slapped it. More reached out, their bodies pressing closer.

Something stirred deep within Birdie, a rage that she had carried with her and nourished every day. A guttural scream erupted from her throat and the rage poured out of her, filling her mouth, her nose, leaking from her eyes and ears, until she was merely a vessel for the primal force. She could no longer see, could feel nothing but the rage passing through her, could hear only her own constant scream.

An interminable second later it passed and she collapsed, Goose's arms catching her and easing her to the ground. Her body dripped of sweat, her lungs labored to move air in and out. Her vision had started to clear, but just as quickly it faded again, and she was lost to the darkness.

* * *

The ravens circled overhead as always, waiting. Morgan stood before her, her wrists slashed and oozing where Birdie had cut her. Birdie waited for the terror to kick in, to paralyze her and leave her screaming, but it never came. She had no voice left with which to scream.

"Just leave me alone," she told her sister. "I can't save you."

Morgan smiled, blood dripping from her mouth, her teeth stained crimson. The ravens descended, flocking around Morgan, perching on her arms and head. On and on they came, covering her until no part of her body could be seen. Then as one they flew skyward, their wings flapping thunderously in Birdie's ears. Morgan was gone, not even a drop of blood left behind to mark that she'd been there.

Birdie watched the ravens disappearing, their forms growing smaller and smaller until they were nothing but black specks in the endless blue, until her eyes could no longer tell if they were there or not, or if they'd even been there at all.

* * *

"I told you to stay with her, Chez."

"How was I to know she'd burst into the midst of them? She should've stayed put like I told her."

"You should never have left her."

Birdie creaked one eye open, nearly blinded by the sun filtering down through the leaves. She closed her eyes again and groaned

"She's awake!"

"Birdie, can you hear me?"

"Yes," Birdie grumbled.

They helped her sit up, and she groaned again. Her entire body hurt, like she'd been crushed between two boulders. She squinted against the sun and saw that she was helped by Pip and Goose. Mr. Chezelwhip sat a few feet away.

"What happened?" she asked.

"That's what we'd like to know," Pip answered. "Goose said you screamed, and the unseelie started dying, winked right out of existence."

"Goose. How did she–?"

"Get here?" The faery shrugged. "I don't know that, either."

"I went through the door," Goose said. "Did I do something wrong?"

"No," Pip assured her. "Mortals aren't supposed to be able to cross the Rift alone. That you were able to is miraculous. The Queen will be most interested to hear about it."

"Speaking of the Queen, we are several hours late,"

Mr. Chezelwhip said. "It'll be miraculous if she doesn't flay us all alive."

"He's right," Pip said, standing. "We must go at once."

Goose helped Birdie to her feet. She felt a moment of dizziness, and Goose helped to steady her. When it passed they took off after Pip and Mr. Chezelwhip. The morning sun saturated the woods with its golden light, and tiny white petals floated through the air. Birdie breathed deep, smelling baked bread and crisp apples. Beside her Goose smiled and squeezed her hand.

Cultivated Hope

By Jordan Phelps

Clarissa trudged up the cement steps and into the Ministry of Deathly Warning, a building she now loathed with a growing passion. She had started working there when she was a young sprite, a recent high school graduate in need of employment. At first, she was only responsible for secretarial tasks such as the filing of paperwork and the fetching of lunchtime ales, but she performed well, and was soon promoted to a "Pre-Death Representative" position.

To humans, a "Pre-Death Representative" was more commonly known as a banshee. This new line of work required that Clarissa transport herself to the human realm and warn individuals of their impending death, usually with a shrill wail that she would administer on their final night—this, she had also grown to loathe. She didn't understand why the faerie realm was responsible for providing such a morbid service, but when she asked her co-workers what their perspectives were, she was given the same response in almost every case. They explained that the faerie realm had been providing this service for countless centuries and that it would be impossible to simply terminate the procedure. Naturally, nobody was even aware of the service's origin, they just continued to go through the motions and collect fat paychecks.

In fact, these paychecks were the only thing keeping Clarissa at the ministry. Though she despised her job, the faerie economy was still recovering from the blow it had taken during the war against the gnomes, and she knew that only minimum wage employment would be available to a woman of her peculiar skill set. So what choice did she have but to keep on wailing?

Clarissa entered the pristinely polished lobby and walked up to the front desk, a loud clunking sound reverberated throughout the room as her high heels hit the marble floor. The scent of citrus and vinegar cleaning solution wafted through the air. Clarissa sneezed.

"Miss Morgan! How are you?" A wee pixie with a wide smile and radiant blue wings sat behind the desk.

"I'm well," Clarissa replied. She had always been jealous of those blue wings. She had been born with none. "Is Mr. Figgleshins ready to see me?"

"He should be. I'll give him a buzz." The pixie put on a headset and pressed down a black button attached to her desk. "Mr. Figs?" There was a pause. "Yes, I missed you very much as well." Another pause. "Oh...Well Miss

Morgan is here to see you." She let go of the button. "He says you can go on up. It's always delightful to see you Miss Morgan!"

"Thanks. You too." Clarissa took the elevator to the top floor and knocked on Mr. Figgleshins's door. It was the only room on the top floor.

"Who is it?" he sang in a too-friendly tone.

Clarissa rolled her eyes. Who the hell did he think it was?

"It's Clarissa," she said. "You wanted to see me?"

"Positively," he sang. "Come on in."

Clarissa walked into the office and he offered her a seat on the other side of his monumental desk. Mr. Figgleshins had a child-like face and huge pink wings that branched out from his black suit.

"Now, I bet you're wondering why I've asked you in today." His tone was now serious.

It was true. They had communicated mainly through e-mail since she had first been employed as a Pre-Death Representative and her visits to the ministry building itself were extremely few. Clarissa nodded.

"I have come to understand that you are not performing to the extent that is required of you by this ministry. We seek a profit, Clarissa. You must understand that."

Clarissa bit her lower lip. She knew what this was about.

"I'm not quite sure I know what this is about," she

said with fake sincerity.

"Your silver comb, Clarissa! You haven't used it once!"

"Oh, the comb! Must have slipped my mind."

"There is a purpose for each and every thing we give you. The comb generates profit. Do you need me to explain it to you?"

"Please," said Clarissa. She knew exactly what the comb was used for, but she thought it would be safer to fake ignorance. It had been given to her years ago along with her silver mirror, but she refused to use it. Unlike many of her coworkers, she had ethical standards.

"The comb, Clarissa, is a dimensional transportation device. It allows you to bring humans back with you when you are returning from their realm. If they so much as touch the comb, they will be spirited back here to us. Understand?"

Clarissa nodded.

"When these humans are sent to us, we can profit by selling them as laborers, either to divergent realms or to local business owners. You have only been doing half of your job Clarissa, and the least important half of the two."

"Don't you find slavery to be a tad unethical?" Clarissa replied.

"Yes. But it's a sacrifice I am willing to make for the success of this company. I like you Clarissa, but we cannot afford to keep you if you don't fulfill your quota. I'm going to mark you down for the successful transportation of five humans this month, preferably children, and if you can't come up with that, I'll have to let you go—regrettably, but positively. And believe me Clarissa, there are others in your position that bring home much more than that."

This disturbed Clarissa deeply, but she simply could not afford to lose her job. In fact, she was surprised she hadn't lost it a long time ago as it was. "I understand, Mr. Figgleshins."

"I'm glad." His tone had returned to its usual chipper state. "Since you're here, I should give you your schedule for the next two weeks." He rummaged through a filing cabinet beside his desk, emerged with a single sheet of paper, and quickly scanned over it.

"To warn," he announced. "Monday night: Timothy Walker, Wednesday night: Elina Walterson, Friday night: Maaria Vanhanen, and Sunday night: Jonathan O'Carroll. Locations are all on the sheet. I have placed you on-call for the following week, but don't worry, I'll make sure some work comes your way." Mr. Figgleshins smiled and handed her the schedule. "Before you go, let's hear that wail of yours. You were always one of the best!"

Clarissa shifted uncomfortably under his watch, then, realizing that it would be best to keep the man happy, she let out an ear-splitting wail. Mr. Figgleshins laughed and applauded.

"Boy, am I glad I invested in shatterproof windows!" he said.

Clarissa laughed, somewhat awkwardly.

"Alright, Clarissa, thanks for your time," he said, giving her a friendly pat on the back. "Keep in mind what we've talked about."

"I will, Mr. Figgleshins," she said dutifully. Clarissa left his office and took the elevator back down to the lobby, where the secretary sat with a panicked look on her face. Her gorgeous blue wings fluttered wildly behind her.

"What happened up there? I heard a scream and I tried to page Mr. Figgleshins and he wasn't responding and—."

"Everything is quite fine," Clarissa interrupted. The wee pixie secretary nodded, only partially satisfied, but she returned to her paperwork anyway. Clarissa exited the building and began her walk home.

Upon leaving the downtown district, she ran into a group of frolicking sprites. Each of them was sprouting a unique and vibrantly coloured set of wings, and as they hopped around attempting to fly, Clarissa couldn't help but feel jealous. She knew that one day they would learn, but for her, that day would never come.

"Hey, sis! Need a lift?" Clarissa's sister, Jenny, was hovering high above the path, her fully developed purple wings buzzed like a hummingbird's.

"Please!" Clarissa said, relieved. She held her arms

out at her sides in a T formation and Jenny swooped down, linked her arms around Clarissa's, and took off back into the sky. They did this with a certain finesse that comes only from years of practice.

"Aren't you supposed to be at work?" Clarissa asked.

"I got off early. Business is pretty slow today." Jenny pointed to the tavern where she worked as a waitress. Two goblins sat on the patio sharing stories and a full cask of ale, but the remaining tables were vacant. "What are you doing out today?" asked Jenny. "I thought this was your day off."

"So did I. I had to go to the ministry for a meeting with Mr. Figgleshins."

"Oh, that creep...." Jenny laughed. "How was it?"

Clarissa told her everything Mr. Figgleshins had said, leaving Jenny as disgusted as she had been back at the office.

"Well, are you going to do it?" Jenny asked, as she flew them back to their home section of the township.

This question made Clarissa uncomfortable. She had understood the importance of what Mr. Figgleshins had told her, but she hadn't really contemplated the reality of it yet. "I guess I don't have much of a choice. We need the money."

Jenny nodded guiltily, wishing she didn't work such a low-paying job.

The two landed just outside of their cabin, which

hosted a living room, two bedrooms, and a kitchenette; it was small but cozy. Jenny announced that she was going to take a "well-deserved" nap, so Clarissa went around to the back and tended to her garden until nightfall. When she entered the house, Jenny was still asleep, so she turned off the lights and went to sleep as well.

The next day Clarissa followed much the same relaxed routine. Jenny had already left for the tavern by the time Clarissa awoke, because, as Jenny had told her many times, the goblins like to start their day with a pint before work. Clarissa preferred to start the day with a plate of honeydew melon, which she did that morning with zest. After a quick trip to the outhouse, she returned to her garden where she could water and weed her troubles away, and she actually had forgotten them, if only for a brief moment before dusk had settled in. A goblin wearing a black suit and tie walked towards her down the path, probably returning from work, she thought. He removed his bowler hat and smiled at her before continuing on his way. Clarissa, realizing she was going to be late, dropped the hose she had been using and scurried to her room where she prepared for work.

She pulled a long, grey cloak from a hanger in her closet, which she changed into carelessly. Clarissa was a good-looking woman, with long blond hair and alluring green eyes, but in her opinion, the grey cloak made her look uninviting; she supposed this was reasonable given her task. Clarissa reached into the top drawer of her bedside table and, from it, retrieved her silver hand-mirror and comb. She looked at the comb with disdain. The time had almost come to give Mr. Walker and his family a visit.

Clarissa tapped her finger on the hand-mirror and a white screen with a loading icon in the middle of it quickly replaced her reflection; while waiting for it to finish loading, she scanned through her schedule and found Timothy Walker's address. The word "Welcome" appeared, scrawled across the face of the mirror, and was soon replaced by a search bar and a touch keypad. Clarissa typed in the address, and when she was asked if she was sure this was correct, she concurred. A glowing beam of light shot from the face of the mirror and she was soon sucked in and transported to a small town in the state of Washington.

She flicked a switch on the side of her hand-mirror and suddenly Clarissa began to fade, giving her an almost ghost-like appearance; she had never gotten completely used to this, but the ministry recommended the feature's use, especially in getaway situations. According to her co-workers, it was often helpful during abductions.

Clarissa walked up to one of the windows and peered into the Walker's home. She always looked into the homes before she started wailing. She wasn't sure why. Maybe it was just to put a face to the name, but she regretted it every time. Tim, his wife, and their three kids were all piled up on the couch, watching television before bed. They seemed to be a fairly average family, but then again, most of them did.

Clarissa trekked back, unnoticed, across their lawn, and positioned herself in the thick woods beyond their home. Then she began to wail his name. She screamed for what seemed like several minutes at the highest octave the human realm had ever heard, but was forced to listen to again and again.

A panicked Tim rushed to the window and searched his yard for what was causing the wretched noise. Of course, he couldn't see her, but she could see him, and it broke her heart. Tim was too frightened to leave his house, and instead, curled up with his children on the couch and told them that the noise would stop soon, that everything would turn out fine. Tim died the next day in a construction accident.

Clarissa had made no abductions that night, and had returned only with a heart full of sorrow. The week continued for her in much the same fashion. She visited the Walterson family on Wednesday and the Vanahanen family on Friday, but returned from both excursions without a single abduction. Clarissa was at a stalemate between her livelihood and her conscience, but she feared that her conscience would eventually win by default. She spent most of her time brooding in her garden, the only place where she could feel at least somewhat at ease.

Soon, Sunday night was upon her, and it was time for Clarissa to visit the O'Carroll family. She put on her gray cloak, started up her hand-mirror, and waited for the search bar to load. When it did, she typed in the address of Jonathan O'Carroll, confirmed it, and was soon transported to a small Irish village.

The O'Carroll home sat on the border of a dark, still lake; its thatched roof shimmered in the moonlit night. The home had a rustic, yet eerie aura about it that made Clarissa feel uncomfortable. She walked up to the window and peered inside. Mr. O'Carroll and his daughter were seated at the kitchen table, eating a late dinner. There was no wife present to share it with them.

Clarissa left the house and walked along the lake's shore until she came across a thick bramble that was far enough away to suit her purposes. She slipped behind it, and, after taking a deep breath, began to wail Jonathan O'Carroll's name. She continued to wail for quite some time, her voice echoing deep into the night before fading. And then she heard the sound of a slamming door. Jonathan walked around to the back of his house, a shotgun in hand, and his daughter trailing close behind. Clarissa sat silently.

"Come out!" he yelled, the barrel of his shotgun changing direction with every passing second. Clarissa continued to wait. Jonathan and his daughter were travelling along the lake's shore in her direction, but she was confident they wouldn't be able to see her through the darkness. Jonathan stopped to inspect a shady section of bramble with the barrel of his shotgun, and his daughter ran ahead. This was Clarissa's chance. She silently took the silver comb out of her pocket and placed it just beyond her hiding place, where Jonathan's daughter would be able to see it gleam.

"Hey, Daddy! I think I found something!" She ran the rest of the way and bent to pick it up, but as she touched the comb, her eyes met with Clarissa's, and those panicked eyes seemed already to know their fate. She was consumed by a flash of white light and sent away from her world before she even had time to scream.

"Don't touch that!" Jonathan yelled, but upon seeing the light, he knew that his daughter was gone forever. Clarissa returned to her realm before Jonathan could reach the bramble she had been hiding behind. She couldn't stand to see his face, or for that matter, ever her own. He would spend his last night on earth mourning the loss of his daughter, and only Clarissa was to blame. She materialized upon her bed and sobbed into her pillow, deep uncontrollable sobs that could not be ignored. And so it was that Jenny entered the room in an attempt to slay her sister's melancholy.

"You did it, didn't you?" Jenny asked. She sat down on the bed beside her sister and placed a hand on her shoulder. Clarissa looked up and nodded, her face wet and glimmering with tears. "Don't cry," Jenny said. "You had to do it. You had no other choice."

Clarissa refused to accept Jenny's comforting words. "What do you mean I had no other choice?" she snapped. "I had choices to no end, yet I chose to steal a young girl's life! If only you could have seen her face, then you'd understand…." Clarissa's rage subsided and she continued to cry.

"I know, Clarissa.I know." This didn't help to settle her sister down at all, but Jenny felt an intense devotion to speak. She continued to rub Clarissa's shoulders until eventually her crying was subdued by sleep. Jenny returned to her room, and, after a quick prayer, she went to sleep herself.

The next morning Clarissa felt slightly better, and a generous helping of honeydew melon heightened her mood to an almost average degree. She went out to her garden with a warm cup of herbal tea and sat down on a bench; ready to take full advantage of the hard work she had put in this season.

It had become her sanctuary. Sunflowers stood tall behind her in a protective fashion, and were joined below by patches of rose and lavender. Ahead, tiger lilies sat with drooping heads that sympathized with her on a deeper level than any communicable being would ever be capable of. Clarissa inhaled the sweet, earthy aroma and savored it. A week of garden therapy was exactly what she needed, and it was within her grasp. Never had she been contacted for work while on-call.

"Clarissa!" Jenny shouted from her bedroom window. "Phone's for you. It's Mr. Figgleshins!" The name wafted out the window and into the fresh garden air, somehow tarnishing the aroma. Clarissa set her mug down heavily on the arm of the bench and dragged herself inside to see what the scheming, baby-faced man wanted now.

"Great job Clarissa," he sang. "Me and everyone else here at the ministry were delighted by your achievement yesterday!"

"Thanks, I guess," Clarissa mumbled.

"You're finally making us some money." He laughed happily through the phone. Clarissa pictured his face bobbing up and down as he laughed. She wanted to hang up.

"Well, you know. I've got to keep my salary." She said this to him, but it was obvious that she was trying to convince herself.

"With more performances like that, you will! It may even go up!"

Clarissa remained silent and waited for him to get to his point.

"So, now that you're brimming with potential, it's time to get you out more often! I have a job for you tonight in Scotland; man by the name of Blane Grant. And if you can pull off what you did last night, I'll have a job for you tomorrow as well. How about it?" Mr. Figgleshins sounded more excited than she had ever heard him, and he was almost always excited.

"Thanks Mr. Figgleshins. I'll try."

"Oh, please! Call me Mr. Figs. And I'll send you a message with the Mr. Grant's full address."

"Great," said Clarissa, although she was disgusted by the mere thought of calling him Mr. Figs.

"I've got to tell you Clarissa, I didn't think you had the heart to pull off what you did last night, but you went and surprised me." There was a brief pause. "A couple more surprises like that and you will flourish with this organization. I know you'll do your best tonight."

Mr. Figgleshins hung up.

"Got another job?" asked Jenny.

"Yep. In Scotland." Clarissa replied. She looked out sorrowfully at her garden, wishing for nothing more than to be there, with an untarnished conscience and a warm mug of tea. Clarissa retrieved her cold tea from the bench and dumped it down the sink, along with the rest of her relaxing plans for that day. Haunted once again by melancholy, Clarissa decided to go to the shoppe. If she couldn't enjoy herself at least she could be productive.

While there, she bought an assortment of groceries—most of which were for Jenny—including a great deal of honeydew melon; this cheered her up momentarily, but the joy was soon forgotten. She paid for her items and carted them back to her house. Later, an employee would walk around their section of the township, collect all of the carts, and bring them back to the shoppe; this was considered a common practice among the faerie realm.

She sorted the groceries into their proper locations, and then spent the rest of the afternoon talking with her sister, who had Mondays off at the tavern. Jenny filled Clarissa in on all the local gossip she had overheard during her previous week of waitressing, most of which had to do with the extramarital affairs of neighboring fairies and goblins—a topic Clarissa wasn't the slightest bit interested in, but it kept her mind occupied. And for that, she was thankful.

As Jenny talked, twilight crept into the sky, and Clarissa began to worry again. She couldn't live like this, Clarissa finally decided. She had to quit. She could live outside in her garden for all she cared. She looked outside the living room window and noticed that someone had come to retrieve her grocery cart. It was the girl she had lured last night in Ireland.

"Jenny," she whispered rather loudly. "It's her! The girl from last night! They must have sold her to the shoppe!"

Jenny looked out the window and saw her too. "Some odds, huh, sis?"

"She saw me before she touched the comb! How am I supposed to live here knowing she could notice me at any moment?"

"It looks like you're going to have to make amends," said Jenny.

"And how do you suggest I do that?" But then, suddenly, Clarissa knew. She ignored her sister's response as a plan manifested inside of her. It felt so natural, like it had lain dormant in her mind, suppressed by melancholy, but was now breaking free with a force that demanded immediate action. Clarissa ran outside after the girl.

Jenny watched from the window as the girl noticed Clarissa running towards her. She began to tear up and flailed herself at Clarissa with a childish rage that was quickly subdued. Clarissa bent down to the little girl's level and spoke. Jenny couldn't make out what her sister was saying, but whatever it was, it had calmed the girl down; she was now nodding with interest. By the time Clarissa had stood up, the girl was trying unsuccessfully to hold back a smile, and Jenny knew that her sister was planning something big.

The two walked back together and joined Jenny inside the house.

"So what was that about?" asked Jenny, feeling thoroughly confused.

Clarissa looked solemnly at her sister. "Jenny, I'm not going to Scotland tonight. You're going to help me fix something I never should have taken part in."

"You're taking her home?" Jenny asked.

"Yes. But not just her."

The room was filled with a thick, beautiful silence.

"Tell me what you need me to do, and I'll do it," said Jenny, and she meant it.

"Thank you." Clarissa smiled and embraced her sister. Jenny returned the hug and waited for Clarissa to speak again. "I need you to look after Lucille while I get the others."

"So she has a name now?" Jenny winked at Lucille who was happily shaking her head as if to inform Jenny that yes, she did have a name. "I think that can be arranged."

"Again, thank you so much. I'll aim to be back here just after nightfall." Clarissa left Lucille with Jenny, and went off in search of the other stolen children.

While Clarissa was gone, Jenny had more fun with Lucille than she'd had for quite some time. A woman can only gossip so much before it becomes routine. They played yahtzee, jenga, and all sorts of other childhood treasures that Jenny kept piled up in her closet; and even though Lucille won match after match, no amount of losses could wipe the glowing smile off of Jenny's youthful face.

Then there was a knock at the door. Jenny guided Lucille to her bedroom with hushed whispers, and then she placed a finger softly over her lips. Lucille nodded and imitated the gesture, leaving Jenny satisfied to seal her in. Jenny walked nervously across the living room to the front door, trying hard to stabilize her composure before opening it. It was Al, the owner of their local shoppe.

"Hey Jen," he said in his usual friendly tone. "How are you doing?"

"I'm well. What can I do for you?" She thought it would be a good idea to smile, so she did.

"I seem to be short one employee. She just started today, so I figure she's gotten herself lost trying to collect all the carts. She's a real young girl, probably about eight years old, maybe this high...." Al held up a hand that hovered just below his chest. "Pretty tall for an eight year old."

"I can't say that I've seen her Al. I've been at home all day."

"Ok. Well if you do, give me a call. I'm hoping to find her before nightfall. I can only imagine how scared an eight year old must be with those drunken goblin bastards wandering around town."

"I'll let you know if I see her," said Jenny.

Al nodded his thanks and flew off to the next house. Relieved, Jenny shut the door and went to get Lucille from her bedroom. Lucille didn't seem to be too flustered by her unexpected confinement. In fact, she didn't even ask what it was about. She was more concerned that their game of Chinese checkers had been suspended, and when Jenny opened the bedroom door, Lucille ran back to the board with her next move still fresh in her mind.

The girls continued to play, long past nightfall, and Jenny began to worry about her sister. She knew the goblins would be too drunk now to even notice Clarissa leading a group of children through town, let alone to confront her about it. But what if she had ran into Al, or, for that matter, any other gossip-loving fairy? Even in the darkness, it was still quite possible.

Jenny tried to cast away her unsettling thoughts and, instead, focused on the scrabble game she was currently losing to Lucille. Then, remembering that the girl was only eight, Jenny decided she was more disturbed by her own deficiencies, and focused her thoughts back on Clarissa; this pendulum of disappointment continued until another knock on the front door suddenly broke its trance.

Jenny hid Lucille in her bedroom and returned to the front door. This time it was Clarissa. She must have had at least ten children behind her, each one of them smiling nervously. She wondered how Clarissa managed to bring that many back unseen, but she decided against asking. Instead, she ushered them inside.

"So," said Jenny. "What's your plan?"

"I'm going to ask each child where their parents live and escort them home using this." Clarissa held up her mirror. "While I'm doing that, I need you to make sure the rest of them stay calm and quiet."

Jenny nodded.

Clarissa asked a tall, awkward child with brown curly hair where he had lived before his abduction, and he was quick to answer. For many of these children, memories were all they had left to live for. And now, hope. Clarissa typed in the address, clasped hands with the child, and they were off to Galway, Ireland.

As they landed, Clarissa felt a cool breeze wafting over the city from the Atlantic. She had worn a bright, green shawl today in lieu of her gray work attire, and she wrapped it tightly around her shoulders. They walked together to the front door of the boy's home, and she knocked loudly on the door. It was eight o'clock at night in Ireland—much earlier than in the faerie realm.

A woman opened the door. Clarissa had prepared to speak, but as the curly-headed boy's eyes met with his mother's, she knew to be silent. The mother embraced her son, many years of lost warmth flowing between them, filling the icy crevices that had formed in their hearts; warmth flowed through them and out into the atmosphere, over Clarissa and over all else who stopped to behold the joyous reunion. Even the Atlantic breeze ceased to blow, and gave way to the powerful heat of affection.

"Thank you," said the mother, her voice muffled by tears. She smiled gratefully at Clarissa, only for a moment, before turning her attention back to her son. But Clarissa would hold that memory forever with delicacy and pride, play it again and again when gripped by melancholy, and be pulled out each time, reminded of absolute bliss.

Clarissa left the son with his mother and returned home. Jenny had turned on the television, and everyone was crowded around it watching cartoons. No curious visitors had come to the house, and for that she was thankful.

Clarissa typed in the next address and was gone. Then she was back. Then gone again. She felt proud each time she reunited another child with their mother—prouder than she had ever felt before. And though no single delivery felt more rewarding than the first one, she returned to her little cabin each time feeling triumphant, knowing wholeheartedly that her benevolence would be remembered forever. Her euphoria evolved with each flight, until soon she had returned from her ninth destination, and only Lucille remained.

"You ready Lucille? It's time to bring you back to mom," said Clarissa. Her glowing smile had transcended reasonable proportions.

"But I don't have one."

"Do you have any family that you know of? Grandparents? An aunt?

"Nope. Just daddy." Said Lucille.

Clarissa's smile shrunk considerably; it had only taken seconds to crush what hours of altruism had built. The two sisters looked at each other apprehensively.

Clarissa placed a hand softly on Lucille's shoulder,

and then, with the same softness, she spoke. "Jenny and I are going to go into the other room just for a moment. If you get bored, go ahead and change the channel."

Clarissa smiled lovingly, and then joined her sister in her bedroom.

"What are we going to do?" asked Jenny. She was pacing back and forth in a horseshoe pattern around the bed. Her wings were fluttering wildly behind her, like they always did when she got nervous.

"Jenny, I think I need to go back with her." Clarissa pursed her lips.

"You mean to live there?"

Clarissa nodded.

"But what about me? What about family? You are loved here, Clarissa."

Tears rolled calmly down Clarissa's cheeks, but only half of sadness. Lucille needed someone just as much as Clarissa needed her. "I love you too Jenny, but this transcends us both. I owe this to Lucille, her father, and also myself."

Jenny ran to Clarissa from the opposite side of the bed and wrapped her arms around her. She cried with her. "Let me come with you."

"Jenny, your wings...you could never live there." Although this saddened Jenny deeply, she knew Clarissa was right. For the first time in her life, she envied her sister for having been born without wings. Clarissa's affliction had become a blessing.

"Don't think I'm leaving you behind, Jenny. We will come back to see you whenever we can. I love you."

The two held each other, suspended in time, both accepting what was to be.

"But what if they find you?" asked Jenny.

"Maybe they will. Who knows? But I would rather be prosecuted for an act of kindness than promoted for spreading evil with the ministry." Finally they let each other go, but their spirits lingered, entwined. "There is one last thing I need you to do for me."

"What is that?" Jenny asked.

"Destroy this. Make sure it is never found." Clarissa took the silver comb that had been given to her by the ministry out of her pocket. Jenny took it without a moment's hesitation.

"I will," she said. And together, they walked into the living room where Lucille sat nervously.

Clarissa turned off the television. "Lucille. I am going to take you back home, okay?"

Lucille nodded happily, either not sensing the tension in the room, or choosing to cast it aside. The two sisters hugged once more, and then Jenny hugged Lucille whom she had grown quite fond of during their time together. Clarissa brought out her silver hand-mirror and entered Lucille's address, which she had still remembered from the night before. She held gently on to Lucille's hand, and together they were swallowed by a dazzling light. Jenny uttered a final farewell to her sister and Lucille.

Clarissa would be a banshee no more. Instead, she would live a life of tranquility, built on love and sustained by selflessness; a dream she had planted in her garden and tended to year after year.

Now it was real.

Seelie Goose

By Eric Garrison

I found the goose girl in Dunn Cemetery, sketchbook and pencil in hand, as she gazed at a stone angel. I watched her draw awhile before I approached. Walking toward her, I made noise so I wouldn't startle her. I've learned that it's easier to talk to people when they don't vanish in fright.

Most won't even see me, at least those in the mortal world. I hate when Skye calls it the "real world" because she can be so...so...human-centric. My world may overlap hers, but that doesn't make it any less real.

I could tell this girl would be able to see me, because you don't see girls like her in Skye's world, unless you're Skye. The girl had a preternaturally long neck, her black feathered hair falling over almost non-existent shoulders. Her wing-arms, feathered and elegant was another telltale. Cream colored skin disappeared into a long ruffled dress that concealed her feet. I wondered if they were webbed, or if she wore shoes. Oh yeah, and the bill was a dead giveaway to her non-humanity. I could see past the glamour mortals would see; this was a creature of my world.

"Oh!" she cried. *Damn, do I need to be noisier, or carry a fluorescent flag, maybe?*

I waved and smiled, but didn't show my teeth; the little fangs that Skye thinks are so cute tend to alarm some folks. "Hello there. Nice day out, isn't it?"

She drew in a breath and nodded, closing her sketchbook. "Yes, maybe the last nice day of the year. I hope it holds out just one more day. Who are you, little one?"

There it is again. Always judge me by my size, they do. Just because a girl's only a foot and change tall, doesn't mean that's what defines her.

I let it pass. "I'm Minnie. I'm new around here. My other half has business in town, and she hasn't got time for me, so I'm puttering around and exploring. Bloomington is such a pretty place, and so full of fairies."

I regretted the word as soon as it was out of my mouth.

She made a face and clacked her bill. "Fairies, hmmm, yes, many of us. You talk too much like one of the mundanes of this world. You mention another half? Minnie, are you married? I am to be married tomorrow myself."

I shook my head and chuckled. "No, it's a bit of a joke. I'm a cast off bit of a mundane's soul. I'm her and she's me, but I live in your realm and she lives in hers."

She nodded, as though this were a common tale. It's not, not even to a goose girl. She clacked her bill twice and looked closer at me. "So you aren't a fai—you're not like me, even though you walk in my world?"

I shrugged. "Even I'm not sure what I am, Sweetfeathers." I gave her a grin.

She set down her sketchbook and preened, seeming to forget me for a moment, then met my eyes again. "Sweetfeathers? Oh! I see, I've been rude; I have your name, but didn't introduce myself. I'm Bernadette Nutte, soon to be Bernadette Gale. Will you accept an invitation to my wedding as apology?"

Courtesy is currency to people like Bernadette. However, this exchange cut both ways. I could refuse her invitation and keep some power over her, and she'd owe me a favor. By the same token, it would be rude to decline, so I'd also be giving her power over me.

So, what the heck, I had nothing else going on. Skye can't even see or hear me when she's sober. Skye's current assignment required sobriety, so I was on my own for the time being.

"Thank you for the invitation, and don't worry about it, Sweetfeathers." I like nicknames, especially when they're funny.

She laughed, but it was cut off by a teakettle shriek as something ripped through the air like a missile. She looked up, and I launched myself into her soft belly like a Minnie cannonball. She folded in and fell backwards, just missing a headstone.

A fiery streak passed through the spot where she'd just stood and smacked into the ground, turning the grass and soil into steam and red-hot glass.

She sat up, catching me as I tumbled from her belly. She honked a couple of times as she fought for breath. She hugged me close to her, enclosing me in her wing feathers. It was a cozy cocoon, but I struggled free to stand on my own. I'm *not* a doll.

When she caught her breath, she stood and said, "Thank you, little one. You saved my life! Imagine if I'd been killed by a shooting star!" Her tone was light, but her voice shook as she looked at the steaming crater in the graveyard.

"I know, what are the odds?" but even as I was about to reassure her that something as incredibly unlikely as that couldn't happen again, electricity prickled my scalp and my hair stood up.

"Get down, NOW!" I yelled, and dove for a flat granite grave marker.

She dropped, covering her downy head with those magnificent wings of hers.

The world filled with light and excruciating noise, and I was thrown ass over head by the blast I'd expected. I passed out, then woke to my ears ringing and blobby afterimages blocking my sight. When I figured out how to breathe, I sucked in air and let it out in gusts, shaking in primal terror. The ringing wasn't only my ears, but also a shrill keening cry.

"Bernadette!" I called out, still unable to see.

"Twice is no coincidence! Tell my love I'm sorry, but I must hide and save my life!"

I staggered and groped around me, but I could not find my new friend, not even as my vision began to clear. Nothing but stones and statues.

Bernadette's sketchbook still lay on the ground, abandoned in her haste to disappear. I hauled it over to a mausoleum, then opened it up to look for ideas as to what to do next.

The last pencil sketch she'd been working on was an intricate likeness of the stone angel she'd been studying when I arrived. Several more pages showed the headstones of this little graveyard.

Another page showed a fountain with a naked woman, surrounded by enormous carp spitting streams of water. Two smaller figures of goose people stood side by side, holding hands, surrounded by other fantastical fairy types of all descriptions. A third goose person, bent and bespectacled, was to one side.

Other pages revealed more fountain drawings, with a nude goose girl floating among the spitting carp, her beauty catching at my heartstrings. I wondered if it was meant as a gift to her intended. She did have lovely webbed feet, if the sketch was any indication.

Earlier sketches included buildings on the Indiana

University campus, and a bust of a beautiful woman with prominent "duck-face" lips and dark hair. Bernadette again, I guessed, in the way she'd be seen by mortals who couldn't see past the illusion of a fairy glamour. I tore this page from the book and folded it again and again until it was thick but just small enough to fit in my shoulder bag.

I shut the sketchbook and slid it into the gap under the mausoleum door for safekeeping.

I took another look around the small cemetery to check for signs of where Bernadette had gone, but I found nothing but headstones and statues, and they weren't telling me anything. So I climbed the low stone wall and hopped onto the trail that led past the Union building. The iron gate was open, but I really didn't want to go near that. I'm not sure if I'm a true fairy or not, but iron *burns*.

Behind me, I heard a chittering, chattering noise, but not made by a bird. I froze, knowing what it'd be before I looked. An orange cat, many times my size, flattened to the ground, ears back, eyes laser-focused on me. An icy bolt of fear shot through me, meeting those eyes.

Oh yes, animals, cats in particular, can see bits of my world, including me if I'm not careful.

The orange tail lashed back and forth as the animal wiggled its butt, ready to strike.

I ran for my life, as fast as my chubby little legs

would take me. I heard the cat's feet scrabble on the pavement as it launched itself after me.

I dodged left. It missed, but got itself in my path. I put my arms up to make myself look as big as possible, bared my vampire fangs and hissed for all I was worth. The cat paused, and I punched its soft wet nose.

The cat poofed from head to tail, orange fur doubling its apparent size. It raised a paw to swat at me.

I knew I was about to become lunch.

A hoof planted itself between the cat and me. The cat arched and hissed, but another hoof kicked at it.

The cat growled and backed up.

The hooves stomped and the cat ran off.

I looked up at my savior and found myself staring at a faun; goat-legged, with a human man on top. This one wore a coarse woven peasant top and a black kilt. He grinned down at me.

"Thanks! I thought I was cat chow for a minute there!"

He bowed with a flourish. "Think nothing of it, my pretty little sprite. That cat's bothered our kind too much lately. I shall have a talk with him. Now, if you need no further assistance, I must be on my way."

"Wait! Uh, please. Sir. I am not local, but I just witnessed a magical attack of some sort, and I need to deliver a message."

He arched an eyebrow and hunkered down closer to my level. "Attack? Message? Go on."

"It's from her," I said, pulling out the sketch of the goose girl in human guise. "She has gone into hiding and asks me to tell her fiancé. I think the wedding is off. I'm Minnie, by the way."

He examined the paper, taking it from me. "From her? My feathered beauty has been attacked?"

Oh!

"So *you're* the fiancé? It's doubly lucky I found you! But she told me…."

He lowered a hand to the ground, palm up. "May I carry you, little one? We must make haste to get help. My name is Panos."

I stared at his hand, and then looked into his eyes. "I prefer to walk, but thank you, Panos."

He sighed and looked off toward the setting sun. "If I promise no harm will come to you?"

Well, say what you want about the fairy folk, they're sticklers about promises. I still don't like being carried by anyone but Skye, but if it could help the poor goose girl….

I nodded and stepped into his hand and grabbed a double handful of his sleeve. He hoisted me up to hold me in the crook of his arm.

Mmmm…cozy. Maybe riding isn't so bad….

I can only imagine how the bad guys in that Star Wars movie felt on those giant walking machines. I rode high above the ground; his feet stomped the ground below. Except this guy could *run*. Hooves kicked up divots of grass and clopped across pavement as he sprinted and leaped through the college campus. Human pedestrians seemed not to see him, and traffic parted ahead of him just in time anywhere he ran.

The pace of the ride thrilled me so much that I failed to pay attention to where he took me. I recognized our destination anyway. As I'd seen it in Bernadette's drawing, a fountain dominated by an enormous metal statue of a naked lady, lying in the water, surrounded by spitting fish.

Reality *bent* here, as it does in many magical places. The fountain stretched out into impossible space, unseen by mortals, becoming a large pond. Fish and merfolk splashed and played in the spray of the fountain. Small white-feathered duck people paddled wing in wing. An island rose out of the center, my eyes aching as it overlaid its overstuffed dimensions in my vision. The closer we approached, the more real it seemed, as the campus bent off into dreaminess outside the borders of the circle.

A small keep stood on the island, and on the shore was an enormous grey-feathered goose, draped in a shawl, wearing spectacles. She honked as she glanced our way, then waded out into the pond/fountain and paddled a straight line toward us. Merpeople and duck people parted to make way, eyes following the great grey goose's progress.

I grabbed Panos's sleeve, flipped over his arm and

leaped to the ground at his feet. I may have let out an "oof". It's a long way down for someone my size, especially since I haven't got wings. I'm tougher than I look.

The spectacled grey goose shimmered as she reached the shore, becoming goose-woman, similar to Bernadette. Only this woman had the elegant bearing of a noblewoman, bill tipped up, eyes peering down with cool detachment at Panos and myself. Her presence hit me like a tangible force. I found myself making a curtsey. I never curtsey.

Who curtseys anymore?

Panos bowed low and his hooves clattered on the paving bricks as he backed up a step.

"Well met, Panos my squire. Who is the doll, we inquire?" The words rang from her as from a grand brass bell, flowing out like a song.

Panos straightened and smiled. "My diminutive companion—."

I interrupted. "—can speak for herself. Who are you, Goose Lady?"

Sometimes people talk about getting an icy stare. They mean it figuratively. Goose Lady's stare literally made me see my breath. Panos hugged himself, clattering a step away from me.

I met her gaze and tried to warm it with a winning smile. Unfortunately, my smile's warmth was only figurative.

After a long chilly moment, she spoke. "Black-haired doll, have a care. I am Mother Gale…Storm if you dare." Her bells clanged a warning that chilled my heart as much as her gaze.

"I…I'm Minnie, Mother Gale. At your service, of course."

A few heartbeats later, it was as though the sun had come out from behind a cloud, the ice melted, and she chuckled. "Very well, Minnie-doll. What brings you to my atoll?"

I saw Panos stand more at ease, arms hanging at his sides now.

I took a breath. "I have a message from Bernadette. I met her in the cemetery nearby. Someone we didn't see attacked her. She said to tell her love she must hide to save her life."

Panos and Storm exchanged a long look, and then Panos said, "I found the little one beset by a cat, and saw no sign of Bernadette, Mother Gale."

"I feared this engagement was cursed," said the imperious goose woman. "Ill fated from the first."

"So," I said, "Someone doesn't want them married? And she's in danger because of that?"

Panos and Mother Gale both fixed their eyes on me, and their scrutiny made me uncomfortable.

"It would seem so," said Panos.

"Then I want to help. I offer my services as a proxy bride, taking Bernadette's place so she can come out of hiding once the vows are spoken."

Mother Gale honked out a throaty laugh, her head thrown back, bill pointing to the sky. "Offer accepted, most intrepid!" she said, with a snap of her bill.

Panos drew a dagger from his belt and aimed it at me, crouching. "You dare?"

I backed up a few steps, hands in front of me. "Listen bud, I may not be your idea of an ideal bride, but it's to help save your feathery lover girl, okay?"

"Bernadette Nutte is not my love, you little meddler! I wish to press my suit for the beautiful Grace Gale, daughter of Mother Storm. There will be blood in the morning. Yours. And then a wedding!"

And with a snap of his fingers, he clip-clopped off, out into the warped space of the more mundane world of the campus.

"Blood?" I said, staring after him.

"He means a duel. His blade is cruel," said Mother Gale.

"And Grace Gale?"

"My daughter, fairest on the water."

Oh!

"I think I know what she looks like," I said, feeling the weight of the sketch in my bag. "Any chance I could just back out of this?"

She shook her head. "Tis her will. A role you will fill."

* * *

Mother Gale found a spare bedroom for me in the keep, and locked me inside overnight for my "safety".

Right.

I noticed they didn't leave me a key.

I glanced at the window and the bed. After some thought, I decided to take some precautions. I wadded up a towel and stuffed it under the bedcovers, making a lump.

Before bed, I scrubbed myself with a minty potpourri I found near a washbasin. I scattered the smelly stuff all around the floor of the room, covering the steps I'd taken.

I climbed into the wardrobe and shut myself in with another towel for my bedding. I slept like a rock for most of the night.

I only woke once, when the window crashed in. From my nest inside the wardrobe, I heard something growl and snarl out in the room. There came a sound of fabric tearing and ripping, followed by snuffling, a sneeze, and a forlorn howl.

Something scrabbled at the window and let itself out, glass tinkling in its wake.

I didn't bother to open the wardrobe. I fell back to sleep for the rest of the night.

In the gray predawn of the morning, Mother Gale made a big fuss over the surprise "animal attack" and apologized profusely. I shrugged it off as nothing, and smiled, knowing she owed me one now.

"Mother Gale, may I ask a favor?"

Storm Gale clacked her bill twice, then nodded.

"May we move the wedding up, to before the duel?"

Her bill clacked once more, then she shook her head. "Impossible, doll. Not proper at all."

Her rhymes are getting weaker, I must be on to something.

"Don't you want your daughter to be happy?"

She hissed. "Don't be smart, you tiny tart."

"If I say the words for Bernadette before the duel, your Grace gets what she wants, Bernadette can be safe, and no blood has to be spilled, especially not mine. I'm doing her a favor, and I've already risked my skin once," I said, pointing at the broken window. "I ask this in return."

I hadn't ever heard a goose *growl* before. Storm said, "Very well, I shall wake Grace and gather the court. If Panos should be early, tis not my fault."

Grace turned out to be a smaller, shyer version of her mother, her feathery hair grey despite her more girlish appearance. She was the face in Bernadette's sketchbook, not a self-portrait after all.

"Thank you for your brave help, Minnie," said Grace after an introduction. She wore a fluffy white confection of a gown, which rustled as she shifted from foot to foot.

I shrugged. "Your girlfriend seemed nice, it was the right thing to do. And I've got nothing else going on for awhile."

Grace and her mother looked at each other and clacked bills.

We joined some bleary-eyed courtiers, some of the goose form, some of pigeon form closer to my size, near a pool of onlooking merpeople.

A fine and proper duck man, nearly morphed into full human form, stepped up to a podium and beckoned us to him. I stood on one side, with some pigeon people to attend me, and Grace and her mother stood on the other.

Both of the goose women peered off into the bent space where reality turned a corner, in case Panos should appear.

I barely heard as the duck read from a book, explaining to those present that I represented the will of the missing Bernadette Nutte, and that the marriage shall be binding in the laws of their community upon Bernadette's return.

I looked up at Grace as she repeated the vows the duck officiant read to her. She stood in her most human form, her bill replaced by pouty lips, her feathery hair touching her slight shoulders, her eyes smiling down at me. I don't have plans to get hitched anytime, but a girl could do worse than Grace. Her name was more than just that, it described her shy beauty and glow of inner strength. The contrast between Grace and her mother struck me. Storm had hard edges and lightning moods, commanding attention and obedience. Meanwhile Grace's nature made me feel the need to keep her safe and happy, despite only having just met her.

She finished up her vows with the softly spoken words, "I do."

My turn.

"I, Minnie, in the name of Bernadette Nutte, take this woman, Grace Gale, to be her lawfully wedded wife. To have and to hold…."

From under her cape, Storm's fingers flickered. She hissed, and a disturbance in the air told me a spell flew toward me.

I had no time to dodge, so I braced for it.

The force of the wave in the air knocked me back into the pigeon man attending me, and he into the pigeon woman behind him.

But like a wave breaking on a cliff, the refraction in the air *bounced* off me and hit Grace, who fell to the ground like a marionette with her strings cut.

Storm Gale let out a honking cry and flapped her winged arms as she leapt to her fallen daughter's side.

"I saw that! You did that!" I said, fighting for breath.

"Hush, you creep. My daughter sleeps!"

"Then wake her, so we can finish. Only a few more words from me and it's done."

She shook her head. "I wish I could as well. Her

sleep is part of a spell."

"Then break it!" I ran up and stood across from Storm, facing her over her daughter's limp body.

Mother Gale honked out a sob. "My daughter's choice in love made me weep. Now it is my fault she sleeps. I wish it to stop, but I can not."

"If you wanted me out of the way, why didn't you just release me from my offer?"

Mother Gale's presence collapsed in on itself as she cried. "If you slept, then more time in this place. Then Panos could marry my Grace. You would sleep until it was done. Grace married to the faun gentleman."

Panos arrived leading a retinue of forest people…a doe girl, some squirrel folk, and an owl man that gave me the creeps.

Sensing trouble, I yelled out for all to hear, "I do!"

"What is this?" shouted Panos, drawing his wicked knife. "I cry foul! A wedding before my challenge shall not stand."

He lunged at me with his knife, but Mother Gale stopped him with a flick of her fingers, freezing him for a moment while she plucked the dagger from his grip.

"Nay fair squire, do not kill the imp woman. She forced my hand and now Grace sleeps anon. Do not stab; you must grab!"

Panos bleated out a curse and his hand darted at me like a striking cobra. His fingers almost met around my middle as the ground fell away and he squeezed the breath from my lungs. He held me to his face and laughed at me.

"Little fool," he began, his nose an inch from my own.

No way I was sticking around for a monologue. So I bit him. Hard. Right on the left nostril. My fangs might be small, but this guy could have put in two nose rings, side by side, as my teeth met in the middle of his flesh.

Panos screamed, and my world went topsy-turvy as he capered around. He tugged once at me, but regretted it, as my teeth held fast.

Man that's gotta hurt!

I heard Mother Gale shouting orders at him from nearby, but he released his, howling as my weight dangled from his newly pierced nose. I tasted blood and could not wait to spit.

I opened my mouth and fell, but halfway down his body, I kicked him in the solar plexus, hard, and launched off him. I hit the ground in a roll, spitting his blood. I leaped to my feet and used the jump's momentum to carry me in a dead run, away from the wedding party. The only sounds behind me were Panos wheezing for breath and Mother Gale honking curses after me. My stomach lurched as I passed the edge of the warped space of the fountain, back in to mortal space. I dodged some human pedestrians and nearly got flattened by a car tire, but managed to lose myself before any fairy pursuit might find me.

My pace wasn't as fast as Panos's hooves had carried me the day before, and I didn't know a direct route to the Union. It took awhile, but I meandered my way back to that huge building and circled it until I found the little cemetery yard. As I approached, I searched for potential weapons. I hoped for a safety pin or possibly a pocket knife, but no such luck smiled on me that morning. Instead, I found a dirty green hair tie, which I tucked into my belt.

I expected to encounter the orange cat, and was not disappointed. It chirped at me and flattened, wiggling its butt, working up to pounce on me. I picked up a hunk of gravel and sat down, looping the hair tie over each foot. I slung the gravel into the elastic band and used it like a makeshift slingshot. I pulled back, aimed carefully, and when the cat tensed to pounce, I let the gravel fly.

The rock bounced off the cat's head, between its ears, and there was a spray of finer rocks and dirt as it scrambled to reverse direction. It kicked me in the side, but I escaped serious injury and the animal darted away from me.

I knew this wouldn't last long, so I sprang to my feet and clutched at the hair tie and sprinted through the little cemetery's open iron gate.

Once inside, I stopped to catch my breath, looking around me. The weathered headstones held their secrets, their moss telling more of a story than the fading words etched into their rough stone surfaces. Two sad concrete angels peered down at me in disapproval.

"I'm...doing my...best...." I panted at the statues. They continued to stare at me, impassive and nonplussed. I gave them the raspberry.

After my heart slowed to something under jackhammer's beat, I gave up the staring contest and made my way to the mausoleum, fished around underneath and dragged out Bernadette's sketchpad. I paged backwards from the end once more. If I stared hard enough, I hoped that some detail in one of the recent sketches might pop up off the page to give me a clue.

The angel in the sketches had as dour a look as the ones near the gate, its gaze at least as accusing as I'd seen on my way in.

I recognized the stones behind the angel and dragged the sketchbook through the graveyard until I was lined up to where Bernadette must have stood to draw it. I left the sketch on the ground and climbed a tombstone; something told me that she had sat her butt here as she sketched. I flicked my gaze between the pad on the ground and the view in front of me. One, two. One, two.

Oh! Two angels, not one!

I leaped down and ran to the left-hand angel and said, "Bernadette Nutte, I know that's you in there. Come out, or I shall tell Mother Gale on you!"

A long silence broke with a sigh from the extra angel, which shimmered and became Bernadette, who clacked her bill at me. “So, you’re working for her now? Did she offer a reward?”

“Nope. She’s the one behind the attacks. When I acted as your stand-in at the wedding this morning—.”

“Wedding!” she honked.

“Calm down. As I said, at the wedding, she cast a spell of sleep on me, but it looks like fairy magic bounces right off me…and hit Grace instead.”

“My Grace? Is she all right?”

I shrugged. “She’s unharmed, just sleeping forever, even Mother Gale can’t undo the spell. I know too many fairy tales not to think that you might be of use waking her up.”

Bernadette flapped her feathered arms in frustration, and the wind pushed me back a step. She said, “What do you think I can do about it if *she* can’t undo her own curse?”

I shrugged. “I figure if I get you to her, maybe something will come to you.”

Bernadette moaned. “She hates me. She’s never approved of her daughter marrying another goose, rather than a gander. Or that faun. She’s not going to let me near her.”

I lost myself a moment in a daydream of interlocking bills clacking together.

“Minnie, do you have a plan?”

I looked at her. "That trick, disguising yourself as a statue. Can you look like anything?"

She nodded. "I can make a glamour that fools the eyes of others to hide myself in plain sight. You saw through it, as no one has done before."

I smiled, not caring if she saw my fangs now. "I have unconventional ways. Can you look like me?"

She clacked her bill once, then plucked a wing feather and handed it to me. I figured the feather was nearly as long as I was tall; I marveled at how light it was in my hand.

"More than that," she said, and the air shimmered. I saw a mirror image of myself replace Bernadette. I realized that as she shrank, I seemed to grow, until I peered down from her height, several feet higher than my usual vantage. I'd love for Skye to see me now! I'd still be shorter than her, but this would even things up a bit.

"There!" she said, in my voice.

"What did you do?" My words honked out in Bernadette's voice, and when I shut my mouth, I heard a bill clack, though I didn't feel it.

"Just a glamour, you're not really that tall, and I'm not really that short. It'll last as long as you hold my feather."

I nodded, still a bit disoriented. "So, here's my plan. Let's go back to the pond like this. Leave your mother-in-law to me, I'll draw her fire while you run up to Grace and kiss her."

"Kiss her?"

"It's the only part of the wedding left to do."

The false Minnie grinned at me. I had to admit; even I thought the fangs made her look creepy.

* * *

As we made our way back, I spied Panos coming our way, a bloody handkerchief held to his nose. When he noticed us, he stopped in his tracks and galloped back toward the warped reality of the pool within the fountain, bumping into a couple of pedestrians in his haste.

Bernadette and I exchanged a glance, shrugged, and kept walking. She said, "I hope we didn't need the element of surprise."

I didn't answer. She'd be better off not knowing that I had no real plan other than relying on confusion to give us an advantage long enough for her to plant the smoocheroo on sleeping Grace.

Space bent around us, and Skye's "real world" squished in on itself like things in a funhouse mirror. The pond swelled before us, and while we steadied ourselves from the transition, hands grabbed Bernadette and me. Slimy, webbed hands.

Frogman guards with spears held us in place, not speaking, just croaking out a victory noise. I saw Bernadette struggle, her seemingly tiny form easily held by the large amphibian-man. Those goggle eyes held a proud glee. Afternoon sunlight glinted off the metal tip of his spear. My own froggy, also dressed in lavender livery of House Gale, seemed more careful in how he handled me. Guess it wouldn't do to harm the boss's daughter's wife.

Just for show, I let out a honk of protest and put up a token struggle.

We were frog marched across to sleeping Grace, now laid out on a featherbed bower. Mother Gale stood over her, stiff and imperious. To one side, Panos stood, dagger in hand, hateful eyes switching between Bernadette and myself.

I made the first move. "I knew you hated me from the start. My only crime is loving your daughter, Mother Gale."

The false Minnie's mouth opened, eyes darting to me. I smiled at her. She shut her mouth and looked back at Storm and said, "Yes! And you wouldn't dare hurt a noble goose like Bernadette!" *Still weird to hear my voice coming from someone else.*

"Crime or not, noble or not, I will not have it! Panos, if that creature comes near, please stab it!"

Her rhyme is off again.

"You can't stop our love," I cried. "Our Grace Gale shall sleep ever and ever on if you harm me." *I might be getting a hang of this fairy tale nonsense after all!*

If geese could grin, I am sure her bill would have

bent into a horrible, wicked, Grinch grin. Her eyes said what her rigid facial features could not. "So be it; if it is a statue you wish to play, then be one evermore starting today! My pond is somewhat bare; a form of stone shall you wear."

Her wings wove tangible neon power in the air and I braced for the magical blast, anticipating the force before the bounce.

Panos let himself smile now as Mother Gale turned to face the real Bernadette, not me.

"Panos saw you switch; take that, you bitch!" And with that, Storm Gale unleashed her spell, which flew like electric spaghetti from her to Bernadette, still in her Minnie form.

I couldn't look. I closed my eyes. My plan had failed. I heard a sharp crackling, like supercooled water freezing in an instant. Silence followed. I opened my eyes to peek.

Mother Gale stood, wings spread, bill open in shock. Bernadette in Minnie form stood free, as the frogman guard had fled after the spell blast. I felt the webbed fingers holding me slacken, and at that moment, all eyes were elsewhere.

Panos had been replaced by a marble statue of himself.

Storm waved her wings and summoned more energy, twisting colorful snakes into the shape of a spell once more, this time aiming at me.

If the glamour is so powerful as to change our properties with each other, that means I'm screwed now, no more immunity for me. Looking like Bernadette, I'm as much a fairy as the rest of them.

I hissed at Bernadette. "Now! Go!"

The paused moment was over. My guard was gone, but I was in Mother Gale's sights. I held my breath and counted down to time this just right. In my peripheral vision, little Minnie-Bernadette scurried toward Grace's bower, forgotten by everyone but me.

The energies grew, a tangled skein of petrifying power.

Wait for it….

Storm let out a cry and flung the spell at me.

I dropped the feather.

The world grew around me as the electric noodles grabbed ahold of me. Magical power began to transmute my flesh into marble, a match for Panos.

Except it didn't. The power flung itself from me like a cat dropped in the bathtub, rebounding onto its source.

Storm Gale spread her wings and screamed, head held high as she turned to stone with an icy crackle.

I shouted to Bernadette, "You may now kiss the bride!"

Behind the statues, I saw Bernadette, back in goose girl form, lean down to press her pouty lips against those of her long-necked lover, their kiss completing the ritual and joining the two of them in matrimony. Grace Gale's eyes fluttered open and she raised her feathery arms to pull her new wife in for a much fiercer kiss.

I looked around the court to give them privacy. My frogman guard followed his companion, webbed feet slapping on the cobblestones as he fled. Pigeon people eyed the new statues with wonder. Merpeople clapped and cheered from the edge of the pond.

"Congratulations, Sweetfeathers," I said, adding, "and Mrs. Sweetfeathers."

I love a happy ending. I knew I had to get Skye to come back with me to visit the fountain later to see Mother Goose and the Satyr added to the naked lady with carp display.

I Knocked Up My Fairy Girlfriend

By Brandon Black

My girl's Moki. We've gone public with our relationship since Faerie established formal diplomatic ties with Man's world. It made things a lot easier in a lot of cases but harder in others. Moki's a pixie, which means she's one of those Tinkerbell-type fairies. She's about five inches tall and has the most beautiful butterfly wings and little insect-like antennae on her head and the most amazing green eyes I've ever seen. She's a short-haired brunette, which I'm told is really rare among pixies, who are usually blonde, green or red-haired. Moki's smart and funny, like really hella funny at times, and we share a lot of the same interests, and I love her, and she loves me. Which is good really, cause she's six months pregnant.

Just walking down the street is tough. When you've got a five-inch tall chick on your shoulder rubbing her swollen belly and complaining about cramps, well, people tend to think the worst of you. There's a lot of ignorance in Man's world, and people look at me like I'm some kind of creepo pedophile. It's not like I'm human-sized and she's five inches tall when we make love. That's not how it works. When a pixie kisses you under moonlight, the moonlight seeps into your bones, and you become a pixie, temporarily, yourself.

Now redcap chicks, redcap chicks are short but about the size of human little people. Oh my God, right, like redcap girls are AMAZING at sex, like even better than Canadian girls. I'm serious. A redcap chick will take your lap rocket on a ride to places you never thought it could go. But she will also *cut* you if so much as look at another girl. So be warned.

Anyway—I know what I just said about redcap girls, and my friends all think I have glitter fever but it ain't like that. Moki and I met at an outdoor rave. I didn't even know she was fey at the time. She was using a glamour she'd borrowed off a friend and was walking around the grounds looking for the world like any other teen girl. She wore her hair short and dyed black and she had on a black t-shirt for my favorite band, this Czech Gothic electronica band called Carodejnice—you wouldn't know them, don't worry about it—and a denim skirt and long, white and purple striped socks with black sneakers.

I was so jazzed to see someone representing my fave band, I forgot my usual shyness with girls and ran right up to her and asked where she found the shirt (a thrift store in Sweden it turns out). So she narrows her eyes at me and asked what my favorite album of theirs was and, I—of course—answered "Dyshexia," and Moki started bouncing up and down for joy. We chatted about bands and listened to dubstep, and made out. She gave me what I thought at the time was ecstasy but turned out to be pixie dust, and we had sex behind the water tower on the hill overlooking the campgrounds. I gave her my number, but she didn't call, and I thought I'd never see her again.

Hina, the redcap girl I was with, she straight up told me she was fey, not that I believed her. We met at a steampunk con in New Orleans and she seemed insulted when I complemented her on her costume. "It's not a costume," she said, "I really am a redcap."

I didn't take her seriously at the time; I thought she was otherkin—you know, the emo ones that think they're werewolves or dragons or unicorns "in their souls" or whatever. It's not like it mattered. She was cute. She was hot. We were horny. That's pretty much all she wrote. She did have these eyes that shifted from green to violet and back again. I didn't manage to put two and two together until after the Fey revealed themselves publicly.

Hina was another girl I didn't expect to see again, but I had hoped to when I went to Walpurgisnachticon the next year and luckily ran into Moki again. She was glamoured again—not that I knew—and appeared to be wearing this cute little Victorian outfit; she smiled and spun in place when I saw her. With this tiny little hat with lace on her head and a parasol, she was utterly precious. We hung out together at the con and after that, we were inseparable.

It was my senior year, and I was working at the Hot Topic in the mall for some extra cash. Moki would just find me at work whenever she wanted to see me. I thought it strange at the time that she never called, nor would let me call her, but I didn't care. She was—is—wonderful. Turns out that fey really, I mean REALLY, don't like electronics, which is why she never called. She would drop by the store and ask me if I wanted to hang out after work, and I'd always say yes, even if it meant breaking plans with friends. I'd spend every minute with Moki if I could.

We hadn't been, you know, intimate, since that first night at the rave. Which makes me wonder, now that I mention it. She was glamoured then—and since glamours aren't real, did we really have sex that night? Was it an illusion, or was it all in our heads? I don't know. But Moki dropped by the store once and told me she had something really important to tell me, and I kinda hoped it was that she wanted for us to be together in that way again. And it was. But it wasn't all she had to tell me.

This was the same day the news of the treaty broke, and I was still totally weirded out by that. We'd made contact with another civilization, but they weren't from another planet, they were from another dimension and they'd been amongst us all this time. Magick was real; fairies were real and now, they were officially talking with the UN. Hell of a thing. Moki and I held hands on a blanket out in the woods, staring up at the stars, talking about the implications for Humanity when suddenly she said that there was something she needed me to know.

"You can tell me anything," I said.

"It'll be easier to just show you," Moki said and placed the softest, gentlest little kiss on my cheek. For some reason, I felt compelled to close my eyes as she did so, and when I opened them again, everything changed. I was small; Moki was small. And—different, with the light and dark blue swirling patterns of her wings at full expanse and her antennae coming out of her head, and I was—the same? The shock of having wings and antennae wasn't half as much as the shock of realizing I was so small now. The whole world looks different from five inches high and five inches high I was, looking up at the Moon and Her radiance like I'd never seen Her before.

And smiling, I turned to Moki and said, "You're fey!"

And she smiled and nodded, "I'm fey!"

Laughing, I took her into my arms, gently at first, mindful of her wings and then hugged her as tightly as I could.

"I love you," I said.

"And I love you," she said.

We made love under the stars, and it was like my first time all over again: awkward and insecure, with questions and passion and laughter, full of amazing, new sensations and utterly, utterly wonderful.

Things were different after the treaty; people knew the Fey were out there, and a lot of people were totally paranoid about the whole 'fey glamour' thing. I mean, it never bothered me. I'd love to be able to just completely change my appearance for a little while, experience what it's like to live life for a few hours as a black woman or a Chinese man or something, but a lot of people get scared when they realize you just can't tell who's fey and who's human just by looking. I mean, really, you never know. Your mailman might be more than what he lets on but then, I guess that's true whether he's fey or not. Yeah, your mailman might be a satyr but then, he might also be a Libertarian or a brony or something so what difference does it make?

Still, I knew it was going to be tough telling the truth to Mom and Dad. We had lunch with them one Saturday to tell them.

"There's something I've been meaning to say," I said. Mom and Dad both froze. I think they were trying to juggle in their minds if I was going to tell them that Moki was pregnant or that we were getting married or both. "You know about all the Faerie stuff in the news?" I asked.

"Yeah," Dad said.

"Well, Moki is a faerie. She's fey."

Mom dropped her tea cup, which broke into pieces on the floor. The tinkling crash of her cup sent Mom into auto-cleaning mode and she ran into the kitchen and came back with paper towels and cleaned up the mess and then sat down again next to Dad. No one said anything for a while.

"She's—fey?" Dad asked.

I nodded. "Yes, Dad, she's fey."

Moki looked at them and quietly said, "Please don't be alarmed."

And then she closed her eyes and canceled her glamour and there hanging in the air before them, her little butterfly wings fluttering, keeping her aloft, was my five-inch tall girlfriend.

Moki curtseyed in the air before them and said, "I'm pleased to meet you, Mister and Missus Peterson, I mean, really meet you. As I am."

Mom took Dad's hands into hers and they smiled.

"She's so adorable!" Mom said.

Moki blushed and flitted a little closer to my parents.

"Well," my Dad said, "it can't be any worse than her being Episcopalian."

Mom smacked Dad on the side of the head. "Roger!"

"Just sayin'," Dad said.

And that was that. If I thought Moki had won my parents over before we told them she was fey, she more than did so afterwards. And later on, when I did have to break the "Moki's pregnant" and the "we're getting married" news to them, they took it well and were happy for us.

It was my day off, and Moki was sitting on my shoulder in her native form, and we went to the Orange Julius for a drink, and the asshole wearing the upside-down cross behind the counter actually told us he wouldn't serve us "cause it's against my religious beliefs." We left the Orange Julius, went to the Smoothie Lyceum in the mall and shared a berry-yogurt smoothie with honey. Moki instantly pronounced it "the best thing in the whole world" and began to kick her little preggers heels back and forth in joy. She was still at five inches height, so I had to draw up the smoothie in the straw and then pinch it off so she could drink but it was utterly adorable.

We were still in the Smoothie Lyceum when this family walked in, and this little girl saw Moki drinking from the straw, and her eyes got as big as saucers, and she beamed this beautiful smile cause I don't think she'd ever seen a fey in the flesh before. And then her older brother leaned down to her and whispered something in her ear, and the smile vanished from her face in an instant.

The father started placing orders with the guy behind the counter and asked the mother what she would like when the little girl slipped free from her mom's grasp and ran over to where I was sitting.

She scowled at me and said, "You stuck your pee-pee in a fairy. You're a bad person." And then she ran back over to her family.

Moki looked at me and started laughing so hard she fell over on to her butt.

Suddenly, Moki hiccuped and at the same time, farted a host of bubbles from out of her backside. The laughter stopped, instantly, and a look of dread and apprehension appeared on her face.

"Oh gods," she said.

The first waft of her flatulence had reached me by now. It was suprisnginly pleasant, even fruity.

"What is it?" I asked.

"Twins."

The Body Electric

By Sarah Madsen

"Why am I even going on this job with you?" I huffed. I was perched on the edge of my desk, my legs hanging and my foot bouncing impatiently.

"Because you never know when your hocus pocus will come in handy," Logan said from beside me, his attention on a floor plan projected on the desk top. "And stop that, it's wiggling the whole desk."

I forced my foot to stop bouncing and hopped to the floor. My soft leather boots made almost no noise on the hardwood as I moved to look over his shoulder. "Seriously, though. Why do you need me on this? Seems like a pretty simple in-and-out job to me."

"Because I would like you with me, just in case. The pay's enough that I'm willing to split it. Or are you saying you want to be short on rent again this month?" I opened my mouth to protest, but he cut me off. "Rose already told me about it, so you can skip the denial part."

"Rose told you?" Rose was my roommate and best friend. She'd *told* him I'd missed rent? I was going to kill her.

"Yeah. In fact, her exact words were 'You should take Alyssa with you on this run. She's late on rent again, so I know she needs the money.'"

"So I'm a *charity* case? Is that what this is?"

"Dial down the indignation there, Alyssa. It's not a charity thing, it's a friend thing. You need money, I need help."

I huffed again. Crossing my arms over my chest, I took a step back from the desk and turned my back on him. I considered telling him no just out of principle, but then I looked around the office of my antique store. My gaze skimmed across my tall bookshelf with actual, paper-bound books, over my worn leather wingchairs and heavy wooden side tables next to my fireplace. I didn't want to have to start pawning things, I really didn't, but my shop just wasn't pulling in enough money lately, even with Retropunk coming into style. The truth was, I needed the money. I might be able to find a buyer for that box of brightly colored MP3 players I got in last week, but this job would bring in more than I could unless I started selling my personal items.

My eyes landed on the large oil painting hanging above my fireplace. It was a scene of a clearing in the woods by moonlight. In the center of the clearing stood a circle of stone arches, and in the shadows you could just make out buildings woven into the branches of the trees, lantern lights winding their way up into the leaves. I'd won it in an auction—or rather, someone else had won it and gifted it to me—and it was one of my prized possessions. The small brass plaque on the wooden frame simply said "Home."

I turned back to Logan and watched him as he studied the floor plan. His blond and cobalt hair was pulled back in a tight ponytail, some of the shorter blue pieces in the front falling loose into his eyes. As I looked over his outfit, I smiled at how differently we dressed for the job; we were both in all black, but the similarities ended there. His cargo pants and jacket were made from a light, rip-stop nylon and had pockets of various sizes just about everywhere. He had on rubber-soled combat boots and had a knit hat tucked into his utility belt.

I, on the other hand, wore leather from head to toe. Soft-soled leather boots, leather pants, and a black tank top under a leather jacket. It made things a little less painful if I had to hit the pavement. Which, unfortunately, I'd been doing a lot more of lately. I sighed and started twisting my long, true-red hair in a tight twist at the back of my head. The style showed off the pointed tips of my ears.

At the sound of my sigh, he flicked his gaze towards me, and I could see the faint, gold spiderwebbing of the Neurolenses on his turquoise eyes. "You're not going to get all 'high-and-mighty elf' on me over this, are you?"

I was silent for a moment before answering, letting a little of the Eldergloom seep through my eyes, causing my golden irises and black pupils to glow silver. "I was considering it."

"Alyssa..."

"I said I was *considering* it. Doesn't mean I'm *going* to." I pushed the Eldergloom back down and my eyes returned to normal.

"Good, cause if you're going to give me attitude all night I'll leave you on the curb as surveillance."

I glared daggers at the back of his head, but he ignored me. Sticking a pin in my hair, I took a long step to the desk and looked down at the floor plan.

It was a simple three bedroom house. The main floor had a kitchen, dining room, living room, and family room. Upstairs held the bedrooms and two full baths. There was a daylight basement, but according to the floor plan it was unfinished. Obvious entrances were a front door, a sliding door to a raised deck, a door from the basement to the back yard, and a door that led from the kitchen into the garage.

"Ok," Logan said, "the mark's name is Giovanni Fantoccini—."

"Giovanni Fantoccini?" I scoffed. "Is this guy in the mob or something?"

Logan blinked at me. "The what?"

"The mob. You know, the Italian Mafia? Chicago,

1920s?" He simply stared back. "Seriously? What do they teach you in school? I know we elves have only been out and proud for ten years, but sometimes I think we pay more attention to your history than you do." I waved a hand, brushing away the argument I could see rising from behind his eyes. "Whatever, you can hook up to the net and do a data-tran on it later."

He watched me for a moment longer, then shook his head and turned back to the plans. "Okay, so, according to my handler, Dr. Fantoccini used to be a developer at Americorp. He quit his job several years ago when his wife died."

"Let me guess. Americorp wasn't happy about losing a talented developer to something as simple as a family tragedy."

Logan gave me a wry smile and continued. "He's been doing freelance work off and on since then. He has two kids, a boy who's eight and a girl who's ten. If we time it right, the whole family will be asleep and we won't have any issues getting in and getting out."

I looked at the silver analog clock hanging on my wall. 9:30 pm. What time did kids go to sleep these days?

"We need to do some recon and locate his home office," he went on. "The plans we need will most likely be on his computer. The guy's smart and doesn't hook up to the net from his work computer, so I can't jack in wirelessly, but I should be able to access it with no problem when I'm sitting in front of it. With luck, the prototype will be there, too, and we can grab the memory chip from it without traipsing all over the house. The client's paying a sizable bonus for the chip, so I want to be sure we get it."

I nodded. "Any idea what the tech is?"

"Nope. I have a file name, K4R4, but that's it. Guess we'll find out when we get there."

"Nothing like a little mystery to keep you on your toes," I said, my voice dry.

He grinned up at me, his eyes sparkling. Dammit, he was going to enjoy this.

To be fair, so was I.

"Oh, and one last thing," he said. "This is time-sensitive. If we don't complete the job tonight, we lose our chance and they hand it off to another set of runners."

"Wow. Why the sudden rush?"

"I don't know," he shrugged. "I just know what I've been told. Tonight is our only shot at this."

"Then I suggest we hurry." I slid a tiny earbud into my left ear, and he did the same. "Lysistrata in," I said. From here on out we were on the run, and would only call each other by our street names in case any transmissions were overheard.

He gave me a thumbs-up. "Grendel in," he replied, and I heard his voice through the speaker in my ear.

"Alright, techie." I grinned. "Let's get rolling."

* * *

We took my motorcycle since it had a run-silent electric engine. I tried not to gloat over the fact that his bike still ran solely on gasoline—mine was a hybrid, so it could do either—but it was rare that I had a piece of tech that he didn't. He had a Neurocomm, Neurolenses, a data jack in his arm—all trademark, patented, and produced by Americorp.

He was quiet as we drove down some of the smaller Atlanta streets and I assumed his mind was on our run. A few minutes later, he said "Ooooh, the *Mob*," and I let out a short laugh. He must have been accessing the net through his Neurocomm and lenses as I drove. Ah, the beauties of technology.

Part of me envied him. My "hocus pocus," as he'd called it, interfered with any tech. If I was lucky, whatever tech I had on me would simply short out instead of reacting violently, but I didn't want to test that luck with a Neurocomm wired to my brain. Crispy tech I could handle. A crispy head, not so much.

We wove our way towards the highway, through the parks district on the east side of the city and into the more modern downtown. Here, the bright lights reflected off the cold metal-and-glass skyscrapers. Projected ads flickered and moved on storefronts behind the crowds of people making their way home from a long day at work or out for a night on the town. Classic suits made of expensive biosynth fibers clashed with vinyl and latex club gear woven with glowing EL Wire. The humid air was made even more oppressive by the press of cars and people, the smell of exhaust fumes and ozone emissions filling my visored helmet. Once we were in the suburbs, I flipped the tinted visor back and spent a few extra seconds at a stop sign taking deep breaths of fresh air before kicking my feet up and continuing down the dark road.

"Ok, turn down this street here," his voice was clear in my small earpiece. I turned into a quiet neighborhood and parked my motorcycle in the empty parking lot next to the pool and tennis courts. I pulled off my helmet and spent a moment enjoying the breeze against my face before following his gaze.

Through the trees behind the pool were the lights of a house. I set my helmet on the seat of my bike and followed him as he walked through the underbrush. A small swell of pride filled my chest as I managed to navigate the leaves and roots without making a sound. He, it seemed, stepped on every dry twig in the small bit of forest.

"You're an elf," he muttered in answer to the grin on my face. "It's cheating."

The house was quaint and unassuming. Black shutters sat in stark but classic contrast to the white siding, and the back yard had a well-tended flower garden bordering a path up to the deck. Large windows showed us a warmly-lit kitchen, with a square table tucked into a breakfast nook.

At the table, facing the windows, sat a man in his late thirties. He had light brown hair, a square jaw, and was handsome. On either side of him sat two children, a boy and a girl, both with the same sandy brown hair. They were in pajamas, snuggled up to their father, and were playing a game that was projected on the table in front of them. With them was a thin, pretty woman with short brown hair. She stood up and walked to the refrigerator, kissing the top of Dr. Fantoccini's head as she passed.

"I thought you said his wife died."

"Girlfriend?" he guessed. "Or maybe he remarried."

I nodded and the woman came back to the table with two cups, handing one to each of the kids, smiling softly down at them. "Let's see if we can find the office."

We crept around the house, giving it a wide berth and sticking to the trees. We paused every time a new set of windows came into view, so Grendel could scan each room with his Neurolenses.

We were back where we started when Grendel let out a *huff* of air.

"Nothing," he complained. "I can't find anything that resembles a workstation in any of the rooms on the main floor or in the bedrooms."

"Which leaves...."

"The basement." We turned our gaze to the door

tucked underneath the back deck.

"Well," I said. "At least it's convenient." The basement door would have been my first choice to pop the lock on anyway, since it would probably go longer without being noticed than the more frequently-used doors. Also, there was less of a chance of walking in on a family member.

Now we just had to wait for everyone to go to bed, and we were golden.

I settled back against the trunk of a tree, instantly comfortable, and laughed quietly to myself as Grendel tried to do the same. Poor city boy was no match for nature. When he finally found a comfortable spot, though, the family at the table turned off their game and made their way upstairs. Lights in the bedroom windows switched on for a few minutes before finally switching off again. We sat in silence for a half hour longer, then crept across the shadows of the lawn to the basement door.

Grendel reached the door before me. He looked at the lock, then took a step back, gesturing for me to go ahead. My momentary confusion was washed away when I saw the lock on the door: A simple deadbolt. If it had been an RFID scanner or a key pad, Grendel would have no problem, but the old-school basics always tripped him up. Basics were my specialty.

I raised an eyebrow at him as I pulled my lockpick set out of my inner jacket pocket and got to work. A few seconds later, we were in.

The basement was a mess, and smelled like plastic and rubber and metal. Large storage shelves stood everywhere, piled with boxes overflowing with wires and scraps of metal. A large worktable stood in one corner, with a 3D printer and tools that I assumed were for metalworking or fabrication of some sort.

Under the table was another box, only this one had an arm sticking out of it.

I nudged the box with my toe. The arm rolled to the corner, the fingers falling open lifelessly. A tangle of wires trailed out of the elbow.

"This guy's in the prosthetic mod business, huh?" I whispered. Grendel slid up next to me, glanced in the box, and shrugged.

"Unless it's the tech we came for, I don't care. Ah, there!" He grinned at the small six by four inch box at the back of the table. "There you are, you little beauty." He reached out a hand and turned it on.

A projected log-in screen appeared on the wall, and a keyboard did the same on the surface of the desk.

"Here we go." He pushed back the left sleeve of his jacket and pressed gently on the skin just below his inner elbow. A tiny square of skin popped open, and he pulled a micro-USB jack from his arm, the thin cord unspooling from under his skin. As he plugged it into the side of the computer, the screen flickered off, and I knew he was viewing it on his Neurolenses.

Nothing for me to do now but wait.

The soft *patpatpat* of Grendel's fingertips against the projected keyboard was almost soothing as I looked around the dark basement. I wondered what sort of prosthetic mods Fantoccini made. There were so many to choose from: Legs that could let you run faster and jump higher, fingers that typed faster or could manipulate things on a level much finer than any human. You could even get an entire eye replaced. It would let you take pictures and video straight to your Neurocomm, and gave you more layers and types of AR vision than the Neurolenses could.

I wasn't sure what a normal person needed all of that for, but it would come in handy for a runner. I knew Grendel had been considering a full-limb mod for a while. I hoped he wouldn't; they always sort of creeped me out.

The typing behind me stopped, and I heard him curse quietly. I turned back towards him just as he whispered "Lys, you need to see this." He pulled his jack out of the computer, and the screen flickered into existence against the wall.

At first I wasn't sure what it was I was looking at. The top of the screen read K4R4, the plans we were here for. It looked like prosthetic plans at first, but this was way more complex than anything I'd ever seen. It wasn't just arms and legs, it was an entire body, the wires and components all laid out with scientific precision. I squinted my eyes and shook my head in confusion, and Grendel lifted his hand and swiped it across the screen. The program flipped to an exterior plan, and my mind reeled.

Half of the face was recognizable: Dark, pixy-cut hair, a pretty brown eye with thick black lashes. The left half of her pink lips were even curved up in a small smile like the one she'd worn earlier. The other half of her face was bare, a plastic and metal skull with a second lidless, brown eye.

"It's his wife," I whispered in horror. It was the woman we'd seen in the kitchen earlier. He hadn't remarried, he'd made a replacement. "She's…," I didn't know what she was. A robot? An android? We didn't have a word for this.

"A Marionette," Grendel whispered.

Marionette. It was fitting. I looked at him, my eyes wide. "What do we do?"

He looked back at the screen, his eyes locked on those of the Marionette, and was silent.

"Grendel," I hissed. "What. Do. We. Do?"

He took a deep breath. "We do the job." He reached out and plugged his cable back in, and the screen blinked off.

"You're going to go through with it?"

"Yep." He reached into his pocket and pulled out a micro-USB drive and plugged it in to the computer.

"I'm copying the file now."

"But...," But what? I wasn't even sure what my argument was. But this felt wrong.

"She's just another set of plans, Lysistrata. Just another piece of tech, just like everything else we ever steal. What makes this different?"

I didn't have an answer for him.

"There." He pulled the drive out of the computer and put it in the small zippered pocket on the front of his jacket. "I've got the plans. Now we just need the chip." Disconnecting his jack, he powered down the computer and started towards the far end of the basement.

I hesitated, my weight on the balls of my feet, then something occurred to me. I caught up with him on the staircase and grabbed his arm.

"How did you know that term?"

He stiffened under my hand but didn't turn. "I don't know what you mean."

"*Marionette*. How did you know to call her that? What aren't you telling me, Grendel? Did you know this was what we were here for?"

He stood for a moment longer, then looked down at me. "No. I didn't know. There've been whisperings of things like this in the tech circles. Marionettes. People that aren't people. Most of us assumed it was just stories. Over-exaggerations of some egotistical techies. But...."

"But it's true."

He nodded, then turned his back on me. "This is

where you come in," he whispered. "The plans said her memory chip is at the base of her skull. You sneak into the bedroom, remove the chip, and sneak out. If you can't do it…." He trailed off, but I knew what he meant.

If I couldn't do it by stealth, we would resort to force.

"I don't like this, Grendel. It's too risky."

"So, what, we leave? No. I'm not ready to hand off my bonus to another runner, thanks. We can do this."

I let my hand drop away from his arm, unease curling its way through my stomach.

We made our way silently through the door at the top of the stairs, passing the kitchen table where we'd seen the family earlier. Up another set of stairs and a quick turn to the right, and we were at the door to the master bedroom.

I put my hand on the doorknob and looked at Grendel, but he was staring intently down the hall, ignoring my gaze. My shoulders slumped in resignation. Just another piece of tech, that's all. I pulled my earpiece out of my ear and handed it to Grendel, then took a deep breath and drew on the Eldergloom.

For a brief moment I saw the silver of my eyes reflected dimly off of the white wood of the door, then I wrapped the eldritch power tightly around me, and the glow faded. My hand on the doorknob looked semi-transparent to me, but I knew to Grendel-and anyone else—I would be completely invisible. I took a breath to steady myself, twisted the doorknob, and silently pushed the door open.

The bed sat in the center of the far wall, and there were two shapes underneath the brocade comforter. The room was dark, the only light was the reddish glow of the digital clock sitting next to a large coffee mug on the left bedside table. I approached the bed, and looked down at the sleeping form of the doctor's wife.

She was lying on her back, the blankets pulled up to her chin and her eyes closed. Her bangs fell softly across her forehead and I could smell the faint scent of powder and perfume. If I didn't know any better, I would have sworn she was alive. I leaned over her, watching for the gentle rise and fall of her chest, just to be sure. Maybe this was all a mistake, and she wasn't a Marionette, but an actual, real person. But the longer I searched, the longer I realized there was an eerie stillness to her that marked her for what she was.

Then she opened her eyes and looked right at me.

I stifled a gasp, fighting the instinct to jerk back. She couldn't see me, I was wrapped in the Eldergloom. I let my breath out slowly and, trying to calm my pounding heart, I took a small step back.

Her eyes followed me.

I froze as she sat up with a gasp. Fantoccini stirred next to her.

"Kara? What is it?" His voice was hoarse from sleep and muffled by the blankets.

"There's someone in here," her voice quavered,

and I heard Grendel's quiet curse from the hallway.

"What?" The doctor sat up, blinking away the sleep and looking around. His eyes passed over me. "There's no one in here, honey."

"Yes there is. She's standing right there!"

He leaned over and turned on his bedside light, squinting in the glare and rubbing his eyes. "There's no one there, Kara. Just—."

She picked up the coffee mug and threw it at me so quickly I didn't even have time to turn away. The mug slammed into the side of my head before hitting the floor with a crash, and I cried out and stumbled from the blow, losing my grip on the Eldergloom. Dr. Fantoccini gasped, and at the same time I heard Grendel's boots on the hardwood floor as he rushed into the room.

"Take it easy there, Doctor," Grendel's voice was low with warning. "We don't want to hurt anyone."

I blinked the stars away from my vision. Grendel stood at the foot of the bed, a small pistol in his hands.

"What *do* you want, then?" Fantoccini wrapped an arm around his wife's shoulder, pulling her to him.

"Her memory chip."

Fantoccini's eyes grew wide, and he stared at Grendel for the span of a few heartbeats. "No," he whispered.

"Come on, Doctor. Just give us the chip and we'll leave. No harm."

"No, you don't understand. It's *her.* It's not just a

chip; it's her memories, her experiences, her emotions. It's her *soul.*"

"She's a mechanical puppet, Doctor. A piece of tech. You can make yourself a new one."

"She's not! She's more than that, she's—!"

A small sound from the hallway startled everyone out of the argument.

"Mommy?"

My heart dropped, and I turned my throbbing head. The children were peeking through the doorway, their hair and pajamas rumpled from sleep.

"Mommy, what's going on?" The girl asked.

"Nothing, sweetie," Kara's tone was light, but she kept her eyes on Grendel, who'd turned his body so the kids couldn't see the gun. "We're fine. Go back to bed."

"But why are these people in your room?"

"They needed to talk to Mommy and Daddy about something. Don't worry about it, ok? It'll be fine, take Tommy back to bed."

The girl's voice caught, and two tears slipped down her cheeks. "But I don't want to."

"Go on. I'll be there in a minute to tuck you back in."

"You promise?"

She pulled her gaze away from Grendel and looked at her daughter. "Yes. I promise."

The girl sniffled once and nodded. She looked at Grendel, and then at me, before taking her brother by the hand and leading him back down the hallway.

"Well," Kara said softly. "And so it goes." She looked back to Grendel, and when she spoke her voice was hard. "I hope you're getting paid well enough to justify me lying to my children."

She stood slowly, turned her back to us, and put her fingers to the back of her head and pushed. A small door opened, revealing a tiny slot.

The memory chip.

The doctor looked from her to Grendel and back again. "Please," he begged. "Please, don't take their mother away from them. Not again."

I can't do this. "Let's go," I whispered.

Grendel stood motionless, the gun in his hand, his eyes on Kara.

"Grendel, let's *go,*" I hissed. "Look at her. She might just be a piece of tech, but she's their *mother*. Do you think those children will understand? Do you think it will matter to them? This isn't just theft anymore, Grendel, it's murder. I didn't sign up for that, and neither did you."

He didn't move, but I could see the muscle in his jaw jump as he clenched his teeth together.

"If it's about the money, I'll handle it. I'll figure something out. I'll sell my painting if I have to. I'm sure I could get a good price for it. If this is about your reputation, suck it up. It's not worth this."

His eyes flicked to me, and I could see shock in his expression. He hesitated a moment longer, then lowered his gun.

"I suggest you guys get out of town," he said quietly. "The people who hired us won't stop with this. When we fail, they'll just hire someone new." He looked at me, his eyes searching mine. "Someone with less of a conscience." He turned on his heel and walked out of the room.

I followed quickly behind him.

We were silent all the way back to the city, neither of us knowing what to say. Once we were in my office, Logan stood next to my small gas fireplace and pulled the micro-USB drive from his pocket, turning it over and over in his fingers.

"What do you think they'll do with this?"

I shook my head. "Make more like her, maybe?"

"And do what with them? Sell them?" He raised his gaze to mine, and I could see a battle raging behind his eyes.

I nodded, and then the battle was over. He pressed his lips into a thin line and, without taking his eyes from mine, he reached out and flicked the switch on the side of the mantle. Fire blossomed, fierce and red and hot.

He tossed the drive into the flames. We watched the plastic melt and bubble until there was nothing left but smoke.

The Last Mission

By Cindy Koepp

With typical elven grace, Commander Zanforil sailed into the hangar and settled his Sabre-class light fighter in its position. Tractor beams deposited Kendoran's heavily scarred fighter nearby.

I have to get over there.

He flipped the generator switches to "Off" with his right hand and slapped the secondary reactor switch with his left hand a moment later. The computer complained with a discordant buzz and refused to let the switch move. He swiped at it twice more, getting the same result.

Zanforil glared at the computer with narrowed eyes. "Identify the problem."

"Allow one-point-two-five seconds between commands or use emergency shutdown protocol."

He rolled his eyes. Finicky system.

If the emergency protocol wouldn't give his tech a long stint of overtime tonight, Zanforil would have switched to that shutdown procedure. He'd have to pace himself better or waste time restarting the sequence.

With apologies to the composer, Zanforil hummed "Moonlight Sonata" at triple the usual tempo and worked his way through the post-flight check list. The first downbeat of each measure was another task completed, and he pressed the canopy release on the last note.

Most of his squadron gathered around Kendoran's fighter. Black gouges marred the blue and silver paint. Kendoran's dwarven tech aimed a pale pink laser beam at the canopy latches melted by a blast that missed breaching the fighter's hull by a few molecules of titanium.

Kendoran scrunched down inside the cockpit and shielded his eyes with his arm. Bits of glass from the gauges and controls pierced the blood-stained sleeve of his gray flight suit.

Belandra and her medical staff waited on the far side.

Zanforil winced and jogged over. Odors of burnt metal and scorched wiring invaded his nose. He arrived a couple beats after the tech cut the last centimeter of slagged metal.

Lieutenant Steven Ruger, one of the two humans who qualified for the otherwise elven squadron, hopped up on the low wing of the banged up *Sabre* and helped the tech pry off the canopy. Zanforil took a few steps back then rushed forward. He jumped, somersaulted over the growing group of techs and pilots, and landed easily on the nose of the ship.

More glass shards pockmarked Kendoran's bloodied flight suit, and his shaky hand fumbled with the catch on his helmet. The face plate of the helmet had gouges worse than the outside of the ship.

Zanforil crouched and slid his fingers under Kendoran's hand. "Here. I've got that."

He deftly flicked the release and lifted the helmet away. Kendoran's fine, blond hair fell around his shoulders. The tips of his ears peeked through.

"What happened out there, Kendoran?" Zanforil handed the helmet to the tech.

His eyes were heavy-lidded and his breathing was uneven. "I got my timing off when I skipped a two-beat rest in the intro. I tried to adjust but couldn't get back on the tempo."

The tech stepped aside and offered Belandra a hand up. Her white medical scrubs did nothing to detract from her easy movements and gentle beauty.

Steven sat on the edge of the cockpit. "I might've been able to help you, Ken."

Kendoran gripped Steve's arm. "Following me in would have been suicidal. That was a risk for me to take alone."

"Oh, yes, if not you, Kendoran, then I'm sure my

husband would have taken the risk." She speared Zanforil with The Look, the one that always started the argument about when he was going to retire from active duty and prepare to be a father for their forthcoming child.

Soon, beloved. Soon. My new position starts in a week.

Belandra pressed the center of the safety harness's clasp. Nothing happened.

"No power." Zanforil slid his knife from the sheath at his hip and slit three of the four belts.

The harness fell away.

Belandra leaned over Kendroran, checked his vital signs, and inspected what injuries she could.

"Well, you don't look too severely battered." Belandra sighed and stood on the port wing. "Let's get you to the medical center and get that glass out of you."

"Can you stand, Ken?" Steven offered Kendoran his arm.

"With some help." Kendoran gripped his wingman's arm.

Belandra caught Kendoran under the left armpit.

The wounded pilot groaned and clenched his eyes and jaw as he stood. His wingman and Belandra helped him to the ground.

Zanforil hopped down and stood aside while Kendoran was situated on a gurney and rolled away.

"Commander Zanf'r'l," General Seth Williams called from behind him.

Zanforil turned to the human. "Yes, sir?"

The general stood as high as Zanforil's shoulder, average height for a human. Seth's brown hair was cut short enough to show his scalp, but he'd allowed the relative inactivity of his current assignment to add a bulge around his middle. Such a shameful lack of discipline.

"I was hoping to assign Kend'r'n for this mission, but clearly that's not going to work now." The general made an abrupt gesture with his hand toward the retreating medics, their patient, and the patient's wingman.

"It was a bad situation out there." Zanforil's cheeks and ears heated up. He unsnapped his helmet and slid it off. "We needed someone to go in and take out the Horde's main gun on the capital ship before it got too close a bead on this station. I was busy holding off a squadron of *Jackals*. Kendoran was the only other one with the right skill rating."

Seth held up both hands, palm out. "Easy, son. I never said you made the wrong call, but Kend'r'n's injuries mean I need you to take the job I had for him. Everyone else with your rating is on another mission or in worse condition than Kend'r'n."

All right. Calm down. At least for the next week, he's still your boss. Zanforil tucked his helmet under his arm and took off his gloves. "What's the mission?"

"Our intel says the Horde has plans for some antimatter missile that would wipe out all or most of our holdings in one blast." Seth set his left hand on his hip and aimed his right index finger at Zanforil. "You need to go in there, set charges to blow the thing, and get out."

He rubbed his forehead. "You know, Belandra's been pregnant for three months. I should have been out of active service that long. She has good reason to be unhappy with the situation."

"Yeah, I know, Zanf'r'l." He scratched under his right ear. "I know, and this'll be the last time. I swear it, but so many of your people left off studying combat for too many years. The number of you elves who can take on this kind of thing is smaller than—."

"—The number of fingers on your hand. I'm aware." *You're a fine one to talk about my people forgetting the art of war.* He glanced at the general's physique, which had been expanding into spherical proportions over the last several months. *We're in the middle of one, and you still haven't gotten back into fighting trim*. Zanforil sighed. "Let me talk to Belandra."

Seth frowned and narrowed his eyes. "Fine, but if not you, then I'll have to send a squad who might or might not get the job done."

"Did intelligence say what progress has been made on the weapon?" Zanforil tucked his gloves into the belt of his flight suit.

Seth nodded once. "Final design phase, which means they could be building on it by now and have it ready before the end of a couple weeks."

Zanforil glanced toward the damaged *Sabre* nearby. "Kendoran will likely recover before then, and he's not a father."

"Yeah." Seth's eyes narrowed further as he leaned closer. "And the Horde could get working on that missile faster than we expect. Is that a risk you're willing to put your family through?"

"I'll talk to Belandra. That's all I can offer for now." He walked away.

"Henpecked elf," Seth muttered.

Zanforil started to turn back but caught himself and kept going. Elven men had the decency to include their wives on decisions that affected them both. That did not make him "henpecked."

Humans. If more of them were like Steven Ruger.... He cut that line of thought short. There were quite a few like Steven.

* * *

Zanforil sat at his desk and drummed his fingers. Blueprints for a new defensive system were sprawled across the whole surface, but they could be pages from a cookbook for all he noticed. He finished humming a tune and frowned. A whole three minutes had passed? How could time be so slow? He started the tune again.

The door of his quarters opened with a soft click.

He stood and met Belandra with a warm embrace.

She pulled him closer and rested her head on his shoulder for a few moments before pushing him back. "No."

He raised an eyebrow. "'No,' what?"

"Whatever Seth asked you to do, no." She shook her head and held both hands up, palm out.

Zanforil took a step closer. "Who said Seth asked me anything?"

She backed up. "I heard him call you over. Then you meet me at the door? Usually, you're so engrossed in your work I could clang cymbals behind your head, and you wouldn't react. So, whatever it is, no."

He wrapped his arm around her shoulders and led her to the soft, green and tan couch. "The Horde is building an antimatter missile that would wipe out our entire area. With Kendoran down and all the others either on missions or on the injured list, I'm the only one likely to get the job done."

She sniffled and brushed her eyes. "Zan, I—."

"I know, but an antimatter missile would just have to get close, and we're all dead." He pulled her into an embrace and rocked.

When she wept on his shoulder, he sang her favorite song at a volume only she would hear. The sobbing eased, and she sat up straighter.

Belandra leaned over and opened the wooden

trunk she'd carved with images from their courtship, wedding, and honeymoon. She picked up the silver helmet inside. "You're wearing your new armor."

He drew a breath through his teeth. "It's still a prototype."

She snorted and cast a sideward glance at him. "Your prototypes are better researched and more stable than most people's production models. You're wearing your new armor. I don't want you in Kendoran's condition or worse."

"He's that bad?" Zanforil winced.

"Yes." She looked in the direction of the medical ward. "Each injury alone wasn't so much, but together, well, he'll be in that healing trance for a week, minimum. He'll need another few days after that to come back up to his proper speed before I can declare him ready for duty."

"Then it really is up to me." Zanforil blew out a breath. "Intelligence suggests that the missile would be ready to fire within two weeks." He stood and picked up the glittering chainmail. "Armor it is."

* * *

Wearing his prototype armor, Zanforil entered the nearly empty hangar. He slid the helmet on and pressed the button on the side. The helmet sealed to the suit with the hiss of pressurized air.

As he crossed the hangar to his fighter, he spotted

Gwalk doing a pre-flight check. The dwarf's long, scraggly beard was tucked into his belt. Between facial hair and the frizzy, brown mop on his head, Gwalk's rugged face was hardly visible.

Zanforil whistled an F-sharp to engage the voice projection system. "Everything ready to go?"

"Yup. Near as I can figger it." He wiped his calloused hand under his bulbous nose and turned. His eyes widened. "Well, don't you look all sparkly! That the armor you said you was workin' on?"

"Yes. I think I'll need all the advantages I can get."

Gwalk slumped. "Yeah. Think y'will."

Zanforil squatted in front of his tech. "I will come back, Gwalk."

"They're sayin' this is a one way run."

He shook his head. "Won't happen that way. I have a wife, a child, and friends in abundance. There are still songs to sing. I will come back."

"Y'better."

Zanforil clapped a hand on Gwalk's shoulder and stood. "Where's the explosive?"

"Left-hand storage, an' I set the armin' sequence to your usual." Gwalk held up five fingers. "The first five notes o' that tune you like."

"Perfect." Zanforil hopped up onto the wing and stepped into the cockpit of his *Sabre*.

Gwalk clambered up after him. "Pre-flight's done. Y'got tower clearance. G'luck, elf."

"See you soon." He triggered the canopy.

The hydraulics lowered the canopy, and the latches sealed automatically. Once Gwalk was out of the way, Zanforil launched. When he threw the throttle to full forward, G-forces pushed him into the back of the seat. The velocity readout raced upward to the ship's maximum. As soon as he'd cleared the range of the asteroid fort, Zanforil entered the coordinates for the Horde base where intelligence had located the missile. He engaged the teleport drive. The star field winked out and reformed as a different set of constellations.

Ahead of him, tracers flew in every direction. Horde capital ships slugged it out with friendlies. *Sabres* and *Jackals* were tangled in a dogfight guaranteed to generate widows on both sides. Beyond the battle, a gray planet shrouded in sickly yellow clouds rotated slowly under the relentless heat of a blue-white star.

Zanforil checked the range counter and did the mental calculation. He'd hit the edge of the battle in three seconds.

His mental metronome clicked off three seconds on the mark when he passed over the near edge of the fight. Zanforil hummed a march as he wove his way through, dodging some battles and taking opportune shots at the enemy. LED tracers embedded in some of the packed uranium rounds zipped past him. Explosions from destroyed fighters bucked his *Sabre* like an unbroken horse.

Passing through the fight felt like hours, but he'd only finished the first verse of the march when he exited the far side.

Forty-eight seconds. Not bad.

He glanced at the radar. A pair of *Jackals* broke away and pursued.

"Don't you sweat it, Commander. We got those dogs," a human pilot from another squadron said.

"I do appreciate it." Zanforil kept the radar in the edge of his vision until a couple *Sabres* overtook the *Jackals.*

He throttled back and adjusted his angle. Red re-entry burn blinded his view outside the cockpit, so he turned to his computer and called up the next phase of the mission parameters. The coordinates for the missile site were a quarter of the planet around to the west. The moment he was through the upper atmosphere, he swung around to the proper heading and continued his descent through the sulfuric yellow clouds.

Zanforil slowed to Mach four as he approached the base's coordinates. An alarm buzzed in the cockpit. He tapped the acknowledgment button. The enemy radar had spotted him, and that meant anti-aircraft fire would be headed his way soon.

Two pings announced a pair of missiles headed his way. Zanforil checked the radar and spotted the incoming ordinance. The system labeled them DF for dumb-fire. Easy to avoid those. He set the metronome in his head to sixty hertz and nodded in time. One-and-a-half beats from impact, he veered hard to starboard. The two missiles blazed past him and kept going.

There'd be no more dumb-fire missiles. The base commander would no doubt accept the extra expense of radar-guided or even image-recognition to make sure they got him.

Two more pings signaled the next volley. The radar labeled them RG. Zanforil reached into the left storage compartment and withdrew the fist-sized explosive charge he'd need to blow the missile silo to subatomic particles and level half the rest of the base. The charge went into a pouch on his belt. His mental metronome continued marking the beats for him. As the missiles closed in, he unsnapped his harness and crouched in the chair while keeping a hand on the control stick. He whistled a D-natural to engage the full life support system.

Two seconds before impact, he let go of the stick and pulled the red ejection lever behind his shoulder. The canopy charges blew and the rocket under the seat shot him straight up out of the *Sabre*. At the top of the arc, he leapt to give himself addition height and distance. The missiles hit the *Sabre* well behind and below him. The shockwave of the explosion slapped into him a moment later, sending him into an uncontrolled tumble. Debris pelted him hard enough to give him professional quality bruises, but nothing pierced his armor.

He willed his heart's staccato rhythm to a legato pace. *Plenty of time to get myself situated for a good landing.*

When the air around him calmed, he whistled an A-flat. A low hum from the armor sounded as wings played out between his legs and between his arms and body. He twisted around to lie spread-eagle, face down.

He whistled a B-natural, and the air shimmered as the cloaking screen engaged. A C-major scale beginning four octaves below middle C played over the helmet's system. Each repeated once before moving up an octave. In two minutes fifteen seconds, the scale would reach four octaves above middle C, and the battery would run out of power.

Try to get a bead on me now.

He studied the layout of the motionless base as he spiraled down. For all the activity below, the place could be uninhabited, but he knew better. As soon as he entered restricted areas, the goblins would boil out of their bunkers. He found the building intelligence identified as the missile silo. Once he set the charges, he'd have a ten-second sprint to the airstrip to confiscate an escape vehicle.

I can manage that in my sleep. He grinned.

The ground came up at him. Zanforil tightened his spiral to circle the building he wanted. At roof height, he whistled the A-flat two octaves below middle C. The wings retracted. He tucked into a somersault before straightening out to land on his feet within arms-reach of the silo door. The countdown timer chimed, and the air shimmered as the cloaking screen ran out of battery.

Zanforil drew the narrow rod at his belt. He pressed a button, and the arms of his bow extended to full length. He unwound the string from the end of one arm and hooked it into position at the end of the other arm. When he drew back the string, an arrow of coherent photons formed. He took quick aim at the door's lock and fired. As the arrow sliced through the lock with a sizzle, alarms echoed from several locations around the base. Zanforil pushed the door open and darted inside. Three goblins ran toward him from the corridor on the right. He turned and ducked under their gunfire. Three arrows from his bow took out all three attackers.

He bolted down the long corridor, passing open workstations and closed offices on both sides. A third of the way to the intersecting hall, the clack-thud of goblin boots crescendoed from up ahead, too many for him to estimate.

Zanforil stopped in one of the workstations and stepped back against the wall. He whistled an E-flat, and the universe went silent except for the sound of his own breathing. He pulled the sonic grenade from his belt and whistled a D-sharp minor scale to arm it. Humming a tune with a tempo of sixty-six, he stepped out of hiding and pitched the grenade down the hall.

The first goblin turned the corner as Zanforil spun back into his hiding place. As he finished the tune, the floor and walls shook. Dust fell from the ceiling tiles overhead.

He whistled E-flat two octaves below middle C. Goblin moans echoed down the hall. Zanforil ran to the crossing corridor and turned left, sidestepping or leaping over stunned, injured, and dead goblins.

The hall ended at a door marked with crossed swords, the goblin symbol for "Restricted Access." Zanforil pressed his back against the wall near the door and listened. No noise.

There is no way they've left the missile unguarded. They wouldn't make it that easy.

Staying out of the doorway, he passed his hand over the sensor embedded in the wall. Gears needing lubrication complained as the door slid open. Multiple bangs and a constant stream of bullets blazed past him. The door closed and rang like a deep-pitched triangle as another couple dozen shots struck.

Zanforil gripped his bow tighter and whistled B-flat. A reddish haze shimmered around him, and the C major scale started at middle C and progressed upward. He drew in a deep breath and blew it out before he triggered the door release and stepped through. Goblin bullets flew at him and bounced off the deflector shield. Zanforil drew his bow and fired one light arrow after another into any goblin that revealed itself long enough for him to get a fix.

The scales reached two octaves above middle C. He'd have to find cover before the other two octaves finished. A nearby computer bank would serve. As he continued firing on the goblins, the scale worked its way upward, and he jogged to the computer and ducked behind it. The reddish haze of the shield winked out with the last note of the scale.

"He's just one elf! Kill him!" a gravelly voice ordered.

Zanforil closed his eyes and recalled a tune from a music style humans called heavy metal. The song played in his mind's ear as goblins hollered a battle cry. He left his bow at the computer station and stepped out into the open to meet the charge. There were five goblins, four grunts and a leader wearing his helmet decorated with scraggly braids made from the hair of dead elves and humans.

On the downbeat of a verse, the first goblin caught Zanforil's boot in the face and reeled back. The rhythm of the song set the tempo of the battle. Each downbeat was a punch or a kick. Upbeats were parries and evasions. At the end of the three-minute song, five goblins lay dead around him.

Zanforil took a deep breath, recovered his bow, and took a look around the room. A columnar mass of circuitry and wires stood in the center.

He studied the project. *We didn't have two weeks. Two days, maybe, but not two weeks.*

Shouts and the clacks-thuds of goblin boots came

from the hall. Zanforil pulled the door barrier from his belt, set it in front of the door. He whistled a B-flat minor scale, and a reddish haze blocked the way. A C major scale started winding its way upward from four octaves below middle C. He returned to the half-assembled missile.

If he put the bomb between the missile and the computer, that should end their efforts. He withdrew the explosive charge from his pouch.

Zanforil flipped the arming switch and hummed the first five notes of the song Belandra had danced to at their wedding. Oh, the grace that dear lady had, and she'd chosen him for a husband? A miracle. Nothing short of a miracle.

The LEDs on the case lit up and started spinning through the countdown. He hummed a tune that would end a couple seconds before the explosion and tossed the charge into the space between the missile and the computer.

Zanforil ran around the missile and stopped, facing the outside wall. He drew his bow and fired arrow after arrow into the wall. Fifteen shots later he had a knee-high, rectangular outline of thumb-diameter holes in the wall. He sat and drew his legs back to his chest then kicked. The remaining parts of the stone in the outlined area cracked. A second kick sent the section of wall flying onto the edge of the airstrip beyond. Zanforil scrambled through the hole, rolled up to his feet, and sprinted toward the nearest *Jackal*. He thumbed the switch that collapsed his bow back to a rod and reattached it to his belt. The tune Zanforil hummed entered the last stanza.

Better not be here on the last note.

"There!" a goblin screamed.

Footsteps ran closer. Gunfire erupted. A heavy impact on his left shoulder pitched him forward. Pain blared down his arm and across his back, but the armor reported no breach. He tucked and flipped back onto his feet and then leapt onto the *Jackal*. Zanforil yanked the canopy release and slipped inside as soon as he had enough space. He closed the canopy and jabbed the engine's cold-start button. The engines groaned and whined their way through warm-up. More gunfire ricocheted off the *Jackal's* armor.

Zanforil lifted off as the song's final refrain began. He aimed for sky and opened the throttle to full. The *Jackal* sped off at three-quarter the maximum speed of a *Sabre*. He hummed the last note of the song. Two seconds later, a fierce glare reflected off the forward control surfaces of the *Jackal*. The shockwave buffeted the fighter. Sparks flew from the instrument panel. The radar and other readouts all went dark, but the engines and controls continued to respond.

The sulfuric yellow clouds gave way to space. Zanforil whistled C-natural to get the armor to broadcast his own transponder.

His helmet communicator chimed.

"Zan, is that you coming up from the planet?" Steven asked.

A faint static riddled the transmission.

Must address that in the next version of this suit. "Yes." Zanforil looked down at the radar to spot the pilot before he remembered his systems were fried. "Mission accomplished, but I lost the *Sabre,* and this *Jackal* is not functioning at full capacity."

"You okay?"

Zanforil lifted his left arm. Pain shrieked a cacophony through his nerves. *That's probably a little more than a bruise.* "I'll be fine. Sound the retreat. The capital ships can provide cover. I'll rendezvous, and someone will have to tow me home."

"You got it, Commander."

* * *

Zanforil landed in the hangar. He closed his eyes and leaned back against the headrest. A strong knock banged on the canopy. He glanced up at Gwalk's huge grin. The dwarven tech slapped the canopy and aimed a thumb at the ceiling.

When Zanforil pressed the canopy release switch, the system didn't respond.

Gwalk rolled his eyes and tugged on the manual release. The canopy popped loose.

The dwarf lifted the canopy back on its hinge. "Well, y'did make it back."

Zanforil kept his injured arm tucked to his side and pressed the button on the side of the helmet. Pressurized air hissed before he pulled the helmet off. His dark hair fell around his shoulders. "I told you I would."

"Yeah, well, Belandra's waitin' fer ya up in the observation deck." Gwalk pointed to the window overlooking the hangar. "Y'better go present yerself whole 'fore she paces a trench in the floor." He climbed down from the wing. "An' show 'er that arm, whatever y'did to it."

Zanforil stood up and jumped to the ground. He waved his thanks to the other pilots who'd had a hand in this mission and jogged to the door. It opened when he arrived and General Seth Williams stood there.

"General." Zanforil stood aside to let the human enter.

"Good work, Commander." Seth drew back to clap Zanforil's shoulder but didn't follow through. "Don't suppose I can convince you to stay on. We need people like you."

Zanforil tightened his grip on the helmet. "No, sir. As was arranged in the treaty, once I'm a father, I'm not available. I should have been out of service for three months now. I'm willing to go back to my engineering efforts and train any human, dwarf, or elf who wants to be trained, but for me, that's it. I will not make my wife a widow nor my child an orphan."

"You're one of the best operatives we have. We

need you." Seth jabbed his finger at Zanforil's chest.

He pushed Seth's hand away. "My family needs me. There are hundreds of other elves who could all do the same thing I can with the right training. If I'm not in active service, I can train three or four people to take my place. You're actually gaining operatives if I retire."

"Training takes time, and in the meantime, we're short someone."

Zanforil glanced toward the observation deck where his gorgeous wife stood waiting for him. "Family first, then job. That's the order of priority."

"That's your final word."

"It is."

Seth clicked with his tongue. "That's a shame. Well, good luck to you then." He continued on through to the main hangar.

Taking the nearby stairs three at a time, Zanforil reached the observation deck and opened the door. Belandra rushed to him and drew him into an embrace, nearly crushing his right side while barely touching his left.

She leaned back and looked up at him. "We'll get you patched up."

"For the last time." He pulled her close and stroked her long hair.

Zanforil trilled the first note of her favorite song. She pirouetted away from him and smiled.

The Beggar-Knight & the Lady Perilous

By Matthew A. Timmins

Once upon a time, there was a knight both brave and true. He lived in a mighty castle and was renowned throughout the land for his strength and valor. Handsome and charming and rich he was, and much loved by his subjects.

There was but one thing the knight lacked and that a lady wife, for though far and wide he searched, nowhere could he find a maiden fair enough to be his consort. Long he brooded upon his trouble until one day there appeared at the castle gate a stranger of strange appearance seeking audience.

"My lord," the elfin man bowed low when he had been admitted, "I have come through seven lands and over seven seas to bring you word of the Lady Perilous."

"And who is this Lady Perilous, and of what account is she to me?" said the knight.

The elfin man smiled. "My lord, The Lady Perilous

is the most beautiful of fairies, more glorious than the dawn and fairer than the day. It is said that she will wed only one of true virtue and courage. It is also said that you are such a one."

"And where is this fairest of fairies?" The knight rose to his feet. "Tell me at once!"

"Ah! That I will, for a small price."

"Name it," answered the knight.

"I will tell you what you wish to know for a small token, a necklace mayhap, or a ring?"

Without a word, the knight pulled a ruby ring from his finger and tossed it to the stranger. "Now speak! Where may the Lady Perilous be found?"

The little man danced a little dance and placed the ring upon his finger. "Follow the moon," he said, "till you came to a forest of swords. Beyond this wood lies a lake of wine. In the middle of this mere floats an island, and at the center of this island stands a tower of glass. Here lives the Lady Perilous."

And with that, the elfin stranger disappeared.

"Ah!" said the knight, "a fairy emissary from a fairy princess! I must have this Lady Perilous for my bride!"

And at once he set out to win her.

Many years he followed the moon, and many dangers did he brave: bandits and lions and trolls and many more besides. At last he came to a forest that sparkled in the sun, for every leaf on every tree was like a sword and every blade of grass was as sharp as a spear.

"This must be the Wood of Swords," said the knight happily, and bravely he rode onward. The blades of grass cut deep his horse's legs, and the branches of the trees assailed the knight like a rain of arrows. Still he did not falter or fail till he emerged from the forest and saw before him the lake of wine. Bloody were both horse and rider, and the knight was sad to see his fine steed so wounded. Dismounting, he tended carefully to the animal's wounds, and when this was done he plunged straight into the lake of wine.

Red as blood was the lake, and the island shore could not be seen, yet the knight dove in and began to swim mightily. The wine stung the knight's wounds like salt and was bitter in his mouth, but he swam on. Many hours he swam till at last he came to a tiny island, and in the center of this island was a tower of glistening glass that reached high into the sky.

The knight wasted no time but jumped from the lake and ran to the tower. But when he reached the base of the tower he stopped in amazement, for by his reflection in the glass he saw that his wounds were healed and all weariness and hunger had left his face. Soon however his amazement gave way to dismay, for the tower was as smooth as silk and he could see neither door nor window.

He sat down with his back to the cool glass and tried to think of a way into the tower. Presently he fell asleep.

At twilight a beautiful singing came to him from the top of the tower, "At the gloaming hour, who and wherefore sits beneath my tower?"

Standing to his feet, the knight answered, "I am the bravest knight in all the land, and I have come to marry the Lady Perilous."

"Then ascend, brave Sir knight," was the laughing reply.

"How might I ascend? For I see neither doors nor windows in your tower."

"It is very easy. Cut off the little finger of your left hand and bury it at the base of the tower."

This the knight did without hesitation. And when his severed finger was buried, there fell from the high tower a single drop of water onto the bloody ground, and instantly the finger bone sprouted like a birch. Up this bony tree the knight did climb till he came to a high window.

Through the window the knight found himself in a room that burned like fire yet sparkled like ice; diamond sand shifted beneath his feet, and a chandelier of gleaming swords swayed above his head. As he surveyed the room, the wall opened mighty jaws and forth stepped the Lady Perilous, more glorious than the dawn, more beautiful than the day. Before her terrible mien the knight's heart did tremble, but his countenance did betray him not.

"You would wed the Lady Perilous?" the fairy spoke, and her soft voice echoed with power. "I have had many suitors and none worthy. Why should I favor you?"

The knight answered boldly, "I am brave and strong and fair. I live in a castle filled with gold and far and wide am I renowned for my virtuous deeds."

"Certainly all you say is true," said the fairy, "but many have come before you with similar boasts."

"My lady," said the proud knight, "set me any challenge, and I will meet it. Name me any price, and I will pay it."

The Lady Perilous laughed. "Your words are the words of your predecessors, and so your answer shall be theirs as well. This doom do I bring to my suitors as dowry: from this day forward every good deed you do, every kind word or act of succor, will bring you misfortune and virtue will be a curse to you." The fairy sighed. "None of your predecessors found this a heavy burden."

With that she disappeared, her and the tower and the lake and the forest. The knight found himself standing in a field beside his horse. Then he laughed and said, "How foolish, to try and wed a fairy!"

But in his heart he was troubled, and thoughtfully did he begin the long journey home.

Soon after, he met a farmer along the road who doffed his cap and greeted the knight.

"Good day," replied the knight. "I hope it sees you

well." But as soon as the words had been spoken his horse stumbled and threw the knight into the mud.

Now the knight knew the fairy's words were true and he thought what he should do. And when he met another man who called to him, "Good day, Sir knight!" he passed by in silence.

Thus he rode for many days, greeting no one and being rude in the inns where he stopped, and no calamities befell him. Still he was unhappy, and the people began to whisper that here was a knight arrogant and mean.

Traveling on, the knight met an urchin girl, small and thin and wearing only a gown of paper against the icy wind. "Please Sir," she said. "I am so very cold."

Without hesitation the knight gave the poor lass his cloak. But when he went to his pack to draw out another he found that all his fine clothes had become filthy rags. Bitterly he wrapped himself in a moldy blanket and continued on.

Much later the knight came upon a river and beheld, on the far shore, a lone shepherd beset by wolves. Immediately the knight spurred his horse into the river but the water swept the animal away, and it was drowned. Swimming on, the knight came ashore and set upon the beasts. With strength and skill, he slew his foes till none remained. But when he drew his sword from the last wolf, the blade was dull and pitted, and where the beats' blood had touched it, his breastplate was rusted, and neither sword nor armor would suffer repair.

The knight walked on, clothed in rags and armed with a useless sword, till he chanced upon a friar standing beside a wagon.

"Good man," said the friar, for he did not recognize the knight as such, "come and help me fix my wagon wheel, and God will bless you for it."

"No," said the knight who looked now like a beggar. "I will be cursed for it, but still I will help you."

So the knight lifted the heavy wagon, and the friar replaced the broken wheel. But woe! When the deed was done the knight wore still the grimace he had made while lifting the load, and he was now quite ugly. Further, his strength had drained away, and he was left as weak as water.

The poor knight now drew near to his castle, and he wished only for his food and his wine and his bed. When he reached the gate, however, the guard would not open it, saying, "Get gone, dirty beggar!"

The knight answered, "I am not a beggar; I am your lord, the knight of this castle and lord of all inside."

Then the guard laughed and called to the kitchen maids and the stable boys. "Come and see our new lord!"

Then all the servants came, and the knight's elderly nurse and his fair sister also, and they jeered and laughed and threw stones at the poor knight. "Our lord is the greatest knight in the land," they yelled.

"The bravest," yelled the fair sister.

"The strongest," yelled the stable boys.

"The noblest," yelled the nurse.

"If you are a knight," said the guard, "you are a beggar-knight. Begone, Sir Beggar-Knight!"

So the miserable knight left his castle and was forced to live in a hovel in the forest outside the village where wolves leered at him and rain fell through his roof. He had to beg for food, and the children sang after him and beat him with sticks. Dogs bit him, and men spit on him. He was known as the beggar-knight and was the reason for much drunken laughter.

Long after, the poor beggar-knight hobbled deep into the forest to find some dead wood for his fire. Suddenly he came upon a green and stinking swamp, and in the filthy bog an old and ugly woman was stuck fast.

"Oh, help me or I shall die in this muck!" she cried.

Quickly the beggar-knight grabbed a branch and held it out to the hag. But no sooner was she pulled from the bog then he fell in himself!

"Help!" he cried. "Pull me out, or I shall perish in the muck!"

"Aha!" said the hag. "I will not pull you out unless you promise to marry me."

"Alas," thought the knight, "what a terrible thing, to marry such an ugly crone. But I am ugly now too. Truly, a lady-hag is a fitting wife for beggar-knight. What choice is there?"

"Very well," said the poor knight. "I will wed thee, old woman."

"Very well," laughed the hag as she pulled him from the bog. "Come to chapel of the glen on the morrow's dawn, and we shall be wed by the priest of the forest creatures. Go now, my betrothed and prepare for our marriage!"

The moon shone brightly that night on the troubled brow of the beggar-knight. For though he thought it a fitting union he had no wish to marry and could scarce remember a time when he had. Visions of flight came to him then, and he planned an escape in his thoughts. "I am the beggar-knight now," he said, "weak and ugly, but still I am a knight, keen of mind, fleet of foot, and bold in action! I know the ways and byways of this and of the lands beyond. Now could I flee to freedom and curse my betrothed from some hidden place!"

But as he was gathering his merger possessions, his words echoed in his ears. He had called the hag his betrothed, and so she was. He had said that he was a knight still, and so he was. He had vowed to wed the hag, and so he would.

At the morrow's dawn, the beggar-knight stood at the appointed place. Not a building of stone or of dead wood, but a green bower grown over the flowered valley, the chapel of the glen shone in the golden dawn. Within waited the priest of the forest creatures, dressed in green vestments and holding a stone bowl in his wooden hands. And beside him waited the bride, wearing a paper gown with a paper veil. The beggar-knight approached the chapel, passed a congregation of foxes and wolves, deer and rabbits. When he reached the chapel and stood beside his bride the green priest began.

The knight heard not the words, for his ears were full of his own misery, but when the priest called for the ring the knight became dismayed.

"I have no ring," he said.

"But I do," said the bride and took from her sleeve a ruby ring that stirred memory in the knight.

The priest took the ring and, placing it in the bowl, commanded them both to drink of the water within. "Of one water," said the priest, "of one stone, of one wood, of one earth, as the water is wed to the stream, as the wind is wed to the sky, so you are wed one to another, here in the sight of all."

But as the beggar-knight lamented his fate, his bride tore off her paper veil and behold! It was not the old hag of the mire but the shepherd whom the knight had rescued from the wolves! And as the knight stared dumbfounded, the shepherd tore off his own face as another veil and was the friar with the crippled wagon! And as the knight stood amazed, the friar threw back this face also and lo! It was the Lady Perilous, and she was more beautiful than the dawn and more glorious than the day!

"You have proven your heart, Sir Knight, for you were virtuous when virtue was poison and did good when it brought you only ill. Now come, be consort to the Lady Perilous!"

Instantly the knight was restored. His strength came back, and his face shone most fair, and the rust fell away from his gleaming armor and his mighty sword. His hovel vanished, and the knight found himself lord of a mighty castle and ruler of a glorious land. He and his fairy queen had many children, and they were much loved by their people.

And as far as I know, a hidden kingdom in an enchanted forest is still ruled by the Beggar-Knight and his Lady Perilous.

The Filigreed Lamp

By Edward Ahern

Once, not so long ago, a young girl named Kestrel lived on a farm. Kestrel's hair was the same gold-brown color as her namesake hawk, and she darted about with the agility of a kestrel in flight.

One day a construction company came to the farm and began to dig a long trench for a gas pipeline. The trench cut right through an overgrown, gnarly gully, good for nothing and left alone by everyone.

After they had laid the pipe and filled in the hole, Kestrel walked down the packed earth as if it were a path made just for her. When she reached the gully she looked down from her path and saw that the diggers had sheared off part of the gully's bank, exposing a little brick wall where none should be. No one had ever used the gully for anything.

Kestrel slid down the embankment to the bricks. She saw that the bricks were laid to seal an opening into the hillside. The bricks were oddly shaped and discolored with age. The mortar between the bricks was half crumbled away. Kestrel kicked at the bricks and they broke loose, falling back into the opening.

A peculiar smell blew out of the little cave, like cooking oil and incense. Kestrel wasn't afraid of mice or spiders, and pushed enough of the bricks aside so she could crawl in. The dirt ceiling brushed against her hair as she crawled. There was nothing there. Well, almost nothing. On a flat rock, in the middle of the little cave, all by itself, was an odd looking pitcher, or gravy boat, or maybe an oil can. It was covered with dust, and the dust had congealed into a layer of dirt.

When Kestrel picked up the pitcher she almost dropped it again. It was really heavy, as if it were solid stone. She picked at the dirt, flaking it off. Underneath were flashes of silver and gold. Kestrel had nothing to use to wipe off the pitcher. She looked down at her pants, already covered in brick dust and dirt. They have to be washed anyway, she thought, and began rubbing the jug on the thighs of her Jeans.

"I think you've rubbed me out."

The voice made Kestrel drop the pitcher. She would have run, but she would have had to crabble around on her knees before she could face the entry.

"Clumsy, I see. Try not to drop that again. It's unsettling."

It was a woman's voice, liquid and soft.

"Where—where are you?" Kestrel quavered.

"Ah yes, a little light on the situation." The words were chewy.

Light swelled up from the thing on the floor, not day light, but the yellow flicker that an oil lamp makes. Kestrel stared at the most peculiarly dressed young woman she had ever seen. Her dark hair was wrapped in braids around the top of her head like a turban. Her slippers were pointed and looked like lake blue silk. She wore red pants and jacket embroidered in gold. She had the complexion of a porcelain doll, with the same pouting lips.

"What? How? Who?" Kestrel muttered.

"Don't babble, dear, it's not becoming. It's my bad luck that you found the lamp and summoned me. All right, let's get started."

"I don't understand."

The woman sighed. "Are you still reading fairy tales?"

"Sometimes."

"What happens when you rub a certain lamp?"

"Oh. You're a Genii—I get wishes! But you're a woman?"

"Don't call me Genii. I am a Jinn. Jeanie is what you call a waitress in a diner. I appear to you as a woman because it's easier for you to grasp. Usually I get a chest thumping man, and he sees me as bigger and meaner than he is."

Kestrel had been poised to jump backward out of

the cave. But this was too interesting. She settled back on her haunches.

"Do I get three wishes?"

"Your requests are unlimited, but there are rules."

"How can there be rules on wishes? I can wish for whatever I like."

"No, you squiggly little eel, you can't. What's your name?"

"Kestrel."

"Listen to the rules, Kestrel." The Jinn waved its arms jointlessly, as if they were made of smoke.

"You cannot ask for what must be freely given—love and friendship, for example.

"You cannot change an inner state—happiness, sadness, pride, greed—in yourself or others.

"You cannot alter the inevitable—such as aging and dying."

Kestrel thought for a moment. "That still leaves lots of things I can ask for."

"Ah, yes, but in addition to the rules there is a caution. The more selfish your request the more likely your wish is to betray you—like lighting a forest fire with the wind howling in your face. Even a good hearted request may have painful consequences."

"But I can keep making wishes until good things happen."

"I can almost hear your monkey mind whirring. Know that none of the men who have disturbed my freedom have ever asked for more than three wishes."

Kestrel was puzzled. "Wait, ah, what should I call you?"

"Alephriel."

"Alephriel, you said freedom. Weren't you trapped inside the lamp until I rubbed it? Aren't you grateful to me to be out?"

"No, sparrow hawk, your fable tellers have gotten it wrong for four millennia. I'm free when I'm not groveling in a cave granting wishes. When you disturbed me I was in the middle of my second century inside a volcano, flowing with swirls of magma struggling to be stone."

"Wow. Do I have to ask for something now?'

"No, the only limit is your lifetime. Take the lamp with you until you know what you want. No one can take it from you until you release me. And you should clean it. It's disgusting looking. Goodbye."

The lamp light went out. Alephriel was gone. Kestrel picked up the lamp and crawled on her elbows and knees back out of the cave. She would have run home, but the lamp was too heavy. Kestrel walked behind their house and used the garden hose to wash off the lamp. The lamp was covered with silver and gold filigree, with symbols etched on its back.

Kestrel put the lamp in the bottom drawer of her bureau, under her tee shirts, and began to think. That night, after supper but before she went to sleep, Kestrel took out the lamp and rubbed it.

"Not even one day and you're already making a wish?"

Alephriel was sitting on Kestrel's bed. She wore a cloak of ink black silk and under it an apple red dress. Her short hair was red and tightly curled. But the face was the same, smooth and serene, with pouty lips.

"Don't you ever dress the same?"

"No, little daughter, when I'm dragged out I like to dress up."

"I know what I want."

"Do you now? No one else ever really did. What is it?"

"Something small, something kind, something not for me. My father broke his big toe when he was a boy, and he's always walked with a little limp because it hurts. Fix his toe, please."

"So you have spoken, so it shall be."

That next morning Kerstrel saw her father pacing back and forth in the upstairs corridor, still in his pajamas.

"What's wrong dad?"

"It's what's right that has me worried, Kes. My toe doesn't hurt anymore. I'm wondering if I have nerve damage or if it's infected."

Kestrel almost giggled. "Gee, dad, maybe you should just be happy that it doesn't hurt."

The doctor could find nothing wrong, and Kestrel's father was so happy that he thought about taking dancing lessons. And then, while walking down the stairs he forgot that his toe was better, stepped like he had a limp, lost his balance, and fell all the way down, breaking his leg.

Kestrel's father came back from the hospital with his leg in a cast. She pulled the lamp out of the bottom drawer and rubbed it so hard her hand hurt.

"Don't wear off the filigree," Alephriel said.

Kestrel was mad. "That's not fair! My dad shouldn't have to suffer because his toe got better!"

Alephriel was twirling around while Kestrel spoke. Her hair was blonde and bouffant, and she wore a green mini skirt with spangled leggings under a pink sweatshirt that said, "EAT GREASE." But her lips were still pouty.

"Kestrel, my child, I warned you about unintended consequences. Everything we do has an effect. But don't worry. Your father's leg will heal, and he'll still take those dancing lessons."

Kestrel waited two more weeks before she summoned Alephriel again. Alephriel was dressed all in black leather, boots up through pants and jacket and black leather cap. Her hair was shaved off, but she had kept her pearly complexion and pouty expression.

"Okay Alephriel, I've got it now. My best friend is Marissa. Her family is really poor, so poor that Marissa has no clothes for school and never has any money for lunch. I wish for her family to become rich, so Marissa can have everything she wants."

Alephriel looked sad. "That's really what you want?"

"Yes, absolutely."

"So you have spoken, so it shall be."

Marissa's family was contacted the next day by a private investigator. An uncle no one had ever heard of had died and left them a big inheritance, Marissa was given clothes, and toys, and jewelry. She was taken from the public school where she and Kestrel went, and placed in a private school. She made new friends, and forgot about the old ones.

Kestrel telephoned Marissa several times, but they never met, and Marissa finally told Kestrel that her new friends and tutors and special lessons left her no time at all for Kestrel. Kestrel cried a little, and waited a week, and rubbed the lamp again.

Alephriel wore a flouncy, white bridal dress, with white satin slippers and a white veil on top of long auburn hair "This is truly uncomfortable. It's no wonder you people only wear it once."

Kestrel started crying again. "How could I make such a mistake, Alephriel?"

"It's not your fault, child. Some people change with their circumstances. But, I strongly suspect that by the time you both go to college you'll be friends again."

"How can you be sure?"

"Her family will have spent all the money. Did you summon me to make a wish?"

"Not a wish, Alephriel. I'm not doing too well with those. But I wanted to ask you about where you go when you're inside the lamp. You mentioned a volcano?"

"Ah child, it's too bad you can't survive these things or I'd show you. Yes, the last time was a volcano, a wonderful, rich mineral soup, so hot things lost their identity, and changed and reformed and changed again. The best hot, soaking bath you ever took would be a tiny taste of where I was.

"And before that for two of your lifetimes I swam in a huge lake under a glacier at the South Pole, an ice shell surrounding a yolk of water older than mankind, with only the faintest memories of the living things that once swam in it.

"And before that for almost two hundred tree rings I rose and fell with the sap of a huge oak that druids worshipped, sharing in the growth and fall of leaves and acorns. So, yes, when I'm in the lamp I'm truly free."

Kestrel made no more wishes, but she thought and thought about what Alephriel had told her. After two long months she rubbed the lamp again.

Alephriel bounced off the bed, clad in bright purple spandex, her white hair sprawling from her head like a shaving brush. "This material should be banned because of body distortion. All my soft parts are squished and my bony bits protrude. Really!"

"Alephriel, I've been thinking."

"A dangerous pursuit for the best of humans."

"I want to make another wish."

"That's a pity. What is your wish?"

Kestrel smiled at Alephriel. "I know that you really love your freedom. But I think you complain a little too much about having to associate with humans. You do enjoy being with us for at least a little while. What you don't like is being yanked around by us willy-nilly. So, what I wish, what I want for you, is that you alone control when you appear to us. You're four thousand years old, you should be adult enough to handle it."

Alephriel's pouty lips broke into a smile. "So you have spoken, so it shall be. I'm actually closer to seven thousand years old. How did you know that once I was free, I wouldn't do you and others harm?"

"Because you don't interfere. You take part, but you don't disrupt things."

Alephriel shimmered, her clothing and hair molting several times in a second. "Free at last. Kestrel, please keep the lamp for me."

"I will. It's just a lamp now, but it's pretty. I can't demand any more wishes, but could you please stop by every once in a while and tell me about your trips?"

"My next trip, Kestrel, will last longer than your lifetime, but I promise that before I leave, I'll come back and tell you about other wishes and other trips."

Keys

By Michael M. Jones

It's after midnight in Club Euterpe as Wednesday night becomes Thursday morning. Jazz dances through the smoky air, our spirits humming with wild energy. The place is packed, the regular crowd bolstered by a bunch of out-of-towners from some pre-packaged bus tour. Tonight: Puxhill. Tomorrow: Poughkeepsie, Memphis, or Minneapolis. They're totally grooving on the music, filling the dance floor with a passion they'll remember as a dream come tomorrow. Up on stage, Gabe's playing the trumpet, an up-tempo tune tugging at the heart. He's backed by Radical Declination, a band of moonlighting math and science professors from Tuesday University. Tonight feels like an especially awesome night; not that I've ever had a bad one here.

The good vibrations make it all the way to the back of the room where, Cerberus-like, I guard a table, snapping a fierce look at anyone wanting to steal one of my chairs. Maria's at the bar grabbing drinks; nonalcoholic all-around, since we're underage. While the establishment is cool with minors here at all hours, they're inflexible where the liquor laws are concerned. No fake ID gets past them. Ever. Fine by me. The music and ambient energy gives me all the buzz I need. Caught up in the rhythm, my fingers drum absently.

Maria returns, taking her chair and sliding me my drink. I grin thanks at her, lifting my glass in salute. Up on stage, Gabe's winding up the set, spontaneously reimagining an old Louis Armstrong song; the band's having trouble keeping up with the improv, but they love a challenge. In the corner nearest us, a gaggle of Funereal Children loiter. They try to look gloomy and solemn in their best mourning clothes, but one girl's lips twitch in an aborted smile, while another bobs his head to the beat. I'm surprised to see them here. They favor more sedate environments, better suited for tombstone dreams and night-shrouded sensibilities. I guess even they need a little variety now and again.

With the set over and canned music taking its place, Gabe comes to grab the third of four seats at the table, settling in with a sigh of relief, planting his horn in front of him. Maria slides a drink his way: ice water with a squeeze of lime, all he ever wants after a stint on stage. He kicked ass out there tonight, and it shows. His cornsilk-pale hair's plastered to his sweat-slicked forehead, while his cool jazz-white suit lies wrinkled against nearly-translucent skin. His eyes, however, are as bright as a summer day.

How a skinny white guy like him managed to master this sort of music, we'll never know. Hell, we don't even know where he came from. Gabe just appeared on the street one day, thin and pale, his only possession an old trumpet. By day, he plays the streets, by night he plays the clubs. He only sleeps in the wee hours of the morning, bedding down in alleys or shelters, on couches or spare beds. Never the same place twice in a row. He refuses to settle into a pattern. He could be twenty, he could be fifty, who knows? He gets along with just about everyone, but he doesn't seem to have any close friends. Maria and I might count, but what we don't know about him could fill a book. Gabe's not one for sharing.

"You were great out there," enthuses Maria, dark eyes shining. She leans forward in the process, her screaming-red blouse dipping to display a generous amount of cleavage. The color looks good against her mahogany skin, and she knows it. She's totally got a thing for Gabe, teasing him every chance she gets. He's never acknowledged it or returned the interest, but she doesn't seem to mind. It's something to do, rather than a goal in its own right. It doesn't affect me either. Even if I was into girls, she's too much like my sister.

"Thanks," returns Gabe, succinctly. "You two are up late, as always. Parents know where you are?" A pair of shrugs answer him. We go through the same question-and-answer every time, and it never changes. It's a lot more satisfying to immerse ourselves in the music and Puxhill's nocturnal culture than it is to play it safe in the daytime. Maria sneaks out because Club Euterpe's the only place where she can get a thrill. She's escaping a feeling of inadequacy and mediocrity earned as the youngest child in a family of scholastic and athletic overachievers. My folks wouldn't even notice if I brazenly walked out the front door in a clown suit, they're so wrapped up in their own set of trailer park issues. Here, Maria and I shed our daylight personas and can be ourselves…whoever we're becoming. That's the common thread among many Euterpe regulars.

Companionable silence falls, the sort that Gabe always seems to inspire. I finally break it. "How about you? Getting a bit late, you heading home anytime soon?" I'm teasing. He's a nocturnal sort; this is early for him.

His chuckle is laced with mild uneasiness, shoulders bobbing in a lazy shrug. "Can't go home. Lost my keys."

That's his idea of a serious answer. Personal questions make him uncomfortable. Ask him a second time, get a different story. He's an orphan from New York, or the youngest of three sons from Las Vegas set out to seek his fortune, or he ran away from the circus, or he was found in a cabbage patch. He won his trumpet in a poker game, he inherited it from his grandfather, he sold his soul to the Devil. And so on. Sometimes, I wonder if he even knows the truth himself. In part, we're drawn by his mystery. That, and he's one of the best musicians I've ever heard. Like liquid silver and moonlight, tied together with cobwebs and kitten purrs. His skills could bring him fame and fortune, but he's absolutely uninterested in anything other than the bare necessities. He lives from day to day, never worrying about the future.

We carry on drinking and chatting—mostly Maria and me, with Gabe contributing the occasional laconic comment as appropriate. Around three-thirty, the club starts to empty out as things die down, about usual for a Wednesday. On weekends, it stays hopping and jazzed up all the way through 'til dawn, when people evaporate with the rising sun. The Funereal Children are long gone, moped back to their hidey-places and pseudo-crypts. The tourists, of course, faded ages ago, the wimps. They're happily tucked into their hotel beds, or possibly already on the bus to their next destination. The place is maybe a quarter-full, soundtrack provided by one slightly inebriated guy banging out Journey on the baby grand piano tucked in the far corner, and it's impossible to miss the moment when Simon Peters bursts in, so frantic you'd think the hounds of Hades were chewing on his Italian loafers.

Simon Peters is a phenomenon worthy of explanation. One of Puxhill's homegrown celebrities, he's a cable talk show host who balances freaks and geeks with character drama, masterminding everything from

KKK family reunions to midget weddings to "Santa Claus knocked up my sister" shockers, all with a ringmaster's flair. Supposedly, he used to be a priest of debatable denomination, until he violated his celibacy with two nuns and a pizza delivery guy. After that, he went into politics, making spectacularly failed runs for everything from PTA board member (neither parent nor teacher) to Mayor (lost in a landslide to a dead guy) to President (of the United States—ran as an Independent, dropped out after two months when he got bored).

Everyone's got a Simon Peters story; it's almost mandatory if you want to be considered a true Puxhill native. They don't even have to be true, just vaguely plausible. No matter what, the stories all agree he's not a bad person. He just answers to a different, somewhat dubious, set of morals. The working girls on the edge of the Gaslight District love him; he frequents this greasy spoon on the corner of Wilhelm and Stratford in the wee hours of the morning after (or before) taping his show, and he'll buy them breakfast just for the company: conversational, or otherwise. If anyone in this city can get into trouble, it's Simon, so we're not surprised to see him on the run for his life.

We are surprised, however, when he beelines for our table, smoothly dropping into the empty chair and snaking out a hand to steal my drink. He guzzles half of it down before stopping. His forehead wrinkles in puzzlement. "I taste the Coke, but where's the rum?"

"Sorry," I say, too startled to be annoyed. "No rum. I drink my Coke like a man." I pry the glass from his fingers while Maria gapes. Gabe remains cool and calm, fingers steepled in quiet amusement. Nothing fazes him.

"Damn," says Simon. "Ah well, beggars can't be choosers. Look natural."

"Oh my god!" That's Maria, helpfully chiming in at last. "You're Simon Pe–"

"Why yes, yes I am. I've also been here for the past, oh, let's call it two hours, shall we? If anyone asks. There's a hundred in it for each if you if you play along." Simon glances towards the door in wary anticipation. I tense, picking up on the strangeness of his mood. Maria bristles like an angry cat at being so abruptly dismissed. I cover her hand with mine, and she deflates a little, quick temper defused. Her sisters set her off the same way.

"Mind explaining what's going on?" I ask, rubbing at the rim of my glass with my sleeve. I wonder if it's safe to drink after him. "And get your own drink."

"Sure, sure, just—." Simon clams up as the front door opens, but it's just Diana, the club's owner. She's a middle-aged Greek woman with the longest hair I've ever seen, curvy and confident, and a world-class flautist who occasionally performs here when she's in the right mood. She's juggling a stack of papers and her flute case as she heads directly for her office in the back. Apparently not the cause of Simon's worries, he starts up again. "If they don't show up in ten minutes, we'll know I'm safe and they lost me when I took that sharp right through Stonejack Park." He refuses to elaborate, instead springing for a fresh round while elaborating on his alibi. "We've been here all night. I'm your beloved Uncle Clarence, in from the country for a night out on the town."

"Clarence?" asks Gabe, sounding rather dubious.

"You don't like it? I thought it tripped off the tongue. Let's see if I have this right. Gabe, Maria, and Danny. Splendid. Now we're all friends."

I'm not so sure, but Simon's got an infectious carelessness that quickly erodes our reservations, no matter how ludicrous it all seems. We make a bizarre group: two high school kids out way past bedtime, the homeless trumpet player in his bedraggled white suit, and Simon Peters with his perfect hair and perpetual smile. This is the first time I've seen him in person, and the stories of his legendary charm are true. I like him, but I make sure I know where my wallet is at all times.

After nine minutes, with no sign of trouble, we've all relaxed, even Maria, who's fallen for Simon's dry humor and "favorite uncle" aura. Gabe alone seems to be holding back, but that's normal. He keeps one hand on his trumpet, and an eye on the door, making him the first to notice when it opens once more. His eyes widen, and we all follow his gaze. Simon curses in dismay under his breath and tenses. Showtime.

Four guys file through, one after another, all

identically dressed in dark suits. Mobsters, FBI, Men in Black, they all have the same dress sense, and I wonder what Simon's gotten himself mixed up in. As one reaches into a pocket, my heart races, sure he's about to pull either a badge or a gun. Maria's hand slides into mine, clammy with worry, and I squeeze it reassuringly. We have to act natural.

Imagine my surprise when, instead of a gun, he produces a palm-sized crystal ball, which pulses slowly with a dull red gleam. He holds it up and outwards, his arm describing an arc across the room, the pulse growing in intensity and frequency. When it points in our direction, it goes nuclear, flashing like a strobe. The guy nods once, barks something to his pals, and they all come our way. I can feel a tiny bead of sweat trickle down my neck. What the hell have I gotten myself into?

"New plan," murmurs Simon. "When I count to three, I run. Anyone know where the back door is?"

"I do," says Gabe. "Sometimes we head outside between sets for some fresh air."

"Splendid. It was lovely meeting you all, but I'm afraid I must now flee for fear of losing life and limb." Even ready to run, Simon never breaks character. Unfortunately, it's too late; they cross the room with unexpected speed. Up close, I'm able to study them in depth. While they're nearly identical, after a moment I can pick out minute differences: one has a thin scar on his cheek; another has slightly more angular features, and so forth. Somewhere, a Swedish family wants its blond, blue-eyed kids back. Strangely, they remind me of Gabe, if he had a few decent meals and got a haircut.

"Simon Peters," says the scar-cheeked one, evenly. His voice reminds me of a sour note in a jazz composition: musical, but *wrong*.

"Me? Oh no. I'm Harvey Walters," says Simon. "This is my nephew, Jack, and his friends, Gideon and Martha."

Zero for three on the names, Simon. Good job. Of course, the alibi was doomed from the start, despite our protestations and reservations. But Simon insisted it would work, and in the crazy heat of the moment, we didn't argue too hard. But there's no way anyone would ever believe we're related, unless there was one hell of a mix-up at the hospital, seeing as how he and Gabe are the only white people at the table. Maria starts to speak, and I kick her under the table.

Scar doesn't hesitate for a second, despite Simon's bold-faced lie. "You are Simon Peters. The crystal is never wrong." He gestures to his companions. "Kill him. Kill the others for helping him. They will all be an object lesson." There's no emotion in his words, just a calm assurance that this is how it's going to be, and that scares me more than any angry threats or bluster would have. Hands drop to hips, and things quickly get complicated.

I'll be the first to admit that I panicked. The second Scar laid down the death sentence, my instincts took over. The next few minutes are a series of mental snapshots, all chaos and confusion. I start by flinging my watered-down Coke into their faces, and my friends follow suit, throwing their drinks as well. The peace shatters as the mystery men reel backwards in surprise and we leap from our chairs.

"Three!" calls Simon, as though this was all his idea, and we follow Gabe on a hell-bent exodus towards the back door, dodging furniture and people alike, most of whom have no idea what's going on. I'm running on adrenaline, fight-or-flight stuck on "flight". Lord knows how we'll explain this to Diana if we ever want to be welcome here again. With Gabe in front and Simon hot on his heels, I drop to the rear to make sure a slower Maria doesn't get left behind. We scramble across the stage and hang a left, bursting through the door to end up in the alley behind the club. We're alone, but not for long.

It's the hazy part of the night where time seems to stand still, outside. Club Euterpe may be winding down to sleep, but all around us are places catering to the hard-core partiers, the insomniacs, the nocturnal. The smells of coffee, fresh bread, and imminent rain drift through the air, while sirens wail in the far-off distance. God, I love Puxhill at night. I refocus on the problem at hand. "Who the hell were those guys, and why do they want to kill you?" I demand, grabbing Simon's sleeve. He's not even breathing hard, and his hair's still perfect.

Unbelievable.

He takes a moment to answer, as we start to half-walk, half-jog away from the alley. We steer clear of Euterpe's front door on Briggs Avenue, instead heading further into the Gaslight District it borders. Here there be cobblestones and ancient buildings, twisty roads and cool little shops which don't appear in travel guides. I've no clue where we're headed, and I don't care, so long as it's away from the men with the glowing ball and the bad attitudes. "I broke two of my personal rules: never play cards with men with pointed ears, and never cheat with someone else's deck. Oh, and I raised while holding two jacks and a joker, but that was just foolhardy on my part."

"What were you playing?" Maria's finally caught her breath, and she gets out the question while trying to match our pace. She stumbles on the cobblestones, and I catch her by the arm. We don't stop moving.

Simon's shrug is careless. "You know, I'm not entirely sure. It was a cross between blackjack, Texas Hold'em, and Go Fish. There were a lot of house rules, and I didn't catch them all. Figured I'd pick it up in play."

We all blink. "So you were trying to cheat at cards…." I begin.

"…without knowing the rules," continues Maria.

"…while playing with complete strangers," adds Gabe, looking faintly ruffled, but otherwise normal. He clutches his trumpet in one hand as he leads the way, long steps carrying him forward into the night. Somehow, he became the leader of our odd little party, and we trust him to guide us to safety. But where's that?

"What were you thinking?" I ask, sadly aware that scolding Simon Peters is an exercise in futility. Thanks to him, we're delving further into the maze-like Gaslight District in the cold hours of the night. Two teens, a musician, and the talk show circuit's version of Peter Pan.

"They told me they had a map leading to the true Fountain of Youth," says Simon, "and I couldn't resist the opportunity. They were very sincere, and obviously saw me coming from a mile away." His sigh is laced with chagrin.

"At what point did cheating seem like a good idea?" asks Maria, tone turned shrill. The blocks are short and the roads come and go with increasing frequency as we take turns at random. Willingham. Vanderhook. Paloma. St. Ives. All I can hear are our voices and footsteps, and I'm not sure I like it.

"It was only the one king, and it fell into my pocket when I went for a tissue," Simon says defensively. "It could have been an honest mistake, really. I didn't know they'd take it so personally."

"Who are they?" asks Gabe. By now, we've all realized that keeping Simon on track is a team effort.

"Transvestites. At least, that's what I thought. They called themselves 'she', so I figured they were women dressed as men. Really, you saw them. Such elegant, refined features, and lovely hair. I love transvestites and transsexuals. They boost the ratings wonderfully. One time, I did a show about 'transsexuals with a secret, and the cross-dressers who love them'." He lowers his voice, conspiratorially. "The secret was they were all Internet porn stars. Oh, the chairs that got flung that day!"

I resist the urge to choke Simon for, well, any number of reasons. He's both the queer community's greatest friend and worst enemy with his bizarre combination of empathy and exploitation. It's like he tries, but doesn't know any better, and yet it's hard to get truly upset with him. Educating him...just doesn't seem to stick. Truly, a conundrum for another time. Instead, I pick up on something from a few minutes ago. "They had pointed ears?"

"Not at first. After a round of their berry wine, they did. I don't know what shape their ears were in the club, since I was busy."

I frown, trying to add things up. Maria interrupts with a worried, "Where are we going?"

Gabe shrugs. "Beats me. I just wanted to put some distance between us and Simon's friends. I know where we are. Mostly." His confidence, such as it is, is not reassuring.

"I'm glad someone does," I mutter, "because I'm lost." All I know is we're deep in the heart of the Gaslight District, and if Simon's enemies don't get us, there's probably a minotaur trapped back here who will. This part of the city is old and strange, a total disconnect from the real world. The streets are narrow and curvy, branching off at all angles and curving back around again, creating oddly-shaped blocks and weird pockets of space. Unplanned, even organic, feeling far older than Puxhill ever should. Some of the shops, all closed for the night, have signs in unfamiliar languages, their meanings impossible to decipher. Butcher? Bookstore? Convenience store? There are churches back here, stern buildings with sharp edges and gloomy exteriors, standing guard over their neighbors, and the streetlights flicker in an eerie evocation of the gas lamps for which this part of town was named.

Static dangles in the air, heralding a change in the wind. Gabe may be leading us, but Simon started this. Are we on a fool's road? The thoughts come to me as though whispered into my ears by a stranger, which I find both unnerving and oddly exciting. The further we go, the clearer things seem. The facts all came together; I know who Simon's pursuers are, but I don't dare say so. I sense them somewhere behind us, and names have power.

Every road has to end eventually, and we run out of ours when the streets spiral and twist together, feeding into a small traffic circle. There's an old fountain in the center, the statue of a young man blowing a horn, eternally frozen in that pose while water, not music, streams forth. The resemblance to Gabe sends a shiver down my spine. I'm not the only one to notice it, either. "Gabe, look," says Maria, voice wavering nervously, "it's your brother."

Her attempt at humor hangs for a moment, before dying on the breeze. We look around. The area's deserted. If there's any life to be found, it's behind locked doors, drawn curtains, extinguished lights. We're on our own.

"Could be," agrees Gabe, wandering closer to give the statue his full attention. I envy his calm, how he can keep his cool even in a crisis. I jam my hands into my pockets, eying Simon balefully. This is his fault.

"What now?" I ask. "I mean, you did have a plan, right? Rather than 'run like hell and hope they never find you'?" I feel like rubbing his nose in it. Petty, but true.

Simon Peters, talk show host and bringer of chaos, shrugs. "I hadn't thought about it. I figured something would come to mind eventually, if I had faith. That's how it usually works. I needed help, I found it."

"Yeah," I say, "but I don't think we're doing so well. You should have found better help."

"I don't know. So far, so good, right? You got me out of the club; that has to be worth something." I'm sorely tempted to punch the careless arrogance right out of the cocky grin he gives me. Instead, I sigh, yielding to his unique brand of logic.

"Something's coming," says Maria, as she joins us.

"Listen."

Hooves clip-clopping on cobblestone. Metal on leather. Rhythmic breathing. They appear one at a time, coming from all sides, blocking every escape. Three, six, a dozen and more. Elegant men and women on horseback, dressed in fine clothes, naked swords gleaming in their hands. They shine like the full moon, but cast no shadows. They're all grim-faced and solemn, long-haired and fierce. Their ears are pointed. Scar and his followers are on foot, glowering at us. I know who we're facing, and I quickly drop my gaze to avoid meeting their eyes.

The Sidhe. The Shining Host. I've read enough fairy tales to know how much trouble we're in. But how can they be here, and why? In the real world? Or are we somewhere less than real, now? I stamp on that line of thinking before it renders me useless.

"Oh!" says Simon. "I forgot to mention the part about the swords. That's why I ran; they were waving the sharp pointy objects at me."

"I'm sure it was on the tip of your tongue," Maria says sarcastically, rolling her eyes in disdain. I suspect she's lost any and all hero worship where he's concerned.

"Simon Peters. We have found you. And now your life is forfeit." The new spokesman is an elegant lord who sits high on his horse, clad all in green and silver. He levels his sword in Simon's direction. "The Host will not tolerate your slights against us."

"Slights? You were cheating!" Simon insists. "There's no way you could have had all the queens!"

"We followed the rules of the game. You violated them."

"But you didn't tell me all the rules!"

"Not our fault. We expect that if you play our game, you know our rules. We should not have to waste time and energy explaining them to lesser creatures."

"But you'll take our money!" Simon protests indignantly. "You'll gamble with us! You sought out us 'lesser creatures'!"

"In order to walk the mortal world, we occasionally have need of funds. Relieving you of yours is a necessary evil and a minor pleasure. Glamouring leaves is no longer sufficient in this age of technology."

They continue to argue, and I ransack my brain. They have superior numbers, weapons, and magic on their side. They're completely amoral and willing to kill to soothe their wounded pride. We're an eclectic quarter of mortals, one of whom's a blithering idiot. I doubt either my Swiss Army Knife or Maria's pepper spray would do much good. What else can we use against angry elves? We're fresh out of four-leaf clovers, pink hearts, and yellow moons, and there's no cold iron (whatever *that* is) to be seen. I think of one possibility, though it's a long shot.

I motion for Gabe and Maria to get closer, and they do, our every movement watched by the Sidhe, who seem content to stay put for the moment. I get the feeling that the Sidhe are enjoying the hunt, the chase, the bargaining, more than they would the actual kill. When you're immortal, you take your amusement where you find it. In a low voice, I share my thoughts, while Simon talks himself further into trouble. He's offering them an appearance on his show. No, a whole week, if they'll just come and be themselves. Sweeps week! Their reply is obscene without being vulgar, the scorn in the Sidhe's voice truly impressive. It gives us time to finish planning, though. We break our huddle, and I give my friends a silent three count on my fingers.

When I hit three, Gabe raises his trumpet, launching into an amazingly defiant version of "When the Saints Go Marching In." Maria adds the words, her tone crystal and vibrant, reminding me why she's in demand for the spring musical every year. She's sung in her church choir for years, and I'm amazed her family never realized this is where her talent lies. It takes my breath away.

I can't sing or play an instrument, but I can whistle, praying that every little bit helps. This is really up to Gabe and Maria. At first, no one pays us any attention. A few seconds later, Simon and the leader of the Sidhe stop arguing, and quickly, all eyes are on us. Simon looks baffled. The Sidhe...don't know what to think. We don't stop. Gabe coaxes heavenly notes from his trumpet while Maria throws her heart and soul into the performance, her voice rich and deep. It's a hell of a duet, passion stemming from desperation.

We have the Host's attention. Horses stamp and whicker nervously, but their riders sit still, straight, and silent. Simon may not understand what we're doing, but at least he's quiet for a change.

Legend has it the Sidhe are vulnerable to certain holy things, like church bells, blessed water, and sanctified ground. Lacking all of those, all we can do is offer up songs in the right spirit.

Minutes tick by, and nothing happens. As the saints finish marching, give Gabe a nod. He segues into a new song, and Maria picks it up without missing a beat. I've never heard "Amazing Grace" done with so much fervor, and it seeps into my bones. The raw emotion drives the Host back several steps, their horses uneasy and rebellious under them. The Sidhe remain silent, eyes wide and luminescent; somehow, miraculously, we've seized an advantage.

Maybe it's a trick of the light, but Gabe's practically glowing, his white suit outshining the dim streetlamps and the Host themselves. I rub my eyes, convinced I'm seeing things, but it doesn't help. Then it's time for a third song. With nothing to stop us, we launch into the last of our initial selections, Maria belting forth the familiar beginning of "Swing Low, Sweet Chariot."

The Host totally lose their composure. A female rider brushes at her eyes, sniffling. Another looks away. The leader lowers his sword. Overwhelmed by Gabe's music and Maria's voice their murderous anger drains away, just like that.

"Enough!" cries their leader, his voice ringing through the area like a silver bell. Gabe and Maria glance at me, falling silent at my nod. "I cry you hold, mortals. Your passion has touched us, stirring up long-buried memories of our ancient, lost home." There's sadness in his voice. Arrogance still, but also an aching sorrow. "We should kill you for awakening the past, but instead, we shall...cherish the moment, the small taste of what was ours, once. And we shall dream of going home, someday." His eyes are far away and distant. "You waste your talents in defense of this silly, foolish little man," he says, flicking a hand at Simon derisively, "but you do so with pure hearts, and we must respect that."

There's a pause, as he locks eyes with each of his companions. One by one, they nod in acknowledgment before withdrawing into the chill night, until only the leader remains. Scar is the last to go, the look he shoots Simon a promise of delayed vengeance and eventual retribution. I shudder at the malevolence contained in those eyes.

The leader, the nameless rider in green, has more to say. "Hear my words, and heed them well. This will not work a second time. Do not seek us out. Do not game with us. Do not assume you can outwit us again." My bones freeze under the weight of his cold words; I *know* a second meeting would prove disastrous. "Simon

Peters, we absolve you of your debt and erase your transgressions. You and your companions are free to lead your fleeting lives as you see fit. Provided you do not cross us again."

We all nod mutely, accepting the finality in those words. Even Simon displays a measure of silent respect. The rider turns and clip-clops away, swiftly vanishing around a corner.

That's not the end of it, though. With the Host departed, it's obvious that Gabe's glowing brightly, a brilliant white light seeping from his pores. His trumpet is like liquid silver in his hands, held in shape by belief. As the three of us watch, he changes, growing taller and more elegant, features sharpening into an exaggerated, inhuman beauty. I meet his gaze, looking away immediately. In his eyes, I saw galaxies.

"I remember," he breathes, voice ringing like crystal. "This is where I fell. This is where I woke."

Maria's the first to blurt out what we're all thinking. "You look like they did! Only not as cruel!" She's right; Gabe possesses a kindness the Host did not.

"Like them," agrees Gabe, "but not the same. We were alike, once, when we all lived together. Our Father had many children, before the Great Argument. Some stayed, some left, and those who couldn't decide were cast out anyway, to find their own way." He lifts his hand to curiously examine his trumpet. Then he takes a deep breath, and blows, unleashing a cascade of music, a freeform jazz piece unlike anything I've ever heard, yet heartbreakingly familiar. It feels like the underpinnings, the very heart, for every song I've ever heard. It feels right and rare and perfect. I'm in the presence of something wonderful.

Lacking the same sentimentality as the rest of us, Simon speaks up. "So close! I almost had them! Real life elves, on my show! Eat your heart out, Jerry!"

I ignore his ramblings, focused on Gabe's continued transformation. The music seems to be burning away the mortal wear and tear and dust and dirt and stress before our very eyes, leaving behind his true essence.

Maria instinctively crosses herself, eyes wide and dark with realization. My knees shake. Just as we know who and what he is, we know better than to sully it with words.

Gabriel lowers his trumpet. Everything human and mortal about him is gone, save for something in his smile. "I've been trying to find this spot for years. It's where the gate was, where I dwelled too closely on Earthly matters until they dragged me down. Where the weight of the mortal world proved too much for my wings, where memory fled and my spirit wrapped itself tight in flesh for its own safety." He smiles, beatifically. "I couldn't have found this place were it not for you, Simon, and your run-in with my lost brothers. You helped open the way."

I recall something I read, once. A theory about the Sidhe being those angels who refused to take either side when Lucifer rebelled against the Lord, and it all makes sense.

"Gabe," I begin, and then stop. What do you say when your mysterious pal with the hidden past turns out to be Not Of This World? I stammer out, "Safe journeys, man." I have a million questions, but the words jumble in my throat and I can't get them out. I'm not sure I want the answers, anyway.

"Danny, you and Maria have always been good to me, and I appreciate it. I'll miss you both. I'd stay if I could, but every second I linger gives the mortal world another chance to drag me down." Gabe's smile is wry and apologetic. "I have to go. I finally found my keys after all." A quick trumpet trill, and he grows transparent, fading away before our eyes. His last words are directed at Simon. "Your help, unintentional and accidental as it was, is still appreciated. But behave yourself, Simon Peters. Luck won't always treat you so kindly. And maybe, if you stay out of trouble, you'll find your way home as well."

Then Gabriel's gone, and the coming dawn is peaceful. No Sidhe, no Gabe, no magic.

With the sun coming up, it's disconcertingly easy to find our way out of the Gaslight District. Once we reach Club Euterpe, we go our separate ways. Simon, who's never met someone he didn't like, claims we should stay in touch, pressing a card into each of our hands. He never does pay us for the alibi. I never expected him to. Maria and I have a Simon Peters story all our very own, and that's worth more than you'd think in Puxhill, no matter how unbelievable or outrageous.

I learned several things that night: never play cards with the Sidhe, always know the rules ahead of time, and never cheat with someone else's deck. You never know what sort of trouble that'll bring.

I also know that sure as day follows night, Maria and I will return to Club Euterpe, though without Gabe, it'll never be the same. I know that somewhere in Puxhill, Simon Peters will be up to his old tricks, getting in trouble and making someone else's life interesting. And sometimes, when I listen to the wind in just the right way, I can still hear Gabriel blowing his horn.

Like a Sister in the Proper Court

By Lisa Hawkridge

Iona ascended gracefully toward the sky a few feet, careful not to cross the protective shield that kept them from human view, which was the main reason she bothered with The Proper Court at all. As a matter of habit, she ran her hand along the edge of the shield, sensing the strength of the magic that made up the shield. When she sensed a weak spot, she concentrated, and lent her own magic to strengthen it. The shield was set up so that magic could be funneled into it from many different faeries, meaning that it only worked because every faerie living within it helped maintain it, making it different from almost every other magic done by the faeries. The only thing like it was the shield protecting The Other Court, which was created for the same reason: No faerie on her own was powerful enough to keep herself completely from human eyes for any length of time, and as humans pressed farther and farther into every part of the world, they were all in danger.

She heard the rustle of another set of wings, and spun slowly to see who it was. She was pretty far out, and in a sparsely occupied area of the outer meadows. She blinked in confusion a few times, hardly believing who she was seeing. There were three groups of Faeries in the Court: Those who pleased The Queen of Light, those who tried to please The Queen, and those who accepted The Queen's authority but stayed out of the Open Court itself and stuck to the outer meadows. Not only was the faerie in front of her, Zeda, part of the second group while Iona was part of the third, but Iona and Zeda had taken a great dislike to each other when they first met, when Iona was petitioning for entrance. Iona fluttered forward a few inches, so she could be sure Zeda could see her.

Zeda clasped her hands in front of her and said, "Don't make me say this twice. I'm here to ask for your help."

Iona opened her mouth to tell Zeda to leave her be, then thought better of it and closed her mouth again. If Zeda, arrogant as she was, needed her help and was admitting it, the least she could do was hear her out. Iona cleared her thoat. "In what capacity?"

Zeda puffed out her chest. "I'm going to attempt a changeling raid." That made some sense. The Queen adored and revered her human servants, and the others followed her example. One of the surest ways to earn

The Queen's good graces was to bring a human child into the fold. "I have some very solid intelligence that tonight is a good night for it."

Iona looked at her and raised one eyebrow. "Why do you need me for that?"

Zeda almost smiled. "Because we're going raiding in Harperville."

Iona's heart-rate skyrocketed and she clenched her fists as she thought about the suburban sprawl that had been built over the glade she'd once called home. She and Phia had lived there for a few years, until hiding from the humans got to be too much, and they sought refuge in the Courts. She was struck by a sudden urge to do something horrible to them despite her place in the Court, and the thought of leaving them without their children filled her with a sort of perverse joy. She swallowed and let out a deep breath. "Alright, I'll be your guide. When do we leave?"

Zeda did smile this time, and said, "Third hour past moonrise tonight. Meet me at the eastward pear tree. Don't be late." With that, she spun around in midair and headed back toward the Open Court.

Iona looked in that direction and sighed. If she was going to go on a changeling raid, she should probably see The Queen. The Open Court was formed in a ring around The Queen's private bower, which was blocked from view by a ring of trees draped with flowering vines. The Throne was set at the Northmost point in the circle, and the human quarters, if such an open space that held no clear separation could be called such, were set up at the southernmost point, although many humans were also to be found attending to the Queen or working by the pear trees, set at the easternmost and westernmost points in the ring respectively, under which faeries congregated to gossip and dine on flowers and nectar prepared by human servants. The western pear tree, peaking over the top of the hedge that marked the border between the court and the meadow, was directly in front of Iona, and beside it, one of the many archways leading into the Open Court.

The sun had yet to set, but the Queen of Light enjoyed holding court in the late afternoon, in defiance of the nocturnal traditions of the Other Court, and was most certainly seated upon her throne at this very moment. If Iona was really to be involved in a changeling raid, the Queen would want to know about it, given the positions humans held in her court. It was by the Queen's benevolence that Iona was allowed to remain in Court at all, and she really couldn't justify withholding the information. Iona sighed and began making her way across first the outer meadow, then the inner meadow, flying low and dragging her feet through the grass. She passed more and more faeries as she drew closer to the court, and even a few humans, gathering flowers. She flitted past them quickly, trying not to draw attention to herself; she had a reputation as an outsider, and didn't do well interacting with the other faeries. She hesitated for a moment, underneath the archway, then rose quickly until she was above most of what was going on, but still within the protective shield. Having gained height, she wove her way along toward the Queen's throne and her explanation.

The throne was a living, growing Birch tree, that extended far above the protective shield of the Court, and the base of which had been shaped by magic, so that there were many crisscrossing protruding roots, which formed perches and steps for any faerie in the Queen's good graces. At the top of the roots, there was an indent in the wood, perfectly shaped so that the Queen could sit there and be above everyone else, with her head just a hairs breath away from the top of the shield, and at the bottom of the roots, several of them lay flat to the ground flush and parallel before dipping below the surface, to form a sort of platform, from which petitions could be delivered. When Iona arrived, the Queen was ensconced on her throne, flanked by her most trusted advisor and consort, Epsilon, one of the handful of faerie males living in the court.

The platform was empty, and Iona alighted on the very edge of it and made sure to speak up and anunciate when she asked, "Might I come forward and speak, Your Majesty?"

The Queen looked at Iona, examining her carefully, and for a moment, Iona was sure the Queen would refuse her, and then be mad because she was not told of the changeling raid. The Queen was silent for a moment, then bent forward to consult Epsilon, and Iona's veins turned to ice. The Queen cleared her throat and said, "Ioma," Epsilon whispered something in her ear, "Iona, please step forward."

Iona did as she was bid, then fell to her knees and said, "Your Majesty, I humbly offer myself in service to you and your Court, which is my Court as well." Once she had spoken, Iona lifted herself off the platform and ascended to the top of the shield. She carefully reached her hand out and pushed a bit of her magic into the shield to increase its strength. "I offer up my Magic for the protection of us all." She then fluttered down and landed in the center of the platform. That ritual or variations thereof were standard procedure when petitioning the Queen, and so it was here by the throne that the protection was at its strongest. Once the formalities were out of the way, Iona began to speak. "Your Majesty, I…that is to say…I was approached by a faerie named Zeda, who…well, suffice it to say that the two of us will be involved in a changeling raid, at the third hour past moonrise tonight."

Having said some semblance of what she came to tell the Queen, Iona fell silent, and waited for the Queen's response.

The Queen was silent for a minute, and Iona's wings tingled with the intensity of her heartbeat. Finally, the

Queen spoke. "I was told of the plan by Zeda earlier, and I understand her motives, given that she is eager to gain my approval. But you, you have not come to court since I granted you protection two cycles of the seasons ago. Changeling raids are not without risks. Why would you undertake this mission?"

Iona bit her lip. She knew that what a faerie said before The Queen could have far reaching consequences. She cleared her throat. "Your Majesty, firstly, I wanted to say that I take the vow of protection I made that day and this one very seriously, and have been constantly strengthening the shield in the outer meadows. Secondly, I know the area the raid is to take place in very well. Knowing this, Zeda requested my assistance, and it was not in my best interest to deny it to her." There was a murmur of understanding among the fairies perched below The Queen. The Court, after all, worked on a system of agreements and obligation. Iona inclined her head and spoke up to be heard over the chatter. "If there is nothing else, Your Majesty, I will take my leave."

The Queen made a sweeping gesture. "Go forth and keep your vow." Iona dropped to her knees again briefly, then fluttered up before pivoting around and leaving the site of the throne as quickly as she could.

She flew so quickly that she barreled into a human without even realizing it. The girl, for Changelings stopped aging before they hit adolescence, fell to the ground and Iona stopped and quickly flew back to hover around the child's knee. The girl slowly sat up. Iona asked, "Are you hurt? Do you need me to heal you?"

The girl sat up and said, "No, I'm quite alright." She stood and dusted off her skirt. "You should be more careful next time.

Iona opened her mouth to admonish the girl, but swallowed her words because the girl was right.

"Perhaps I should." She wasn't sure what to do. She had been staying in the outer meadow to try to avoid the humans, since that was the subject of the argument between herself and Phia and the reason she had chosen this court, although she almost regretted it. She took a moment to study the young girl before her. She had never thought to really look at any of the humans, mostly to avoid painful memories, but this child was interesting. Curious, she asked, "What's your name?"

The girl looked at her quizzically. "My name's Maureen."

Iona noted that it was a very human name, for a resident of The Court. And suddenly, a peculiar thought struck her, "Do you hate The Court? I know it can't be pleasant being a servant, but everyone has to contribute something, and since you have no magic...." She trailed off.

Maureen frowned. "It's not bad really. And I...I owe you everything." Tears started to form in her eyes; she hiccupped.

Iona flitted forward and lay a hand gently on Maureen's cheek. "Why don't you sit down and take a deep breath."

Maureen plopped down and sat cross-legged in the grass. Iona landed lightly and stood in front of her so that they were eye to eye.

Maureen wiped a tear from her cheek and blinked. "I...I was six when they took me. They were going to take the baby next door, but I was there, trying to stay away from my father, and I begged them to take me instead. My mother died when I was born, and my father, he hated me. And I did what I could to please him, but it was never enough, and then he...well he kept forgetting my sister and I existed when he wasn't mad at us, or at least it felt like that. The one thing I miss is my sister." More tears started streaming down her cheeks. "Her name was Wilma."

Iona reached forward and gently wiped the tears away as best she could. "I miss my sister too."

Maureen sniffed. "What was her name?"

Iona looked up at the sky, tinted slightly beneath the shield. "Her name was Phia. She...when we were little, we lived with our father, our mother having left for the...Other Court." She lowered her gaze to Maureen's face. "We stayed, even as the humans came closer and closer, but then...my father was killed by a human hunter, and we both knew then that we would be better off in Court. Only…we argued. She thought humans were inherently evil, and I knew that was… impossible, although later I wasn't so sure." Maureen's eyes widened. "I am now though." Iona hastily added, before continuing. "She, she stormed off to join the Other Court. She always was hot headed. I haven't seen her since, and I never will."

Maureen cocked her head to one side. "The Other Court?"

Iona sighed. "I suppose the best way to explain would be to explain how the Courts were formed. A long time ago, almost a thousand cycles of the seasons, faeries began to be hunted by humans with iron. They had been hunted before that, but it was then that a solution was proposed. The Queen had—has—a sister, and the two of them worked together to gather enough faeries to forge the shield and form the Court. It was only one Court in those days, and The Queen and her sister ruled together, joint Queens of a unified Court. Only… they argued. Over the same thing Phia and I argued over, whether humans could be reasoned with or not. The Queen said they could and she and those who agreed with her brought humans, like you, to Court, and even occasionally granted humans boons, if they offered something in exchange. The Queen's sister and her followers, on the other hand, went out of their ways to play tricks on humans, or offer them deals that they knew would get them into trouble. Eventually, the fighting got so bad that the Court split into our Court, the Proper Court, and the Other Court, ruled by Queen's sister."

Iona looked around them to where other faeries were talking and flitting about. "Every faerie was forced to pick a side, and every faerie since who's been forced to join this Court or the Other Court has had to make the same decision. Nobody has ever crossed between the two, for fear of being branded a traitor in both."

Maureen frowned. "Did you ever consider joining the…Other Court?"

Iona pursed her lips. "Once my head had cooled, and I began to miss my sister, I thought about it, but it was too late, and…I couldn't bring myself to hate humans, not like Phia did."

Maureen narrowed her eyes. "Then why do you bring them here?"

Iona cocked her head to the side. "I thought you said you asked to be taken here?"

Maureen began to fidget with her skirt. "I did, but… my next door neighbor was a very nice woman, if a bit dumb, and she loved her baby very much, and he… he would have been happy. He was happy. And they were just going to take him, and I wondered, but I never asked, because I was so grateful. But why…"

"Because they didn't know," said Iona quickly, cutting her off. "And because he was young enough that he wouldn't miss his mother, or his sister, and because they only take Changelings to please the Queen. And because...horrible things happen to humans outside the Court. You get sick and hurt and have no magic for healing. And even if you don't, you age and die and... we don't let any of that happen to you."

Maureen burst into tear then, and Iona tried to stroke the tears from her cheeks. After a few minutes, Maureen sniffed. "Have you ever taken...." She trailed off.

Iona thought for a moment, wondering how much to tell, but ended up saying, "No, but tonight...tonight will be my first."

Maureen's eyes grew wide. She held out her hand and made a fist with all her fingers except her smallest. "I want you to promise me you won't take a baby who someone wants. There are babies and children that parents hate. Take one of them. Promise me."

Iona dropped to her knees and put her hand over her heart. "I vow to you that I will find a child that is unwanted, and bring him to the Queen, who wants him."

Maureen nodded. "Thank you." She stood up, yawned, and began walking toward the human quarters. "There are plenty of humans around to serve. I'm going to take a nap." Iona rose up to hover right around her shoulder and followed. She watched Maureen lay down on one of the patches of extra thick flowers grown for the humans benefit and decided that a nap might be in order for herself as well. The sun was just setting, after all, and there were hours left until their departure.

When she awoke the moon had risen and Zeda was hovering a few feet above the lily in which she had curled up. Iona blinked and shot up a few feet in the air before settling down to hover right next the other faerie. "You startled me."

Zeda shrugged. "I heard you went to see the Queen."

Iona sighed. "Would you withhold information from the Queen?"

Zeda pursed her lips. "We leave in one hour." With that, she spun around and flew off, leaving Iona to perch on the edge of one of the lily petals and think.

After a few minutes she gave a few flaps of her wings and headed back across the outer and inner Meadows to the hedge. Rather than go through the archway, as was typical, she decided to fly along the top of the hedge, looking in at all the activity under the western pear tree. Not looking to go by the Throne again, Iona headed toward the human quarters, hovered just long enough to notice that Maureen had woken up, and then continued to fly along the top of the hedge, keeping low to avoid flying outside the shield, until she came to the western pear tree, a tree grown to be short and wide, reaching barely over the hedge at its tallest point.

To avoid running into a branch, Iona ducked, only to end up inside the hedge itself, under the top layer of evergreen leaves. She was about to extricate herself when she heard voices coming from down below. One of them said, "Okay, why in the name of the Queen did you ask that crazy faerie Iona to help you?"

Curious as to who was talking about her, Iona ceased her efforts and listened. The voice that answered, as she was half expecting, was Zeda's. "She knows the area, and she has reason to want to cause trouble among the humans there. The raid will be successful."

Whoever Zeda was talking to sighed. "Oh I'm sure it will be. But she has a sister in the Other Court."

Zeda gasped. "What?"

"So I've heard." The other voice said then continued smugly, "And Delta saw her make a vow to a human."

"How does that?" Zeda asked, sounding almost disgusted, and Iona swallowed.

"I don't think you should go near her," said the other voice.

Then it was Zeda who sighed. "It doesn't matter. I asked her for help, she agreed. I can't back out now. Besides, once this raid is over, it's unlikely that she'll ask for my help for a long time yet. She stays away from... pretty much everything."

"Why are you even going on this changeling raid anyway?" The other voice asked.

"The Queen wants more humans," Zeda said, as if

it were the most obvious thing in the world. "She will be pleased if I bring her one."

"For a little while," replied the other faerie. "Anyway, I need to get back to the throne."

"Wait, Gamma, let me come with you." said Zeda.

"Well hurry up," said the other voice, who Iona now knew belonged to Epsilon's sister Gamma.

Neither of the two said anything for two minutes, and when Iona was sure the two of them were gone, she began working herself free. Although originally unintentional, it would not do for Gamma and Zeda to know she had been eavesdropping. When she finally managed to work herself free, Iona flew down, and approached the pear tree from the inside of the hedge. When she finally came to the trunk, she sat down with her back against it and waited.

Soon enough, Zeda came, flying from the direction of court with a small smile on her face. She had changed, and instead of wearing the delicate gown made out of bluebell blossoms she had been wearing earlier, of the type favored by those in the thick of The Court, she was wearing a simple dress made of fused leaves, similar to the dress Iona herself was wearing. Iona jumped up and gave a few flaps of her wings to keep herself in the air. Zeda said, "You're early."

Iona shrugged. "So are you. Do you want to leave now?"

Zeda considered it. "Alright." She slowly began to

rise, easing her way toward the shield. Iona followed suite, keeping pace exactly with the other faerie. Zeda paused when they reached the shield and gestured to Iona. "Go on."

Iona took a deep breath and flapped her wings. The Shield was cool to the touch and spread a tingly sensation all across her body. Her wings started to feel stiff and hard to move but she kept going and then her wings were fully above the shield and she kept rising and with a slight tingling tug at her ankles, she was out. She took a deep breath in as Zeda followed her through the shield. Even the air outside smelled like danger, like bullets with iron alloys; it wasn't soft and heavy, but quick and light like the flashing blade of a knife. Zeda finally came through. Iona turned to her and asked, "Well?"

Zeda took a deep breath and blinked. "You go first. You're the one who knows the way."

Iona nodded and looked around. She did indeed know where the Court was in comparison to the place that had been her home, and she was sure she could find her way back there tonight. After glancing up at the stars to make sure to her position, she headed off to the south. She looked over her shoulder once, to make sure Zeda was following, and didn't look back again.

Perhaps because of the very nature of the air, full of danger as it seemed, or perhaps because they merely had nothing to say to each other, the two faeries remained silent through the entire trip, as they crossed highways, and strip malls and small patches of forest. Iona let the way: half by the stars and half by instinct.

Harperville was not the town that Iona remembered being built, although it was a bit of a blur of pain and anguish after her father died. She certainly didn't remember there being rows and rows of square homes made of iron here. She stopped at the edge, hesitant to go any further. There was a huge bonfire that was lit, and human males were gathered around it, laughing and drinking. Zeda stopped next to her, and the two of them looked around. Zeda cleared her throat. "Bonfires are always known about, and this should mean there are some unattended children somewhere."

Suddenly, there was a wailing, and the two of them looked for the source. About ten houses away from the fire, a woman was sitting on a chair in front of her rectangle. About a hundred feet away from her was a bassinet, or some twisted modern equivalent thereof. The woman heard the baby screaming and said, "Oh shut up would you?" with such casual malice, that Iona knew that this was the child they would take. Before Zeda could stop her, Iona darted forward and put a silencing spell over the child. The human woman snorted and turned her attention back to the spectacle the males were making of themselves.

Zeda hurriedly caught up with Iona and snapped, "What the hell were you thinking?"

Iona jerked her head toward the woman. "She

won't notice her child missing and raise a fuss."

Zeda pursed her lips. "Fine." She cast an invisibility spell over the infant, and grabbed his arm. "Help me carry him." Iona moved forward to grab his other arm, and that's when she noticed a young girl, no more than five of six years, perched on the steps of the house, staring with wide-eyed horror at the place where, from her perspective, her little brother had just vanished. Zeda snapped, "Hey," and Iona took up the baby's arms and lifted him into the air.

The two of them flew back they way they had come, again silently. When they came to the tree that marked The Court, the two faeries slowly sank down, lowering the child feet first through the shield, using a spell to take away the usual effects it had on humans. And in the reflection that the sparks of magic made on the outer surface of the shield, Iona saw the wide-eyed horror of a sister left behind.

Gnome Games

By Saera Corvin

The blaring of the alarm pierced through the membrane of drowsiness that threatened to roll Esther into the comfort of sleep. She jolted out of her trance, too disoriented to remember where she was in those few seconds, and cracked her forehead painfully against the edge of the folding table.

"Son of a bi–" she cried, her mind catching the curse as it left her mouth and transforming it into something more appropriate for the daughter of a Lutheran minister; she wasn't even aware she did it: "–scuit! Biscuit, biscuit, biscuit!"

Esther rubbed the dull red line forming over her eyebrows, the area all the more painful where it had struck a cluster of angry pimples that had been choosing that particular site for forming since pubescence. Despite the dull throb announcing the headache to come, she snatched her phone from the floor next to her, scraping her fingernails against the concrete in her haste and cracking a nail in the process. She drew breath in a painful hiss and a small whimper escaped her lips. Although she'd never thought much of girls who were overly preoccupied with breaking nails she had to admit that it really *hurt*.

She sucked at the bleeding middle finger as she flipped her phone open and shut the alarm off. It was now 11:32, a fact Esther noted with disgust as she closed her phone with a soft click and settled back against the cinderblock wall. Half an hour to midnight and she'd dozed off only fifteen minutes after taking up her post!

From the floor above Esther could hear the constant beat of her roommate's new favorite band seeping through the walls, and every once in a while she could pick out a few words sung in the driving voice of Lizzy Hale, punctuated occasionally by a separate female voice. Josie thought the loud music masked her nightly mating rituals, but it ultimately only added more noise to the symphony. Usually this was a great source of annoyance for Esther, but tonight she didn't mind too much. It actually kind of helped. More resolved than ever, she leaned back and fixed her stony gaze on the ancient Sears Kenmore dryer across the room.

When Esther first realized that someone was stealing her underwear, she'd been very frightened. The first thought that came to mind painted a grainy, film noir style picture of a beady eyed pervert creeping around the small two-bedroom home she and Josie rented.

When she finally voiced her fears, Josie had laughed.

"C'mon, Essie! If someone was going to steal anyone's panties, don't you think mine would've gone missing, too?"

"Well, how do you know yours aren't gone?" Esther challenged. "Or what if he's not stealing them, just sniffing them, or fondling them, or, or…."

"Esthie-pestie, you're such a little spaz," Josie crooned. "Think about it; if someone were breaking in and stealing underwear, why would they want yours? You wear cotton grannie panties, for Chissakes! Perverts want *sexy* things."

Esther had to admit that Josie had a point, but she was still unwilling to let it go. It scared her to think that someone might be in their home while they were sleeping (or at least while Esther was sleeping). "I think we should report it to the cops."

"Don't you *dare!*" Josie warned, her good humor gone. A malicious sparkle lit her eyes like demon's fire. "They might want to go through the house, and I got stuff in here, understand?"

Esther nodded; she knew about the pot.

"Besides," Josie went on, "we don't really know for sure if anyone's been in here. If it keeps happening we'll talk about it then, but really Essie, I think you're just being a dumbass about all this."

Esther had been cowed by her metal studded roommate before, but that wicked gleam never faded, and it told Esther that if she called the cops she would be very, very sorry for it. She believed that Josie could very well make her sorry, too.

So, Esther had kept her mouth shut, Josie had not said another word about it, and underwear kept disappearing. Although cotton panties were much cheaper than the lacy postage stamp sized thongs Josie wore, it was beginning to add up when she had to buy a new package of underwear twice a week, plus the extra cost of laundry detergent needed to wash her new purchases. She thought about suggesting they call the cops again and again, but every time Esther thought about that look in Josie's heavily mascara lined eyes she held her tongue back. No matter what she said Josie would never believe her unless she could actually prove there was someone sneaking into their laundry room, and there was no way to do that unless she could find a way to show her hard evidence....

And like a set of headlights popping out of the fog, a brilliant idea presented itself. Esther's grandfather, an avid hunter and trapper, had bored her on several occasions with still pictures of deer taken from the wooded acres behind his house where he'd set up feeding stations. These images, he'd explained with an excitement his granddaughter could not reciprocate, were taken with a trail camera that snapped a series of pictures when it detected motion. Esther had been nervous about asking, but as it turned out Gramps was only too happy to lend her one of his old cameras, and in three days Esther had the pictures she needed to prove that someone really was stealing her underwear.

The only problem was that she would never show Josie the images captured in the laundry room on January 13th at 11:57 p.m. No one besides her would ever see the stills because after reviewing them several times to make sure she wasn't simply seeing things, Esther deleted them.

The trail cam had revealed the culprit to be a little man no taller than three feet with a tight pot belly protruding over a gaudy belt buckle. A bulbous, crooked nose hung low over thick lips framed by an untamed mass of hair. The pudgy little face leering over a pile of Josie's unwashed clothes gave off the impression of being incapable of any emotion besides malevolent mischief. Though she could not distinguish color in the digital images, Esther could see that his clothing was pieced together from various undergarments, and a pair of white boxers with heart shaped patterns sat perched on his shaggy head like a hat.

It looked like a hideous little lawn gnome, and that's exactly what she decided it was. A *gnome* had been stealing her underwear this whole time and making *clothes* out of them! Esther clicked through a fantasy world saturated in hues of ethereal bluish green, trying to insist that she had it wrong, that it was a joke, a horrible joke! The images showed the little man rifling through the dryer and pulling out chunks of cloth that she knew to be underwear, and then briefly inspect them before tossing them into a small sack. A joke, it had to be a joke!

But it wasn't. Even if Josie had known about the camera, how could she have pulled off an elaborate prank like this in such a short amount of time? She supposed it could be done, but Josie had spent the entire weekend with her boyfriend. There was no way it could have been her.

Unreality left Esther dazed in front of the computer, and she began to giggle. The giggles turned to wild, mad wrenching laughter and then melted into tears. She sat like that for what could have been hours or minutes, her mood alternating until she was not even sure if she was laughing or crying anymore. She thought absurdly that if this was what it was like to go crazy that there were probably worse ways to go.

After a while, she began to come back to herself, though periodically something would strike her as funny and off she would go into the wonderful land of madness again. And to think she had almost called the police! It occurred to her that not a soul could know about this, and suddenly Esther felt very alone and frightened. If there had been someone to tell, would they have believed her anyway? Of course not.

When her composure returned, Esther tried to deliberate the situation rationally. She finally came to the conclusion that, for the sake of argument at least, if she could accept the existence of a faceless omnipotent being like God, perhaps she could also accept the existence of gnomes. It seemed almost blasphemous to compare the two, but she had to find some rocky bottom of sanity to anchor her poor brain to. After all, she reasoned, the two weren't really *that* different when you thought about it.

Having tentatively accepted the possibility of the gnome's existence, she turned to the tangible problem at hand—her underwear. She weighed her options carefully. She could not simply guard her laundry and lock her room at night, because if the little man could break into the basement, then he could probably break into her room, too. The thought of the gnome lurking around her dark bedroom while she slept raised goose flesh over her arms, and she trashed the idea. She *could* go commando like Josie did most of the time, but the very thought of doing so went against the grain of her upbringing. No dice on that one, either.

There was only one answer: Esther had to confront the situation. Confrontation also went against her grain and made her stomach curl, but it seemed like the only good solution. After some debate, she had decided on a note. Her father had told her once that a note was the most polite and reasonable way of reaching someone with whom she might find herself in a conflict with. Yes, a note would do very nicely. It was very reasonable, very adult-like. There was no need to get emotional over this.

That night Esther sat hunched over a yellow note pad and wrote:

Dear Sir– I know you have been taking my underwear. I would like to ask that you please stop doing this. I am not a rich girl, and the thefts are beginning to show a toll on my finances. Though I do not know why you would want my under garments, I would be willing to compromise if you are unwilling to stop completely: you may take ONE garment per month. –Sincerely Yours,

Esther Larson

Esther paused with the pen clicking against her teeth, and a malicious glee that felt alien and extremely pleasing tickled the underside of her ribs as she added:

P.S.– My roommate has many undergarments much nicer than mine. Perhaps you could take a few of hers? I do not think she would miss them.

She felt a bit guilty when she placed the note in the dryer. It wasn't very Christian to do such a mean thing to Josie, but it was technically the truth; Josie had twice as many panties as she did, and they *were* nicer than hers. Besides, if Josie never wanted to do her own laundry it was her own fault.

Two days later, there had been a response scribbled

onto the back of her note. A wave of faintness nearly made her swoon. The sloppy handwriting confirmed what up until that moment Esther was still willing to believe was some kind of hoax. After taking a little time to recover from the shock, she read the response the little man had left for her:

Dear prune faced troll- Go find a bridge and take a dive! Do you really think I want your slut friend's butt-floss? I can't clothe my children in those things! Listen, troll, you're the only one around here that wears real cloth since the old hag on Beecher Street kicked the bucket a few months ago, so get used to it! I'll take what I want, when I want, and if you don't like it you can come down here and suck my hairy turnip!

By the time she'd finished reading the note a second time Esther's hands were shaking so badly that she had to set it down before she tore it to pieces. Never had she known such humiliation, such anger! Josie tormented her as often as she could, that was one thing, but this...this....

Her father's calm voice told her that anger was never the solution: "Retribution is the child of anger, and anger is not His way. Always follow His way, Esther."

Yes, His way. Esther felt her nerves begin to calm. She had been insulted and snubbed, but she did not have to ignore it. There was something else she could do. A note had not worked because it was not direct enough. She decided that she had to handle this in person, and as she sat on the cold floor that night after finding the note, listening to her roommate screw her latest fling upstairs, she imagined the satisfaction she would taste when the little man appeared. It would taste like communion wine—sweet and cheap.

She took the note from her pocket and read it over and over, letting herself feel just the tiniest bit of anger to build confidence over the foundation of cowardice that usually ruled her. Esther told herself she felt sure, she felt strong, and she tried to push away that little pest whispering in her ear that she would inevitably fold, just as she had always folded when she tried to stand up for herself in even the most trivial situations of injustice—like trying to get Josie to do her own damned laundry. But, as familiar as she was with her failures, Esther remained intent this time that she would succeed.

She watched and she waited.

Time was a sloth, pulling midnight along with the painfully slow speed well known by those who wish to thwart sleep. Esther's eyelids became heavy drops of syrup trying desperately to ooze shut. She pulled her fist in a death grip around the note and willed her eyes to remain open. Soon…he would come soon….

But he didn't come soon enough, and when Esther jerked awake the laundry room was too bright, and the small storm window above the washing machine was lit with the glow of a gray morning. She groaned in harmony with every stiff muscle, flinching as she relaxed. She had spent the entire night on the laundry room floor, gotten a thudding headache and a nasty bump on her head, a sore bleeding finger, and all so she could fall asleep here instead of in her bed. He probably hadn't even—.

And then she saw the hump looming up from the floor in front of the dryer. Her jaw dropped, and all pain was forgotten.

The gnome had come after all, and he had left her a little present in the form of a giant middle finger sculpted from the tattered remains of the clothes she had left in the dryer. Her shocked gaze traveled upwards from the floor, tracing along the erect rainbow contours almost a foot wide and reaching three feet towards the ceiling. Although it was nothing but an inanimate creation, it seemed to be leering at her of its own volition, as if the gnome's contempt alone had given it life. The strong reek of Mountain Breeze stung her nostrils, and she realized that in order to achieve the fine detail of the large raised finger and the two folded digits flanking it he had soaked the rags in detergent. *'He even gave it a nail,'* she thought in dazed wonder and then burst into weary tears.

What had she been thinking? There was no reasoning with this creature. He was foul, he was disgusting, and he had *won!* Esther knew she would have to move, and even then she wondered if the little devil would follow her if only to torment her further. Yes, most definitely he would follow her, follow her right up to her dying day, and then he'd dance all over her grave, maybe mold a big cock out of the dirt they would throw over her coffin....

Her father's voice tried to break in, tried to calm her, but Esther slammed the door and locked the deadbolt on it.

Do unto others, huh? *Bull*-shit!

Follow His way, her father said. And just what was His way? Mercy and compassion? Had it been compassion that drove Him to bring Sodom and Gomorrah to ruin, or mercy that sent the flood waters to swallow the sinners? It had been anger, the black mother of retribution, and *that* had always been His way. She had been a fool to let herself think otherwise. She had been a fool her entire life.

"*Retribution is the child of anger....*" Oh, she had anger alright, and if only she could think of a fitting retribution, to make the gnome pay, make him *hurt* as she hurt, if she could only do something....

But couldn't she? A cold wave of sweet serenity blanketed her boiling rage, not containing it but controlling it in a much more useful direction. The tears slowly faded, and eventually Esther began to smile gently, her honey colored eyes sparkling and dancing. If Josie had walked into the basement just then, it would have been her turn to be afraid.

* * *

"What are you so happy about?" Josie asked when Esther walked through the door that afternoon, stomping fresh sheets of snow from her boots. In the two years they'd been rooming together, Josie didn't think she'd ever seen the other woman smile fully. "Does Esthie-pestie finally have a date?"

Esther set down the brown paper bag she'd carried in with her as she shrugged off her heavy coat and began peeling away the rest of her winter gear. The smile didn't fade in the face of the teasing, but widened. "Yeah, you could say that."

Josie wasn't sure she really cared for that smile. There was something about it that made her uncomfortable, but then again Esther always was kind of a putz. She settled back onto the sofa with her copy of *Rolling Stone* and went back to flipping through the pages.

"Well, whatever. Just don't keep me up if you decide to let him bust your cherry—whoops! Sorry, didn't mean to offend your Jesus freak purity." She smirked and gazed over the top of the magazine to enjoy the blush that would be creeping up Esther's neck only to find that she was still grinning fit to split. Disappointed and a bit unsettled that her insult didn't have the desired result, Josie went back to her magazine. She ignored her roommate as she opened the door and went into the laundry room.

* * *

Josie didn't bother to ask what was in the bag. Esther knew she wouldn't.

It only took Esther fifteen minutes to get everything ready for that night. She hummed a Linkin Park song under breath as she piled clothes into the dryer, careful to keep the underwear at the bottom. Her voice was an odd but lovely contrast to the drabness of her mundane features. Esther was really beginning to enjoy rock music. Maybe Josie could lend her a few of her CDs... Ah, yes, Josie; she had plans for Josie, too. Still humming dreamily, Esther placed the pièce de résistance on top of the pile of clothes:

You win. Take whatever you want.

The evening went by like a delightful dream. Josie went out for the night, leaving the house drenched in silence. Esther hummed as she lay in bed waiting. She had no problem staying awake that night and when the hollow metallic snap of the trap finally came she did not feel the slightest bit drowsy. She smiled at the sweet song of pain echoing from the basement. Gramps had set the Connabear trap with extra weight for her—enough he'd said to take fingers clean off. Esther hoped the little bastard lost his whole hand.

SNAP! There went the second trap. This time the

gnome didn't howl; he shrieked like a demon from Hell.

"Fuck me?" Esther said sweetly as she closed her eyes. "No, little buddy—fuck *you*."

The Goat Man's Garden

By Marten Hoyle

For well over a century, the family of the Goat Man had received a trophy in the yearly competition for having the most beautiful garden in the town, and on the day when all of this began, the last of the proud family sat piping away at his flute one day to sooth and please his greatest friend, the centaur Orion.

While his friend played, Orion gazed as he always did in wonder at how alive his companion's garden appeared. Everything sparkled with an ethereal, almost divine glow. The humming birds drank themselves to intoxication in the Erich's shimmering roses, the bees sang hearty songs amid the flamboyant tulips and butterflies wished their wings could be half as beautiful as the petals of the daisies. Worms did not eat the crimson apples, but stood still, admiring the perfection of every fruit. Lightning bolt veins of ivy embraced the walls and the cold stone rejoiced for every brick felt the joy of the vines. The weeping willows shed tears of laughter into the little stream where petals of flamingo and onyx swam over the heads of fish who knew well how all the other fish and brooks of the world envied them, for they lived in the Goat Man's garden where all the leaves danced to his song.

When Erich ceased playing to gather his breath, Orion said (as he said every day), "My how beautiful your garden is!"

This was the one thing which stood between the hearts of these loyal friends. Every year, Erich took first place in the competition while the centaur took second. Day and night in his home, Orion looked upon row after row of second place trophies. He did not hate his friend, but oh! He envied him! Every time he sat on the patio admiring the flora, he asked, "O! My darling companion, what is your secret?"

"That," the Goat Man always said, "I shall never tell."

And he resumed his playing until Orion quite forgot the enquiry, lost in melodies as sweet as the peaches Erich grew and shared with all the village along with his homemade bread, butter, and cream. The glowing milk his cows produced surpassed the flavor of all others, for they ate well of the emerald grass and golden hay of his—some might say "magical"—stock and store.

That day, however, was the day before the day before the announcement of the year's winner, and when Goat Man played, Orion for the first time did not become sleepy and did not lose the question in the pleasure of the song. He knew well that his friend cared for the garden only at night when the garden was most gorgeous, for the moon seemed always to be full when it smiled on the house. So, Orion decided that the following day, he would watch his friend from dawn until dusk and at last discover the secret. The following year, he told himself, he would have a garden ten times as brilliant as the fawn's. He might take second this year, but next year! Next year he would win!

* * *

The following night, Orion entered the regal Hall of the Elders. He was most distraught and could not form his sentences properly. The only intelligible words he uttered were, "I saw it! I saw it with my own eyes!"

At length the thirteen Elders managed to calm the centaur. By their order, guards poured glasses of the deep forest mead and ordered Orion to drink. When at last his nerves settled into the warmth of the liquor, he sat before the elders and confessed to following Erich the Goat Man throughout the day in hopes of learning how to make his garden the best in the village.

"In the morning," he said, "I watched Erich gather his flute and several articles in a large bag. I thought this rather queer, so I crept along at a safe distance as he walked not through but around the village. I figured I would at last learn his secret! So, I kept following (again, at a safe distance) and soon found myself standing in the grasses on the border of the Starlight Forest."

"The Starlight Forest?" asked the one who sat at the centre of the great table. This hybrid was the Elder of the Elders, a Seker named Piktas.

"Are you sure, Orion?" he said.

Even in the full, golden glare of the daylight hours, the sky above the pine, ash, willow, and redwood slept in perpetual moonshine, and stars formed constellations of all life forms outside its winding paths and silver streams, clusters of nova which do not exist in the night sky outside the forest's borders. What made Orion pause was the law as Piktas now reminded him:

"No village dweller may enter the Starlight Forest unless the time has come to bid farewell to the dead."

"But he did!" Orion insisted.

"So," said Piktas, regarding his fellow elders, "The fawn entered with a sack over one shoulder, but brought no dying relation with him." He turned his attention to Orion. "Is that what you are saying?"

"Yes."

"And you dared to enter as well?"

"I hesitated!" Orion said. "I wasn't going to. But when he disappeared into the night, I galloped after him. I wanted to tell him to come home! So I ran after him and slackened my pace when I found him again. He was taking the path to the lake!"

"To the home of the fairies?" said Piktas. "Or, I

should say, the forbidden home of the fairies."

"I followed him to the lake," the centaur confessed.

"What did he do?" Piktas said.

"He," the Centaur began and suddenly, under the pale eyes of the Seker, regretted coming here. Nobody in the village knew much of anything about the bird-man. He was very old, wise, and (though none would say so out loud) cruel. When laws were broken, their penalty was usually something simple—such as being placed in a private chamber overnight. The worst penalty was said to be banishment. But (again, though nobody would say so out loud) the truth was that the worst penalty was to have one's fate in Piktas's hands. Fear prevented most of the villagers from breaking any laws because it was unlikely that Piktas would show any semblance of mercy.

"He sat watching the fairies," said Orion.

"That is not all he did," said Piktas. "You came here for a reason. Tell me what he did."

For a moment, the centaur thought of running from the hall, to Erich's house and telling him to run, run far away from the village. But when he looked over his shoulder, he saw that not one, but two trolls stood in his way, their grey husks coated in the scars left by whips, their eyes empty of all emotion, of mercy, and their hands wielding black truncheons.

"Say what you saw," Piktas demanded. "And do not lie. We will know if you are lying."

"I," the centaur began. "I thought of approaching and asking what he meant by entering the wood. I was going to tell him to return to the village with me and promise never to tell a soul I saw him go there.

"But then, he brought the flute to his lips and piped a song I never heard him play before. It was the sweetest nectar! My ears drank deeply of it and so too did the fairies. Together, we (the fairies and I) became drowsy, for we danced both frantic and merrily to every note. Under his brilliant notes, some high as the heavens and some as low as my spirit every time my garden has lost to his, the stars seemed to shine brighter, the man in the moon grinned and (I swear to you) I saw his eyes grow heavy with sleep. But the spell broke from me when I saw several of the fairies approach Erich! I became afraid."

In those days, the dead were not buried. No, when mothers, fathers, children, and friends neared death's door they were brought to the fairies and sent floating, prostrate, to the heart of the lake. The fairies descended upon them and with little pearly fangs bit into the breast of the nearly departed. From failing lungs, the sprites inhaled deeply of the last breath, of blood and precious fluids of the body; of the essence and the mind, leaving only a shriveled, drained hulk behind to sink down, down to the cemetery below. When the fairies approached Erich, Orion feared they would suck the breath from his instrument and that his friend would die before his eyes.

"But I did not go to his aid, for I saw that the fairies

left the air to sit on the grass at his feet. And then, the light faded from their wings, and they each drifted into slumber.

"I wished at that moment to reveal myself and applaud. I believed he had only recently composed this song and wished to congratulate him on such a crowning achievement.

"Before I could do this, Erich laid his flue aside and took from the bag a tremendous silver pale. This he set at his side closest to me so that I could see perfectly the instrument he brought out of the container. I watched speechless and suddenly rooted to the spot as he lifted one of the slumbering creatures, took its head in his grasp between his thumb and forefinger, and break its little neck. It was only a slight, popping sound barely audible over the small ringing of the water as ripples bust from under fallen leaves. With the tool taken from the pale, he then carved the wings from the dead thing's back. He did not flinch as the gore spurted from the lacerations. He laughed! A cacophonous utterance which pained me to hear as he cast the cadaver into the lake. After this, he took up another and repeated the process."

"Disgraceful!" one elder cried.

"A law has been broken!" another said.

"By a heathen!"

It was from the final breath and substance of mortality that the wings sparkled with the divine light which maintained the balance of the Starlight Forest, preserving it in this dimension under a night sky which praised all life forms with the faraway flames of the cosmos. To kill them was to kill the forest. For this the penalty was exile.

Mortified though he was, the centaur followed the fawn to his home, hoping for an explanation to this blasphemy. He watched from the window which overlooked the patio where he sat many a day dreaming under the songs of the Goat Man and witnessed all the lovely wings ground into a fine, glittering powder. From the other side of Erich's gate before Orion ran for the hall of the elders, he watched as handful-by-handful, the fawn sprinkled his garden with the magic of the sacred forest.

Upon learning this, all save one of the elders burst into anger and commotion.

"Heathen!" they cried. "Murderer! Cheat! False!" and a thousand other things, sometimes raising in curses, sometimes muttering methods for exposing the fawn, and when the idea that banishment was not enough came about, they thought of execution.

"No!" Orion cried. "Please! Please don't hurt him!"

"Why?" one elder, a dwarf, asked.

"Because," Orion didn't need to think about it, "I love him. He's my friend."

Of all the elders, Piktas remained silent. Deep in thought, running his humanoid fingers up and down the sharp curve of his beak, he eyed the centaur.

"And you believe he feels the same way?" the troll said.

"I know he does," said Orion.

This seemed answer enough for all but one of the Elders.

"So," said one, a serpent maiden. "If we banish Erich, would you follow him?"

"Yes," said Orion.

The serpent smiled. "Your love touches my heart."

"Do you think he would do the same for you?" Piktas said.

"I—."

"Then why," Piktas continued, "would he not share his secret with you? Look at yourself, centaur! You grow old. We all grow old. Yet he and his garden remain young and full of life. Full of the lives the fairies drink."

With this, Piktas made some private decision, rose from his seat, took his gavel in hand, and struck the gong before him.

When all was quiet, he said, "My friends. We have much to discuss this night. Tomorrow is the day we announce this year's winner for 'best garden.' We have learned that the family who has earned gold for over a hundred years has done so through methods of a most vile nature which this disgusting bloodline has deemed a "secret." Thanks to our friend before us, we have discovered this secret. We know a law has been broken, and the breaker of that law must be punished.

However, while you spoke just now, an idea came to my mind."

"What is that?" they asked.

Casting his gaze on Orion, Piktas said, "Young centaur! Go now and rest."

Orion rose and turned toward the door.

"No, no, no!" Piktas said and shouted, "Guards! Show Orion to our private chamber. Do not be alarmed!" he said when Orion turned his head and looked in fear upon the elder as men in armor of shimmering silver approached him, each bearing a spear and with a sword at his side.

"You are our witness," Piktas explained. "We will need you here. Goodnight, Orion. I will see you in the morning."

* * *

That night, alone, Piktas gathered the guards and what he called his "personal assistants," the trolls in the Hall of Elders.

"The End," he said, "rises with the dawn. The people must be warned."

"What will the Elders do?" someone asked.

"The others, you mean?" Piktas said. "They cannot be trusted. It is they who wish to bring those beasts out from the wood. They must be stopped."

It required no persuasion. Like his father before him, Piktas held the soldiers of the village under his power.

They guarded him and believed his words when he told them night after night that a day would come when the twelve others must die.

"On this night," Piktas told them, "they have learned the secret of the Goat Man's family. They will use this secret to bring the Soaring Feast. There is only one punishment for such a crime. They must be dragged from their beds and fed to the very horror they would unleash upon us!"

With the dawn approaching, Orion remained much in the same position as when he entered the private chamber. Grey, naked, and cold, the room seemed to swallow him whole, the warmth within him snuffed out by the cadaverous breath of this cell. Shortly after his arrival, a guard arrived with a cup for him to drink. Sniffing the amber liquid, Orion determined it to be more of the forest mead.

"I think I've drank enough," he said.

"Please drink it," said the guard. "I'll get into trouble if you don't."

So, the centaur drank. But before he could swallow the last sip, his vision blurred. All about it, the bricks took on the quality of a painting ruined by water, melting from a canvas of darkness. Sleep filled his head, making his skull heavy, far too dense for his shoulders. He slumped downward, saw the floor peel away as a curtain from a stage. Blackness here, blackness there, blackness inside. When he woke, he found the sky through the bars of the only window grow pale as the sun approached. He rose and found he could not move far. His hooves stamped, and he tried to walk, but round each ankle the guards fastened a cuff attached to chains fixed in the wall.

"Oh, Erich!" he groaned. "What have I done? What are they going to do to you?"

When the chains denied him so much as a single step forward, he raised his arms and reached for the window. If he could just grasp the bars and look outside—he didn't know how it would happen, but in his mind, he imagined this simple act might be instrumental in rescuing Erich from the decree of the elders. In his head, he heard Piktas saying, "Do not be alarmed!" which told him "Be alarmed! Be very alarmed!"

"Oh Erich!" he cried. "I'm so sorry!"

From behind him, he heard the latch snap, and the door creek open.

"You're awake," a voice said.

"Who are you?" he asked.

Circling round his tremendous form, a guard presented himself to Orion's gaze. From behind, the centaur heard two others enter. Each held truncheons of a form smaller but similar to that of the trolls above.

"I'm very sorry," the first guard said and raised his weapon.

Orion closed his eyes and waited for the first shock.

"Erich," he thought. "What are they going to do to you?"

* * *

Erich loved nothing more than to greet the new day. He sat on his patio with a steaming cup of his morning brew in his hands and his flute on the table beside him. He took inspiration from the mist hovering so delicately above the ground as the distance paleness brightened to crimson and gold. With eyes closed, he listened to the birds singing their salutations as they woke from their nests, the song of every fresh ripple in the water as the fish stirred beneath. All the night long, after sprinkling the garden, he had sat with his flute and composed a new song, one he hoped he might not have to play. But when the gate creaked open and he did not hear the familiar clip-clip-clip of Orion's hooves, he knew he must perform today. Opening his eyes, he saw dressed all in black, leaning on a cane with one hand while tipping his hat with the other, the very elder he knew would come.

"Good morning," said the elder.

"Good morning," Erich returned and lied, "I know you, but I'm afraid I have forgotten your name."

"Perhaps that is a good thing," clicked the elder's beak. "Only law breakers remember my name. It is Piktas."

"Ah, yes!" said Erich, pretending to be surprised. "The Elder of our Elders."

"That is correct," Piktas returned his hat over the fading feathers of his crown.

"And what brings you here this morning?" Erich said.

"Well," said Piktas. "I'm afraid I have been very busy. Or, rather, my servants have been busy all night long. It seems we shall have to postpone the day's ceremony. There is a bulletin on every door."

"Not on mine," said Erich.

"No," Piktas said. "I thought you deserved a more personal touch. I have heard much of your garden over the years, though I have never seen it with my own eyes. I have approved every first place trophy for you, but I never delivered one. I thought today, I might see it, meet you and—If you are not busy—invite you to play a song for me."

Setting his cup aside, Erich took his instrument and brought it to his lips, but Piktas raised a hand to stop him.

"Not here!" he said. "No. I say 'if you are not busy' because I wish for you to take a walk with me. And then play."

"Well," said Erich. "Since the ceremony has been cancelled—."

"Postponed," Piktas corrected.

"Postponed," Erich echoed, "I should think I am quite the opposite of busy. Yes. I will walk with you."

He rose and in swift, great strides came eye-to-eye with the hawk who looked upward. They stood beneath one of Erich's apple trees.

"Do you mind?" Piktas reached for the nearest fruit. "I have not eaten."

"By all means," said Erich.

Piktas plucked the apple and with one great crunch bit down and swallowed the whole thing.

"Delectable!" he said. "They taste even better now than when I was a lad. Long before you were born. I wonder—," he said, offering his arm for Erich and leading the way out into the road of cobblestone. "Whatever happened to your father?"

"He died of course," Erich said.

"Yes," Piktas said. "But he seemed so very young, did he not? Even when I came of age and took my father's place in the Hall of Elders, he looked hardly a day over...well, whatever age he was when I first saw him, nearly fifty years before that. And you. How long has it been now? Twenty-five years? You don't look a day older than the day you carried your father to the woods."

"My grandfather was the same way," said Erich. "We like to say we age well in this family."

At his side, the hawk cawed in laughter.

"That you do," he said. "That you do. Come! I am old. See! My feathers fall from my face at the slightest touch! But let us walk quickly! I am eager to hear you play."

Of course, Erich knew precisely where they were

going. He could tell by the red marks painted on every door. These marks did not say the ceremony was postponed. They meant the village was in danger. And the villagers feared only one thing: the Soaring Feast, the hunger of the fairies which Erich and his father, and his father before him prevented.

When they reached the meadow, and the twisting, glittering boughs of the wood came into view, he halted and feigned confusion when he stopped and the elder insisted he follow.

"But, Elder of my Elders," he said. "That is the Starlight Forest."

"Yes," said Piktas. "Don't be alarmed. You are with an official. The official. You will suffer no penalty for entering as long as I am with you."

Together, they entered. Leaving the sun and outside world behind, they traveled beneath the full moon. When at length they reached the turning to the path which led to the lake, Piktas said, "And besides," he cawed his laughter. "There is a funeral. And you are cordially invited."

"Whose funeral?" Erich said.

Without warning, Piktas struck Erich across the back with his cane, and the fawn fell.

"Stop pretending!" the elder hissed. "You know perfectly well why we are here. You know who I am and what I am, and you know that your friend came to me!"

With great strength in his old frame, Piktas raised

Erich and pushed him along the path. In the spaces between leaves, the fawn saw the twinkling lights of countless fairies, but soon forgot them when the lake came into view and he saw, lying chained to the ground, covered in gushing abrasions and with one swollen eye blackened and closed, Orion panting.

Crying his name, Erich rushed to his friend and knelt by his side.

"Orion!" he said. "Orion! What have they done to you?"

Every breath brought the centaur pain. Several of his ribs had been broken, and now jutted out of the auburn flesh as the lungs filled with fluid. In a weak voice, he heaved the words, "I'm sorry Erich."

Erich turned to face Piktas, but his eyes first fell upon the lake. Floating prostrate beneath the fairies, twelve forms over which the fairies hungrily swarmed.

"The Elders," Erich whispered.

"All but one," said Piktas.

"You fool!" Erich cried. "Do you see what you have done?"

"I've gathered them," said Piktas. "All of them! At last! My father's dream! He suspected. He suspected for so many years how your family's garden managed to thrive so like the Starlight Forest. He died leaving the task to me, and now it is my dream!"

"Your dream?" Erich asked.

"To rule! Your family has used them for what

purpose? To make a pretty garden. Did you not realize the power you held in your hands?"

"You idiot!" Erich cried. "We didn't use the power to make our garden pretty and win in your stupid contests! It was the only thing we could do to control them, and the only way to dispose of them. You don't know what they are!"

"I know," said Piktas. "You killed them. Little at a time. Perhaps you even took pleasure in it. Your friend said he heard you laughing."

"I laughed," Erich said, "because I knew he followed me. Because I knew he would go to you. I laughed because I don't have to do this anymore."

"Yes you do," said Piktas. "One last time."

Raising his head, the Elder cawed three times. From the brush around them, Erich discerned the stomping of heavy feet, the cracking of branches and saw the figures of trolls come into view, each bearing a carcass in his hand: no doubt, he figured, the guards who killed the elders for Piktas.

"Immortality," Piktas said. "That is what you will give me."

"You cannot have it!" said Erich.

"I will," said Piktas. "Either you sing them all to sleep, or they will drink themselves into a frenzy. Every last one of them, and all your family's efforts shall have been in vain. You say I don't know what these things are? They are the End of Days. Imagine, Erich! You send them to sleep, and I slaughter them all. I bring them to the village, declaring the state of emergency is over and reveal myself as the savior this world hungers for! I shall rule, the one elder. And my son shall follow me. And his son after him, and his after him, and all the while there shall hang a portrait of the Piktas the Great: The One who saved the village and all the world beyond from the Soaring Feast."

"You can't kill them all," Erich said. "That's impossible."

"You mean it is impossible to try killing them all alone," said Piktas. "Why do you think I've brought trolls? I can crush two at a time, they can crush twenty—under each foot. Or, once the fairies have drank the elders dry, my friends here will give them one soldier. Just one. This will not satisfy them. With the others, the trolls will lure them from the lake and out into the world. You can prevent the Soaring Feast, or you can cause it, boy. It's your choice."

"I won't help you," Erich said. "I won't let you kill them."

Piktas laughed, and approached one of the trolls. From the soldier's corpse slung over the beast's shoulder, he withdrew a sword.

"Either you sing them to sleep," he said, slowly walking with the tip of the blade pointed toward Orion's throat. "Or your friend dies."

Looking into Orion's eyes, Erich saw many things:

Love, fear, hatred for the Seker and something else. Something which stirred memories of his father.

Sitting, Erich said, "My father told me I might live to see this day. But, my grandfather told him the same thing. He didn't think he actually would, I didn't either. Not until last night. I told you I laughed because I was caught."

"Yes, yes," said Piktas. "Spare me the reminiscences and do what you're told."

"I'll play the song for the fairies," Erich said. "But first, I want to tell you something. My father taught me the song that has been passed through our family from generation to generation to hold the Soaring Feast at bay. This forest, it moves. And when it moves to hide from us, we follow. Giving them the dead satisfies them for a little while, but they won't be satisfied until the life of every beast is in their wings. Then, they will die and this forest will die. That is the end.

"But my father once told me that there are many different meanings to 'The End.' One he told me is a song called 'The New Beginning.' It is a song that will never be taught. It will be played only once by whoever brings the end."

He looked to Piktas.

"You cannot stop the end," he said. "You can only make it happen."

He placed the flute to his lips and blew a single note, high and shrill. Within this single cord, countless voices seemed at once to sing. The fairies, heeding, drifted above the bodies; some pried their fangs free while others froze, their teeth within the flesh, drinking nothing, only listening.

Piktas lowered the blade, the trolls dropped their cadavers and the glazed eyes of Orion roved, for the fairies burst suddenly into brilliant life, rising and circling, ring upon ring of winged hues. The silver of the trees dimmed, their trunks transparent as the time of this place ended, and the full light of the outside world's new day devoured the night.

"What is happening?" Piktas demanded.

The fairies, hearing him, descended, soaring and landing upon him. For a moment they lingered, and in the next leapt into the air and pursued with their kin the trolls who ran in fright from the shriveled husk of what once was their fearless leader. They too fell, and so too did the villagers who opened their doors, for they heard from far away the song of the new beginning. The Starlight Forest, its shine had disappeared, swallowed by melody inviting them to a slumber eternal, a rest without pain as little silver fangs sought their last breath. Whether the wood truly died or returned to the dimension to which it belonged nobody knows, but it is said that when he finished his song, the last Goat Man crawled below the swarming colors, and as the teeth sank into his flesh and his essence drained into hundreds of hungry fiends, his fingers touched the palm of his friend who clasped them.

"I'm sorry," he heard a weak voice sigh.

"Don't be," he whispered, his last breath, a golden haze greedily consumed into the lips of the plague. "This is only the beginning."

About the Editor

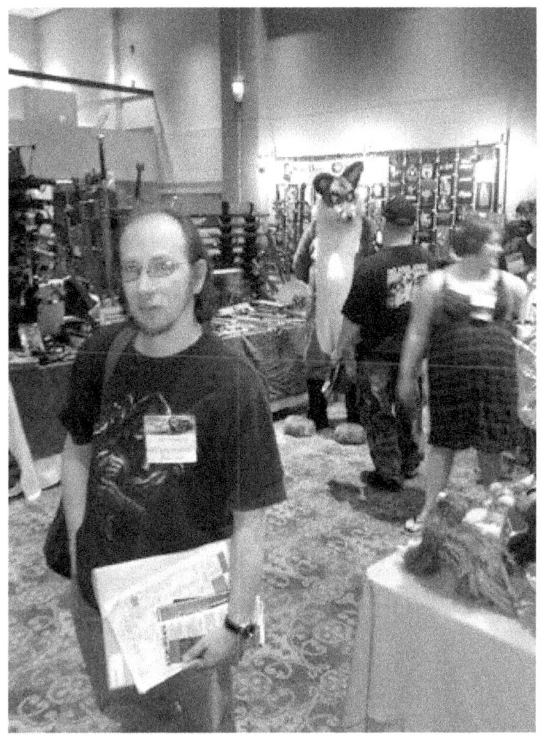

Scott M. Sandridge is a writer, editor, freedom fighter, and all-around trouble-maker. His latest works as an editor include the Seventh Star Press anthologies *Hero's Best Friend: An Anthology of Animal Companions*, and the two volumes of *A Chimerical World, Tales of the Seelie Court* and *Tales of the Unseelie Court*.

For more on Scott and his work, please visit:
http://smsand.wordpress.com

Check out the following pages
to see more from

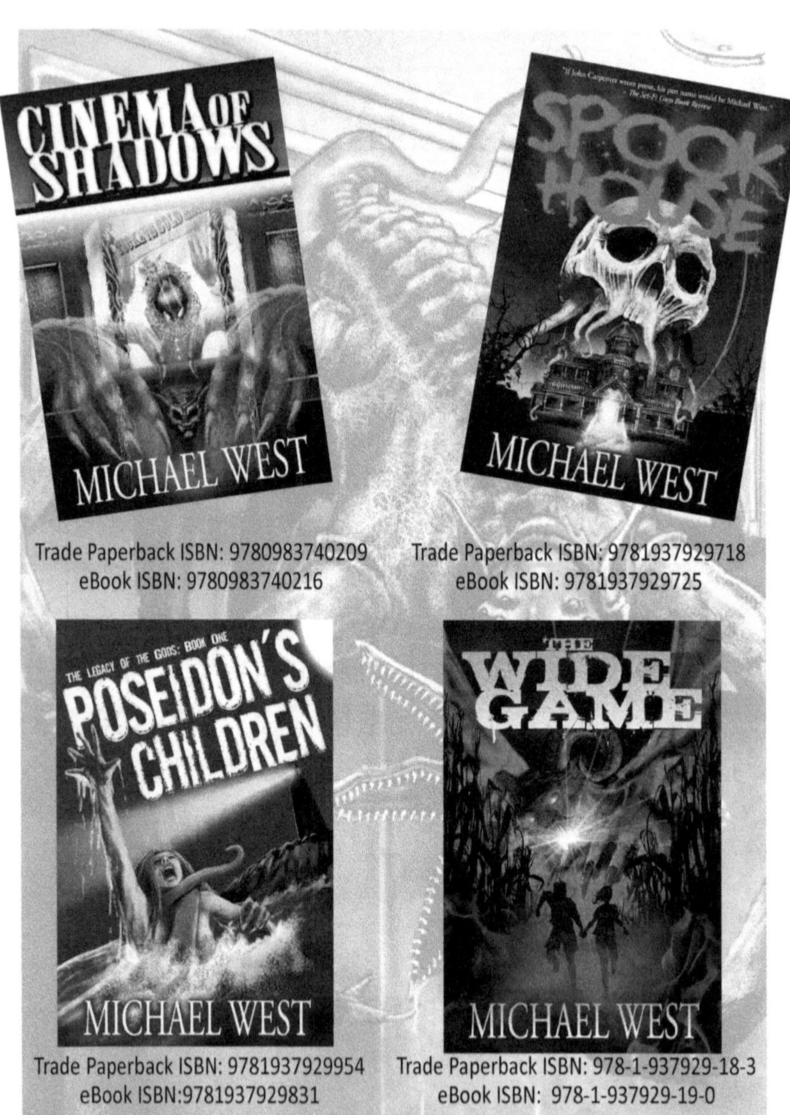
CINEMA OF SHADOWS
MICHAEL WEST
Trade Paperback ISBN: 9780983740209
eBook ISBN: 9780983740216
SPOOK HOUSE
MICHAEL WEST
Trade Paperback ISBN: 9781937929718
eBook ISBN: 9781937929725
THE LEGACY OF THE GODS: BOOK ONE
POSEIDON'S CHILDREN
MICHAEL WEST
Trade Paperback ISBN: 9781937929954
eBook ISBN:9781937929831
THE WIDE GAME
MICHAEL WEST
Trade Paperback ISBN: 978-1-937929-18-3
eBook ISBN: 978-1-937929-19-0

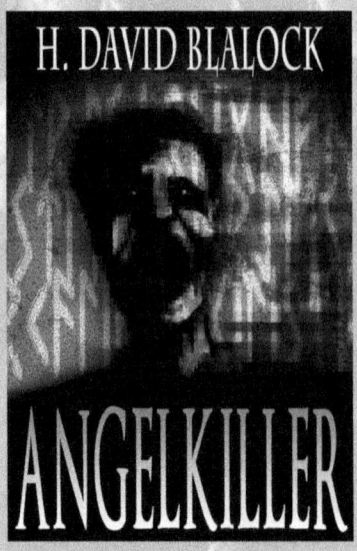

16 Tales of the Paranormal and Ghostly from editors Alexander S. Brown and J.L. Mulvihill!

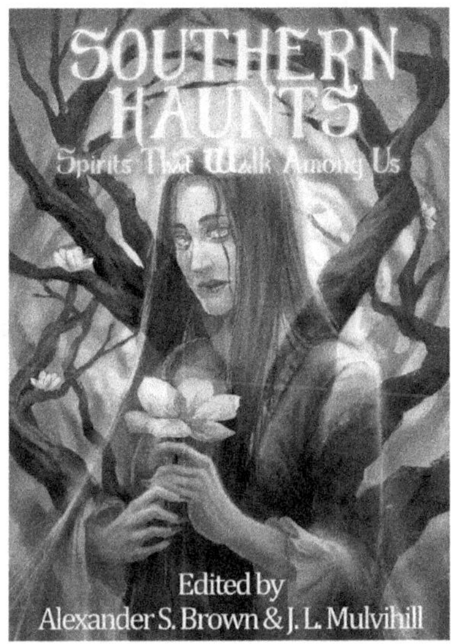

eBook ISBN: 978-1-937929-14-5

Softcover ISBN: 978-1-937929-12-1

From the shadowed realms of the paranormal comes 16 chilling tales that dwell in the South and South West. From 16 authors, learn of haunted homes, buildings, landmarks and roads where restless entities from beyond the grave desire acknowledgement amongst the living. Become acquainted with the aftermath of an eclipse that awakens the dead in a Memphis cemetery, see what horrors dwell in the woods at Hell's Gate, learn the dark secrets of Sidney's Cotton, and dare to travel down Ghost Road. These and many other tales are sure to keep you awake as you are introduced to what makes the South and South West so unique.... History and GHOSTS!!!!! So, sit back, dim the lights and prepare yourself to face the spirits that walk among us.

Urban Fantasy from John F. Allen!

Meet Ivory Blaque!

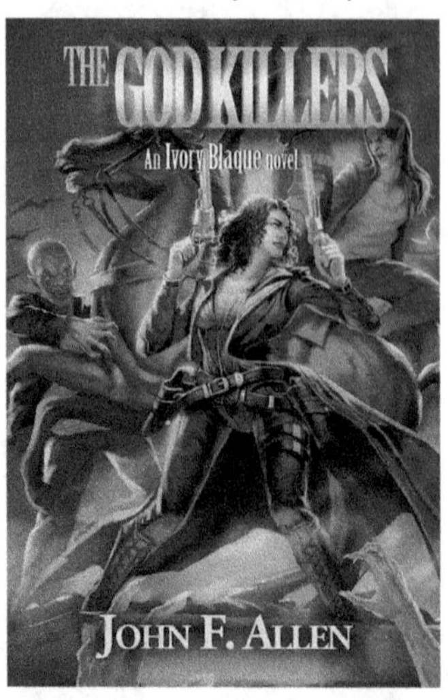

Softcover: 978-1-937929-16-9

eBook: 978-1-937929-17-6

In The God Killers, the first book of The God Killers Legacy, former professional art thief Ivory Blaque is hired to procure a pair of antique pistols and gets much more than she bargained for when several attempts are made on her life.

Her client turns out to be a shadowy government agent who reveals that she is descended from a race of immortals, and that the pistols are linked to her unique heritage and the special psychic gifts she possesses. He uses the memory of her father to guilt her into working for him.

Ivory eventually gives in to his request, and in return, he presents her with her father's journal, which was written in an unbreakable code. Bishop believes that she is the only one capable of breaking the code and unlocking the plans of the vampire hierarchy. But when the city's top vampire is a sexy incubus with an attraction for her and she's assigned a hot new lycan enforcer to protect her, she finds herself caught between two sets of rock hard abs.

To regain her autonomy, clear her name, unlock the secrets of her past, and protect the lives of those closest to her, Ivory must play along with the forces trying to manipulate her. Ivory's life is rapidly spiraling out of control and headed for an explosive conclusion which she just might not survive.

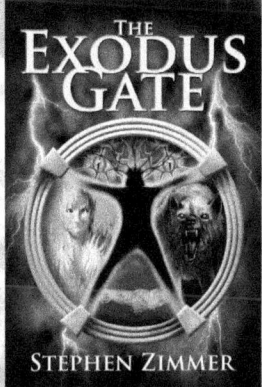

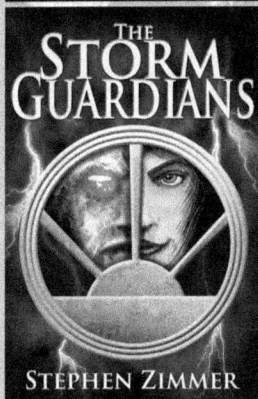

Virtual Blue from R.J. Sullivan!

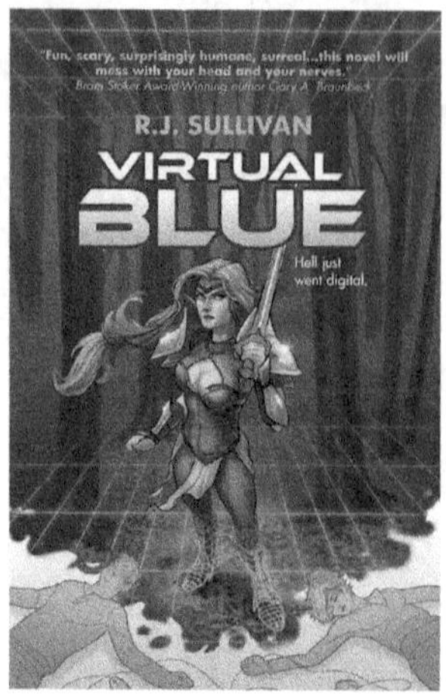

Softcover ISBN: 978-1-937929-32-9

eBook ISBN: 978-1-937929-33-6

Did you ever wish you could escape to a virtual world? What if you could...but then couldn't get out? Two years after her deadly clash with a vengeful ghost, Fiona "Blue" Shaefer still can't shake off the trauma of that night. Moving to New York with her father didn't help. Neither did absorbing herself in her college classes. Not even her poetry provided the solace it once did. She convinces herself that ending her relationship with Eugene "Chip" Farren, her long-distance boyfriend and final tie to the horrors of that night, might bring the closure she needs. Blue travels to Bloomington to break the news to Chip in person, but her timing couldn't be any worse. The Sisters of Baalina, vengeful cultists who practice a new form of "techno-magic," have targeted Chip's multi-player videogame as the perfect environment to cast a dangerous spell to free a demoness from the very pits of hell. In the process, their plan may trap Blue in a prison of the mind with no locks, no bars, and no escape.

A paranormal thrill ride from Eric Garrison! Four 'Til Late is Book One of the Road Ghosts Trilogy!

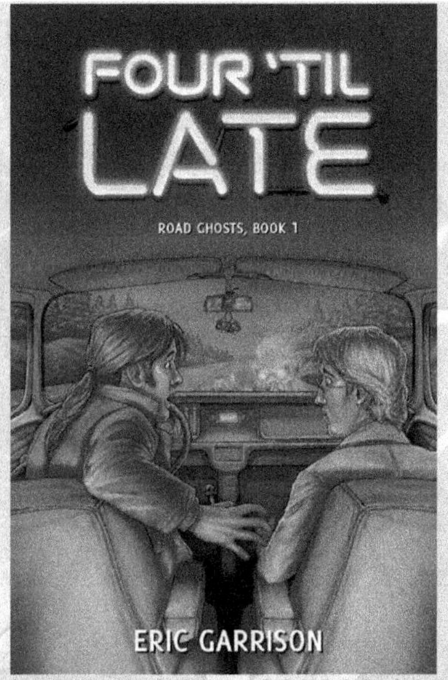

Softcover: 978-1-937929-22-0

eBook: 978-1-937929-23-7

In Four 'Til Late, amateur ghost hunter Brett and his friends Gonzo, Jimbo, and Liz are on a road trip with dangerous detours, dreadful dreams and dire warnings. But that won't keep them from reaching their goal: New Orleans. Along the way they discover that some spirits leave you with more than a hangover and regrets. Can they get there in one piece, or will they be stopped and rest in peace? The bags are packed, the engine's running. Turn up the radio and get moving because the road ghosts are waiting, and it's Four 'Til Late.

Hellscapes, Volume 1
Venture through the infernal, where angels fear to tread!

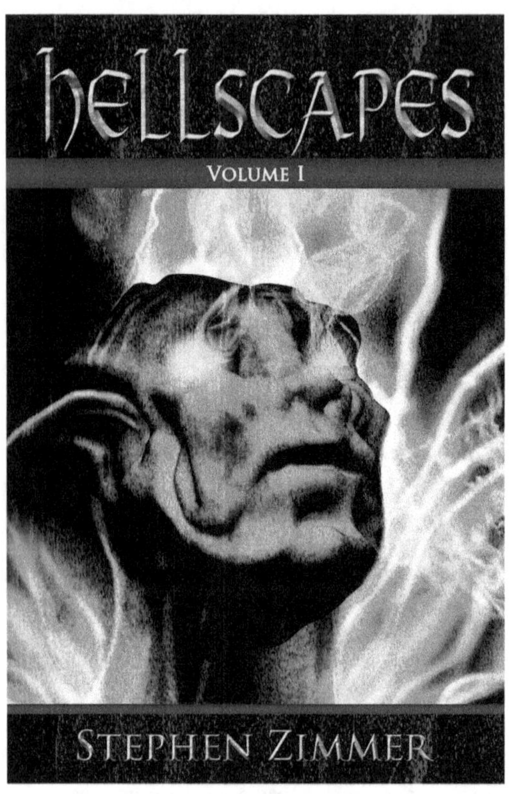

From Stephen Zimmer, a new horror series set in realms where the inhabitants experience the ultimate nightmare!

softcover ISBN:
eBook ISBN:

www.ingramcontent.com/pod-product-compliance
Lightning Source LLC
Chambersburg PA
CBHW071143020726
47502CB00002B/245

* 9 7 8 1 9 3 7 9 2 9 4 7 3 *